THE GUARDSMEN OF RAMMSIHAAR

A Novel

J. CAMERON MILLAR

Order this book online at www.trafford.com
or email orders@trafford.com

Most Trafford titles are also available at major online book retailers.

© Copyright 2011 J. Cameron Millar.
All rights reserved. No part of this publication may be reproduced, stored in a retrieval
system, or transmitted, in any form or by any means, electronic, mechanical, photocopying,
recording, or otherwise, without the written prior permission of the author.

Printed in the United States of America.

ISBN: 978-1-4269-9662-7 (sc)
ISBN: 978-1-4269-9661-0 (hc)
ISBN: 978-1-4269-9660-3 (e)

Library of Congress Control Number: 2011918960

Trafford rev. 12/02/2011

 www.trafford.com

North America & international
toll-free: 1 888 232 4444 (USA & Canada)
phone: 250 383 6864 ♦ fax: 812 355 4082

Also by J. Cameron Millar

The Van Der Meer Dossier

Man is not going to wait passively for millions of years before evolution offers him a better brain.

Corneliu E. Giurgea, PhD

For Michelle

THE GUARDSMEN OF RAMMSIHAAR

The potential military application of a new intelligence-enhancing drug is explored in this tale of an experiment run out of control, rising political tension between the Eastern and Western worlds, and a seeming solution to the global energy crisis. An adventure set truly out of this world leads to a frantic search amongst ancient ruins in order to save the peoples of Earth from the forces of tyranny and ultimate annihilation . . .

PROLOGUE

South Western Chryse Planitia, Mars, July 1976

The vast barren reddish-brown desert of the Martian surface extended away towards the horizon in every direction. A few gentle but as yet unnamed hills in the middle distance were the only geographical features that broke up the otherwise flat expanse of the great empty plain. Even in the midday sun the temperature hovered around twenty degrees Fahrenheit, little influenced by the thin gentle breeze blowing in from the south-west, composed as the atmosphere of the entire planet of mostly carbon dioxide and a little nitrogen and argon.

It had been twenty four hours now since the NASA Viking I Lander robotic probe had reached the surface of the red planet. Launched from Earth some ten months earlier, the Viking I Orbiter had achieved Martian orbit on June 19. An initial landing had been planned for July 4, the same day as the bicentennial of the United States of America, but initial imaging of the intended landing site had shown it to be too rough to provide reasonable assurance of a safe touch down. Some sixteen days later, after a more suitable site had been identified, the lander, replete with its aeroshell had finally separated from the orbiter on July 20, while moving at around nine thousand miles per hour. The aeroshell's retrorockets fired in order to begin the lander deorbit maneuver, which had then been reoriented for atmospheric entry one hundred and eighty-eight miles above the planet's surface. The aeroshell went on to slow the lander as it plunged through the atmosphere, all the while protecting it from burning to a crisp with its ablative heat shield. On reaching an altitude of three and three-quarter miles, while still descending at a rate of five hundred and sixty three miles per hour, the lander's parachutes deployed. Seven seconds later the aeroshell was jettisoned, and eight seconds after that the lander's three legs were extended. In the planet's marginal atmosphere it took the parachutes three-quarters of a minute to slow the lander to one hundred and thirty five miles per hour. At just under one mile above terrain, the lander's own retrorockets fired and within another forty seconds slowed the craft to a little above walking pace, just before it finally reached the surface of red oxide dirt in western Chryse Planitia, coming to a complete stop during a late afternoon, with just a little left-over fuel.

Upon learning of the successful landing the mission control specialists on Earth at the Johnson Space Center in Houston, Texas had let out a series of combined whoops and cheers. This day would prove to be a historic one indeed as the very first images of the Martian surface were expected to be received within a quarter of an hour. The lander was already in the process of acquiring an initial visual photograph, which would take around four minutes to complete. Following that, for a period of seven minutes, a three hundred degree panoramic photographic scan would take place. Additional experiments were planned also, involving a gas chromatograph-mass spectrometer, as well as an x-ray fluorescence spectrometer, pressure, temperature, and wind velocity sensors, a three-axis seismometer, a magnet on a sampler observed by the cameras, and various engineering sensors. But everyone associated with the mission cared only at this moment how the surface of the red planet would appear.

When the first visual images were received by Houston, taking around three minutes to traverse the some thirty-five million miles back to Earth, the mood in the control room could only be described as awe-struck. The dusty and in places rocky blasted moonscape appeared on the monitors in front of the team, who became the first humans ever in the entire history of Creation to glimpse the landscape of an alien planet.

The subsequent panoramic scan was received approximately twenty two minutes later. As it started to appear on the monitors, section by section, the excitement intensified, as progressively more and more images were revealed. In excited tones, Mission Engineer David Orloff was the first to articulate a proper sentence in his clipped British pronunciation.

"Do you realize we are the first human beings ever to be witnessing this? I mean, my God, this is broadcasting on location from Mars. From bloody Mars!"

"Well let's hope we don't find any little green men," the Mission Chief responded.

Orloff laughed loudly.

"I'm quite sure that-"

He stopped abruptly as the final frame of the scan came into view.

At first nobody was sure as to what they were seeing. But after a few more seconds had passed, it became clear and unmistakable.

"What the hell?! Olivia! Are the frequencies from Vidicon One banded correctly?"

Viking scientist Dr. Olivia Streeten was busy staring wide-eyed at her monitor and checking various systems on the camera.

"Everything checks out!"

"Try Vidicon Two! Let's see if that one sees the same thing!"

But the image received from the other camera showed the same unexpected phenomenon, just from a different angle.

Streeten was not happy. She didn't know what else to do, how else to explain what they were apparently seeing.

"What the hell is this?"

Her voice betrayed a sense of rising panic, bordering on a touch of real fear.

"Is this some kind of joke?"

But no-one was laughing. What everyone at Mission Control had just seen lying on the great Martian plain had left each individual stunned into confused silence.

The Mission Chief finally spoke again.

"I want those images cleaned up so that we do not see any of this! Do you understand, people?! These monochrome images had better be completely wiped."

Orloff immediately objected.

"Sir, we can wipe the monochromes, but not the color photographs that we will receive tomorrow. The software won't allow for that!"

The Mission Chief frowned.

"And anyway, sir," Orloff continued. "Would that be wise?"

He paused, his brow furrowed in thought.

"Would it even be moral? I mean, the people of Earth have a right to know? Don't they?"

But Orloff's suggestion only caused the Mission Chief's anger to pique.

"Get one thing straight, David. I don't give a damn about the rights of the people of Earth. If this were to get out it would be a disaster! A fucking disaster, do you hear? All kinds of shit could come down on our heads! Either you do your job, or if you can't, you will be replaced by someone else who can. Is that clear?"

The look on Orloff's face gave the Mission Chief the answer he was seeking.

According to NASA records, when the initial color photographs were received on Earth the following day, the very first in the series was shortly afterwards classified as having been officially lost from the records.

CHAPTER 1

Boston, Massachusetts, May 2008

The jet black Audi TT pushed on south through the rain and the gloom along Interstate 93 towards the suburbs of Quincy and Milton through the city's early evening traffic, which within another twenty minutes or so would reach full rush hour proportions. Considering the time of year the weather was not good. For almost the entire month now temperatures had been in the high fifties to low sixties and rain had been pouring down on the city from the banks of gray rolling cloud that had encircled the entire New England region. Today had been no exception.

Sitting behind the wheel, staring ahead through the drizzle at the red tail lights of the vehicle in front, thirty-eight year old Captain Dawn DeFaller was in a pensive mood as she contemplated the outcome of the meeting to which she was traveling. Lying beside her on the passenger's side seat was her black leather briefcase, containing the orders she had just received concerning the naval exercise involving several ships in which she was to participate as overall commander. She groaned as a radio news anchor issued predictions of yet more bad weather in the immediate forecast.

She glanced at her watch. It was 4.48pm. Within one hour and forty-two minutes she had to be at the naval base at Groton, Connecticut, some seventy miles distant, to meet with the British

Naval Attaché to Washington, Vice-Admiral Sir Phillip Bailey, who had already indicated to her in his orders that there were to be some special considerations relating to this exercise that he felt unable to discuss with her except in person. It had so happened that he had flown up to Groton by helicopter from Washington DC on one of his many trips that he made there throughout the year, so on this occasion Dawn's attendance at the meeting could easily be accomplished by her making the journey south by car. In truth she felt a little stab of trepidation at the prospect of taking command for the first time of an entire naval squadron, albeit a small one. And the prospect of additional irregular and probably secret considerations did not sit comfortably with her either, despite the fact that this represented, as she well knew, standard military procedure. She could not help but cast her mind back to the last time she had been ordered to participate in such an exercise when she had been commanding officer of the British destroyer HMS *Wildcat*. Things had not gone according to plan then and she hoped that the Vice-Admiral did not have something of a similar nature in mind for her now. Of course, Vice-Admiral Thomas Powers of the United States Navy, who, as a Rear-Admiral had been flag officer in command at the time, had since assured her that, under a hastily crafted agreement, all American and French apparatus and equipment, as well as all blueprints relating to the project which had led inadvertently to her ship being projected more than two hundred years into the past, had been irrevocably destroyed. And of course she had also been assured that the original and all copies of the secret van der Meer dossier, the document that had rendered all of this possible, were no longer in existence either. There was therefore no possibility of the navies or any other branches of the armed services of the United States, the United Kingdom, or France of ever dabbling in such a dangerous experiment again. But then she smiled to herself as she considered that had she not been engaged with Vice-Admiral Powers' project, she would never have met her husband, Matthew. Captain Matthew Revere, formerly of the American Continental Navy. There were times when she still found it utterly incredible to think that she was married to a man who had been born in 1740, and whom she had met in 1776. And yet here they both were in 2008, each aged just thirty-eight years. She smiled to herself again for a moment as her thoughts shifted to the recent e-mail message she had received from him. He had departed from New London, Connecticut, six days previously and was currently cruising down towards the eastern Caribbean islands of Trinidad and Tobago in the sailing training vessel USCG Cutter *Eagle,* engaged in training some mostly teenaged cadet hopefuls looking to build a future career in the United States Coast Guard. He had reminded her of the beautiful weather that he and his crew had been experiencing, somewhat to her chagrin, and had gone on to praise the modern gadgetry aboard his ship, as he seemed yet still wont to do, despite his having been living in the early 21st century for about two years chronologically at this point. Radios had impressed him greatly and continued to do so, but in particular he had expressed deep and continuous admiration for his ship's GPS system, which at the push of a button would tell him or any of his bridge officers their vessel's precise location on the planet, down to the last second of longitude and latitude. Dawn had been amazed by his explanations as to how a ship's captain from his era could estimate latitude to a high degree of accuracy from the position of the sun or the pole star, but longitude was still something of a matter of experience coupled with guesswork, a process to which he referred as 'dead reckoning'. Dead reckoning had been known to give rise to many shipwrecks. She could not imagine attempting to navigate a modern 21st century warship in such a manner. The problem had been technically resolved in 1761, after the invention of an accurate marine chronometer by the humble northern English carpenter John Harrison. But the device had not become generally available until 1773 after King George III had finally persuaded the British Admiralty Board that Harrison should receive the prize money they had promised for his invention, despite his not being, in their view, a 'gentleman'.

Dawn arrived at the naval base in Groton at 6.20pm. She showed her clearance to the security guards at the main gate, who then waved her on through. She would have just enough time to spare to park her car and walk over to Vice-Admiral Bailey's meeting, which was to be held, somewhat unusually, not in his office that he maintained there, but in a nearby lecture room. She took a moment to check the meeting itinerary for its number.

Upon reaching the room itself, she knocked on the closed door. Bailey's clipped aristocratic tones responded at once.

"Enter!"

She stepped through the door.

"Ah. Captain DeFaller. Do come in. Glad you could make it. May I offer you a drink?"

"A coffee if you have it, sir, thank you."

"Certainly. One moment please, Captain. I will go through the introductions presently."

Dawn glanced around the room. It was at this point that she realized she and the admiral were not alone. Seated around the lecture room were a number of other naval officers, all belonging to either the United States Navy or the British Royal Navy, and all turned out as Dawn in dress uniform.

Bailey crossed the room and poured some coffee from a large urn into a paper cup.

"If memory serves, you take it black, with no sugar, Captain?"

Dawn smiled. "Yes sir. Thank you."

He brought the coffee over to Dawn and then stood straight, facing her squarely.

"Captain. May I introduce these officers?"

The other officers all rose from their chairs in unison. Bailey proceeded along the line.

"Commodore Keith Lambert, United States Navy."

"Captain. I am pleased to meet you." He extended his hand in greeting.

"Sir."

"And I believe you know this officer?"

Vice-Admiral Thomas Powers rose from his chair and stepped forward enthusiastically. Recognition suddenly registered on Dawn's face.

"Captain! It is a great pleasure to meet you once again! Glad you could make it. How are you and that husband of yours?"

Dawn laughed.

"Sir. I'm sorry, please forgive me. I didn't recognize you at first. We're getting along just fine." She grasped his outstretched hand and shook it vigorously for several moments.

"And you, sir?"

"Well, I'd say there's a little mileage left in this old body yet!"

Dawn laughed, just as Bailey interrupted them.

"I apologize, but I must hurry you along, Captain."

Bailey indicated a trim man in his thirties, a little under six feet tall.

"Commander Donald MacPherson, Royal Navy."

"Commander."

Macpherson saluted.

"Ma'am."

"Commander MacPherson is officer commanding HMS *Rosshire,* British Type 23 frigate."

Bailey then turned to a thicker-set, stockier man, probably around her own age, she thought.

"Commander Allan Wood, officer commanding HMS *Daring,* British Type 45 destroyer."

"Commander."

"Ma'am. It is a privilege to meet you." He saluted and then extended his right hand in greeting.

"And then we have Commander Jack Tylon, Royal Navy, officer commanding HMS *Skirmisher,* Trafalgar class nuclear attack submarine."

Tylon, a little shorter in stature, seemed to Dawn to present something of a Eurasian appearance, although she could have been mistaken.

"Commander."

She immediately picked up on his apparent charisma. Tylon saluted her.

"Ma'am."

"And finally, may I present Lieutenant-Commander Elizabeth Burleigh, Royal Navy, officer commanding HMS *Dardanelles,* British Sandown class minehunter?"

Burleigh, a young blonde woman, about the same as Dawn's five feet four inches in height, in her late twenties, with very blue eyes and a rather Nordic appearance, straightened her back and stood hard to attention. She simultaneously fixated her gaze on a point just above Dawn's head, while inclining her eyes slightly to her left. She saluted stiffly and barked like a parade ground cadet. She seemed very keen.

"Ma'am!"

"Lieutenant-Commander." A momentary sense of awkward silence ensued, broken only when the admiral continued.

"Now that the introductions are complete, I suggest we all take a seat, as I have some adjunctive information to discuss with you all. I might remind you that everything you hear from this point forward is classified as top secret. Nothing is to be repeated outside this room."

He pulled down a screen, and pushed a button on a remote control unit. A ceiling-mounted projector whirred into life. A moment later a slide appeared, depicting what appeared to be the main campus of a company of some sort.

"This is an aerial photograph of the new but highly successful Brodmann Corporation, a pharmaceutical company located near Rahway, New Jersey. For several years now, scientists at this company have been working on a project to develop an effective marketable prescription oral medication for cognition enhancement."

"Cognition enhancement?" Dawn was uncertain of what this meant.

"Cognition enhancement. In essence, Captain, scientists at Brodmann Corporation have been working for the last eight years to develop a drug for the treatment of Alzheimer's disease.

Something that will help stimulate the brains of patients slowly losing their minds to this devastating condition, perhaps in the hope of retarding or even reversing the chronic degradative effects. But along the way, one of their several research teams engaged on this project stumbled upon a discovery that attracted the interest of the military."

At that point Bailey nodded at Lambert.

"Commodore Lambert is a biochemist by training, and will take over from here. He heads the United States Navy's Research and Development Section of Biological Research. He is much better qualified to explain the relevant details."

Lambert stood and walked up to the front of the room. He took the controller and laser pointer from Bailey and then advanced to the next slide, which showed a schematic of the human brain.

"Alzheimer's disease is known to be associated with a progressive synthesis and deposition of a substance known as beta amyloid in the brains of sufferers."

He spoke in soft tones, each word carefully considered.

"In addition, there is progressive loss of brain tissue itself. Eventually enough of the brain is compromised by both the amount of beta amyloid, and the loss of overall mass, that the cognitive or reasoning capacity of the affected individual is significantly and noticeably compromised. As indeed is short-term memory function."

He stopped to take a sip from a glass of water.

"Research dating from the early 1990's has suggested that one of the principal features of the disease process is loss of function of what are called cholinergic synapses, that is, nerve endings within the brain that under appropriate stimulation release a substance called acetylcholine. So, efforts at treating the condition naturally enough were directed at, amongst other things, attempting to restore the presence of acetylcholine by the use of drugs, engineered to enter the central nervous system, and cause the release of more of the required acetylcholine at the affected nerves. But as we headed into the late 1990's it became apparent that in addition to restoration of cholinergic function, further research efforts were beginning to show that some drugs were also able to block the synthesis of beta amyloid. And, they were also able to cause that which had already been formed to regress, over time. There have been many experimental success stories with this line of research, but there has been very little which has yet made it into clinical use. However, eight years ago, a pair of university-based scientists in the field, Drs. Ernst Brodmann and James McLeod, both Associate Professors at Yale University, identified business potential in this area of endeavor and decided to quit academia and start their own company. This they did in April of 2000. Of the two, Brodmann was able to invest several times as much start-up capital as McLeod, thus making Brodmann the *de facto* senior partner and hence the company was dubbed Brodmann Corporation."

Dawn's expression became visibly quizzical. Lambert paused momentarily as his eyes met Dawn's directly.

"Are you with me so far, Captain?"

"Yes sir. But I am not certain I understand where the navy comes in."

He smiled.

"Bear with me, Captain. I am coming to that."

He cleared his throat.

"So, as I was saying, Brodmann Corporation has been in business now for eight years. In that time they have indeed made good on their promise to get some drugs into the clinic and there are now two fairly effective drugs available to clinical neurologists with which to, at least temporarily, slow the progress of Alzheimer's, perhaps by as much as five to seven years, in effect. However, although these drugs retard the course of the disease they do not arrest it altogether and eventually the patient will succumb. But Brodmann Corporation have continued pursuing their research endeavors vigorously, and have recently expanded their operation. In late 2005 a new building was added to their campus in Rahway and by mid-2006 it was fully operational. Approximately one hundred additional neuroscientists, approximately one-third of whom are educated to doctoral level, were hired and they have all been actively engaged in attempting to find ever better ways to attack this disease. But in 2007, just last year, a completely unexpected but fascinating discovery came to light. At first the company kept it to themselves, but the information was leaked to the press and attracted the attention of our Section of Biological Research. While testing a series of seventy-six chemically related new candidate agents, labeled as BC-66940 through BC-67015, for their potential to exploit a particular pathway discovered in the brain, it was found that one of these agents, BC-66996, not only appeared to arrest the effects of Alzheimer's as simulated in animal models, but actually appeared to enhance the intellect and reasoning capacity of those same animals to an unnatural level, that is, a level not found in nature. Further studies with BC-66996 on normal healthy animals had a similar, but even more profound effect. Now the pharmacological name for BC-66996 is cholyltriazofemproterone. But Brodmann Corporation have recently been given permission by the United States Food and Drug Administration, more commonly known as the FDA, to sell the drug under the trade name Chotone. Due to the nature of the discovery and its potential military applications, the FDA approval process for Chotone was greatly accelerated, in a matter of months versus the more usual period of around ten years. But this took place under the condition that it will be marketed exclusively to the United States military for a period of not less than sixty months, or five years. However Brodmann Corporation will be able to charge a considerably larger price for the product than could be obtained on the civilian market, anywhere in the world, even in North America. During that time it will not under any circumstances be made available to the general public, even via special prescription as an experimental agent to treat an otherwise fatal condition. However following expiry of this sixty month period this official FDA position will be reviewed. If performance profiles of Chotone as established within the context of extensive military testing have proved satisfactory, without any overt signs of toxic or otherwise undesirable side-effects, the drug may be given FDA approval for general sale in the United States as a prescription-only medication. As for its mechanism of action, Chotone is a nootropic agent. It enhances cognition, memory, intelligence, motivation, attention, and concentration. It does so by combining the activities of benzodiazepines and cholinergics, and also incorporates non-feminizing estrogenic and androgenic hormones."

Dawn had a question.

"Can you explain what you mean by the term, 'nootropic'?"

"Yes. The term was coined in 1972 by the Romanian chemist and psychologist Dr. Corneliu Giurgea. It is derived from the Greek words *nous,* meaning mind, and *trepein,* meaning bend, or turn. Chotone apparently works by altering the availability of the brain's supply of neurochemicals, those being neurotransmitters, enzymes, and hormones, and also by improving the brain's oxygen supply, probably by increasing blood vessel production, and by actually stimulating nerve growth. The latter activity it does to a tremendous degree over time, resulting in an eventual near-doubling of the brain's neuronal mass but without any increase in volume. There is a corresponding reduction in the mass of the supportive glial tissue, but by no more than fifteen percent and probably less. The precise mechanism or mechanisms of action of Chotone however remain unknown at this point."

He advanced to the next slide, which showed a still photograph of a guinea-pig standing in a miniature maze. He clicked on a 'Play' button displayed at the bottom right of the screen and the image leaped into life.

"As you see here, this normal guinea-pig negotiates the maze only with considerable difficulty, but is eventually able to find the food reward hidden within. Repeated attempts with the same animal indicate that he has some capacity for learning to negotiate his way through the puzzle, but even at best, it takes him several minutes to achieve his prize."

The movie jumped to repeated tests showing the animal's overall performance improving a little each time.

"But this next guinea-pig was treated once-daily with Chotone for a period of one week prior to a similar set of experiments, and continued treatment on a once-daily basis thereafter."

The next slide showed another similar-looking guinea-pig standing at the entrance to the same maze.

"This animal had no prior exposure to the maze."

Lambert clicked on the 'Play' button once again. The animal this time ran through the maze in about ten seconds. Dawn raised her eyebrows, particularly as the animal's expression seemed to suggest a focused and protracted determination not typically seen in rodents, at least as far as she was aware.

"As you see, the animal on Chotone shows significantly enhanced performance. But I must emphasize, he is not in any way aware of how to find the prize, he is simply running through the maze by trial and error, just as his untreated counterparts. The essential difference is that he is able to do so much more quickly. And after his first time through, on subsequent attempts he remembers which turn to take, every step of the way, without error, so that he is able to knock his time down from about ten seconds to just three."

The next sequence corroborated Lambert's statement.

"Remember the best time an untreated animal could attain, even after having experienced the maze some sixteen times over in four days, was two minutes and twenty-one seconds, or forty-seven times longer."

"That is indeed quite remarkable, sir."

"Yes, isn't it indeed, Captain? But now, consider this."

The next slide showed a dog, an adult black Labrador.

"This is Frieda-May. Frieda-May was treated similarly with Chotone once-daily for a week prior to the tests to which she was subjected, highlighted here in this demonstration."

Lambert clicked the 'Play' button again. Immediately Dawn heard the voice of what was presumably a researcher asking the dog some questions.

"Frieda-May, what is two plus two?"

There was a brief pause, after which Frieda-May responded with four distinct barks in rapid succession.

"Frieda-May, what is ten minus three?"

Another pause, followed by seven barks.

The researcher, a woman in a white coat then entered the frame, and placed a rubber knife, a rubber gun, a wooden stick, a ping-pong paddle, a large dictionary, and a doll about three feet in front of the dog.

She then issued further commands.

"Frieda-May, pick up the gun and place it on top of the dictionary."

Frieda-May duly responded.

"Frieda-May, take the ping-pong paddle and use it to bat away the doll."

Again Frieda-May obliged, this time taking the paddle in her mouth and batting away the standing doll so hard it went flying out of the picture.

"Frieda-May, place your right front paw on the handle of the knife, not its blade."

Again, a brief pause, followed by perfect compliance.

A giant keyboard with large violet-colored buttons was placed in front of the dog. It became clear a few seconds later that it was hooked up to a wall-mounted display monitor. The keyboard included both letters and numbers, as well as certain simple mathematical operators.

"Frieda-May, what is the square root of seven hundred and sixty-nine?"

After a brief pause, during which it appeared that Frieda-May might not have understood the question, she stood up and approached the keyboard, and gingerly lifted her right front paw. She then carefully touched in succession the appropriate number keys to type out the digit '769'. She then checked the display, apparently to make sure that the correct number had been entered into the system. She then returned her attention to the keyboard and again with her right paw carefully hit the square root key.

The answer 27.73084925 immediately appeared on the screen. Frieda-May then barked once and fixed her gaze on the answer.

Another question.

"Frieda-May, what is the odd-one out in this sequence? Dog. Monkey. Spider. Human. Gorilla.

Frieda seemed to consider the question carefully, but then she lifted her paw over the keyboard and typed out the word, 'SPIDER'.

Several murmurs and gasps of amazement had started to develop by this stage. But Lambert simply invited his audience to continue watching, with the promise that it was going to get even better. He advanced to the next slide. This time a chimpanzee could be seen seated in what appeared to be the pilot's left seat of a flight simulator built to resemble the cockpit of a jet airliner. Once again, he clicked 'Play'. Dawn saw the camera pan back, and immediately it became apparent that the chimp was 'flying' the simulator, along with a human pilot in the right seat. The human pilot spoke.

"Benji, you have the aircraft."

Immediately the chimp placed his hands gently on the control yoke in front of him.

"Benji, steer course 340 degrees."

The chimp responded by applying a little left aerilon and watching the direction finder in the virtual display edge its way over to 340. Just before reaching the required heading he started to gently level the wings, all the while keeping his eye on the artificial horizon. As he completed the maneuver the plane came right onto the desired heading.

"Benji, we have been directed by Eastern ATC to adjust to flight level 140. Do we need to climb or descend?"

Benji glanced at the altimeter readout tape on the virtual display. It read 15,530 feet. Benji then turned to his fellow pilot and indicated the thumbs-down signal with his right hand.

"Very good, Benji. Take us down to 14,000 feet. During the maneuver maintain airspeed 260 knots, and rate of descent of no more than 500 feet per minute."

Benji responded by pulling back the thrust levers to the flight idle position as he applied a little forward pressure on the yoke. He kept a careful eye on the artificial horizon and the vertical speed indicator as the plane entered a gentle dive. At one point he applied just a touch of speed brake in order to prevent the aircraft's speed from exceeding the mandated 260 knots. On reaching the required altitude he leveled out and increased the thrust once more.

"Very good, Benji. I am going to engage the Flight Director and Auto Throttle now."

The human pilot then pushed a series of buttons causing some green lights to come on under a selection of panels located on the upper area of the dash, displaying parameters of speed, direction, and altitude, and then selected the F/D and A/T switches to the 'On' position.

"Flight Director and Auto Throttle engaged."

Immediately Benji took his hands off the yoke and sat back in his chair.

The scene then jumped to what appeared to be a final approach to landing. Through the simulator windows, over Benji's head it was becoming apparent that the plane was coming in close to an airport.

"Benji, you are cleared for a non-ILS landing on runway 04 Right. Flight Director off. Select flaps twenty five. Arm speed brake."

Benji immediately complied with the instructions.

"Select flaps thirty."

Benji reached over and moved the flaps lever to '30'.

A little later came another command.

"Gear down. Select flaps forty. Set Auto Throttle Vref plus five at 145 knots. Insure proper rate of descent for landing.

"Gear down and locked for landing?"

Benji glanced over at the landing gear indicator lights and then gave the thumbs-up sign. Moments later they crossed the runway threshold and Benji flared the aircraft to three degrees nose-up as the radio altimeter indicated that the main gear was fifteen feet above the tarmac, all the while applying gentle pressure on the rudder pedals to keep the nose of the airplane barreling straight down the center line of the runway. He reached over without taking his eyes off the runway ahead and pulled the thrust levers back to idle. A moment later a rumbling sound and a visible shaking of the cockpit confirmed touchdown, as the speed brake lever automatically shot back to the fully deployed position. Benji then applied gentle forward pressure to the yoke and brought the nose gear down on the runway, while at the same time selecting the reverse thrusters before engaging full reverse power. Moments later, as the full 'weight' of the aircraft settled on the gear, he pushed down on the toe brakes to further bleed off speed with perfect symmetric braking. As they approached taxi speed he engaged the nose wheel steering switch, and then, using the rudder pedals, maneuvered the aircraft off the active runway at the next available exit. He reached out his right arm and moved the flap selector lever to the 'Inboard' position, and also selected the Speed Brake lever to the 'Park' position as he commenced 'taxiing' to the Apron.

Lambert stopped the video.

"That chimpanzee had been with his human instructor you saw there in the video for three weeks, and actually at the controls, albeit of the simulator, for a total of about thirty-two hours when that sequence was shot. The simulator was incidentally that for a Boeing 737-800. Since then he has piloted, under supervision, in a similar manner to that which you saw here, three flights in real Boeing 737 aircraft."

Dawn was by this point completely aghast, as were several of her fellow officers. Noting their reaction, Lambert smiled, as Vice-Admiral Powers joined him on the podium. Powers spoke up as Dawn still tried to take in what she had just witnessed.

"So you see. Brodmann Corporation scientists have discovered a drug that causes immense enhancement of the mind. In the case of the dog and the chimpanzee, sufficient enhancement that they were able to learn, albeit with intensive and imaginative training over a period of time, to read, type, and understand spoken English and mathematics, in aside to the tasks you saw them perform. The United States Navy has acquired some of this drug from Brodmann Corporation, under the special licensing agreement with the FDA, along with all details currently known concerning its production, pharmacokinetics, pharmacodynamics, toxicology, dosing posology, and side-effects."

"Yes sir," said Dawn. "But what do you intend to do with this? Why is the navy so interested?"

"Can you imagine, Captain, what would be possible if a ship's commander, a squadron commander, or even a fleet commander were to be mentally enhanced in a manner similar to that which you saw in those animal tests?"

Dawn immediately became leery of where Powers was going with all of this.

"But sir, would that be safe? I mean to give this to a human? Has it been properly tested?"

"Absolutely safe? No, of course I cannot say with certainty that it is. But it is as safe as we can reasonably assess with the data we have to date. And we have already performed some limited testing of our own with this drug, under the direction of Commodore Lambert. It seems that as long as any animal subject is on the drug they will experience enhanced intellectual capacity, but following discontinuation the intellect slowly returns to normal. We have no reason to believe that it is inherently dangerous."

Dawn just stared at him, unwilling to buy in to what he was saying.

Powers advanced to the next slide. It showed a British naval officer, wearing the uniform of a Commander.

"This is Commander Garry Hunt, Royal Navy."

Dawn nodded her head.

"I have heard of him, sir, although I have never met him."

"Commander Hunt has agreed to be our first human guinea pig for our initial tests with Chotone."

"But sir, I must protest, has Commander Hunt even-"

Powers cut her off.

"He has seen all of the data we have. He is ready and willing to go through with the tests. We will have our finest physicians on hand at all points during the testing phase to monitor his health regularly. If at any time anything goes wrong, the test will be ended. In addition, Commander Hunt is single, has no children, and all of his immediate family are deceased. He is informed and fully aware of the risks he will be running. He is prepared to accept them, and has already signed all relevant legal documentation and releases to that effect."

Bailey spoke up again.

"Commander Hunt has been given command of HMS *Diamond,* the first of three new Type 45 destroyers to have been launched at Scotstoun in Glasgow. A flotilla consisting of *Diamond* and those vessels represented by the respective commanders with us this morning will be assembled in the North Atlantic Ocean where an exercise in simulated convoy protection, code named *Ankara,* in which several merchant ships will also be taking part, will be conducted under your overall command, Captain. In addition there will also be an element of anti-submarine warfare."

Dawn was prompted to ask another question.

"These merchant ships, what types will they be, and how many?"

"We are still finalizing the arrangements with the relevant civilian companies, but most likely you will be dealing with three empty British and American oil tankers, running in ballast, and two ocean-going salvage tugs. The tankers will be diverted from their more usual run to Bahrain in the Persian Gulf. They will delay by a number of days to assist in *Ankara.* The salvage tugs we are renting from British and Dutch companies, they will be out of London and Rotterdam respectively, and will be scheduled to arrive on station at about the same time as the tankers. When the tankers depart, so also will the tugs."

"I see, sir. And will I have an opportunity to meet with their commanding officers beforehand?"

"Yes indeed. That you will, Captain."

"Very good, sir."

"Vice-Admiral Powers will also be present during *Ankara* to assess outcomes. Commander Hunt will enter the theater of operations under the influence of BC-66996, while all the other commanders here this morning will be drug-free. Hunt's performance will be compared with that of his fellow officers."

"Why two Type 45's sir? Aren't they still rather scarce, considering that only three have so far been launched?"

Dawn was of course referring to the Royal Navy's new larger 7,350 tonne replacement for the 5,200 tonne Type 42 destroyer, to become officially active in 2009.

"Yes they are, Captain, but we want to make conditions for the test as fair as possible. Hunt will be in command of a Type 45, so we want another one in the theater as well, commanded by an officer as much like Hunt from the point of view of command ability and psychology as we can find. And that officer of course is Commander Wood. And besides, it will be a good opportunity to showcase the new joint UK-US Rolls Royce Northrop-Grumman Gas Turbine engines in these vessels. The Royal Saudi Naval Reserves have expressed interest in ordering two or three of the class. So we can kill two birds with one stone, so to speak, by having two of these vessels active during *Ankara,* affording every chance to demonstrate their performance and handling characteristics."

"I see sir."

In reality Dawn was a little envious that some other commanders were to get to captain the new Type 45, which promised to be a significant step up from *Wildcat* in numerous different ways.

"And as for Commander Hunt. He will be delivered aboard *Diamond* just prior to the commencement of the exercise, when the lab people and the medics say he is ready."

Bailey smiled at Dawn reassuringly.

"Don't worry, Captain. Hunt will be at the peak of physical and mental fitness."

Dawn just looked directly at him, her expression impassive.

"I certainly hope so, sir."

He in turn regarded her for a moment, without saying anything. But then he continued.

"Some other details. You will be operating in waters traversed by active merchant shipping, so exercise all appropriate precautions. We don't want any kind of mishap. I might add that both yourself and Vice-Admiral Powers are at liberty to install yourselves aboard either *Wildcat* or *Daring* for the duration of the exercise. But I would like you both to remain off *Diamond,* and also off the submarine."

"Yes sir," Dawn acknowledged. Powers just nodded knowingly, as if he had heard all this detail earlier.

Bailey faced the room once more.

"Well. That concludes the briefing for this morning."

With that, he stood up straight and faced the room once again.

"Are there any final questions?"

"No sir," came the reply.

"Then thank you all for attending, and at such short notice. Good luck in Operation *Ankara.* You are dismissed."

But as each officer stood and commenced filing out of the room, he turned to Dawn.

"Please wait behind, Captain. There are some additional issues I would like to discuss with you, in private."

When they were alone, and the door was once more closed, he turned to her again.

"Captain. As I said, you may choose to be based aboard *Wildcat* for the duration of Operation *Ankara.* Your old executive officer, Malcolm Callaghan, will be in command."

Dawn broke into a smile.

"It will be just like old times sir. I am very much looking forward to going to sea again, more especially aboard my old ship."

"Yes Captain. Commander Callaghan has also expressed that he is very much looking forward to working with you again too. But be aware. You are entering uncharted political waters here. There is much riding on *Ankara.* The outcome of the cognition enhancing drug that Commander Hunt will be taking is of the utmost importance, make no mistake."

"Yes sir."

"And there is another thing that I wish to discuss only with you, Captain."

"Sir?"

Bailey appeared to become a little uncomfortable for a moment.

"Captain, I did not make it clear earlier, but Commander Hunt is in fact already under the influence of the experimental drug. Indeed he has been now for over one month."

"One month, sir? But I-"

"During most of this time he has been working in close association with engineers from the British-American conglomerate company United Kingdom North American Systems, or UKNAS. UKNAS evolved about fourteen months ago from BAE Systems, the company that produced the Sting Ray Mod 1 torpedo, as I am sure you are aware."

"Yes sir."

"Well, for several years now UKNAS has been working on a top secret project to develop an upgraded version of the Sting Ray. Their engineers however ran into a variety of technical difficulties which they were unable to solve, despite devoting nearly three years of focused and intensive work to the issues involved. But with Commander Hunt's assistance over these last few weeks, UKNAS now say they stand ready to commence general delivery of the upgraded version of this weapon, which they have dubbed the Sting Ray Mark 3, or Super Sting Ray. Commander Hunt's success represents the first real evidence that this cognition enhancing drug really works."

He lifted a fifty page report from his desk and handed it to her. Across its cover it was clearly marked 'TOP SECRET'.

"This is a detailed dossier outlining the Super Sting Ray. I think when you read it you will agree that it is a truly remarkable weapon. As part of *Ankara,* I also want you to test this new weapon. All relevant details and orders are included in the dossier.

In aside to Vice-Admiral Powers, who has been fully appraised of the technical specifications of the torpedo, this dossier is for your eyes only, Captain. But I will leave it to your discretion to discuss details of the new weapon with your officers as you see fit. But the bottom line is this. The Super Sting Ray had better work. A lot of money, and I mean billions of dollars, are at stake here. Especially for UKNAS, who must secure the contract for supply of the torpedo to the Royal Navy, which will almost certainly lead to smaller but still very lucrative spin-off contracts for supplying the navies of Canada, Australia, and of course Saudi Arabia. Not to mention the United States."

He faced her directly.

"I know I can count on you Captain."

"Yes sir."

"Do you have any further questions?"

"No sir. I believe I understand fully."

"Then until next time. Thank you for taking the trouble to drive here, and at such short notice."

"Sir."

She shook his right hand he extended to her, saluted, and took her leave.

CHAPTER 2

O n her way out of town, Dawn stopped at an independently-owned coffee shop she knew and for which she had a particular liking, just off the interstate highway, on the outskirts of Groton. She felt in the mood to sit alone in a comfortable chair and study the dossier that Vice-Admiral Bailey had given her, while sipping some strong hazelnut flavored coffee which was a particular specialty of this establishment.

A short time later she was relaxing with a large mug of her favorite brew, the dossier resting in her lap. After studying the cover once more, with its reminders regarding the top-secret nature of the material contained within, she opened it and turned to the first page. There she found a color photograph showing a view of the corporate offices near Washington DC of the British-American conglomerate company United Kingdom North American Systems, or UKNAS. Underneath there was a block of text.

United Kingdom North American Systems (UKNAS)

UKNAS, the corporate offices of which are shown in the photograph above, is a company which evolved approximately fourteen months prior to the date of the present report from BAE Systems. BAE Systems was a previous manufacturer and supplier of ordnance to the British

Royal Navy, including (but not limited to) the Sting Ray Mod 1 torpedo which is currently in service aboard British warships of selected types. Engineers at UKNAS have been working on a top-secret project to develop an upgraded version of the Sting Ray Mod 1. As of May 1, 2008, UKNAS now stand ready to commence general delivery of the upgraded version of this weapon, termed the Sting Ray Mark 3, known colloquially as the Super Sting Ray.

On the next page there was a two-panel color diagram. The panel on the left outlined in considerable detail the schematics of the Sting Ray Mod 1. Comparative schematics of the Mark 3 version were indicated on the right. The text continued underneath.

Sting Ray Mod 1 Torpedo (BAE Systems (Left Panel)) and Sting Ray Mark 3 Torpedo (UKNAS (Right Panel))

The present Sting Ray Mod 1 has a maximum speed of 45 knots, mounts a 99lb Torpex warhead, and has a range of 4.3 nautical miles before its magnesium/silver chloride sea water battery is spent and the torpedo is dead in the water. The weapon is acoustically guided, agile, dives well, and homes independently on target, so if fired on an enemy vessel or submarine it stands a very good chance of scoring a hit. And of course its electric powered pump jet renders it fairly quiet.

Dawn shifted uncomfortably in her chair. Images of burning men flying through the air from USS *Connecticut,* the sailing ship that she had encountered in the North Atlantic Ocean and sunk while in 1776 flooded through her mind.

But the Sting Ray Mark 3 represents a radical departure from torpedo design to date. This torpedo in fact is the first truly 'smart' torpedo that has ever been developed.

Smart torpedo? Dawn was perplexed.

After firing, the torpedo is able, completely independently, to distinguish between enemy and friendly ships or submarines by detection and analysis of their precise acoustic signatures, as well as via use of its periscope-mounted on-board electronic eye sensitive to all wavelengths of the electromagnetic spectrum. The weapon also possesses an electronic 'nose' or olfactory system, inspired from that of the shark with which it can literally smell-out enemy vessels, as well as a range finding radar system. The torpedo takes stock of ship type, position, heading and speed, land proximity, water depth, and overall numbers of ships in the theater of operations. It can remain on the surface or dive to a depth anywhere down to 2,000 feet, thereby bringing any fleet submarine from any naval service in the world within range, no matter that it may be deeply submerged. Using its on-board computer, it can make decisions concerning which ship or submarine to attack, and precisely when, in order to achieve the greatest tactical advantage. The torpedo can be loosed when within 150 nautical miles of an enemy formation, and then left to its own devices. It can be trusted to make completely independent assessments regarding how best to damage enemy interests. The torpedo may be recalled or neutralized after having been launched (see below).

Sting Ray Mark 3: Abort Mode.

If, following launch of a single torpedo or any multiple number of torpedoes, a commander wishes to recall a single torpedo, or any combination, or all of them, each individual weapon's recall code simply has to be transmitted by radio, or sonar, as appropriate. Each torpedo so addressed will then immediately abandon its mission and return to whichever ship it is instructed, or to whichever set of co-ordinates specified (if for example there is insufficient power remaining for a return journey to a ship). On arrival it will hold position adjacent to whichever area of the ship is desired, until lifted from the water by crane or net. If preferred, the torpedo can be instructed to detonate immediately at whatever location at which it happens to present in the ocean, or to proceed to new co-ordinates and then detonate. The recall codes are encrypted so that an enemy cannot take advantage of this feature.

Warhead Options

The weapon may be fitted with either a 250lb Enhanced Torpex Warhead (ETW), or a small Tactical Nuclear Warhead (TNW) of 5 kilotonne yield. Because of the more advanced design of its pump jet, it runs in almost complete silence, at a maximum speed of 85 knots, nearly twice as fast as the Sting Ray Mod 1 version. The Sting Ray Mark 3 can remain dormant and at large under its own power for a period of up to 50 hours after firing. It can also run at full speed for 8 hours and 15 minutes. It is expected that this weapon will prove extremely useful in the fight against illegal drug trafficking and international terrorism.

Sting Ray Mark 3—Preliminary Testing

Initial tests of the Sting Ray Mark 3 torpedo have already taken place at the Royal Naval Armament Depot at Coulport, Argyll, Scotland.

Sting Ray Mark 3—Testing During Operation Ankara

The first sea-trials of the Sting Ray Mark 3 torpedo will take place in the North Atlantic ocean off the western coast of Shetland as part of Operation Ankara (Flag Officer Commanding, Vice-Admiral Thomas Powers, USN; Fleet Commander, Captain Dawn DeFaller, RN).

Potential Spin-Off Contracts

The following naval forces have expressed interest in the Sting Ray Mark 3 torpedo which they may recommend for purchase if the weapon successfully completes sea trials during Operation Ankara.

United States Navy
Royal Saudi Naval Forces
Canadian Armed Forces (Maritime Command)
Australian Defence Force (Royal Australian Navy)

Dawn continued reading. There was information regarding the intention that the Sting Ray Mark 3 be placed aboard the new Type 45 destroyer as part of the standard weapons complement. There was mention of the interest of the Royal Saudi Naval Forces in potentially purchasing two or three ships of this class. An interest that would no doubt be much enhanced once the Sting Ray Mark 3 had been approved for entering regular service with the Royal Navy, she thought.

But nowhere was there any mention of the assistance rendered to UKNAS engineers in their development of the Sting Ray Mark 3 by Commander Hunt. However Dawn was not entirely surprised. She supposed that Hunt's artificial cognition-enhancement was presently simply too secret even for a dossier such as this.

She turned to the latter part of the dossier and studied her orders in detail in regard to the testing requirements for the new weapon. A new weapon which on paper at least appeared to be extremely impressive.

CHAPTER 3

The glassy calm water of the Caribbean Sea perfectly framed the elegant form of the United States Coast Guard Cutter *Eagle*. She sailed on through the warm night headed south-south west out of Bridgetown, Barbados, bound for Port-of-Spain, Trinidad, a distance of some two hundred and twenty nautical miles, or around sixteen hours sailing time. On her darkened bridge, peering out into the starlight twinkling from the cloudless sky, her commander, Captain Matthew Revere, USN, was engaged in conversation with his First Officer, Lieutenant-Commander Jim Hackett of the USCG.

"A beautiful night, sir," Hackett commented.

"Yes indeed. I have had occasion to sail these waters in the past and have always been fortunate to enjoy a tropical ambience, almost each and every time."

Hackett furrowed his brow for a moment.

"When did you first come here sir?"

Revere thought for a few seconds before answering. He did not want to lie, but he could hardly be transparently honest either.

"Quite a number of years ago," he said finally, as he thought of the time he had sailed through this general area aboard the fishing schooner *Jawn Henry*, back in 1761.

"I was with a different vessel at that time."

But in truth, although he had first plied these waters around two hundred and forty-seven years ago, to Revere the look and feel of the ocean did not seem much different. Even some of the towns at which they had stopped along the way, from Basseterre, St. Kitts, to Fort-de-France, Martinique, had hardly changed. There were of course roads, modern amenities, pleasant hotels, and even small airports. But for all that the islands and their principal population centers presented an appearance that was to Revere still recognizable and in essence similar to the way they were as he remembered them from the latter part of the 18th century. Even the specific locations that had apparently morphed out of all recognition, like Nassau town in the Bahamas where the crew of the *Eagle* had spent two nights about one week before, were not really so different from a cultural standpoint, once one took a little time and looked beneath the surface. Perhaps it had to do with island lifestyle and culture that seemed to him even now still conservative and resistant to modernity.

Revere decided that now would be an opportune time to change the subject of their conversation.

"So tell me, Jim. From where do you hail?"

"Key West, Florida, sir."

"Ah. Key West. I have spent a little time there."

Revere thought carefully about his next comment. He made a concerted effort to remember what he had read about the development of Florida through the 18th and 19th centuries.

"Key West was at one time the largest city in what is now the State of Florida."

"Yes sir. At that time Miami and Fort Lauderdale were just swamp land. Although Saint Augustine and Pensacola were the capitals, back when Florida was divided into two separate territories, east and west."

"Yes."

Revere remembered this well, but once more chose to remain quiet on the issue.

"Of course, Tallahassee is the capital now," Hackett went on.

In truth Lieutenant-Commander Hackett, as an Ivy-League graduate, was something of an intellectual. He liked to talk but most people quickly found him to be a bore. But Revere was different, and this was one reason why Hackett enjoyed his company.

"Originally Key West was isolated from the rest of the State, which was accessible only by boat, until Henry Flagler built his railroad across the Straits of Florida all the way from Miami via Key Largo to Key West, using the various keys along the way as natural staging points. The railroad was later badly damaged during the Labor Day Hurricane of 1935, one of the worst hurricanes ever to hit the Gulf coast. The railroad company could not afford to reinstate the service, which had been losing money right from the start. But Flagler's bridges were of sound construction and later gave rise to the overseas highway that now runs down to the city."

"Yes, indeed. I have read about that."

"So tell me sir, where have you been in Key West?"

Revere thought for a moment.

"One of the main thoroughfares in the city. I am sorry but I do not recall its name. It was a street running approximately north to south, located towards the western end of the island."

Revere did not mention the fact that he was there last in 1761, stopping for a couple of days sheltering from a storm while engaged in another fishing trip aboard the *Jawn Henry*. Nor did he mention that the town was a lot smaller than the size to which it ultimately grew, or that it had just come under the rule of the British Crown, and was dubbed *Cayo Hueso,* a name given to it by its Spanish settlers which literally meant *bone key,* so named for the many Native American burial grounds supposedly to be found there. Revere did remember however that at the time, the British were busy deporting the local Native Americans and Spaniards to Havana in nearby Cuba in an effort to clear the land for incoming settlers from England and the British Bahamas. But in the end the settlers never materialized in significant numbers. He had witnessed some of this first hand and had found it to be most distasteful, even distressing. Families who had lived there their whole lives were simply evicted at musket and bayonet point and forced aboard waiting ships, while their homes, property, and livelihoods were confiscated, and all in the name of His Britannic Majesty King George III. Indeed Revere had almost got into trouble with the Royal Navy when he rescued a young Spanish woman and her three children from the ravages of a particularly brutal British sailor, and smuggled them aboard the *Jawn Henry*. He later dropped them with a friendly and hospitable community with which he had some familiarity on the Netherlands Antilles. He could still remember her face. Her dark complexion. Her flowing black hair. Her name. Anna. He had never seen her again, but often wondered what had become of her.

Hackett interrupted his thoughts.

"Perhaps Duval Street?" Hackett was still trying to guess the name of the street Revere had been on.

"I do not recall. It was a long time ago."

"When you were there, did you go to the Ernest Hemingway house?"

"No, regretfully I did not."

Revere did not understand what Hackett had just asked him. But as he gained more experience of life in the early 21st century he had learned not to be so immediately honest with his thoughts. Hackett did not seem to notice.

"It is worth a visit, sir, especially if you enjoy reading some of Hemingway's stories."

"Ah. Hemingway is a writer."

"Was a writer. He is dead now, sir. But he was a very famous novelist. I am surprised that you haven't heard of him."

"I apologize. Unfortunately I am not an avid reader of the novel genre."

That answer seemed to satisfy Hackett. He continued.

"Well, he won the Pulitzer Prize for fiction in 1953 and the Nobel Prize in Literature the following year. He maintained a permanent residence in Key West, where he wrote *To Have and*

Have Not, although he was originally from Oak Park, Illinois. He committed suicide in Ketchum, Idaho, in 1961."

"I must read some of his work."

"Yes sir. I would recommend *The Old Man and the Sea,* or *For Whom the Bell Tolls.*"

Revere still was dissatisfied with the direction the conversation was taking, so he made another attempt to change the subject.

"Do you hail from a military family?"

"Yes sir," came the proud and immediate response. "My father was in the navy, and also my grandfather. My grandfather saw action in the Pacific aboard an aircraft carrier during the Second World War as a lieutenant-commander fighting the Japanese during the so-called Great Marianas Turkey Shoot, when an American carrier fleet went toe-to-toe with a Japanese carrier fleet and won, hands down. He survived all that unscathed but later was injured and sent home, back in early 1945, a few months before the atomic bombs that were dropped on Hiroshima and Nagasaki."

Revere balked inwardly a little as he contemplated what it must have been like to have been caught in the blast propagated by such weapons. Since his appointment as a captain in the modern USN he had been through some intensive and imaginatively designed training to bring him up to speed with modern naval officer standards, training which had included a somewhat in-depth study of nuclear weapons and their effects on structures, and human populations. He had studied the work of Dr. Robert Oppenheimer, chief scientist, and General Leslie Groves, US Army, as they had led the Manhattan Project in Los Alamos, New Mexico, and the test detonations of the very first atomic bombs at Trinity Site in the early 1940's. But he still had a hard time envisioning what would possess obviously very highly intelligent men to devote their gifts to the design of such an infernal device.

Hackett continued in his explanation, interrupting Revere's thoughts.

"I also have a brother in the army. He's a lieutenant in the Corps of Engineers. Right now he's in Iraq, taking care of all these improvised explosive devices that are being set by the insurgents."

The situation in Iraq had been a source of puzzlement for Revere. The more he had studied it, the less it had seemed to make sense to him.

"So tell me, what do you think of the way things are developing in Iraq?"

Hackett thought for a moment.

"Well, sir, I see it like this. It seems to me there are several factors involved, including the need for the advanced world to have continued access to the giant oil fields that exist in that whole area of the Middle East. Saudi Arabia possesses the largest proven global reserves of crude oil, and Iraq is not far behind. There is the added advantage that the Iraqi fields are largely undeveloped at this time, especially in the south of the country. The global economy depends on the continued flow of oil from the Middle Eastern pipelines. There is much talk at this time of alternative energy sources, but the numbers don't seem to add up, at least for a country as large as the United States. We are going to continue to have a need to import large quantities of oil, for the foreseeable future."

Revere pondered that last statement but could only respond in the affirmative.

"Indeed."

"And then there is the issue of terrorism. The events of September 11th, 2001, were terrible, and extraordinary. Subsequent attacks on London and Madrid were no picnics either. I cannot see how any rational person could argue against the idea that something big has to be done to address the problem of Al-Qaeda and its terrorist training activities, both within the Middle East and other nations, especially Western European nations. But then, all but one of the terrorist pilots who hijacked those airliners which attacked New York and Washington were Saudi nationals. The sole exception was Egyptian. In my opinion sir, the ringleader of Al-Qaeda,

Osama Bin Laden, a Saudi national himself, had purposely selected Saudis to fly that suicide mission because he was trying to create discord between the government of the United States and the House of Saud, which he hates for their allowing liberal decadence to spread across his country, not to mention its pro-US stance. In fact, Bin Laden seeks to destroy Saudi Arabia along with all other Arab nations and recreate an Islamic kingdom, or caliphate, extending from Egypt to Indonesia, and administered along the lines of very strict interpretation of Sharia law. He and others of his ilk believe that only then will Moslem peoples attain power and wealth in this world, when they return to the proper practice of Islam, which will be pleasing to Allah. This instead of the present situation whereby many Moslem nations, especially the non-Arab Moslem nations, are practicing a more liberal form of Islam, often without full Sharia law, or any to speak of at all in the cases of Turkey, Egypt, and Indonesia, which even accept to a certain degree the 'evils' of Western civilization and philosophy. In Bin Laden's eyes, this is an offense to Allah and incurs His judgment and wrath."

Revere was listening, but now he had a question.

"So why not send the military into Saudi Arabia instead of Iraq?"

"Because, sir, America in particular, and the West in general depends in part on Saudi oil supplies, and indeed the whole structure of the Western economic system is built around the price of a barrel of Saudi crude. Thus he who controls the Middle Eastern oilfields controls the Western, and hence the global economy. Also, despite their extremely conservative Wahhabist form of Islam, Saudi Arabia is arguably the most powerful and advanced country in that whole region, with the possible exception of Iran, and may well represent the key to restoration of some form of stability to the Middle East. The Saudi government are fully aware who the major players are in Al-Qaeda and could take effective steps to stop them. Perhaps in the end more effective steps than we in America can take, despite the obvious fact that America now possesses the largest and most powerful military machine on Earth. I daresay it is axiomatic that some problems respond better within the context of a diplomatic or political as opposed to a military solution. Although relations are somewhat strained between our two countries, the Saudis are the closest thing we have to friends over there, sir. Even though they are now charging around one hundred forty dollars for a barrel of oil, when back in 1999 they were charging ten. I suppose they are also thinking of their own national economic future, and perhaps they are trying to stem the increased demand for oil that the American and European governments are making upon them, as well as increasingly those of China and India."

"Perhaps."

Despite all of his recent studies, Revere still found it all very strange that the extraction, sale, and movement of crude oil, this thick and dirty black sludge now being extracted so vigorously from beneath the Earth's surface, was so vital to modern global economics. He had however learned not to say as much as he had quickly found that most people considered this, to say the least, a peculiar point of view. He also thought it odd that the world seemed intent on boosting its production and consumption of the same ever more into the future, when yet it was presumably a finite natural resource that surely must one day start to become depleted, all over the planet.

"Now Iraq by contrast is and has always been a mess. It is true that under Saddam Hussein things did operate in some semblance of an orderly society, but in essence, ever since its creation by Britain in 1920 following their initially unsuccessful invasion of the country early during the First World War, and then their later capture of Baghdad in 1917, it has never really worked. Modern Iraq was born out of the Anglo-French Sykes-Picot Agreement, a deal also involving Imperial Russia, which defined respective spheres of influence and control in West Asia following the downfall of the Ottoman Empire which had controlled Iraq up until that time. In November of 1920 the country became a League of Nations Mandate under British control. In the name of freedom the British imposed a Hāshimite monarchy on Iraq and defined the territorial limits of the country without taking into account the politics of different ethnic and religious groups, in particular those of the Kurds and the Assyrians to the north. During the British occupation, the Shi'ites and Kurds fought for independence. Perhaps inevitably, the cost of the occupation for Britain spiraled. There were numerous public protestations, many of which were published as letters in the *London Times.* In October 1920 Britain replaced Arnold Wilson with Sir Percy Cox as the new Civil Commissioner. Cox did for a time quell a brewing rebellion growing within Iraq, but was also ultimately responsible for implementing a policy of close co-operation between the British government and the Iraqi Sunni Moslem minority. Ultimately the British supported the Sunnis over the growing, urban-based nationalist movement. The Land Settlement Act which the British then implemented gave the tribal Shaykhs the right to register tribal lands in their own names. In addition the accompanying Tribal Disputes Regulations conferred upon the Shaykhs judiciary rights. But the Peasants' Rights and Duties Act of 1933 punished tenant farmers, forbidding them to leave their land until such time as all debts to their respective landlord had been settled. In 1941 British interests were threatened, for example during the Rashīd 'Alī al-Gaylānī coup, and Prime Minister Winston Churchill responded with a military invasion of the country with a force made up of the British Indian Army and the Arab Legion, based in Jordan. In fact, one leading historian has opined that the British invasion of Iraq in 1941 can be linked to the regime change debate over Iraq that took place in 2002. In some essential respects, the American posture against Saddam Hussein and Osama Bin Laden plays out like a reprise of Churchill's 1941 crusade against Rashid Ali and the Grand Mufti. Three fundamental arguments advanced by the Bush administration in support of a regime change in Iraq: the need to pre-empt Saddam Hussein before he acquired weapons of mass destruction and the means to deliver them; the requirement to strike a blow at terrorism; and the notion that a region of the world that possesses one-fifth of the global oil supply must not be allowed to fall under the control of a demonic regime that will use those resources for nefarious purposes; mirror almost exactly points stressed in an eerily similar historical context by Churchill sixty-one years earlier. In a nutshell, the British government of the 1920's thought little of the potential problems of marrying the Kurds to the north with the Sunni and Shi'ite Moslems to the south in a sort of shotgun wedding. And in fact Churchill even advocated using poison gas against the Kurdish people at one stage. Iraq was for all practical purposes created by Britain as a kind of garbage can state to house all of the Middle East's surplus troublemakers and undesirables. I agree that bringing down Saddam Hussein was a good thing. Saddam after all threatened global oil supplies when he invaded Kuwait in 1991, and was threatening to do something along similar lines again, as well as prosecute other attacks on Iran, or even Israel, of a magnitude that could destabilize the whole region and hence gravely threaten world security and badly damage the global economy. Although it is worthy of mention that the United States installed Saddam in power in the first place, and then supplied him with sufficient weaponry to enable him to remain so. But nevertheless, in my view his execution for the catalog of vile crimes he committed against his own people was richly deserved. But I am not at all convinced that democracy will ever be made to work in that country, sir. People forget that the British attempted to bring democracy to Iraq from the 1920's through the early 1940's, but the results were nothing short of disastrous. Hundreds of thousands of local people and tens of thousands of British servicemen died, but at no point was there ever any meaningful resolution to the inherent problems of the region. The current very similar American-led military intervention against the region has run into essentially the same issues."

Revere pondered this last statement thoughtfully. He seemed momentarily pained. When he spoke he sounded a little pressured and intense.

"Indeed. You know, America was not intended to develop into this. The intention of the Founding Fathers was to build a nation free of war, corruption, inequality, moral turpitude, murder, and strife. America was to be a nation lifted above the yoke and shackles of empire under the heel of monarchy, a safe haven if you will. America was not to become a nation seen by others around the world as a superpower, intent on building an empire of her own."

Hackett momentarily stared at Revere, surprised at this statement. In Hackett's mind Revere was sounding as if he had actually lived through the revolutionary period. But of course this was nonsense. After an awkward, pregnant pause, lasting another few seconds, he responded.

"Well yes, sir. But remember that the intention of the United States is only to spread freedom and democracy."

Revere simply returned Hackett's stare, shaking his head as if he were dealing with a child.

"That was exactly the argument of certain cabinet ministers within the British government of the 18th century, and of His Grace King George III. They were going to spread freedom and democracy, not to mention Christianity, even if they had to build the biggest navy and army the world had ever seen, and kill every single dissenting person in North America and elsewhere to achieve their aim. But what they failed to grasp at that time is the simple lesson that people will always ultimately reject governance from a foreign power, no matter how fair, equitable, or prosperous it may prove to be. Human beings do not want our notions of freedom and democracy foisted upon them. What they want, and in the end will have, is self-determination. The British learned this in North America, in India, in Africa, even in Asia. The Dutch for that matter learned this in Indonesia. As did the French in Indochina, and the Portuguese in Brazil. All of these nations at the height of their imperial powers suffered terrorist attacks. And they all ultimately lost their superpower status, although not, ironically, because of terrorism, but because of a combination of military over-extension and economic collapse."

Hackett did not really know how best to respond to this. Revere, surprisingly, seemed all of a sudden agitated and serious.

Hackett did not wish to start any kind of an argument with his commanding officer. So he decided simply to continue with the line of reasoning he had been developing.

"I think instead, after taking down Saddam we should have recruited the standing Iraqi army as a force to police the country with a zero-tolerance policy on violence and law-breaking, rather than disband them and then try to recreate a new local force which has not proven to be very effective. Attempts to placate the local populace with Western values have made us seem weak and ineffectual in the eyes of many Iraqis. Only the Ottoman Turks ever ruled effectively there, and they achieved this with the iron fist of totalitarianism, not modern Western notions of democracy, equality, and civil rights which to many Iraqis and others in that region are anathema."

Hackett seemed to have said his piece about the Middle East. But then he had more, this time in regard to Western Europe. Revere just remained silent.

"Then of course there is the issue of the growing populations of Moslems within France, Holland, Belgium, Sweden, and England, who increasingly are rejecting the cultural mores and traditions of their host countries, in favor of Islamic Sharia law."

At the mention of France Revere felt a slight jolt as he remembered the glimpse of an alternative world that he had been afforded. A world in which France as a theocratic and dictatorial Islamic superpower, governed by the dictator Prime Minister Alain DuLac, controlled North America and most of the developed world.

"For the first time in these countries since the advent of the Enlightenment Period and the Industrial Revolution, relatively small minorities representing a particular religious viewpoint have been able to impose their will on the majority, and are doing so to an ever greater and greater degree. In England for example one can no longer take one's dog, or alcoholic beverages, in taxi cabs or certain buses. In major French cities Islamic ghettoes, the *banlieues,* have sprung up. Local police forces regard them as no-go areas. Honor killings of young women by their husbands, fathers, and brothers are sharply increasing. On public transport in Malmö, Sweden, gangs of Islamic youths have been reported to beat up and sometimes even murder innocent travellers, in the full knowledge that they will most likely escape prosecution. And things seem to be worsening with each passing year. England now has more than eighty-five Sharia tribunals up and down the country, whereas just five years ago there were four, and ten years ago there were none. The Moslem population in that country is still a minority but is the fastest growing segment of society by a considerable margin. If one factors in the reduced birth rate among non-Islamic Britons, it would not be beyond the bounds of possibility to imagine that within the next half-century or so the British will waken up one day and find themselves living in a Sharia state. It is in fact quite bizarre when one considers that countries such as Turkey, Egypt, and Indonesia are Moslem and yet have embraced democracy and a modicum of separation of religion and state. And yet in England, where approximately four hundred years ago ideas underpinning modern democracy first started to form and incubate, where the Enlightenment and later the Industrial Revolution was born, the present generation are apparently intent on trading their hard-won freedoms, fought for against successive monarchies since the beginning of the 17th century, and then later Nazi Germany, for theocratic totalitarianism. A form of theocratic totalitarianism not unlike that which we see currently in, for example, Sudan, Saudi Arabia, and Yemen."

Revere gazed squarely at Hackett, thoughts of his past adventures flashing through his head making him shudder.

"I would sincerely like to believe that this is not so."

Glancing at the bridge chronometer, Revere noticed that it almost three o'clock in the morning.

"Come, Mr. Hackett. Your watch ended almost an hour ago. We shall be docking in Port-of-Spain within seven hours from now. I suggest that you turn in and get some rest. I will keep watch until Lieutenant Hunter reports for duty, which should be at three o'clock sharp."

"Yes sir. Good night sir."

"Good night, Mr. Hackett."

With that, Hackett saluted, took his leave, and made his way back to his cabin and his bunk. Once in Port-of-Spain the crew of the *Eagle* would enjoy another well-earned shore leave.

CHAPTER 4

North Atlantic Ocean, 0730hrs, June 4, 2008

Dawn peered through her binoculars at the four warships lying ahead of them in the mist of the early morning. Despite the time of year it was looking as if it was going to be another cool day, in the high fifties to low sixties only, according to meteorological reports. Not entirely surprising, given their current position west-north-west of Scotland's Shetland archipelago. She was standing on the bridge of *Wildcat,* her old command, the ship in which she had experienced some of the strangest and most exciting adventures of her life. It felt good to be back aboard, once more amongst familiar surroundings, and yet not to be in command any longer was still for her an odd experience. *Wildcat's* new captain, Commander Malcolm Callaghan came back onto the bridge after having taken care of some business that had occupied him outside on deck.

"Malcolm."

"Ma'am. Are you comfortable in your cabin?" His Scottish brogue was still distinctive but yet perhaps a little more refined than since last they had met.

"Your cabin now, Malcolm." Dawn smiled. She was of course referring to the captain's cabin, which had been her personal space aboard this ship. Malcolm's space now, but one which he had gladly vacated as soon as he had heard that Dawn was coming aboard.

The Communications Officer, Lieutenant Gray, called out.

"Ma'am! *Daring* is hailing us! Vice-Admiral Powers would like to speak with you!"

"Thank you." She crossed over to the opposite side of the bridge console and picked up the radio handset.

"Captain DeFaller speaking. Over."

"Captain. Powers. The merchant contingent of *Ankara* are now twenty nautical miles from our position. They will be stopping within the hour. I have already arranged a boat from *Daring* to ferry the respective captains across to *Wildcat* so that you may meet with them. Also, Commander Hunt will be arriving on board *Diamond* at 0800hrs tomorrow morning. Over."

"How is he, sir? Over."

"So far his physical and mental conditions are first rate, according to the medics who are with him. Also, I spoke with him myself just a few minutes ago. He says he's chomping at the bit and rearing to go. Over."

"Excellent news, sir. Over."

"Yes indeed. We will give Commander Hunt one hour following his arrival on board *Diamond* to settle in, and then we go. Stand by for further orders. Over and out."

Approximately two and a half hours later Dawn found herself once more in *Wildcat's* officers' mess, facing the commanders of the merchant ships for the first time. Malcolm was busy performing the introductions. From their reactions it seemed as if they were finding their experience aboard *Wildcat* perhaps a little too stiff and formal.

"May I introduce Captain Martin Grant, commanding officer, tanker *Exxon Lion.*"

"Captain Grant."

"Captain DeFaller."

"And then we have Captain Bryan King, commanding officer, tanker *Saskatchewan Star.*"

"Captain King."

King, a large-framed but well-proportioned man in his early forties of perhaps six feet four inches, smiled disarmingly, and extended his right hand. He seemed immediately to project a most pleasant demeanor.

"A pleasure to meet you, Captain." He annunciated his words in a pleasant cultured Texan drawl. "I am very much looking forward to assisting you with your exercise in any way possible."

Dawn smiled.

"Thank you, Captain. It is most kind of you to agree to work with us."

Callaghan moved along.

"Captain Richard Alexander, commanding officer, tanker *Brent B.*"

Alexander, a short stout man in his early sixties, just stared at her impassively.

"Captain," she said, politely.

"Captain."

Unlike the American accents of Grant and King, Alexander was English. From the north, judging by his accent. Perhaps Sheffield. There seemed to be just a touch of surliness about him. He did not seem overly enthused to be a part of the proceedings.

Callaghan then introduced a slender brunette woman in her early forties.

"Captain Barbara Brown, commanding officer, ocean-going salvage tug *Lloydsman II.*"

Brown faced Dawn directly.

"Captain. Thank you for inviting us aboard your vessel."

She came across as educated, polite, proper. Perhaps a little cold.

"Captain. It is a pleasure to meet you."

Callaghan then turned to another dark-haired man, also in his forties, about five feet ten inches tall.

"Finally, ma'am, Captain Pieter Pronk, commanding officer, ocean-going salvage tug *Smit Texel.*"

Pronk stood to attention, clipped his heels, and bowed his head politely.

"Captain. Ma'am."

"Captain." She took an immediate liking to Pronk. As with many Netherlanders he was polite to a fault. "Once again, thank you for joining in our little exercise."

"I am very glad to be of assistance."

Following the introductions Dawn asked everyone present to be seated, and began her presentation.

"The exercise in which you have all agreed to participate, Operation *Ankara*, will begin at 0900hrs, that is, nine o'clock, tomorrow morning. I must stress once again that your participation in this exercise is voluntary, but we greatly appreciate your assistance. I would also add that, unlike regular naval rules and regulations regarding operation of STUFT vessels, that is, merchant Ships Taken Up From Trade, there will be no complement of Royal Navy officers aboard your vessels. So it will be up to you to maintain communications with myself as Commander of the Task Group, or CTG."

Dawn quickly scanned the room as she made this last statement, hoping to see evidence that the civilian commanders would be set a little more at ease to know that there would be no direct naval presence aboard their ships. But if any such evidence were present, she didn't detect it, more to her chagrin.

"At 0900hrs you will be asked to form up as a convoy, the three large tankers will be spaced fifteen nautical miles apart, facing due west, with *Saskatchewan Star* in the lead. As formed up, *Saskatchewan Star* will be positioned at sixty-one degrees north, seven degrees west. All other merchant vessels will calculate their start positions from *Saskatchewan Star*. *Exxon Lion* will lie astern of *Saskatchewan Star,* in a due-easterly direction. *Brent B* will then lie another fifteen miles due east of *Exxon Lion*. For the purposes of this exercise, it will be assumed that *Exxon Lion* is carrying a more valuable cargo than either *Saskatchewan Star* or *Brent B*. To this end, the salvage tug *Smit Texel* will be positioned, also facing due west, one mile due north of *Exxon Lion,* and *Lloydsman II* will be positioned, again facing due west, one mile south of *Exxon Lion.* Thus the entire merchant convoy will be formed as an elongated diamond, with the most valuable vessel, for the hypothetical purposes of the exercise, in the very center, with some modicum of protection from the front, rear, and both flanks."

As she spoke she marked the relative positions of each ship on a whiteboard, with a felt-tipped pen. She turned to address the two salvage tug captains, both of whom were seated together.

"Be aware, that your duties will include mounting an additional lookout to help guard *Exxon Lion,* and also be ready to provide a rapid towing response should any of the three tankers become crippled, or a rapid rescue response should any be 'hit' or even 'sunk', although the navy would also provide very rapid assistance in the latter situation. You will, for all practical purposes, be acting as goalkeepers. But also be careful to maintain your one mile separation. This latter requirement will be relatively easy for you, whereas for *Exxon Lion,* which is much less maneuverable, even despite the fact that she will be carrying no cargo and will be running only in ballast, it will be practically impossible. It will be up to you."

Dawn's last statement prompted a comment from Brown.

"Thank you for your directions and instruction, Captain. However Captain Pronk and I are in fact already very well aware of the issues and special concerns when running with large tankers. But that aside, what of the naval vessels? Where will they be located, relative to us?"

Her voice poorly masked an element of mild irritation. Perhaps even annoyance.

Dawn eyed her for a moment. Why did she get the sense that this woman was trying to compete with her? Was she just imagining it? She decided to ignore it.

"That is the clever part. Convoy escort today is a more complex business than during the Second World War. We have in our naval flotilla five surface vessels available, including this one, and a nuclear attack submarine, but at any given time no more than two surface vessels will be within sight of the convoy. The other three will be anywhere from fifty to one hundred nautical miles distant, in any direction from your position, and thereby visible only on your radar. And since the submarine will remain submerged for most or possibly all of the exercise, you will not detect her at all, except perhaps briefly. I am assuming that your vessels are not equipped with anti-submarine sonar."

Brown, who had been staring at her incessantly, looked away at this last statement.

"The distant ships will be actively engaged in hunting and perhaps intercepting potential threats while they are still relatively far from the convoy. The warships within sight will act in the role of final defense should any attack successfully penetrate our outer screen."

Pronk had a further question. His whole demeanor was much more pleasant than Brown's.

"What form might such an attack take, Captain?"

"An excellent question, Captain. At selected times one or more of the warships, perhaps even the submarine, may act in the role of aggressor, in order to test the defenses arranged by the others. Also we will, in addition to maintaining a defensive screen around about the convoy, at various times be firing some highly advanced torpedoes."

Brown seemed immediately alarmed.

"Torpedoes?"

"Torpedoes, yes Captain. But do not be concerned. These weapons will be unarmed. They are also of a very sophisticated design, and they should be well able to provide an additional modicum of significant protection for the convoy, in the form of monitoring for enemy vessels or threats, completely independently. That is another thing that we shall be testing tomorrow. But the bottom line is, the torpedoes will be there to protect the merchant convoy. Not attack it."

She decided against adding that these torpedoes were still in the experimental stage.

"These bloody torpedoes of yours had better not cause any trouble," Alexander stated flatly. "I have a crew of fifty-eight people to worry about."

"Please, Captain, be assured that they will be carrying no explosive warheads. They will be incapable of detonation. You will never see them. That I promise you."

"I hope so. Just so that you are aware, I was against taking part in this exercise. My ship is here only because Royal Dutch Shell informed me that we would be helping out the Royal Navy. By rights at this time I should be steaming towards the Persian Gulf. Not sitting it out here in the freezing waters of the North Atlantic taking part in this bloody exercise."

Inwardly Dawn sighed. By this point in her career she had sufficient experience of British Merchant Navy officers to be aware that for some there was no love lost between them and the Royal Navy, which could make them difficult to work with, but she had rather been hoping to avoid such potential problems. It seemed however that Alexander was determined to make his displeasure known. She was also beginning to get the feeling that Brown was not entirely happy to be participating in *Ankara* either. She hoped that over the course of the ensuing days this would not grow to become a concern.

"All will be well, Captain Alexander. You have my word."

But for all of her assurances, Alexander still seemed unimpressed.

Activity aboard the tankers had been kept ticking over all night at a low level, but things had intensified after 0530hrs as the vessels started firing up their engines, an involved process requiring a period of over an hour to complete. When their engines had finally been made ready, the vessels had then slowly moved into their respective positions, and held at their assigned co-ordinates using their computer-controlled thrusters, which worked in combination with their on-board GPS systems. The two ocean-going tugs had then finally taken up their respective stations also, but only after the tankers were settled in position. By 0830hrs all stood ready with the convoy.

On *Wildcat's* bridge, with Callaghan standing beside her, Dawn stood looking out at the merchant ships through a pair of powerful binoculars. She marveled at the size of the tankers. *Exxon Lion* was the closest to *Wildcat* at that moment. But even although she was about a mile and a half distant, she looked huge, decorated from stem to stern with a variety of white and colored lights, causing her to resemble, superficially at least, a floating city. She remembered well her experiences two years ago aboard the giant American aircraft carrier USS *Enterprise,* but even that ship would seem only moderately large when compared to one of these vessels. These big tankers needed thirty miles of sea-room to stop, even with all engines in full reverse, and had a minimum turning circle of ten miles radius. She had heard that the crew used motor scooters to traverse the main deck between the for'ard and aft sections, for to walk this distance might take as much as from fifteen to twenty-five minutes.

Presently a younger man whom Dawn did not recognize, wearing the uniform of a Lieutenant-Commander, stepped onto the bridge from the deck outside. He addressed Callaghan.

"Sir, the ship is ready to get under way. All electronic and weapons systems are nominal, sir, as is the Lynx."

"Very good, Commander."

Callaghan then indicated Dawn.

"May I introduce our flotilla Commander, Captain Dawn DeFaller? Captain DeFaller will be in overall command for the duration of *Ankara.* Ma'am, please allow me to introduce my executive officer, Lieutenant-Commander William Shirer."

Shirer immediately snapped to attention and saluted.

"Ma'am!"

She returned the salute.

"Lieutenant-Commander Shirer."

"Two years ago Captain DeFaller was officer in command of *Wildcat.* At that time I was her Executive Officer."

"An honour to meet you, ma'am." To Dawn, as a native of the English West Country, he sounded as if he hailed from Cornwall. Perhaps Bodmin. Or Padstow. "Commander Callaghan has often spoken of you."

She smiled.

"I hope he has not been too honest."

Callaghan immediately spoke up.

"I have shared with Commander Shirer something of our adventures and exploits together, ma'am."

"Quite. Well, Mr. Shirer, you are in excellent hands. Commander Callaghan is a fine officer."

"Ma'am."

As their brief exchange came to a conclusion, Shirer snapped to attention once more.

During the run-up to 0900hrs, voices on the radio started coming through from the merchant ships indicating their states of readiness to commence operations. Dawn glanced at the radar screen. In aside to *Wildcat* which was now standing approximately two miles to the south of *Lloydsman II*, *Rosshire* was positioned three miles to the north-west of *Saskatchewan Star*. *Daring*, by contrast, was standing ready to sweep the ocean ahead for submarines, and was presently about ten miles south of Reykjavik, Iceland, rendering her much more distant. And *Dardanelles* was standing ready at a point twenty miles west-north-west, from where she would be ready to commence sweeping the ocean ahead of the convoy for mines using her sophisticated detection equipment. For her part, *Skirmisher* was presently submerged and, according to Dawn's current information, somewhere within a one hundred seventy-five mile radius of the convoy, but she did not know where. The SSN, during this initial phase of *Ankara* was to act in stealth mode, and possibly mount an 'attack' on the convoy. It would be up to the commanders of the individual surface vessels to locate and 'destroy' *Skirmisher* before she would be able to strike at any targets. Both destroyers, *Wildcat* and *Daring*, each of which was especially suited to antisubmarine warfare, would have their work cut out for them.

Ankara commenced at precisely 0900hrs. The convoy started steaming on a westerly heading that would take them south of Iceland, then on past Cape Farewell and Sydproven, on Greenland's southern coast, to eventually reach the Hudson Strait lying between Northern Québec and the giant bulk of Baffin Island in north-eastern Canada. Only conventional detection equipment and weapons would be in use during this phase of the exercise. On reaching the Hudson Strait, which would be some two thousand miles from their starting point and would take about five days to achieve, the convoy would stop and rest for a couple of days. During that time the navy would assess how things had gone up until that point, including addressing any concerns the civilian captains might have. Also at that juncture the performance of Commander Hunt of *Diamond* would be assessed, and compared with that of Commander Wood of *Daring*. Following this, the convoy would in essence turn around and make the return voyage to the starting point. It would be during this second, easterly voyage, that the ability of the Sting Ray Mark 3 torpedoes to defend the convoy on their own would be tested. Dawn would also soon have to brief the naval captains, as well as her own officers, on the specifics of the new torpedo as she had not yet done so. At present all any of them knew, with the exception of Commander Hunt, was that they would be testing some kind of enhanced weapon. It would soon be time to get everybody up to speed.

Throughout the return voyage Commander Hunt's abilities would continue to be tested. Following their arrival back at their starting position, Dawn would have to comment officially in the form of an extensive report on the performance of both the Sting Ray Mark 3, and Commander Hunt in his cognition enhanced state. For now she could only hope that things would turn out well.

By the end of the initial twenty-four hour period of sailing, the convoy was passing approximately two hundred miles south-south-east of Reykjavik. The weather had been good with easterly winds blowing at no more than Force 1. During this period *Skirmisher* had made three approaches, each from a different angle as she had circled under the convoy, but in every case she was intercepted and 'sunk' before coming within sixty miles of the tankers. Although in the final attack she had, after initial detection by *Daring* very nearly been able to evade continued tracking by the destroyer's sonar array. Fortunately *Dardanelles* had been able to pick up and maintain the contact long enough for *Daring* to regain the positive sonar fix. On reflection of the circumstances which had led up to the development of this scenario, Dawn had decided to recommend instigation of corrective procedures regarding the performance of Commander Wood of *Daring*. But she had commended the quick thinking and rapid actions of Lieutenant-Commander Burleigh of *Dardanelles,* which, had this chain of events played out in earnest, would undoubtedly have saved lives. So far Commander Hunt had achieved nothing truly spectacular, but it was clear even before any detailed analysis of events had been performed that he was making decisions more rapidly and with a higher degree of fidelity than any of his competitors. In the various preliminary exercises, whether as attacker or defender, acting either alone or in tandem, and adjusting for all other factors it was obvious that Hunt had the upper hand. It was not so much that his performance belied a greater degree of intellect as such, but simply that he was able to assimilate and process information significantly more effectively than his fellow officers, all of whom were similarly experienced and in command of similar, or in the case of Commander Wood, identical vessels. Hunt had even been able to anticipate as if by some sixth sense the thought processes and decisions made by Jack Tylon, the attack submarine skipper. And all this despite the subtleties and nuances of Tylon's Perisher's training, required of every British submarine skipper, but which Hunt himself lacked.

Dawn had spent part of that first evening sitting in her cabin with Malcolm and Powers, who had come over from *Daring*, discussing Hunt's performance.

Malcolm had piped up with a question for Powers.

"So what did you make of the day's events, sir?"

"More or less as expected, Commander. Commander Hunt's ability to recognize and assess situations seems to be undoubtedly enhanced, as is his ability to put his thoughts into practice. But this is as we predicted."

"How is he feeling so far, sir?"

Dawn was still concerned that there might be some side-effects to the experimental medication.

"Medical reports indicate that he is in tip-top condition, Captain. Really, there is nothing here that has not been anticipated. But although Hunt is clearly experiencing enhanced mental abilities, we have seen nothing to suggest the comparative level of enhancement that was found in the animal tests, at least not yet. We have spoken with some of his own bridge officers, people who have worked with him and know his professional persona. In fact I spent about thirty minutes this afternoon talking with his executive officer, Lieutenant-Commander Ewan MacRae. He is of the opinion that Hunt is entirely the same as he has always been, in every respect that counts, but is simply sharper and virtually error-free in his thinking, like a well-oiled, highly efficient machine. He said in fact it was a sheer pleasure to work with him today. But Hunt is continuing on daily drug treatments and so we will see how things develop."

Callaghan had another question.

"If I may ask something else, sir?"

"Shoot."

"Why the Royal Navy, sir? If this drug that we are testing has been developed by an American company, and the interest that has been expressed in it for military purposes thus far has come from the USN, why is it that the entire flotilla is composed of British ships?"

Powers laughed, and looked at Dawn.

"I seem to remember you asking a similar question about two years back, when we were about to attempt to project *Wildcat* half way across the globe."

In response she just stared at him wanly.

He faced Callaghan and addressed his question.

"Well, Commander, the reasons are political. As indeed they nearly always are. The present CEO of Brodmann Corporation, Jon Noble, is British. An Englishman, I believe."

"I am still not sure I entirely understand, sir."

"Well you see Commander, Dr. Noble insisted on one condition. Which was, he would agree to turn over the fruits of Brodmann Corporation's labors to the armed services for testing, only if it were to be performed initially, and satisfactorily completed, in his estimation, by a British contingent. It seems that Dr. Noble does not trust us Americans to refrain from using his drug as a tool for waging war. So of course, being the obliging folks that we are, we acquiesced to Dr. Noble's wishes."

Dawn grinned.

"You know, sir, I cannot help but be reminded of the previous experiment that involved a British ship. This ship, in fact. I do hope things do not go awry this time."

"I think we can safely say that this little exercise is going to prove much more pedestrian than our previous forays into warp field generation."

They continued talking for a short time further, until Malcolm was called away to the bridge. Dawn had then offered Powers one more drink before he himself would have to be getting back to *Daring*. But in the meantime they continued to chat for a little while longer.

"So how are you finding married life, Captain, if I may be so bold?"

"You know sir, for some time I imagined I was simply not the marrying type. That is, until I met Matthew. Life with him, sir, is just perfect. I cannot think of any other way to put it. We are so right for each other. And of course, it is only because of the warp field experiment that I was ever able to meet him at all."

"How is Matthew adjusting to life in the early 21st century?"

"Well, sir, reports have all been most favorable, and psychological-"

"I am not asking for your summary of a pile of psychological mumbo-jumbo authored by a cadre of PhD's. What is your personal assessment? As his wife?"

Dawn smiled, then just shook her head gently from side to side.

"It is marvelous how he has adjusted sir. Truly marvelous. It is as if he was born to live here in this time, with us."

"No issues?"

"Issues?"

"Sudden bouts of apparent anger? Depression? Homesickness for his own world and time?"

"I have kept a watch for all that, sir, as I was advised to do. I have also discussed it with him on numerous occasions. But he seems more than happy and content with his present lot."

Powers fell silent for a moment, as she took a sip of the brandy in her glass.

"So tell me, sir, are you married?"

Powers' expression grew more serious. He didn't answer immediately. When he did, his voice sounded a little more grave, his normal upbeat disposition temporarily on hold.

"I was once. Jean and I were married in 1980, back when I was a very junior lieutenant. Our son Anton was born two years later, in September 1982. He would be coming up for his twenty-sixth birthday."

"Would be, sir?"

"If he had lived."

Dawn was suddenly embarrassed.

"Oh, I'm so sorry, I didn't mean-"

He stared for a moment directly into her eyes, as if seeking an absolution.

"That's quite all right. Anton died in late 1988 in a car accident. A friend was bringing him home from her child's birthday party when a drunk driver coming the other way lost control of his vehicle, crossed the center median, and hit them head-on. Our friend was all right, suffering from minor injuries only, but Anton was rushed to a local hospital. He never recovered consciousness, and died there about four hours later. Jean died three years following that after having been diagnosed with a particularly aggressive brain tumor. A glioblastoma multiforme of the parietal lobe, the doctors called it, if memory serves."

Dawn felt crushed. She wished she had never raised the issue.

"People said, and continue to say that I should remarry. But Jean and I were, how did you put it, so right for each other. After her there can be no-one else. Of course I have met others over the years, but it is always immediately clear that no matter how well we get along, no matter what we might think and feel about each other, I could never be married to anyone else. There can be no-one else to replace Jean. What she meant to me. It all happened a long time ago, but of course I still remember them both as if it were yesterday. I sometimes wonder what would have become of Anton had he lived. Would he have followed me into the navy, done something else entirely, or what? But there it is. Life throws a curve ball sometimes, knocks you down. You just have to get back on your feet and move on."

A solitary tear welled in Dawn's eye and ran down her cheek.

"I'm so dreadfully sorry."

"Don't be. My life has played out as it was intended, and will end when my time here is done, just as for each and every one of us. Of that I have no doubt."

Despite her feelings of awkwardness and embarrassment, Dawn found herself looking at Powers with new-found respect and admiration for his sheer strength of will. For in spite of the terrible pain he must undoubtedly have suffered, he was invariably friendly and upbeat, and yet a thoroughly committed and professional officer.

The following four days brought essentially more of the same for Operation *Ankara*. Additional approaches by *Skirmisher* were warded off in much the same manner as before. *Rosshire* played a prominent role on day three of the exercise, winning Commander MacPherson a commendation. By the time the convoy was pulling into the Hudson Strait Dawn was beginning to get the impression that things were going to be largely routine. During the two-day period that the ships were to remain there, the civilian officers and crew were to be allowed to go ashore for some rest and recreation, however the naval vessels were to remain on station, guarding their charges and taking stock of their performance thus far. During their down-time, Dawn was going over the initial part of her report on the outcome of events, and noted with satisfaction that Commander Hunt had been able to triumph in all permutations of possible scenarios with the small flotilla at their disposal. No matter how the other ships or the submarine had attempted to attack him, either alone or in combination, he had not only spotted the weakness in their plan and acted rapidly and accordingly, but in addition he had never once failed, in the role of sole merchant ship escort, to maintain a highly effective defensive screen around *Exxon Lion,* despite her massive bulk and relative lack of speed and maneuverability. And the medical officers looking after him had about an hour earlier provided her with yet another update of his physical and mental condition, which checked out as nothing short of excellent. They also noted that his overall mental clarity and sharpness did appear to be slowly improving as the days rolled on.

During the second, return phase of the exercise a number of additional attack maneuvers were to be mounted against Hunt's ship, and he was to essentially repeat his previous performance of defending his vessel, but this time with the benefit of the Sting Ray Mark 3 torpedoes which would shortly be stationed at various points around *Diamond,* each weapon independently weighing and assessing the situation, ready to strike any 'enemy' at a moment's notice. As each torpedo was tipped with a dummy warhead only, any strike against a ship would simply register as a blip on an on-board computer on the bridges of *Wildcat* and *Daring* and the vessel 'hit', and also cause an alarm to sound. There would be no audible explosion, no damage. Just the knowledge, privy only to the bridge officers, that a hit had been achieved. The level of enthusiasm for the new Sting Rays was extremely high, now that Dawn had revealed their details to her officers and fellow commanders. In truth everybody could hardly wait to see if they would, or even could, perform as promised.

Two days after arriving at the Hudson Strait, the merchant vessels weighed anchor and departed for their starting position on the other side of the Atlantic. Immediately following their departure, the naval vessels powered up and moved out behind them. Soon after departing Canadian coastal waters, and at precisely the appointed time, *Diamond* launched forty Mark 3 torpedoes, one after another, on command from *Daring*. Dawn watched the scenario developing from the radar on *Wildcat's* bridge which had been configured to track the telemetry outputs from the weapons. Her initial impression of them was that they did indeed seem able to deliver on the claims of their manufacturer. Following launch, the torpedoes veered away from *Diamond* at breakneck speed, but then seemed to slow and come to an almost dead stop in the water after they had run out some ten miles.

"This is the point where they start monitoring," Dawn commented. "At this moment the torpedoes, using their on-board GPS, are establishing the positions of each vessel in *Diamond's* vicinity. They have of course been programmed to recognize *Diamond* as friendly, but not the rest of us. They are also taking into account the bottom profile of the ocean in this general area, and all coastlines within 150 miles."

A question occurred to Callaghan.

"What about if they were to encounter other vessels, ma'am, not included in their programming?"

"Then they would regard them as friendly, unless given specific instructions to the contrary by a naval vessel which possessed their access codes, or unless the vessels were to assume a posture potentially threatening to their principal. Although even in that case they would, if there was time, broadcast a warning on all standard international communications frequencies, affording the potential hostile or hostiles an opportunity to stand down, before committing to an attack."

The torpedoes really were impressive. Over the course of the next two hours, Dawn watched as they zig-zagged around within ten miles of *Diamond,* forming a protective screen and at the same time looking out for enemy infiltration. Dawn contacted Tylon of *Skirmisher* with the instruction that he was to commence, at his discretion, an attack on *Diamond.* Dawn did not know of *Skirmisher's* current position, but this apparently mattered not. The submarine ascended from her position at depth and within twenty minutes Callaghan called out from the radar.

"Torpedo number two has established contact, ma'am! Number five is also moving in to offer assistance!"

The new torpedoes were not only able to function independently, but they were also able to communicate with each other, precisely as outlined in the UKNAS dossier that Dawn had read. In this case, of the forty torpedoes launched, number two had detected the threat posed by *Skirmisher* and had immediately signaled the others with the updated information regarding the position, depth, direction, and speed of the SSN. Following analysis of this new development, number five had made the decision to assist. The others evidently were remaining on station to continue to provide cover for *Diamond.* It was not long thereafter that Tylon became aware that his vessel had been detected by two incoming torpedoes but by that time it was too late. He instigated standard evasive maneuvers but the Sting Rays were rocketing towards his boat, which was still six hundred feet below the surface, in a converging path from two different directions. They had run so silently as to be undetectable by his sonar array until twelve seconds before impact. Number five was the first to strike in the for'ard section, followed a half second later by number two which struck aft. When the torpedoes hit there was a loud dull thud, clearly audible to the crew inside *Skirmisher's* hull. The weapons then disengaged, activated their transponder beacons and strobe lamps, inflated their buoyancy control devices, and floated up to the surface. There they awaited later retrieval by *Wildcat,* after the termination of the day's exercise. They were then to be stored until they could be delivered back to UKNAS for detailed inspection.

Skirmisher went on to make several additional attacks from different positions and depths, but even with the constantly improving skills of her sonar operators in dealing with the incoming threat posed by the weapons, she was hit each and every time, always by at least one and sometimes two, and always in a vulnerable position which would have resulted in a massive inrush of water that would certainly have sunk her. Even an attempt by her technicians to improve the sensitivity of the sonar equipment resulted only in her being able to detect the incoming torpedoes up to two seconds earlier than she otherwise would, an improvement in performance that Tylon assessed as 'almost negligible under the circumstances' in his interim report.

Next, Dawn ordered *Skirmisher* to make an attack run while submerged, while *Wildcat* and *Daring* also mounted additional, simultaneous attacks. This was attempted, at first with all three vessels coming in from the same general direction, then repeated from completely different directions. The pattern was repeated again, with all vessels attacking at the same time, and then once again but with each vessel attacking sequentially. But the end result was always the same in every case. Despite the best efforts of their commanders, *Skirmisher, Wildcat* and *Daring* were invariably hit just a few seconds after they became aware they were under attack, and always by two or three weapons. In one case *Daring* was hit while standing only a quarter-mile from *Diamond*. One of the torpedoes that struck her actually circumscribed a path around *Diamond,* bypassing her by the narrowest of safe margins, but then homed in on *Daring*.

Dawn was very happy with the performance of the new torpedoes thus far. She felt fully able to deliver a glowing report to Vice-Admiral Bailey and the UKNAS-RN Joint Committee, with whom she had been informed she may be meeting in a few days time.

Day five of the second phase of *Ankara,* the last day of the exercise, commenced with the launch of the remaining ten of the test Sting Rays. By now everyone was becoming quite accustomed to the weapons' modus operandi and it was simply a matter of completing the obligation by the Royal Navy to test all fifty of the initial batch of weapons delivered. A few final attack scenarios were set up and executed. In each case, just as previously, eight of the torpedoes, operating completely independently, found their mark. At the conclusion of the exercise, Dawn finally brought all proceedings associated with *Ankara* officially to an end, and instructed Callaghan to recall the final two weapons that had not engaged any target but which were still at sea. He had turned to Shirer and relayed the order as a simple matter of routine. Shirer had then seen to it that the communications officer was taking the situation in hand. Dawn had then turned to Callaghan once more.

"So what do you think, Malcolm? How do you rate these new Sting Rays?"

Malcolm took a deep breath.

"I think they're bloody marvelous, ma'am, bloody marvelous. The engineers who designed them are extremely ingenious. My only fear is that once they enter general service, there won't be a job left for us."

Dawn smiled.

"My thoughts too, Malcolm. It would seem that not only have they successfully defended the convoy, but they have actually performed the job more proficiently than even Commander Hunt managed to do during phase one of *Ankara*. What would you suppose if-"

"Sir!"

The tone of Shirer's voice betrayed a sense of controlled urgency. Callaghan looked over at him.

"Yes? What is it?"

"Torpedoes nine and ten, sir! The one's we launched today! They are not responding to our recall signal!"

Callaghan rushed over to the communications console.

"Do you have the correct codes?"

"Yes sir! Both torpedoes acknowledge the signal, but in effect have refused to obey!"

"Refused to obey?"

"Yes sir! And they're headed towards one of the tankers!"

He stared at the radar scope, on which he could make out the somewhat alarming sign of the two remaining torpedoes speeding towards the massive bulk of *Brent B.*

"Well try again! Enter the codes manually this time!"

"Yes sir!"

But even as Shirer typed the recall codes at the keyboard in front of him, both torpedoes suddenly increased to maximum speed, and then ran themselves headlong into the tanker.

They struck her simultaneously amidships and astern.

CHAPTER 5

"What the hell are you fucking people playing at?" Alexander had still not calmed down after nearly twenty minutes meeting with Dawn in Callaghan's cabin aboard *Wildcat.*

"Did I not make it clear that I have fifty-eight crew members to think about? What do you suppose would have happened if our fire fighting apparatus had not taken care of the explosion that you caused? We are an oil tanker, for God's sake! Running in ballast, with fumes! Flammable fumes! We could have been blown to kingdom come!"

Alexander was referring to the torpedo that had struck his vessel amidships, on the starboard side. The weapon of course had been carrying no warhead, as Dawn had repeatedly assured him, but because of its speed had burst through the merchant vessel's relatively thin starboard hull plates, entering the empty Number 5 Cargo Tank. It had then shot right through to the opposite side, damaging a tank baffle in the process, and slammed against the port plates of the hull, finally coming to rest. Indeed the internal baffle probably robbed the torpedo of enough speed to prevent it from exiting the port side to the ocean as it most probably otherwise would have done. The resultant concussion had sparked a small explosion, fueled by the air/petroleum fume mixture present in the tank. Ordinarily the empty tank would have been filled with inert gas, rather than air, to quell any explosive tendencies, but there had not been time to sort this out before commencement of *Ankara*. By a stroke of bad luck, Number 5 Tank had just a few hours before been filled with air to facilitate an urgent and legally mandated inspection by two members of *Brent B's* crew. Only a rapid and, Dawn thought, thoroughly efficient response by *Brent B's* fire fighters had prevented a more serious situation from developing. The tank had of course flooded with seawater, but at a rate wholly insufficient to quell the fire. To compound the error, the other torpedo had hit the tanker astern, badly damaging her solitary rudder and screw, and bending her propeller shaft. Alexander had been obliged to shut down his engines in a hurry to avoid the need for further costly repairs. In the high seas in which *Brent B* had found herself she had rapidly gone into a high-speed drift, in water much too deep to drop her anchors. Rapid action by *Lloydsman II* which had been on station had resulted in *Brent B* being brought under partial control following the tug's third attempt to fire a hawser line over to her. The tug's water cannon had also played a role in extinguishing her tank fire. In the meantime *Exxon Lion* had increased speed and steered a new course in order to afford her more sea-room in which to maneuver, and just in the nick of time as it turned out. Had she not done so, a collision between her and *Brent B* could very possibly have taken place. But the 211,000 ton *Brent B* had not finally been brought completely under control until *Smit Texel* had been able to reach her and join in on the act. With the two giant tugs now exerting a combined 85,000 horse-power, *Brent B* was safe, although not before Barbara Brown of *Lloydsman II* had contacted Dawn over the radio simply to give her a piece of her mind. Like Alexander it seemed that she had little patience for the Royal Navy. Or with Dawn. In fact, out of the three vessels involved in this incident, only Pieter Pronk of *Smit Texel* had maintained an air of professional courtesy and civility towards her.

"I assure you, Captain Alexander, I have no idea why this incident occurred and the Royal Navy will leave no stone unturned until we establish the cause of the problem."

Alexander was still unimpressed. Indeed his face was so red Dawn thought he might actually burst a blood vessel.

"I am so thoroughly sick of you navy people, with your arrogant airs and graces, your self-importance as you swoon around, expecting everyone to jump to attention in your presence. And all because you carry guns and munitions over which, like the petulant adolescents that deep down you all are, you quite obviously have no real control. This is not a game, you know. People could have been killed. My ship is going to be out of commission for weeks. And who, exactly, is going to pay for her repairs? Tell me that! If you can!"

Dawn felt a growing sense of anger at Alexander's wholly unreasonable and stinging comments, but somehow managed to retain her composure.

"Captain Alexander. Under the terms of the agreement between the Royal Navy and Royal Dutch Shell, your ship will be repaired in a yard of Royal Dutch Shell's choosing, at the expense of the Royal Navy. And yes, I accept that there could have been casualties. But please, be thankful that there were not."

She stared at him imploringly.

"And please, Captain. Will you accept my sincere apologies?"

Alexander responded by simply returning her stare while at the same time slowly shaking his head, as if he was dealing with an errant child. Dawn offered to have him flown to any destination he wished on the mainland United Kingdom, but he insisted that he had to return to his ship as his crew needed him.

Within the following ten minutes he had boarded *Wildcat's* Lynx helicopter standing ready on her stern helipad deck. A few minutes later he had arrived safely back aboard *Brent B*. He did not, however, deign to thank the pilots for making the trip, instead just jumping out and running off as soon as the machine touched down on the tanker's deck. All that remained for Dawn to do now was to return to the bridge and notify all civilian officers that *Ankara* was at this point officially over and thus the merchant ships were now released from their obligations and free to depart. *Exxon Lion* and *Saskatchewan Star* were to sail for Bahrain in the

Persian Gulf, while *Brent B* with her escorting tugs was to cut a southerly course for the Irish Sea between south-west Scotland and Ulster, from where she would be towed to Scott Lithgow's yard at Greenock on the Clyde, one of Scotland's few remaining shipyards with the capacity to handle such a large vessel. There she would be laid up for repairs. However Captain Bryan King did extend to Dawn an invitation for her and her fellow naval captains to dine with his officers aboard *Saskatchewan Star* the following evening. He would not, apparently, be departing for Bahrain until the morning after that, as he was required by maritime law to afford *Exxon Lion* plenty of sea room. Despite the circumstances Dawn decided to accept, and then made a mental note to have one of Callaghan's people make the necessary arrangements with MacPherson, Wood, Tylon, and Burleigh. Hunt would not be joining them as he was to remain aboard *Diamond* undergoing numerous physiological and psychological assessments.

After Alexander had gone, Callaghan approached Dawn.

"We have performed a preliminary diagnostic, ma'am. We can't find anything wrong so far. According to all data to which we have access, the torpedoes functioned normally. But of course-"

"But of course they did not, did they, Malcolm?"

Her tone implied that she was a little annoyed. She softened a little.

"I'm sorry, Malcolm. I know it's not your fault. It's just that I'm going to have to soon write a report detailing all of this. Something to which I am not particularly looking forward."

"Quite so, ma'am." He inhaled. "Look, it's a long shot, given our limited understanding of these new Sting Rays, but Lieutenant-Commander Shirer has a strong background in computer engineering. If he could examine the main hard drive from the torpedoes retrieved from *Brent B,* he might be able to glean some useful information."

Dawn considered this for a moment. She mulled over the idea that these torpedoes were the property of UKNAS, and that she should not interfere with them. But then she weighed this against the reality that two of them had just disabled a large oil tanker, caused a potentially very dangerous on-board fire, and very nearly caused it to collide with another. The outcome of all of this could easily have been catastrophic. In her view, opening a torpedo casing under such circumstances would not represent overstepping the bounds of her authority. Even when considering that the weapons were still classified as top secret.

About two hours later Dawn sat with Callaghan and Shirer on the bridge, while Shirer verbally delivered his report following his foray into the inner workings of the Sting Ray Mark 3.

"Well, ma'am," he started. "It's complicated. But in principle, I think, based on my incomplete understanding of the system, there may be a flaw in one of the integrated circuits in a silicon chip on this circuit board, here."

He picked up a circuit board and handed it to her, indicating a particular chip located upon it, one of perhaps about sixty or seventy.

"Based on the way this chip tests compared with the others, I would say that it has within its electrical circuitry a flaw. A flaw that theoretically could go back to the initial design phase. But more likely one that resulted from some kind of power surge. Because of the multiply redundant way the circuitry is configured, it seems that most of the time adequate compensation can be made to accommodate this problem. But under certain circumstances, such as those which developed while *Wildcat* was between one of the attacking torpedoes and *Brent B,* there was an overload which manifested as an effective melting of a small area of the chip. This led to a number of short circuits, resulting in the torpedo incorrectly identifying *Brent B* as a target, and ignoring all of our recall commands."

"What about the other torpedo? Did you examine that too?"

"Yes ma'am."

"Does the same fault appear in that one also?"

"No ma'am. That one appears to be intact, however my guess is that it started taking orders exclusively from the first, failed torpedo. Orders which somehow overrode its programming that *Brent B* was supposed to be regarded as friendly."

"So why would this overload have occurred in the first place, Commander? And only on this one torpedo?"

Shirer shook his head.

"I don't know, ma'am. Perhaps there is an additional fault that I am missing, or perhaps the weapon's circuitry encountered an unusual constellation of momentary stresses. But that is only a guess."

Dawn sighed and rose to her feet.

"Well, Malcolm. Commander Shirer. I had better go and prepare my report."

Both men also rose immediately and saluted as she took her leave.

But as she was leaving, she had a few more words for Shirer.

"Lieutenant-Commander Shirer."

"Ma'am!"

"When you are finished with your examination of the torpedoes, completely re-assemble them. And be sure to let me know if any further information comes to light in the meantime."

"Aye ma'am!"

As Dawn left her spirits were lifted a little as she thought of her first meeting with senior UKNAS executives that she had now been informed she would be attending the following morning. She would at least have the opportunity to present her case and delay delivery of live versions of their new torpedo to the Royal Navy.

CHAPTER 6

The first meeting of the Joint UKNAS-RN Committee convened at the Company's head offices in Britain, located in the Whitechapel area of London, England. No research, development, or manufacturing was carried out here, that was the exclusive purview of the main UKNAS campus in Norfolk, Virginia. But the meeting had been scheduled for the London location in view of Dawn's proximity to the city by helicopter, where she had flown directly from *Wildcat* early that morning. The flight in the navy Lynx had taken some two and three-quarter hours and had not been the most comfortable experience, more especially as she was wearing her dress uniform. Moreover flying, especially by helicopter, was not something Dawn enjoyed, and never had. But there was the advantage that the aircraft was able to set down right on the roof of the UKNAS building, which was equipped with its own helipad. The pilots were simply to wait with their aircraft while she was engaged in the meeting.

Once there she was met by a junior representative of the company and was shown quickly to an elevator inside a roof top doorway, in which she was taken down some seven stories to the twenty-eighth floor of the building and then ushered directly into the meeting room itself. Upon arrival she had but a moment to settle into her assigned chair as every other invited attendee was already present. In aside to Dawn there were nine additional people, a mixture of American and British, all men, senior in one capacity or another with UKNAS, including the Vice President of Research, Frank Boozman, and a Senior Director of the Marine Systems Division, Dr. Evan Gardner. Boozman, who was chairing the meeting, commenced the introductions. After he was finished, he turned to face Dawn directly and launched into a lengthy explanation of how she had spent the best part of the last two weeks engaged in an exercise to put the company's new Sting Ray Mark 3 torpedo through its initial sea-trials.

"In essence, this presentation is based on Captain DeFaller's report that she submitted to UKNAS yesterday at the conclusion of Operation *Ankara*. During this operation she tested our new Sting Ray Mark 3 torpedo and its ability to provide superior protection to a convoy consisting of three large oil tankers and two accompanying highly capable ocean-going salvage tugs."

Boozman was a highly energized New Yorker who had flown in that very morning from Kennedy airport. He presented the image of a high-powered business executive for whom flying across the Atlantic for a meeting was all in the course of a day's work. He distributed handouts to each person present as he continued.

"The Sting Ray Mark 3's tested, fifty units in all, performed virtually flawlessly throughout phase two of *Anakara,* which lasted . . ."

He consulted his notes.

"Five days. During that time the units were able to demonstrate a very high degree of efficacy in distinguishing 'enemy' from 'friendly' vessels, and were able to plan, communicate, and ultimately mount successful attacks. None of the escorting warships, or the submarine, acting in an 'enemy' role, were able to avoid being hit."

Boozman of course was not aware of the other aspect to *Ankara*. The test of the cognition-enhancing drug administered to Garry Hunt.

"The weapons functioned equally well on the surface or at depth. In their defensive role they exceeded the performance of the navy vessels that had been engaged in convoy protection during the initial part of *Ankara,* before any of the torpedoes had been launched. All of this information is summarized in the first two pages of your handouts, if you will turn to them now."

Dawn peered at the front of the bundle of papers she had been given, bound up in a neat bright green cover, emblazoned with the title, **Sea Trials of the Sting Ray Mark 3 Torpedo: Operation Ankara.** Also printed across the cover running in a diagonal were the words, **CLASSIFIED: UKNAS Confidential, Security Access 1A Required. FOR AUTHORIZED PERSONNEL ONLY.** She opened the cover, revealing the first page that showed a schematic, replete with diagrams of the main internal components of the Sting Ray Mark 3, similar to the ones she had seen before. The following pages consisted of text, some of which she noticed had been lifted from her own report, as well as a series of bar charts, graphs, and tables, outlining the relative performance of the new torpedo and its capacity to identify and attack 'enemy' vessels.

Gardner looked up from his report that he had been casually leafing through. He ran his hands through his hair.

"So what's your conclusion, Frank?"

Boozman smiled, his features belying a hint of triumph.

"I say we are a go. We can commence production immediately."

"All the production run machinery is in place?"

"Absolutely. It has been for nearly two weeks. We have just been waiting for the go-ahead from the British navy."

Dawn was beginning to wonder when one of these men was going to come to the issue of the accidental torpedoing of *Brent B.* She also could not help but notice that Boozman and Gardner were doing all the talking, while everyone else present in the room was remaining silent. She felt the compulsion to speak.

"Gentlemen," she began, but it seemed nobody was listening to her.

"Yes," Boozman intoned, to no-one in particular.

At first Dawn thought he might be responding to her, but apparently, he was not.

"If we deliver the initial main inventory, excluding the pilot inventory ready to go now, to the Royal Navy within a month, then we will see initial before-tax profit margins being turned by the beginning of the second quarter next year. That would be-"

"Gentlemen!"

Dawn was becoming a little more insistent now. Boozman looked over at her, his facial expression and body language suggestive of a somewhat condescending demeanor.

"Yes? Captain DeFaller? You have something to say?"

Dawn sat up in her chair and squared her shoulders.

"You are aware, are you not, that two of your Sting Ray Mark 3 torpedoes inadvertently attacked and damaged one of the tankers in the convoy? A vessel which their on-board computers had been clearly instructed to recognize as friendly?"

There proceeded an awkward silence. Boozman stared at her, a little incredulous, as if he had just been insulted. Gardner appeared all of a sudden a little annoyed. The faces of several of the remaining men in the room turned an awkward red color as they commenced staring at their shoes, in a sort of collective embarrassed silence.

"I did allude to this incident in my report, quite carefully, I believe. On the final day of *Ankara* two of the Sting Ray torpedoes apparently malfunctioned and struck the tanker *Brent B,* despite all attempts by the ship tracking them to neutralize the threat that they posed."

By now Boozman was looking a little helpless. Gardner spoke up. He made an effort to sound at once apologetic and unconcerned.

"Not malfunctioned, Captain."

Dawn found his uncultured cockney drawl a little irritating.

"The torpedoes were simply not preprogrammed correctly, as per instructions. That is why they misidentified the tanker as a threat."

"The torpedoes were preprogrammed correctly, Dr. Gardner, of that I can assure you, as were the other forty-eight that we launched over that period. In each and every case UKNAS programming instructions were followed to the letter, and double checked by two independent observers prior to execution. And I can further assure-"

"Ah, but you must not have punched in the correct codes to your launch computer. I can assure you, Captain, that this minor glitch was nothing more than an error by the navy."

"Minor glitch? *Brent B* was set on fire and had her propeller shaft and steering gear damaged. She had to be towed to western Scotland for repairs. And our technicians were able to isolate a specific chip from one of the two torpedoes involved that seemed to exhibit a serious-"

Boozman interrupted her, holding up a single page document that she had not seen previously.

"Captain DeFaller. I have here a letter from Captain Barbara Brown, the commanding officer of the ocean-going tug *Lloydsman II* that was involved in operation *Ankara*. She sent it to senior management at UKNAS following the conclusion of the exercise. In her letter, Captain Brown alleges that during the opening phase of *Ankara*, she found you to be somewhat arrogant and unwilling to consider the advice of fellow professional officers, be they military or Merchant Marine."

"What?!" Dawn was completely taken off guard. She could not believe that Brown would have done such a thing.

"In particular, Captain DeFaller, Captain Brown feels that you marginalized and trivialized her own professional opinions as an experienced officer and commander. She goes as far as to suggest that your poor leadership skills combined with an attitude that could best be described as bull-headed may very well have contributed to the incident involving *Brent B*."

He handed Dawn the letter. She peered at it. It was indeed signed by Brown, and did outline the issues Boozman had stated.

The bitch, thought Dawn. *How could she make such obviously untrue allegations?*

But before Dawn could sufficiently collect her thoughts and offer up further comment in her defense, Boozman spoke again, his tone very final and matter-of-fact.

"If there is nothing else, I would like to wrap this up? As I said, production can commence in a month." He sounded all of a sudden confident and self-assured, as if Dawn had not just spoken up. "Captain DeFaller has highlighted for us a minor hiccup of the type that we see with most new technologies but we are aware of the issue and have already taken steps towards its resolution. Is that not correct, Evan?"

"Yes indeed. We have in fact sorted out the problem and have our pilot inventory standing by ready for delivery. We are only awaiting a green light from you, Frank."

"Very well. We shall begin supplying the Royal Navy immediately. Only the Type 45 destroyer *Diamond* will receive weapons for now. She is the only vessel with experience of handling them. The other Type 45's will be supplied by the end of the month, after *Diamond* has had further opportunity to become familiar with them. Clear?"

"Crystal clear, Frank. I will initiate delivery now. They will be flown out by heavy helicopter. *Diamond* will receive her torpedoes by this evening."

"Please remind me again Evan. How many torpedoes will *Diamond* be receiving?"

"Sixty. That represents the total of our current production inventory, bar two units that we are holding back for further calibration."

Boozman stood, and the other men in the room immediately followed his lead.

"Congratulations, gentlemen. When this contract matures fully, we shall soon be realizing projected before-tax profits of around two billion, in US dollars. Thank you for your attention."

He was clearly attempting to imply that the meeting was over. He was also ignoring Dawn. Avoiding eye contact with her. Speaking and acting as if she were not in the room. But unlike the men she remained defiantly in her seat. She paged through the handout in front of her for an explanation of the events that had transpired with *Brent B.* But she could find none. It seemed that senior management at UKNAS was intent on making light of the whole issue. And she could not understand why Gardner, an engineer, with an academic doctorate, and who had specialized knowledge of the computer guidance systems for this torpedo would not speak out at so crucial a meeting. As the men started to file out of the room, she had but one final comment to make, as she handed Brown's letter back to Boozman.

"I sincerely hope you are right in your assessment that the problems encountered were only, as you put it, a minor glitch. Remember that we are potentially talking about peoples' lives here. The production torpedoes will be mounting live warheads. I'm sure I don't need to remind you gentlemen of the devastating consequences should one end up running into a friendly vessel."

It was at that point that Boozman apparently lost his patience and expressed his annoyance at her disrespectful attitude. He proceeded to directly ask her to leave the meeting, and depart from the premises. To her disbelief he added a demeaning comment regarding his attitude to women holding military rank. This proved to be much to the amusement of the assembled company who variously chuckled and smirked like a group of overgrown schoolboys in a highly self-satisfied manner. She felt the hackles rise on the back of her neck as she offered up an angry retort, but it seemed that all that was left for her to do now was leave. On her way out she could have sworn that she heard one of them add a further comment, intended for her ears, about it obviously being the wrong time of the month. But when she shot an angry glance back at them they were all tight-lipped and silent, but still grinning like Cheshire cats.

On the return journey to *Wildcat* she was so angry with the apparent arrogant stupidity and foolishness, coupled with the highly self-aggrandizing, almost megalomaniac desire for the realization of rapid and enormous profit she had encountered that morning, that she hardly noticed the almost three-hour flying time required. With a few exceptions, Dawn did not generally dislike men, and held a number that she had encountered professionally over the years in the highest esteem. But she could not help but think that had there been a few women in key positions on the Board of Directors of UKNAS, then perhaps the decision-making process that morning, as well as a willingness to entertain her point of view as an involved expert consultant, may have developed in a somewhat different manner. How could Boozman behave in such a selfishly irresponsible and overtly sexist manner? And how could Brown have taken the action that she did? Because of this *Diamond* was now going to be restocked with a further sixty of the new torpedoes, live versions in this case that could, for all anyone really knew, prove to be extremely dangerous. Her anger intensified as images of another powerful man from her past who had displayed similar tendencies flooded through her mind. Vice-Admiral Sir John Wentworth-Tailleur, Royal Navy. A misogynistic fool whose blinding arrogance and religious bigotry had led to tremendous problems, and ultimately serious threats to world security. Ultimately it had presumably cost him his life, as well as the life of young Kevin Ledbetter, a valued member of her junior officer complement while she had been in command aboard *Wildcat*.

She was still angry when the Lynx touched down on *Wildcat's* helipad late that afternoon.

CHAPTER 7

T hat evening, Dawn, along with her fellow senior officers were preparing for their visit to *Saskatchewan Star* as per the invitation extended to them by her master. Even as they were boarding the inflatable launch which was to ferry them across, she was still fuming from the outcome of her meeting with UKNAS. In particular she was still smarting from Brown's obvious betrayal of her trust. She had certainly noted clearly that Brown had not warmed to her at the beginning of *Ankara,* but this was beyond the pale. And because of her absurd and wholly false allegations, Dawn had no chance at all of persuading the UKNAS committee that delivery of live versions of the new Sting Ray torpedo to *Diamond* should be delayed. She determined that if ever she encountered Brown again, as unlikely as that might be, she would force her to explain herself. Thoughts of legal action had crossed her mind too, but that seemed unlikely to be a viable option as technically Brown had only expressed an opinion, and in any event, military personnel, and especially commissioned officers, were held to a higher standard of account than their civilian counterparts. But for now Dawn resolved to make a serious effort to put the incident behind her as she feared that otherwise she would not prove to be very pleasant company for her hosts.

From their vantage point by *Wildcat's* side, the tanker appeared to be very large indeed. But at close quarters the ship was quite simply enormous. Approaching aboard the inflatable she loomed so huge as to resemble not so much a ship as a floating metropolis. Her colossal length was almost overwhelming. And as if that were not enough, her superstructure towards her stern, directly ahead of them, seemed as tall as high buildings in the middle of any mid-sized city's central business district.

King was present to welcome each officer aboard as they climbed the long steps running up his vessel's port side. He personally shook hands in turn with Callaghan, MacPherson, Wood, Tylon, and Elizabeth Burleigh, before finishing up in front of Dawn. He was standing straight up at his full height, peering down at her. Up close, like his ship, King was quite a giant. Despite his being probably around two hundred and thirty or two hundred and forty pounds in weight, he seemed trim and well proportioned.

"Captain DeFaller. I am so pleased that you could attend our little soiree."

He smiled down at her. Once again Dawn could see that he was possessed of an immediately pleasant, disarming manner, combined with a cultured, well-spoken voice.

"Captain King. Thank you for your kind invitation."

He broke into a beaming smile. "Please. Call me Bryan. We do not stand on formality, except when strictly necessary, of course." He turned on his heel. "Please, ladies and gentlemen. Follow me."

King led them to a large open room four decks above the spot where he had first welcomed them aboard, along one side of which was a counter set up replete with a bar tender and a selection of beers, wines, hard liquor, and soft drinks. In the center of the room was a long table, carefully set for dinner. There were several other officers standing at the bar when King entered the room, but, as Dawn was quick to notice, they maintained a casual demeanor. In fact they did not appear to acknowledge his presence in any way. To her this was noticeably different from the way things were done in the navy.

"Please first allow me to introduce my fellow officers, and then help yourselves to whatever you would like from the bar. Dinner will be served in forty-five minutes."

King then went through a quick introduction of each of his officers, four men and two women, who simply smiled and nodded as their names were called in turn. To the other naval officers present also there did not seem to be the same level of discipline in the presence of the ship's commander.

As Dawn stood slowly sipping a glass of red wine, King came over to her once again.

"So, Captain," she started.

"Bryan, please."

She smiled.

"I am sorry. Bryan. How many weeks per year would you say you spend aboard?"

"That varies depending on the price of crude oil, and where we are taking it from and to. But it averages out at around thirty-five weeks each year. The crew would work perhaps about half of that as they each have a relief counterpart aboard, but I as captain have no such relief. Whenever the *Star* sails, I sail with her. Of late we have been running up into the Persian Gulf, either Kuwait or Bahrain, to collect most usually a full load and then carry perhaps sixty-five percent of it to New York City. The remainder we then often take to Buenos Aires, Argentina. All that of course can be subject to change. But that's what we've been doing these past few months."

"And how much oil would represent a full load?"

"Well. That depends on several factors, including oil grade, current price on the major global markets, distance to travel, predicted and actual meteorological conditions on the sea lanes over the course and time of the proposed journey, and so on. It typically comes in at around 150,000 tons. But that figure can vary up or down by as much as fifteen percent."

Dawn decided to change the subject for a moment.

"So what do you do when you're not aboard?"

"I go home to see my wife and dogs."

"And where do you live?"

"In Fort Worth, Texas, in the United States."

Dawn smiled.

"What does your wife make of your being away at sea for so much of the year?"

"She seems comfortable with the arrangement. But I do believe my dogs are less happy. We have two Scottish West Highland Terriers."

"Oh? Black or white?"

"Black. Both of them. Tenacious little devils. But we regard them as family. I think my wife—Victoria—likes to have them around, especially when I'm gone. So, Captain, how long have you been in the Royal Navy?"

She smiled again.

"If I am to address you by your first name, then I insist you please call me Dawn."

"Dawn."

"Sixteen years."

"May I inquire if you are married?"

"I am. My husband is also a naval captain. However he is an officer in the United States Navy."

"So how does that work? Do you see each other often?"

"We have a house in Boston, and I am Assistant to the Chief British Naval Attaché in Washington, DC. We actually see each other much more frequently than you and your wife apparently see each other, from the way you described it."

And so their conversation proceeded, up until it was time to take their seats for dinner. They variously discussed such topics as life in England versus the United States, Pink Floyd, gender equality in the workplace, the complex details of the four major types of tanker charter contracts, and the differences between day-to-day life aboard a civilian versus a military vessel. Dawn had also commented on the sheer size of the *Saskatchewan Star,* but had been startled when King had pointed out to her that, large though his ship was, there were even larger oil tankers currently plying the world's oceans, those of the Ultra Large Crude Carrier, or ULCC, class. He had even been able to reel off their names from memory: the *TI Asia,* the *TI Europe,* the *TI Oceania,* and the *TI Africa.* Each of these ships had a deadweight capacity of a little over twice that of the *Saskatchewan Star,* at 441,500 tons, and measured nearly one-quarter of a mile in length. The thought of being in charge of such a colossal vessel left Dawn feeling simply aghast.

Dinner itself was served in the form of five courses, by a small army of white-jacketed stewards. It consisted of shrimp cocktails, followed by a beef, chicken, or fish entree, then desserts. There was then a selection of fine cheeses and port wines, and the whole affair was finally rounded out with excellent coffee. The food was in fact very good; Dawn was quite surprised at the standards of service aboard a tanker. Indeed the accommodations aboard seemed more in keeping with what one would expect to find aboard a cruise liner than a working ship. After dinner was over and everyone had had ample time to talk and get to know one another, King offered to take anyone who might be interested up to the bridge. Dawn, of course, as well as all of her fellow officers, jumped at the chance.

The bridge turned out to be raised at a very high level above the surface of the sea. Standing looking out of the windows, the visiting officers felt as if they were inside the control tower of a major airport, rather than aboard a ship. The total area was also sufficiently large such that the dinner they had all just enjoyed could have been held here, right in front of the ship's steering and navigation instruments. Dawn wished Matthew could have been aboard; she felt he would have found everything to be fascinating. The officer of the watch stood as King along with his six naval officer guests trooped in. The forward control console was covered with an array of advanced navigation instruments and computers, and the view out onto the lighted enormous deck area far below and the darkness beyond was very pleasing. Dawn however felt a sobering feeling at the prospect of having to maneuver such a large vessel. From here it seemed entirely believable that such a ship would need about ten miles of sea room just to make a turn.

She felt a little twinge of unease as she could now see more clearly the predicament in which *Brent B* had been placed by the rogue Sting Rays, and could perhaps understand Alexander's earlier anger a little better.

Despite that, however, the evening had turned out to be a success. In particular, the unmarried Commander Tylon, known in the navy for his having many lady admirers, using his innate charisma had got on very well indeed with one of the tanker's female engineering officers, an attractive young woman by the name of Toni Wright. She had spent the last thirty minutes explaining to him much of the details of the tanker's operation, including crude oil loading and unloading procedures, loading pressures, potentially dangerous topping off procedures, associated ballast trim procedures, tank cleaning using crude oil washing systems, and specifics of single versus double-hull tanker designs. As she continued to explain these different aspects of the operation of the ship her monologues became progressively more and more complex and technical, but Tylon was intrigued. He seemed especially interested to learn that the *Saskatchewan Star* was of a newer double-hull design, which had its advantages and its disadvantages, but the crippled *Brent B* was of an older, single-hull design. According to Wright, the International Convention for the Prevention of Pollution from Ships had decreed that all single-hull tankers were to be phased out by 2026. And the United Nations had agreed for its part to phase out single-hull oil tankers by 2010. As Dawn overheard this she realized that this could have been another potential source of Captain Alexander's annoyance at having his ship damaged by the Sting Ray Mark 3 torpedoes. Since his vessel would quite soon no longer meet maritime regulations for hull design, perhaps her owners would elect not to have her repaired but instead simply sell her for scrap. He and his officers and crew may then find themselves out of a job.

Dawn could not be certain but she was left with the impression that before it was time for everyone to return to their respective vessels, Tylon and Wright had exchanged business cards. Not a practice that was strictly encouraged according to naval regulations. But when she considered how she had met her husband she could hardly in good conscience object.

CHAPTER 8

Brodmann Corporation, Rahway, New Jersey, June 15, 2008.

The atmosphere in the Investigative Research Principal Conference Room was so tense that morning it could have been cut with a knife. Chairing the meeting was Dr. James McLeod, Vice-President of Research and Development. Also in attendance were Drs. Laurie Griffin, Greg Dillon, and Ritchie Clark from the Departments of In Vivo Pharmacology, Pharmaceutical Chemistry, and Molecular Genetics. Also present was the Chief Veterinarian, Sherrie Walton. The subject of the meeting, which had been called on an emergency basis by McLeod after receiving the disturbing news from Griffin, had been expressed most clearly in the short video clips they had all just witnessed. In the first, lasting about a minute, Frieda-May, the black Labrador who had been receiving the cognition-enhancing drug treatment, and who had performed phenomenally well in her previous tests, was seen to be exhibiting, for no apparent reason, some very aggressive and unreasonable behavior. From the video, and also the reports of the veterinary technicians who had been dealing with the dog, it was apparent that she had become determined to hurt any person who tried to approach her, even if they were only attempting to leave food. The dog would lunge at anyone who entered her compound, but most tellingly would wait until the individual was far from the cage door, so she could circle around, thus cutting them off from a rapid exit. She would then make a determined attempt to bite that individual in particularly vulnerable areas of their body, including the ankles, the knees, and the inside of the thigh. One technician who had run to the aid of another had been savagely bitten in the stomach. He had doubled up in pain, and then received more bites to the face and ears. And stopping the dog had been difficult, she seemed always to be aware of the need to defend her own space, moving her body from its very core, always in exactly the manner that made her the hardest to restrain. In the end, after two technicians had been taken to hospital, Frieda-May had been shot with powerful tranquilizer darts and was currently unconscious. She would remain so until it could be determined what had gone wrong. And what could be done about it. The other video clips told essentially the same story.

Dillon had asked Griffin if the chimp was in the same condition.

"Yes," had come the reply. "Actually worse. It's interesting really. None of the rats have exhibited any symptoms beyond a mild tendency towards antisocial behavior towards adult members of their own species, and also a tendency towards killing and eating their young. Actually not entirely unusual behavior in rats, but their reaction to humans seems completely normal. But the dog has become quite dangerous, although clearly she has retained her enhanced powers of reason. But the chimp's behavior lately has been quite frankly bizarre. In a routine flight simulator test he started purposely 'flying' on the wrong heading, or at the wrong altitude. A couple of times he even purposely and in a seemingly calculating manner 'crashed', on both occasions into densely populated areas. It's as if the higher the innate intelligence level, the more dangerously affected the drug-enhanced mind is likely to become. But unlike the dog, the chimp is still able to maintain an outwardly relaxed and calm disposition, without any indication of the homicidal tendencies that he is obviously contemplating.

So I would say that, although the same basic premise applies, the higher mind is affected in a qualitatively somewhat different manner."

McLeod cut in.

"So what do think is going on? Psychosis?"

"In a manner of speaking, and yet, not ordinary psychosis, for the powers of reason and rationality, as well as the enhanced IQ, seem entirely unaffected."

Walton chimed in, all the while shaking her head.

"I would say that, with all three species, but especially with the chimp, the behavior we are looking at here is not so much dangerously psychotic, as dangerously psychopathic. Although up until now I had always understood that only humans could be afflicted with such a condition."

At that, McLeod became visibly alarmed.

"Who exactly knows about this?"

Griffin was adamant.

"With the exception of everyone in this room, just the three animal technicians who have been working on the project."

"You are certain?"

"Yes. And I have impressed upon them the need for absolute secrecy. They have not talked, and nor will they talk to anyone."

McLeod's countenance grew very stern.

"Make certain that it stays that way. A report will have to be submitted to the FDA, and then they will have to decide how to deal with this. Especially since this project is under special military jurisdiction. I don't want anything to leak out before then. The legal consequences do not bear thinking about."

CHAPTER 9

North Atlantic Ocean, June 17, 2008

"What the hell do you mean *Diamond* is missing?" Powers' expression was grave. He seemed to be looking to Dawn for answers, seated as he was on the bridge of *Daring*, where Dawn and Callaghan had been summoned to join him earlier that following morning.

"I'm sorry sir, but try as we might, we have been unable to raise *Diamond* on the radio, or identify her on radar. I think Commander Hunt must have left the exercise zone and turned off his transponder. He apparently has no intention of responding to any attempt to contact him or his ship at this time. Or at least that is how it appears. Although I fail to understand why he should be pursuing this course of action. As best we can determine, and based on our last known contacts with *Diamond*, it seems to have happened at some point during the melee with *Brent B*. It's as if Hunt used the opportunity to slip away at that time. But how he could have done so unnoticed is baffling. He cannot have made it so terribly far, though. We are bound to locate *Diamond* sometime soon from one of the helicopters that we have up right now searching a wider field."

"Well? What do you suppose he's doing?"

Dawn just shrugged. "I don't know, sir. I was only informed of this myself just fifteen minutes ago by Commander Callaghan, who himself had only just been appraised of the situation."

She shook her head.

"It's as if he has taken leave of his senses. We had just wrapped up *Ankara* and were preparing to depart from the area and head for home when *Diamond* disappeared from our radar screens."

Callaghan spoke up.

"Do you think it's possible that this has something to do with the drug he has been taking? Some kind of bad reaction, perhaps?"

Powers just glared at him impatiently. Callaghan decided not to pursue his point any further.

"We will find him soon, sir. Of that I am certain."

"I hope so, Captain."

Powers was obviously not happy with the present situation. Not happy at all.

But Dawn's optimism turned out to be without foundation. For try as they might over the course of the ensuing twenty-four days, *Diamond* could not be located anywhere. Not even when the search had expanded to involve all major areas of the world's oceans on which ships typically traversed, and had enlisted the assistance of tracking satellites, spotter aircraft, and surface and submerged vessels from the navies and air forces of both the United Kingdom and also the United States.

HMS *Diamond*, it seemed, had simply vanished.

CHAPTER 10

Arabian Sea, July 11, 2008

"This is the Officer of the Watch, ocean liner *Rohollah Samimi,* out of Abu Dhabi. Sailing under the Iranian flag. Requesting permission to run out of the Gulf of Oman into the Arabian Sea. Over."

The British voice crackled on the radio in response.

"*Rohollah Samimi,* what is your ultimate destination, over?"

"Bombay, to stop and pick up passengers. Over."

Moments later the sought-after permission was granted.

"*Rohollah Samimi,* you may proceed. However please be advised you are passing close by an area in which a British warship is engaged in a military exercise. Please steer course one-three-two degrees, hold and maintain. Also, please advise of your position every twenty minutes. Over."

"Thank you. Over and out."

As the *Rohollah Samimi's* passengers basked in the sun by her several luxuriously appointed swimming pools, or shopped in her duty-free mall, or simply relaxed in one of her many lounge areas or restaurants, they paid scant attention to the British destroyer, barely visible through the hazy heat, on the distant horizon. Nor did they entertain any inkling whatsoever of the fate which awaited them.

CHAPTER 11

IRANIAN CRUISE SHIP SUNK IN BRITISH NAVY 'FRIENDLY FIRE' INCIDENT

The banner headline in the July 12 edition of the *New York Times* said it all with stark clarity. The headline in *The London Times* was worded with a little more sensitivity:

ACCIDENTAL SINKING OF IRANIAN PASSENGER VESSEL: 1,200 REPORTED MISSING

The article following was run in almost exactly the same format in all of the major American and British papers that morning.

Eastern Arabian Sea, July 11, 2008. At least one British warship was engaged in an exercise in this region of the Arabian Sea off the coast of western India. Details are still poorly defined, but it appears that the Iranian cruise liner, Rohollah Samimi, *with 1,468 passengers and crew aboard, was heading out of the Gulf of Oman towards Bombay, where she was scheduled to stop and embark an additional number of passengers. While en-route early reports indicate that she was struck by two or possibly three torpedoes, which according to eye witnesses emanated from one or possibly more British warships allegedly present in the area.*

A spokesman for the British Royal Navy, Vice-Admiral Sir Phillip Bailey, British Naval Attaché to Washington DC, denied that any British warships were operating in this area at that time. However Admiral Bailey had no comment when questioned on the possible disappearance of one of the Royal Navy's newest and most advanced warships during the middle of last month while engaged in an earlier naval exercise in the North Atlantic Ocean off the coast of Scotland. Eyewitnesses, including a number of fishermen said that a large warship flying the British flag was seen in the area close to the Rohollah Samimi. *They added that she appeared to be launching torpedoes immediately prior to the sinking. Several witnesses added that the* Rohollah Samimi *sank so rapidly that there was time to launch only a very few of her lifeboats and rafts. It is estimated that of the 1,468 passengers and crew aboard, only 271 were saved, some of whom are in very serious or critical condition.*

Early reports suggest that the Rohollah Samimi *suffered a broken back after being struck amidships and astern by two torpedoes which exploded on impact with a very high degree of force, sending the ship to the bottom in some 2,400 feet of water in a matter of minutes. Several of those who survived were seen running across her decks, some of whom were on fire, immediately prior to jumping into the sea. Amongst those aboard were 14 British nationals and 6 Americans.*

In Tehran the President of Iran has denounced the sinking of his nation's vessel, personally offering his condolences to the families of all those who lost their lives. The Iranian President has also condemned the Americans and British as terrorists who have perpetrated yet another murderous and wholly unprovoked attack against innocent Iranian people. He added in a statement yesterday that Allah will, in his infinite wisdom and mercy, punish the Western Godless infidels for their arrogance.

CHAPTER 12

Riyadh, Saudi Arabia, July 13, 2008

The late morning sun had already caused temperatures to soar to over one hundred and five degrees, and it was still to become hotter yet in the bustling metropolis of over four million people before the day would be over. In the bustling Olaya business district at the northern end of the heart of Riyadh, in the city's Kingdom Centre, several thousand people were going about their daily business, from shopping in one of its one hundred and sixty one stores in the mall, to worshipping in the mosque, or checking in to the hotel or one of the many apartments, all contained within. The Kingdom Centre tower, at 992 feet was the highest skyscraper in the country and currently the 37th tallest building in the world. Its mosque also had the distinction of being the world's highest. On the skybridge, a group of tourists had already gathered as they always did each day, to enjoy panoramic views of the entire city.

Riyadh's name had been derived from the Arabic word *Rawdha,* which roughly translated into English as *A Place of Gardens and Trees.* Riyadh had certainly been for more than 1,500 years a fertile settlement within the Arabian Peninsula. For a very long period of time there had been a small walled city here, but by the early 21st century this had developed into a dynamic metropolis, rendering it one of the fastest growing cities in the world, as well as a center for travel and trade. The city boasted many financial, educational, technical, and cultural institutions, as well as much fine architecture, top-tier accommodations, dining, shopping, and entertainment. Riyadh had become by 2008 a model for other Islamic cities both in the country and around the globe.

But none of these particular thoughts permeated the mind of Captain Dan Murphy as he prepared to pilot his Federal Express McDonnell Douglas DC-10 freighter out of Riyadh's King Khaled International Airport. About to take off from runway 33 Left at 11.07am, he had been given clearance to make an immediate climbing left turn and head out over the north west of the country, reaching cruising altitude as he crossed over into Jordan and Israel, and thence out over the eastern Mediterranean. As Captain Murphy accepted clearance for take-off from the tower, and advanced the thrust levers, thereby commencing his take-off roll, he allowed his mind to wander a little to the recent past when he had been approached by representatives of what had turned out to be a rather radical organization. Captain Murphy was a particularly devout Christian and had for many years been very active in his Southern Baptist church as an elder. His devotion had indeed caught the eye of a number of very senior people. So much so in fact, that a week earlier he had represented America's Southern Baptists at a large convention held in Toronto, arranged by the great Canadian soul saving and well-funded organization, the Toronto Blessing. He had been involved in intense discussions concerning the future of reformed churches across North America, the United Kingdom, and Australia and New Zealand. The convention had proved to be a great success for Captain Murphy, so much so in fact that he had been approached by a small group of senior people who had then invited him to meet with them in what had seemed to him very clandestine circumstances. During the meeting itself, which had taken place in a private hotel suite, away from the Convention Center, many questions had been asked. Did he consider as a Christian man that the United States government was doing enough to combat the Islamofascist threat? Al-Qaeda? What about the general decline of morality over the last hundred years or so? The rise in American and Western European society of such anti-social mores and norms as selfishness, needless and cruel litigation, sloth, hedonism, pornography, and violence? What was the government doing to secure future access to global petroleum and hence safeguard the economy? One of the men had finally asked Murphy outright if he would be interested in joining with them in the organization which they represented, an organization named God's Christian Soldiers, or GCS, hidden from the public eye and the prying of the press only in so far as was necessary in order that it be able to carry out His will without let or hindrance directed against it from agents of secular government. Could he find the strength within himself, despite his being a family man, to carry out God's purpose as one of His warriors, according to instructions that He had sent to the senior membership of GCS by angelic messenger? Or if instead would he, as most men, lusting after power and mammon, and cowardly by nature, shy away from Him and His true purpose? But following his apparent willingness to carry on with God's work, Murphy had been introduced to yet another man, who within a very short time had left him utterly convinced he was now in the direct presence of his Savior. For this man had seemed to be possessed of an almost preternatural intelligence and awareness of events; past, present, and future. It was as if he had access to the sensorium of God Himself. It was this man who left him utterly convinced of the task he must soon carry out. It was this man who had assured him, more so than all of the others, that he would receive a special place in the heavenly hierarchy for his sacrifice.

Following take-off Captain Murphy commenced his climbing left turn as he raised the landing gear and started the process of running the slats and flaps inboard. But instead of settling on a north-west heading, he continued holding on left aileron until his aircraft had turned to face almost exactly south-east. Almost immediately the agitated voice of an over-stressed air traffic controller started blaring in his headphones, but, to the growing astonishment of his co-pilot, Murphy simply leaned over and calmly flipped the master switches on the communications and navigation radios to 'Off', as well as those on the Flight Director and Auto-Throttle. Now flying the aircraft entirely by himself, and heading towards downtown Riyadh, at an altitude of a mere three thousand feet above the underlying desert, his considerably younger co-pilot, who was at this point beginning to experience mild alarm, started reminding him about the fact that they had deviated from their proper flight plan. He added, rather unnecessarily, that they had prematurely discontinued their climb, and that there was now the possibility of conflict with other traffic. Murphy appeared to hear, but responded simply by bowing his head and starting to pray, quietly at first, but gradually increasing in intensity. His co-pilot in the meantime stopped talking and simply stared at him, shocked and uncertain of what to do next. Murphy's prayer intensified further as he appealed to God for forgiveness while he rapidly withdrew a pistol which he had secreted in his pocket, took aim, and discharged a single bullet through his co-pilot's head, splattering blood, bone, and brains over the cockpit right-side windshield. As the co-pilot's lifeless body jerked rightward and then slumped forward in its harness, twitching and quivering, Murphy calmly resumed looking straight ahead. By now he could see that Riyadh AB military airfield was visible to his left, and downtown Riyadh was looming out of the desert. He made some minor course adjustments, lining his aircraft up precisely between King Fahd Road and Olaya Street, as if he were intending to land on some imaginary runway that might theoretically exist between the two thoroughfares. He then pushed gently forward on the yoke and put the big jet into a shallow dive. As the unmistakable shape of the Kingdom Centre appeared dead ahead of the DC-10's nose, Dan Murphy knew that his life on earth was almost done. He once again started to pray, very much more earnestly this time. Murphy then advanced the thrust levers to full power, while ignoring the increasingly insistent Ground Proximity, Gear, and Over-Speed warnings.

But in his last few seconds of life, Murphy was gripped with a sudden sense of growing alarm that rapidly morphed into panic as he realized that he had been duped. Purposely flying his aircraft into a busy downtown building would not serve God, nor indeed any worthwhile human purpose. He found himself in a state of clear-headed sanity once more, faced with the realization that he was about to crash and that there was absolutely nothing he could do to prevent this. How could he have been so stupid? He frantically pulled back on his control yoke while simultaneously forcing it over to the left. But it was too late. He was only able to let loose a piercing heart-wrenching scream, before a moment later the heavy jet, fully laden with highly explosive aviation fuel, rolled to the left and then slammed into the north side of the Kingdom Centre, at about the level of the large and busy shopping mall.

The aircraft struck the tower at a little over 400mph.

CHAPTER 13

The evening news reports around the globe from CNN to the BBC and Al-Jazeera were all dominated by the crash of the Federal Express DC-10 Freighter into the Kingdom Centre in Riyadh. CNN attributed the cause to an engine unexpectedly going into reverse thrust during flight shortly after take-off, thus causing the aircraft to veer off course and become progressively more and more uncontrollable. The crash had killed upward of three thousand people, mostly Saudi nationals, although citizens of up to thirty nations had been involved, including some Britons, Continental Europeans, and Americans. The Kingdom Centre had been very badly ravaged by fire, its upper portion completely destroyed, but the lower part of the tower still stood as an ugly ruined charred and broken stump in the center of the city. In addition to those killed, some six thousand more had been injured, both in the tower itself and in some areas within a radius of about a mile, as a result of falling debris, explosions, and fire. The BBC, while giving credence to the early interpretation of events that the crash had been an accident, did allude to the message sent to their head office in London by an organization calling themselves 'God's Christian Soldiers', or GCS, who, according to the message, had claimed responsibility for the incident. The message had been accompanied by a five-minute video tape, but the BBC had decided not to reveal either the existence or the content of the tape at this time. Al-Jazeera, who had also received a copy of the same tape, had chosen to respond somewhat differently. They had, as the BBC, presented the theory that the Federal Express aircraft had experienced an engine malfunction, but had then gone on to devote considerably more time to a character study of the senior pilot, who was known to be a devout Christian and church elder. The station had also played an edited version of the GCS video tape to Middle Eastern audiences. The tape itself, the full version of which Al-Jazeera had posted on their website, consisted of a long statement from a middle-aged professional man, identified as being a Canadian national, sitting addressing the camera, in English. In his statement he said that the destruction of the Kingdom Centre in Riyadh was regrettable, but a taste of things to come unless Moslem terrorists under the auspices of Al-Qaeda desisted in the prosecution of their evil and Godless attacks against the West. The commentator went on to deride the inaction and apathy of Western governments, especially those of Britain, Canada, the Netherlands, Belgium, France, and Sweden in dealing with Islamofascism. He further talked of the alleged involvement of the House of Saud in financing and otherwise encouraging the global Islamic terror network. He had then praised the heroism of Captain Daniel Murphy of Federal Express, and extended his sincere condolences to Captain Murphy's wife and family, and also the next of kin of First Officer James Harper, who was also killed in the crash. As God's soldiers, he had said, these brave and majestic souls would be lifted up to heaven, there to sit by the right hand of God and Jesus. His final statement had been chilling: any further prosecution of Islamic attacks on the West, or any further toleration of Islamofascism by Western governments would lead to all-out war. A war in which the righteous Western nations would prevail.

At that point the tape ended abruptly.

CHAPTER 14

Arabian Sea, July 14, 2008

It had taken *Wildcat* three days to reach the vicinity of the Arabian Sea, whereupon she had immediately commenced the search for any evidence of the previous presence of the still-missing *Diamond*. Despite the convening of several British and American naval and governmental committees, each of which was empowered with substantial authority and all of which had met several times by this point, the whereabouts of *Diamond*, or Commander Hunt, was no closer to being established. But a brief encrypted transmission, believed possibly to have emanated from Hunt himself, had led rapidly to the conclusion that a British or American naval presence should be established in this region of the world. That plus the recent shocking reports of the Federal Express crash in Riyadh had facilitated the decision that, for the sake of attempting to salvage international relations, the governments of the United Kingdom and the United States should be seen to be taking action. In response *Wildcat*, with Dawn and Powers aboard, had been dispatched to the area.

Wildcat's communications officer, Lieutenant Gray, was the first to spot the flashing stroboscopic beacon of the life raft of which they had been made aware earlier that morning by another, unknown, encrypted transmission that *Wildcat* had picked up on her radio. The message had indicated the presence of a single life raft, its approximate location, and the fact that it would be carrying one of *Diamond's* engineering officers, twenty-six year old Lieutenant Clarissa Devlin, who had purportedly jumped ship. The message was thought to have perhaps originated from *Diamond* herself although that had been impossible to immediately verify. The rescue of Lieutenant Devlin had taken another twenty-five minutes, after which she was taken to *Wildcat's* sick bay to recover from the trauma of having been afloat in an open raft at sea for three days. Dawn, along with Powers and Callaghan had gone to visit with her, as soon as she had been seen by the Medical Officer.

Devlin was in surprisingly good spirits when Dawn had commenced the debriefing.

"Lieutenant Devlin, please tell us in your own words what transpired aboard *Diamond* immediately following the termination of Operation *Ankara* up until the moment you were rescued by us."

"Well ma'am, it was very strange. During *Ankara* itself all ship board activities and procedures seemed normal, although there was a sense of elation, at least amongst the officers, that we had done exceptionally well throughout. The word was that our captain, Commander Hunt, was proving himself to be extremely adept and proficient in dealing with the tasks we faced. But after the announcement that *Ankara* had ended, and-"

"How long after?"

Devlin thought for a moment.

"About twenty minutes afterward." Devlin looked at Dawn quizzically for permission to continue.

"Please continue, Lieutenant."

"Well, about twenty minutes after the announcement that *Ankara* had ended, and the advisement that we had all been stood down from duty, another announcement came over the intercom that we were all to return to duty immediately. On return to station I found the Chief Engineering Officer, Lieutenant-Commander McLellan, engaged in a serious discussion with Commander

Hunt. Nobody spoke directly to me about anything, but it appeared they were going over a collection of drawings that, if I understand things correctly, Commander Hunt himself had prepared earlier."

"Drawings for what?"

"As far as I could tell, drawings indicating a method for the manufacture of a variety of devices, using only parts and materials available from on-board stores."

"And so what happened after that?"

"Lieutenant-Commander McLellan set us all to work on building additional units that would function as radar jammers and even a very clever device indeed that would project images of the open ocean, captured by a series of cameras, onto panels suspended along each side of the ship's hull and up into the superstructure, so that, when activated, *Diamond* would be for practical purposes invisible when viewed from a short distance of say at least a mile."

"And was all of this made to work?"

"Yes ma'am, as far as I am aware."

Callaghan looked at Powers.

"My God, sir. Hunt has turned *Diamond* into a stealth vessel. That's why we have been unsuccessful in our attempts to find her. She doesn't send a transponder signal, and she is invisible both to radar and also the naked eye."

Dawn thought for a moment.

"So how did it transpire that you were able to get off *Diamond,* Lieutenant Devlin?"

"Well, ma'am, Lieutenant-Commander McLellan informed me that Commander Hunt wished to speak with me personally in his cabin, and that I was to cease all work and report there immediately. Which I did."

"And how did you find Commander Hunt? Did he seem normal to you?"

Devlin furrowed her brow for a moment.

"No, ma'am, I wouldn't say he seemed normal. He seemed if anything, extremely focused on some lofty purpose, but he wouldn't say what. He asked me if I liked to drink gin. I responded by telling him that I did indeed, but that I was presently on duty. He told me not to be concerned about that and he poured a glass, and then offered it to me. He invited me to sit. At first I wondered what his intentions might be."

"Did you get the feeling his interest in you might extend beyond the merely professional, Lieutenant?"

Devlin chuckled. But Dawn remained serious and focused.

"Well he is a very attractive man, ma'am. And I am a woman, after all."

She chuckled again, but cut short her mirth when she saw the expression on Dawn's face. Dawn was well aware of Devlin's reputation within the fleet concerning her predilection for certain extracurricular social activities, but did not want to hear a single word about it.

"But actually no. He simply started off on a rapid and very intense monologue about a whole series of highly technical issues, ranging from how to construct very complex circuits from standard ship-board supplies that would yield this impedance, that resistance, such-and-such a voltage drop, and so on. In all honesty I found it next to impossible to keep up with him. He must have been thinking at the speed of light, so to speak. He asked me if I considered as a marine engineer that it would be technically feasible to render a warship such as *Diamond* invisible to the naked eye during daytime. Both from the vantage points of other ships, and also aircraft. I said that I could not see how. He responded by telling me to open my mind and allow the possibilities to flood in. Then he changed tack and started going on about global political issues and where in my opinion the world would be in ten years, twenty years, fifty years from now, if current geopolitical trends were to continue. He asked if I considered that as a naval officer it might be a part of my remit or duty to do something about this. I remember I just laughed and suggested that all of that was beyond my control, that I was just a junior officer aboard a destroyer and that there was nothing I could do to influence world politics. But I added as an afterthought that geopolitical trends never continue in a truly linear fashion, but rather always exhibit some unexpected twists and turns as time goes on. That last comment seemed particularly to excite him, as if it had caused some circuit in his brain to light up. But then he looked at me, in a very strange manner indeed. But not the way a man normally looks at a woman, but more like . . ."

"Like what, Lieutenant?"

She paused for a moment, as if collecting her thoughts. Her features had adopted a somewhat serious, even grave appearance.

"Like a wolf might look at his prey. There was such an intensity and focused intelligence in his eyes. And yet I felt no danger, just more as if I was in the presence of a mind of almost superhuman ability. It was a strange feeling. A strange feeling indeed."

Devlin paused, and simply stared at all three of them. Dawn found this last comment poignant, as Devlin was wholly unaware of Commander Hunt's drug-induced cognition enhancement.

Callaghan prompted her further.

"So then what happened, Lieutenant?"

Devlin sighed.

"Well that's it, sir. I don't remember anything else. Except that I was floating in the life raft, adrift at sea, with one month's rations of food and water, extra clothing, a radio transmitter with charged batteries, and the strobe and transponder. At first I was afraid, afraid that I might not be picked up, but then after three days I saw *Wildcat* homing in on my position and I felt a great sense of relief."

"It seems that perhaps your gin may have been drugged."

"Yes sir, I expect so. I must have lost consciousness very rapidly. And I do remember waking up in the raft with a severe headache and feeling extremely groggy. As if I was suffering from a bad hangover."

About seven minutes later Powers had put out a call to the United States Eastern Seaboard Command in Groton, Connecticut, that they were now on the lookout for a rogue British destroyer which had been jury-rigged for stealth operation and was not going to respond on the radio on any frequency but was believed to be operating in the northern Indian Ocean or the Arabian Sea. Dawn and Callaghan had tried to make the case that *Diamond* was a vessel of the Royal Navy and therefore the problem of finding her fell to the United Kingdom armed forces, but Powers had simply shaken his head.

"No Captain. This problem has become much too big to be left in the hands of the British. We have a rogue vessel of the most modern type, at large and for all practical purposes invisible on the high seas, armed with the very latest in stealth torpedo technology. She is commanded by a superbly trained officer who is under the influence of a cognition enhancing agent, the long term effects of which we still do not yet fully comprehend. And an agent supplied by an American company, incidentally. Remember too that *Ankara,* even although operated by vessels of the Royal Navy, was an American operation from the start. Hunt may be responsible for the sinking of the *Rohollah Samimi,* and with the destruction of the Kingdom Centre in Saudi Arabia, a terrorist act for which, for all we know, he may also be ultimately responsible, it seems we could be teetering closer to an international incident of such proportions that the possibility of major war looms closer. No, Captain. Hunt must be stopped. Global security is at stake. We expect official Presidential approval any time now, but it is known that the President concurs with this view of the situation, which he has judged an extremely grave threat to world security."

Powers engaged Dawn in direct eye contact, a sincerely apologetic expression on his features.

"I am sorry, Captain, and please understand that I mean no disrespect to either you or the Royal Navy, both of whom I hold in the highest regard, as I believe you know. But this has become an American problem now. From this point forward your role is merely supportive."

Dawn managed to avoid appearing a little crestfallen as she replied.

"Yes sir."

CHAPTER 15

New York City, July 16, 2008

The Secretary General of the Assembly of the Security Council of the United Nations stood before the Chamber of Delegates amassed in New York City from every major nation on the globe. He stood to introduce to the Chamber the President and spiritual leader of Iran, who had been invited to Manhattan to address the Security Council, following a majority vote by Council members. The President stood at first in silent courtesy while the Secretary General reached the conclusion of his introduction with the words,

"Delegates of the United Nations, I present to you the President of Iran."

The President stepped over to the podium, placed the microphone in the lapel of his tan colored corduroy jacket, and began to speak.

"Delegates of the Security Council of these United Nations."

His English seemed flawless.

"I come to you today to share some of my views as to the state of affairs in this world of ours as we find it at this present time. As I am quite certain you are all aware, I represent a nation that follows the teachings and tenets of Islam, one of the world's three major religious doctrines, and, as I hope to persuade you here today, the only correct doctrine that all of mankind, without exception, must come to follow."

As he continued speaking, a strange lull seemed to fall over the assembled delegates in the Chamber listening to him that afternoon.

"But first, allow me to establish a little of the background of Islam. Islam itself of course means nothing more than 'submission', that is, submission to Allah, and all of His teachings. Islam began, on the Christian calendar, in the early 7th century in what is today known as Saudi Arabia, when the prophet Muhammad wrote the Islamic holy book known by its name as the Qur'an, or 'Recitation'. The Qur'an describes within its pages the revelation of the Angel Gabriel which he gave to Muhammad. Muhammad spread the word to the peoples of that region of the world and in consequence Islam enjoyed unparalleled growth and success, and remained wholly unified under Allah while Muhammad remained alive. But then, upon our blessed prophet's passing in what would be called AD 632 on the Christian calendar, Islam suffered a schism, a split, if you will, into two main sects. This most grievous of tragedies, which was and continues to be an insult to Allah and His laws, led to the development of the Shi'ite sect, comprised of those Moslems who recognize that only descendants of Muhammad, who was as Allah's messenger, infallible, may interpret scripture and rule all of the peoples of the world. But it also led to the development of the Sunni Moslems, who believe that rulers may be drawn from a much wider group. This of course as you might imagine, led to much discord and disharmony amongst the Moslem peoples. This finally came to a head in October AD 680 on the Christian calendar, near that city now known as Karbala, in present-day Iran. Now one of Muhammad's descendants, Ali, had an adult son named Hussein. Hussein was named by the Shi'ite Moslems to lead them into battle against the Sunnis. However, in the fight which ensued, Hussein was decapitated. But Hussein's passing was a victory for the Shi'ite Moslems. Because you see, he became a martyr for his peoples. Indeed even today in the People's Islamic Republic of

Iran, the annual mourning that takes place for Hussein, known to the Moslem peoples as Ashura, is by far the most important ceremony for the Shi'ite Moslems. During Ashura, young men wail in baleful sorrow for Hussein as they strike their own chests and flagellate themselves with whips, knives, and even swords!"

His tempo and intensity growing by the moment, the President had already succeeded in mesmerizing most if not all present at his speech.

"And after our prophet Muhammad passed, he was followed by a series of his male descendants, known as Imams, or Leaders. But even amongst the Shi'ite righteous, in time controversy took hold, as regards the specific number of Imams to succeed Muhammad. There were those who believed that there were but five Imams, such Shi'ite Moslems became known as the Zaydi, or Fiver, Shi'ite Moslems. Then there were those who believed that there were seven Imams, those Shi'ite Moslems then became known as Ismaili, or Sevener, Shi'ite Moslems. And then, there were those Shi'ite Moslems who recognized and believed the truth. The truth as revealed to them by Allah, that there were twelve Imams. Those righteous Moslems became known as the Ithna Ashari, or Twelver, Shi'ite Moslems. And because Ithna Ashari is the truth as revealed by Allah to all of mankind, Ithna Ashari Shi'ite Islam is the official religion of the Peoples Islamic Republic of Iran."

The President paused for a drink of water. His audience simply waited for him to resume his speech. At that moment it was so quiet with anticipation that one could have heard a pin drop.

"The twelfth Imam, Abu'l-Qasim Muhammad, also known as Muhammad al-Muntazar, or 'Muhammad the Awaited One', was born in Iraq in Samarra, in the year AD 868 on the Christian calendar. His father of course was the eleventh Imam, but he passed in AD 874. History tells us that the leaders of society at that time were unaware of the birth of Muhammad al-Muntazar, and so they did seek the counsel of the eleventh Imam's brother, Ja'far, in the hope that he would accept the role of twelfth Imam. Ja'far was willing to assume this role and did enter the deceased eleventh Imam's house to commence the funeral proceedings. But the Qur'an instructs us that a young boy, Muhammad al-Muntazar, stepped before him saying, 'Uncle, stand back! For it is more fitting for me to lead the prayers for my father than for you.' But still no one present was aware of the boy's true identity. Later there were those who inquired of Ja'far as to whom the boy had been, but the boy by then had disappeared. The Qur'an teaches us that from that year onward the boy went into hiding, or occultation. Thus in the year AD 874 on the Christian calendar, the true twelfth Imam went into hiding without sons. And thus, the twelfth Imam did not and has not passed from this Earth, but remains in occultation, in order to protect his life from those enemies of righteousness who would seek to do him harm. Indeed the Qur'an also tells us that the twelfth Imam passed from the sight of man in a water well, Bi'r al-Ghayba, or 'Well of Occultation', located in a cave in Samarra. A House of Worship, the Jamkaran Mosque, has since been built to cover the cave. Ithna Ashari Shi'ite Moslems regularly gather in rooms of the cave to pray for the return to Earth of the twelfth Imam, also known today as Imam Mahdi. That is why, after I myself personally visited Jamkaran Mosque, to pass a letter to the Imam Mahdi by way of the well, I ordered commencement of construction of a railway link directly from Tehran to the Jamkaran Mosque so that those who seek the Mahdi may find him. Indeed those who visit Jamkaran forty Tuesdays in a row to pray, without interruption, will be granted an audience with Imam Mahdi."

He paused once more for another sip of water, to great dramatic effect.

"Now the period of occultation of Imam Mahdi is divided into the Lesser Occultation, lasting from AD 874 to AD 941, on the Christian calendar, when Imam Mahdi communicated with the outside world through four successive agents, and the Greater Occultation, which commenced when the last of these agents passed. Since the commencement of the Greater Occultation, until this very day, the Imam Mahdi has desisted from all communications with men. The Greater Occultation continues.

Imam Mahdi is waiting for the time that Allah has set aside for his re-appearance to the world."

The President paused again, raising a finger to his audience.

"But be assured, my friends. The twelfth Imam, Imam Mahdi, will appear when Allah wills it. He will be revealed as the divinely guided Mahdi, who will vindicate his followers, restore the faithful community, and usher in, at the end of time, a perfect Islamic society of justice and truth. These are the signs that will herald the Imam Mahdi's return: He will appear suddenly. He will be joined by three hundred and thirteen of his most devoted, enlightened believers, who will pledge loyalty to him. Although only Allah knows the exact time of Imam Mahdi's appearance, it will occur on a Friday, or in conjunction with the autumn equinox. Jesus, peace be upon him, will also return and serve as Imam Mahdi's lieutenant. Imam Mahdi will establish the seat of his global government in Constantinople, now known as Istanbul. The earth will know true justice and peace, as Islam shall become the pinnacle of faith. All shall convert to Islam. It will become the one, pure lasting world religion, practiced by all of the world's peoples. At the same time the world will experience astounding growth in science and technology as Imam Mahdi corrects all of mankind's scientific mistakes and errors. The Earth will experience abundant rain, and vegetation will flourish. There shall be eternal spring. Now the Qur'an instructs us that the Imam Mahdi's return may be hastened by the bringing about of the end times, the tribulation of the world, that is, the destruction of that insolent Western bridgehead called Israel, impinging without mandate into Palestinian territories, and the concurrent reduction of the Western arrogant powers to their knees. Only then will Imam Mahdi return and usher in an unprecedented era of justice and peace, and transform the world entire into a caliphate, an Islamic Republic. For you see, dear friends, the lessons of history tell us that repressive and cruel governments do not survive. Allah has not left the universe and humanity to their own devices. Many things have happened contrary to the wishes and plans of governments, which tell us that there is a higher power at work, and all events are determined by Allah. Can one deny the signs of change in the contemporary world? Is the situation of the world today comparable to that of ten years ago? Changes happen fast and come at a furious pace. The peoples of the world are not happy with the status quo and pay little heed to the empty promises and comments made by a number of influential world leaders. Many around the world feel insecure and oppose the spread of war, corruption, dubious policies, and are protesting the increasing gap between those who have, and those who have not. Many are also protesting the increasing gap between the rich and poor countries. Peoples around the world are angry about the attacks on their cultural foundations and the disintegration of families, and the fading of care and compassion. The peoples of the world have no faith in international organizations, because their rights are not advocated by these organizations. Liberalism and Western-style democracy have failed to realize the ideals of humanity. Those with insight can already hear the sounds of the shattering and fall of the ideology and thoughts of the liberal democratic systems. We see increasingly that the peoples of the world are flocking towards a main focal point—that is, Allah, the Architect and Creator of all things. Undoubtedly through faith in Him and the teachings of the prophets, the people will conquer their problems. My question for you is this: 'Do you not want to join them?' For whether you like it or not the world is gravitating towards faith in Allah and justice and His will shall prevail over all things. *Vasalam Ala Man Ataba'al hoda!*"

With that, the President of The Peoples Islamic Republic of Iran concluded his speech.

That evening the news at six o'clock aired on CNN started with a lead story about the resumption by Iran of activities commensurate with the development of nuclear capability.

"Inspectors for the International Atomic Energy Agency have concluded that Iran appears to have solved most of its technological problems and is now beginning to enrich uranium on a far larger scale than before, according to the Agency's senior officials. According to diplomats familiar with the inspectors' report, at the present pace, Iran could have three thousand centrifuges operational by June—enough to manufacture the equivalent of one nuclear weapon per year. The sprawling underground nuclear enrichment facility at Natanz in the Esfahan province, a little to the north-west of the center of the country includes a centrifuge pilot plant, approximately half the size of the Pentagon, that has been in operation since January 2006. The centrifuge pilot plant could hold as many as fifty thousand centrifuges, enough to manufacture the equivalent of one nuclear weapon every three weeks. Natanz itself is supplied from a huge facility that converts uranium yellowcake into uranium hexafluoride, the feedstock for centrifuges."

The news item went on to report on the President's speech at the UN that afternoon, at which he had spoken at some length on his views concerning Islamic theology. The item concluded with a few seconds of footage of the scene outside the UN building when the President had emerged to face a sea of reporters, all eager to be the first to ask him a question.

"Mr. President! Is Iran resuming the pursuit of its nuclear ambitions so that a bomb may built?"

The President had responded with a disarming spread of his arms and a smile to match.

"Should a nation not be allowed to pursue technology for peaceful purposes from which it can benefit greatly, merely because the technology could conceivably be corrupted by a perverse individual seeking to develop a weapon?"

"So you deny any intention to attack Israel?"

"I deny nothing. And if I may be so bold as to remind the American people, America was the first nation to build atomic weapons, and to date is the only nation ever to have used them against large civilian populations, in Japan. But the Iranian peoples seek only peaceful ends from their nuclear program, for example, the generation of electricity by nuclear power stations."

Another reporter yelled out a question.

"Mr. President! What are your views on the sinking of the *Rohollah Samimi* and the attack on the Kingdom Centre in Riyadh? You said nothing of this in your speech earlier."

The President's countenance became more somber, more pensive. He seemed to be considering his answer with care.

"The British and American terrorists will pay dearly for their unprovoked assaults on both the peaceful peoples of Iran and their brothers in Saudi Arabia. The Saudi peoples are our natural allies because the twelfth Imam, Imam Mahdi, will journey to Mecca upon his return. For it is written. The unrighteous will rise up against Allah's people and make every effort to subdue them, but the sword of Islam shall rise victorious. To intentionally attack with torpedoes our unarmed civilian ship is a morally heinous crime, the attack on our Saudi brothers in Riyadh is the work of cowardly infidel dogs. But Allah will take His revenge at the appointed time, and make no mistake, the hand of Allah when He has been moved to anger and vengeance shall strike with mighty force such as to spread terror and panic in the hearts of the infidels, and the time shall be very soon! America and her pit bull terrier Britain belong to Allah, not to the Americans, not to the British! Soon Allah will make clear once again as He has done so many times in the past that all peoples of planet Earth are Moslem, whether they would believe this or not!"

CHAPTER 16

The familiar voice of the evening anchor for CNN, after introducing Mr. Larry Shayler, spokesman of the pressure group *Concerned Christians International,* or CCI, cut directly to the salient questions.

"So, Mr. Shayler. You have read a transcript of the Iranian President's speech which he delivered earlier this afternoon at the General Assembly of the United Nations in New York City."

"Yes I have."

"Can you summarize your main problems and concerns with his address?"

Shayler cleared his throat.

"Yes. The President of Iran is clearly insane. His world views are most definitively not biblically based, but rather based on a skewed and highly suspect theology as espoused in the Qur'an, the Islamic holy book."

"You particularly dislike the manner in which Jesus is portrayed within this theological doctrine?"

"Most certainly I do, as do all members of CCI. Jesus is described by the President as coming back to Earth sometime in the future, a view with which we agree, of course, but only as a lieutenant to the twelfth Imam Mahdi. It is with the latter point which we take issue, indeed we find highly offensive. Jesus Christ is no follower of a Moslem prophet. He is the King of Kings, the

Lord and Savior of all mankind! The twelfth Imam, should he even truly exist, is no more than a man, just like you or me! Jesus is God incarnate, the proof provided by His coming to Earth in human form to die on the cross in atonement for all of our sins! His is a free gift to be granted to all those who ask! The very idea that Christ Jesus is but a follower of an ordinary man strikes at the very heart of all that we as Christians believe. The President has caused grave offense to Christians all over the globe with his blasphemous comments this afternoon!"

"And what do you think of his plans to develop a nuclear program?"

"Obviously Iran intends to attack Israel and cut off her people from their birthright!"

"By birthright you mean their land? The nation of Israel herself?"

"Indeed yes! What other possible reason could there be for his development of a nuclear capability?"

"There are those who say he merely wishes to use nuclear power for peaceful means. That his aim is only the construction of enough nuclear power stations so that Iran can provide electricity to every private home and business within her borders."

"Well that is just nonsense. Listen to what the man is saying! He has made it crystal clear he intends to destroy Israel, and the West along with her! He clearly believes that he can usher in the end of the age according to Moslem belief by ridding the world of its Christian and Jewish peoples. Already Moslems have practically succeeded in taking over certain western European countries. The President and those of his ilk are now setting their sights on the United States! Mark my words! The third world war has already started. And if we do not prevail, the sun will set on the Western way of life, along with all of the values that we cherish here in America."

"Values such as?"

"Freedom of speech! Freedom of expression! Freedom of the press! Democracy! Presumption of innocence until found guilty beyond reasonable doubt by a jury of one's peers within the context of a properly organized and overseen adversarial trial! Freedom from cruel and unusual punishment! The Bill of Rights! The Constitution!"

"And what do you suppose the President meant when he said that, quote: 'The hand of Allah when He has been moved to anger and vengeance shall strike with mighty force such as to spread terror and panic in the hearts of the infidels, and the time shall be very soon?'"

"I think quite obviously he means to organize another attack against a Western target somewhere, probably a city along the eastern seaboard, perhaps even New York."

"An attack along the lines of some we have seen previously? Another 9-11?"

"No, nothing that dramatic. There will never be another attack like 9-11. That was a one-off. It'll just be some suicide bomber or something. Probably a handful of innocent bystanders will be killed, and the event will be reported on the news for a few days. That kind of deal."

The anchor decided to switch rapidly to the next item on his agenda.

"There are those who are suggesting that the Federal Express plane crash into the Kingdom Centre in Riyadh was a deliberate act. That this was an attack against Islam. Where does CCI stand on this issue?"

"After examining all of the news reports in detail, I would concede that this was most probably a deliberate act of sabotage, rather than an accident. However the pilot was operating of his own volition. No American government agency would sanction such an action. He was an independent agent. And also a lunatic, in my opinion."

"What about the sinking of the *Rohollah Samimi?* A deliberate act, as the Iranian President seems to imagine?"

"No, of course not. Although the ship from which the torpedoes emanated was foreign and therefore not operating to the standards of professionalism that we expect of the United States Navy. But the sinking was merely an act of incompetence, a mistake. In fact I heard on the news that the captain was a woman. Women have no place commanding warships."

"And why is that?"

"Because as the Bible says, the woman submits to the man, who in his turn submits to Christ. Men do not submit to women. As a consequence of this violation of God's law, a liner lies at the bottom of the Atlantic Ocean, and-"

"Actually the Arabian Sea, was it not? And according to the latest news reports I have heard the woman commander to whom you refer was not involved in the sinking of the Iranian liner."

"Yes, well whatever. The point is that God punishes those who transgress His laws, whether purposely or otherwise. But it was an accident. There could be no possible reason for that cruise liner being deliberately attacked."

At that point the interview was brought to a conclusion.

"Well I am sorry but I must stop you there as we are out of time. Thank you, Mr. Larry Shayler, of Concerned Christians International, for agreeing to appear with us here tonight."

CHAPTER 17

London, England. July 18, 2008.

The early July morning was much like any other in central London. Temperatures were already in the high sixties with the promise that they would climb substantially higher by lunch time, perhaps getting past seventy, and the day was to be free of rain, unlike the immediately preceding several weeks that had proved somewhat fickle from a meteorological perspective, as is so often the case in the British Isles, even during the summer months.

By 9.30am the city streets were thronging with commuters making their way to work, variously by train, bus, underground subway, or private car. The United States Embassy in Grosvenor Square was preparing to open its doors to the many applicants for employment and immigration visas who had by now formed neat but long lines by the barricades which, along with police officers wearing Kevlar vests and armed with MP5 submachine guns, kept them well back from the building itself. Many were leaving family members or friends to hold their spots in the line so that they could run to the nearby cafes and shops to purchase food and coffee for their breakfast.

The dull thud that shook the air moments later caused a few hundred heads to turn towards the north-west. At first nobody seemed to be aware of what was happening, but shortly thereafter shouts and screams started to permeate the morning air. Police officers who, seconds before, had seemed as nonplussed as the members of the general public surrounding them suddenly started running in the general direction of Marble Arch underground station, where there had, it seemed, just been a large explosion. In the face of this however people continued simply standing still in their lines, beginning to feel uncertain, afraid, not knowing what else to do, as the sound of police, and, a little later, ambulance sirens started wailing across the city from the underground station just a couple of blocks distant.

But within minutes there was the sound of another blast, this time emanating from Hyde Park Corner underground station, followed about a minute after that by another from the station at Oxford Circus, and then finally, another from Piccadilly Circus. By now, some eleven minutes from the initial blast, several police cars and vans had sped to the Embassy and large numbers of officers jumped out as their vehicles screeched to a halt on the pavement. A Metropolitan Police chief superintendent immediately started addressing the by-now badly startled crowd with a loudspeaker, instructing everyone present that the Embassy was now closed and would remain so until further notice. As such all those who could quickly disperse should do so, but not by subway as following the morning's developments all London Transport Trains were no longer running, again until further notice. The superintendent further strongly suggested that those who had accommodations within eight miles of Grosvenor Square might consider, for their own safety, returning there on foot. He advised that clear passage would be open along North and South Audley Street, but Park Lane, Piccadilly, and Regent Street, as well as part of Oxford Street would now be closed to all but emergency personnel. He suggested that those heading north should proceed on foot to Marylebone station, while those heading south should consider using Victoria.

But his carefully planned suggestions were cut short by the tremendous flash that emanated from inside the Ford Transit van that was parked at the corner of Grosvenor Street and Park Lane. The roar of the blast that came but a fraction of a second later, and the mushroom cloud that went up five thousand feet into the atmosphere came too late for any who had been present on the scene only moments before to witness. All present within a radius of three city blocks had simply been vaporized, as the buildings around about them had been instantly pummeled to rubble and dust. The 600mph winds as hot as two thousand degrees Fahrenheit that instantly shot out in all directions thereafter immediately set fire to other structures lying further out from the explosion's epicenter, almost a half-mile in every direction. People not under cover or inside sturdy constructions were subjected to burns, varying in intensity from mild first degree over exposed skin only, to rapid although not instantaneous incineration, often accompanied by agonized screams. In the final aftermath of the blast, the damage extended from Blandford Street to the north, just touching Green Park to the south and part of Hyde Park to the west, and New Bond Street to the east. In just moments, approximately five thousand six hundred and fifty people had lost their lives, including four hundred police officers and all of the staff of the United States Embassy. A further estimated nine thousand had been injured to the point where they would require immediate hospitalization. A substantial proportion of those, given the extent and severity of their burns and blast injuries, were not expected to live.

It was later that day that a video was posted on an Al-Qaeda website condemning the British and American arrogant Western powers for their continued acts of international terrorism in the barbarous sinking of the unarmed ocean liner *Rohollah Samimi* and the attendant loss of one thousand two hundred innocent lives, followed shortly thereafter by the wanton destruction of the Kingdom Centre in Saudi Arabia, with the loss of many more innocent lives. The veiled commentator on the video was of course speaking in Arabic but a translation indicated that the blasts at the four Underground stations in London that morning had been of the conventional type, and as the bombs involved had been relatively small, only fifty pounds each, they had been intended more as a diversion than a serious attack. The diversion was to occupy the emergency services with attending to the involved stations before unleashing the new weapon, a first for Al-Qaeda, a nuclear briefcase, one of around twenty-seven such devices originally manufactured in the old Soviet Union for potential use by KGB operatives, but had since, according to Western analysts, gone missing. The commentator on the video then cut to Osama Bin Laden himself, who appeared looking rather thin but in otherwise good health. Bin Laden commenced issuing a plea, again in Arabic, to governments of all Western nations that they and their people immediately convert to Islam otherwise there would be more such atomic blasts in busy downtown districts, brought about with the specific intention of causing as many casualties and as much destruction as possible.

Initial outrage and calls for revenge against the terrorists by members of the British cabinet and opposition gave way to indecision and confusion over the course of the following two days. Was a military or diplomatic response appropriate? Who was responsible for the blasts, exactly? Did Al-Qaeda really have access to ex-Russian nuclear briefcases, or was this simply a hoax? Did such briefcases even really exist? Perhaps Iran was the real culprit? If so, continued sanctions against that country might be the most effective way to prevent them from purchasing any more nuclear briefcases on the international black market, and/or manufacturing their own nuclear devices. What was the American responsibility in all of this, given that it was their Embassy that was destroyed, and some of their people killed? Washington responded simply by issuing a formal statement that the war on terror would continue as before and that the perpetrators of this act would be brought to justice and punished for their crimes. Unsurprisingly, this position drew the usual howls of protest from the American political Left, who insisted that fighting was not working and it was time to sit down at the table with Al-Qaeda and talk about this, before another nuclear blast like the one that had just taken place in London occurred in a major American city.

They emphasized again the need to exercise greater sensitivity to our Islamic brethren if such future attacks were to be avoided. The Islamic Council of Great Britain for their part stated in the news media that they did not support the terrorists and reiterated that Islam is a religion of peace. However this proved insufficient to dissuade a large and very angry group of British National Party skinheads from petrol-bombing several north London mosques during prayers, resulting in several dozen more burn injuries and two deaths as well as the total loss of one mosque, and the vicious beatings of several police officers and firefighters who had responded to the scenes.

CHAPTER 18

The letters that arrived simultaneously at the White House in Washington, DC, and No.10 Downing Street in London, the residence of the British Prime Minister, addressed respectively to the President of the United States and the Prime Minister of the United Kingdom, were brief and cut straight to the point. They each were comprised of only four short paragraphs, presented in standard military style.

July 19, 2008

Dear Mr. President/Prime Minister.

1. At this point it cannot have escaped your notice that the present state of tension in relations between certain nations of the Middle East (notably Iran and Saudi Arabia) and the West are such that the potential for touching off a Third World War has now become very real. Any further attacks, either real or perceived, by one side against the other could very easily bring about the realization of this nightmare scenario.

2. I am fully aware that you have been attempting to hunt down my vessel in the vicinity of the Arabian Sea and the Indian Ocean. However I must inform you that the

efforts of each and every branch of your armed services will meet only with failure. My intelligence quotient or IQ I currently estimate to be 236 and continues to increase. Consider the IQ of Dr. Albert Einstein, author of the theories of relativity and special relativity, at the peak of his mental fitness was approximately 160 (incidentally a most impressive figure in of itself). In addition, my powers of processing are enormously enhanced, such that I anticipate your every move even before you do. I have no doubt that by now, one of my engineering officers, Lieutenant Clarissa Devlin, RN, rescued on July 14, 2008 by representatives of the Royal Navy in the Arabian Sea has informed you of my adaptation of HMS *Diamond* for stealth operations. I would confirm that at my command HMS *Diamond* was seen by eye-witnesses aboard local fishing vessels in the act of launching Sting Ray Mark 3 torpedoes which resulted in the deliberate sinking of the Iranian cruise liner *Rohollah Samimi.* I further confirm that during Operation *Ankara* held in the North Atlantic Ocean this year in June, the supertanker *Brent B* was struck intentionally by two non-live Sting Ray Mark 3 torpedoes, the normal functioning of which had been hijacked by my intervention. In addition, in part in person and in part by means of various third parties, I engineered the attacks against the Kingdom Centre in Riyadh, Saudi Arabia, the conventional bombings of the subway stations, and the nuclear attack on the American Embassy, both in London, England.

3. Although I have not yet provided conclusive proof, I must warn you that at this time I have at my disposal a number of tactical nuclear weapons which I can at any time bring to bear on targets in the Middle East.

4. I strongly urge you to view the video presentation which can be found at: http://www.commandergarryhunt. co.uk/. There you will find an in-depth explanation of my insights and details of how to prevent any further

escalation of hostilities between the Middle East and the West. Failure on your part to follow the demands as laid out in my presentation will result in a full-scale atomic attack against selected targets in Iran and Saudi Arabia, for which the governments of the United Kingdom and the United States of America will appear, in the eyes of the world, wholly and jointly responsible.

I remain sirs, your obedient servant,

Garry Hunt

Garry Hunt, Commander, RN
Officer Commanding
HMS *Diamond*

After considered debate and discussion in each case, both the President of the United States and the Prime Minister of the United Kingdom arrived at the conclusion that it would be prudent to watch the presentation as Commander Hunt had suggested in his missive. They settled themselves in their respective offices and ordered that key members of their cabinets do the same and concentrate on viewing Hunt's presentation. All members were of course to remain in constant contact while doing so. Upon opening the web site, they saw Hunt himself, appearing in his dress uniform, seemingly aboard *Diamond*. As far as anyone could guess, the ship was most likely at sea, possibly somewhere in the Indian Ocean, but really could have been anywhere for all anyone knew. The filming was of professional quality and included only Hunt, delivering a simple presentation while standing at a lectern.

"Good morning," he started out. "I am very pleased that you could join me. This is of course a recording that was made a number of days ago now, but let us not quibble about such details."

He pushed a button on a controller and immediately a screen, clearly visible behind him, indicated what appeared to be a map of several islands, possibly very large in geographical area.

"I would like you now to focus your attention, if you would be so kind, on this map shown here."

Both the Presidential Staff in Washington, and the Prime Ministerial Staff in London peered at the map for some time, but not a single person was able to identify which area of the world it might represent. The only thing anyone was able to indicate with any certainty was that the map appeared to be old, probably dating back several hundred years. It appeared to show a number of unfamiliar land masses, lying very close to one another.

Hunt smiled.

"Do not be embarrassed if the map appears unfamiliar to you. It does to all those who see it. Although I can assure you, this is an accurate map of a land mass here on planet Earth."

Hunt went on.

"This is a photograph of a map drawn in 1513 by Admiral Piri Reis. Admiral Reis was a senior officer in the navy of the Ottoman Turks. However the admiral did not actually draw *de novo* the map you see here, but rather he copied it from a number of extant originals left from an earlier time period, dating to around 4000 years BC. This map shows the detail of a part of the Palmer Peninsula, and Queen Maud Land, in the continent of Antarctica. Now I know what you are thinking. This looks nothing like Antarctica. But in fact it would be more accurate to say that it looks nothing like Antarctica, as it appears today. However Antarctica was not always covered in ice as it is now. In point of fact, advancing ice sheets covered the continent around six thousand years ago, and as a result its topography has remained largely hidden to the eyes of the world. That is until 1949. In that year a joint British-Swedish cartographic expedition revealed a glimpse of the geography of the land masses underlying the ice, during their very extensive seismic survey. And do you know, the odd thing is, the survey revealed a topography that is to all practical intents and purposes identical to the features indicated on the Piri Reis map, despite the inescapable fact that, back in 1513, Antarctica was covered in an ice sheet approximately one mile thick, in places even thicker. In any event the continent was not rediscovered by Europeans until 1818, some three hundred and five years after the Piri Reis map was drawn. On the original of Admiral Reis's map are handwritten notations indicating that he had copied it from much earlier maps he had obtained from some source, or sources. A source, or sources, that must have existed at least six thousand years ago, before the continent was covered in a thick layer of ice. But the very strange thing is, the earliest known civilizations on Earth, those of Sumer and Ancient Egypt, are considered by conventional wisdom to be no more than five thousand years old at most, perhaps a little less. So it would seem that conventional wisdom is perhaps not entirely correct. In fact it may well be the case that there were skilled cartographers in the world predating Sumerian and Ancient Egyptian societies by at least one thousand years, who could produce maps every bit as accurate as those produced during a survey carried out in the middle of the 20th century. And further. It would seem that there was not only a cache of skilled cartographers in the world at that time, but in fact there existed an entire advanced civilization, quite possibly every bit as advanced as our present civilization, on the continent that is presently covered in ice and which we now call Antarctica."

Hunt paused for effect, before framing his next statement as a question.

"But how could Antarctica ever have been ice-free? It lies at the bottom of the Earth, where for approximately half of the year the sun's rays almost never permeate. The answer is simple. Things were not always that way. Think, if you will, of the Earth's crust. The hard, rocky outer layer covering its interior and making up its surface, upon which all land masses, all oceans, all seas rest."

At this point Hunt's audiences in both Washington and London were listening intently.

"The crust varies anywhere from about ten to twenty-five miles in thickness, under which lies the hot mantle, comprised of semi-molten rock, a viscous, plastic layer if you will. And of course underlying the mantle are the even hotter and truly liquid outer and inner cores. Now imagine the skin of an orange as representing the crust of the Earth. And imagine if at all points immediately underneath that skin was a viscous semi-liquid layer that allowed the skin to slip or slide as a single complete unit over the entire underlying structures of the fruit. So perhaps now you begin to see the picture. From time to time, geologically speaking, perhaps every six thousand years or so, the Earth's crust slips in a quite sudden, rather cataclysmic event that has the effect of altering the terrestrial co-ordinates of every single point on the surface of the planet. As well as the climate. Admiral Reis copied his famous map from an earlier map that was drawn just before the last such slip occurred, around six thousand years ago. At that time the continent we now call Antarctica was occupying a position in the southern hemisphere but was not in the southern polar region, and was blessed with a temperate climate. And therefore was not covered in ice. And not only was the continent ice-free, but it was home to an advanced civilization, similar in many respects to present-day advanced societies. But this civilization was brought to an end by the sudden movement of the crust, which repositioned its component land masses to their present position, plunging them into an ice age from which they have still not recovered."

Hunt took another brief pause.

"Now it is my belief that if we were to investigate the land as it exists today under the ice, we would find remnants of this advanced civilization. Indeed several relatively modest but nevertheless fascinating collections of artifacts have already been recovered by some minor drilling expeditions that have been mounted to date. But what is even more fascinating is the fact that some of the same artifacts have been found in the Mayan ruins in Mexico, the great plain of Nazca in Peru, and the pyramids of Egypt. In fact it is my belief, based again on a considerable body of evidence, that following the last cataclysmic shift of the Earth's crust representatives of the inhabitants of this ancient society went out into the world to find other lands to colonize.

The ancient and so-called first civilizations of Mexico, Peru, and Egypt are all direct descendents of the earlier civilization that existed in Antarctica. There are very many lines of evidence to support this. For example, the design and construction of the totora reed boats found on Lake Titicaca on the border between southern Peru and north-west Bolivia are virtually identical to those that are to be found on the River Nile, in Egypt and Sudan. And historical evidence teaches that this has been so for centuries, if not millennia. Remains of dry batteries have been found in all three countries, and also in Antarctica, that are all exactly the same in design and are all of indisputably ancient origin. There are even more fascinating lines of evidence. The Inca constructions in Peru, for example, those of Macchu Pichu, and the Mayan, Aztec, and Egyptian edifices still extant, all share very compelling parallels with one another, as well as those of Puma Punku in Tiwanaku in the Bolivian Andes, most especially a curious stone structure known as the Gateway to the Sun. And incidentally these are constructions which, in the opinions of many, were far too advanced to have been built by the ancient Egyptians, or the Incas, or the Aztecs or Mayans. Or for that matter, even by modern human society. The Incas of Peru constructed temples and dwelling places from giant boulders weighing very many tons apiece that were often carried miles up hills or mountain sides, even sheer cliff faces. These blocks were intricately and precisely cut, so as to fit together rather much like giant jig-saw blocks. And, being of a very hard stone indeed, in the case of Puma Punku, for example, composed of a mixture of andesite and diorite, the blocks were presumably cut with a blade fashioned from a substance harder than the stone itself, such as carbon steel or diamond. As it happens they fit together so well that in many if not most cases even a single sheet of paper cannot be slipped between any two of them. And as if that were not sufficient, such constructions are also earthquake-proof. When the Spanish Conquistadores invaded Peru, they destroyed an Inca temple in the town of Cusco, and built in its place a Catholic cathedral. Twice in history that cathedral was destroyed by earthquakes, but subsequently rebuilt. However despite the destruction of the cathedral each time, the Inca foundations upon which the edifice was constructed did not suffer any significant damage whatsoever. In Egypt, the pyramid of Giza is built to mathematical tolerances that can only be described as remarkable, and once again using enormous but precisely cut and positioned blocks of stone, assembled in such a manner that many of the inner blocks could not have been placed without the outer blocks to support them. But strangely the outer blocks, if positioned first, would have precluded the subsequent insertion of the inner blocks. And because of the nature of the very limited internal spaces inherent in the design, logic dictates that temporary supporting elements would not have been feasible either. Remember once again that many of these blocks weigh literally over one hundred tons. A conundrum if ever there was one. In fact it is wholly impossible to imagine that this is the work of a relatively primitive people. Also, within an internal passage deep inside the pyramid there exists what appears to be a time-line, depicting global history from the birth of Christ to around the turn of the 21st century. The walls of the passage are inscribed and indented or built outward or inward with various symbolisms, irregularities, and three-dimensional reliefs that seem to parallel precisely major tumultuous events in human history, from the crucifixion to the crusades to the English civil war, the American and French Revolutions, the Boer war, the First and Second World wars, the Vietnam and Korean wars, the Cuban missile crisis, Watergate, and so it goes, each step of the way along the passage representing another ten years in the history of the planet. That is until one reaches the end of the 20th century. At that point the passage simply drops, very suddenly, and without warning, into a seemingly bottomless pit. It is as if the pyramid has an inbuilt system alerting those of us living on earth at present that the end of the present age is imminent. This, if it indeed represents an accurate representation of our immediate future, could be a warning transmitted to us by the ancients concerning the major geopolitical issues of our epoch. Issues such as spiraling economic problems, national debt, endless war in the Middle East, a terminal and irreversible peaking of global petroleum production, the end of cheap oil, the rise of militant Islam, global warming, or a thousand other things. It may even be that we are due for another crustal slip which may plunge at least part of the developed world into a new ice age. There are several apparent warnings of an astrological nature to be found in Mayan, Aztec, Egyptian, and Inca ruins that as the planet's polar axis shifts from pointing toward one constellation to another, cataclysmic climatic changes will take place, and very suddenly. And even as I speak, the polar axis is shifting from alignment with the constellation Pisces to the constellation Aquarius. The shift will be complete in approximately four years from now, in December 2012. Interestingly too, the Mayan calendar predicts that the end of the current age will occur at that same time. There are also numerous Biblical prophecies that describe the end of times and the final battle of Armageddon, the conflict between the forces of Gog and Magog, and the coming of the new Israel. Many believe that these prophecies are now being fulfilled. They say that levels of decadence and immorality and crime have exploded across the face of the globe. Left to his own devices man will soon pass from history. And none of the three so-called major monotheistic religions; Judaism, Christianity, or Islam, possess any answers. Instead they seem intent only on mutual destruction. Indeed the sinking of the Iranian cruise liner, the *Rohollah Samimi,* the destruction of the Kingdom Centre in Riyadh, and the small but quite devastating atomic blast in London are but a taste of things to come. If no countering action is taken, then I predict that from this point forward history will unfold, in broad terms, as follows: OPEC nations will continue to increase the price of each barrel of oil, which has already hit one hundred forty dollars and will soon rise to one hundred fifty, and from there continue to two hundred, and then two hundred fifty, which will be a reality on or around 2010, two years from now. That will translate to spiraling gasoline prices, especially in the United States where costs until very recently were held artificially low. The US government will announce to the world, both directly and also via various forms of news media that the price increases are as a result of the obstructionist policies of various Middle Eastern nations, as well as Russia, who will be seen to be attempting to set the price of a barrel of oil at too high a level in an attempt to severely weaken the economies of America and her allies. As a result there will be considerable animosity felt by ordinary Americans and Western Europeans towards these countries, which will be fueled by continued negative reporting by mainstream journalists. Sometime between 2010 and 2011 governments of the world will finally be forced to admit that the oil reserves in over sixty percent of all countries will have peaked, that is, more than half of the available oil will have by then already been pumped. Remaining oil will be more difficult and costly to extract, and ever smaller yields will be realized, which will cause a growing loss of confidence by major investors. Stock markets will therefore crash, further driving up the price of a barrel of crude. Panic will set in with alarming rapidity in both the US and Western European economies as the supply of affordable oil will soon start to seriously diminish by well over five percent in the space of perhaps two to three years. Of course there will be the many arguments from various pundits presented in the mass media with regard to reserves in the Jack field in the Gulf of Mexico, as well as fields in Venezuela, western Africa, and 'vast' reserves of Canadian shale, but in reality all these sources combined will keep the US economy solvent for perhaps a further year or two only, even at current rates of US consumption of around twenty two million barrels per day, of which about sixteen million barrels are imported. Following that, it will quickly prove impossible to maintain supplies at anything like current prices. So the inevitable reduction in crude oil imports will result in a severe economic recession, or more likely a series of recessions, which will eventually develop into a depression, as Western currencies are progressively devalued to the level of say, the Indian rupee, worth around two cents, or even the Indonesian rupiah, worth around one-hundredth of a cent, at current exchange rates. Business after business in Europe and North America will permanently close their doors, yielding unprecedented rates of mass unemployment. Power stations will fail, leading to increased frequency and severity of blackouts, especially in urban areas. Shelves in the stores will become empty as deliveries of all kinds of goods and commodities will start to dry up as trucking companies are put out of business by gasoline prices exceeding twenty dollars a gallon. Without continued deliveries or shipping of products the pharmaceutical industry will collapse, and in turn hospitals will run short of essential medicines, medical devices, and other supplies. One by one the airlines, which collectively have lost more money since 2000 than they have earned since 1950, will go out of business until there are none left flying. The United States Air Force and one or two other Western air forces, however, will continue to fly their planes on synthetic kerosene, manufactured via the environmentally dirty, costly, and slow Fischer-Tropsch process, using coal or natural gas as a starting point. In the US and Europe, mass migration from the suburbs to the cities will take place, in order to avoid the by-now very expensive and scarce transportation, by people still hoping to find work. But rioting and mob rule will break out in inner cities as law and order progressively collapses. Those left in the by-now deserted and decaying suburbs, which will become the new ghettos, will form armies of beggars. People will be attempting to eke out a living twenty or thirty or even more to a house, using what was the front lawn for growing simple crops. And of course, they will be attempting this without power, running water, proper sewage facilities, lighting, heating, or cooling. Western governments will by this point have begun to instigate serious inroads into alternative energy programs, including those based in space. But it will prove too late to save millions from terminal unemployment, homelessness, and starvation. In the final analysis, major governments across the globe will be forced to consider previously unthinkable strategies to drastically reduce their respective populations that can no longer be supported, by utilizing such things as military death squads, or release of deadly pathogens into the environment. In the meantime, the Middle

East with its still relatively massive oil reserves, and Russia with its natural gas, and even some countries in western Africa will be able to enjoy the proceeds obtained from the sale of oil to the by-now desperate West, at huge profit margins. And as India, Pakistan, and particularly Israel continue in their policies of proliferation of nuclear weapons, others will increasingly follow suit, notably China, Iran, and North Korea. At this point militant Islamists in the Middle East and Western Europe will perceive an opportunity to bring about an end to the Western economy once and for all by obtaining some of these nuclear weapons for themselves, which by this stage will be relatively easy, and setting them against key targets in North America and Western Europe. Once detonated, the severely weakened economies of those countries will face final ruin. There will of course be a response in kind from the West, which will in turn devastate the economies of the Middle East and Asia. And thus with the advanced economies gone, man's mastery over the Earth will be broken."

Hunt stopped, and spread out his arms in an imploring gesture.

"So you see, Mr. President. Mr. Prime Minister. My ability to bring about a third world war in reality represents only catalysis of the inevitable. It will happen, with or without my intervention. I should take this opportunity to point out that I have the launch codes of a number of American and British nuclear missiles currently stationed in silos around North America and Scotland. And I have modified and enhanced the ship-board computer systems aboard *Diamond* to such an extent that I can hack into any of your systems I choose, including, but not limited to, your military command systems. At this point I could quite literally cause you to destroy yourselves."

Hunt stopped, leaned back, and inhaled slowly and deliberately, as if deep in thought.

"There is however, an alternative scenario. It would involve indulging a certain proposal that I have been entertaining in my mind for some days now. I would urge you to devote some serious consideration to the ideas I am now about to espouse. For this may well represent the salvation of all of humanity."

CHAPTER 19

Hunt's declaration that he held the immediate fate of the world in his hands, that he could start a third world war in earnest, met with a surprisingly muted response in Washington. Consensus opinion at that point tended to advise that the President and his staff should continue listening to Hunt's presentation, in particular to discover what his alternative proposal to all-out war might entail. The response in London however had been less passive. The Prime Minister had put into words first what everyone present was thinking and feeling.

"Who the hell does this arrogant bastard think he is? Chief of Naval Operations! Please explain to me again why we can't simply send some ships out to his position and blow him out of the water!"

Slowly and carefully Admiral of the Fleet Sir Anson Howe explained once again why such a course of action was not going to prove practicable, since Hunt had jury rigged his command as a stealth vessel, replete with full radar jamming capability as well as effective invisibility. Not to mention that he apparently had access to the mainframe computers that controlled nuclear missile launch capability all across the United Kingdom and the United States. Access that could not be blocked or locked out. There was nothing to do but to continue to hear out Hunt.

And as if to prove the point, upon resumption of the presentation, Hunt first of all announced that on July 20 at 10.00am, GMT, he would arrange for a little demonstration of his capabilities. He would send up an intercontinental ballistic nuclear missile, or ICBM, from a silo in the US or the UK which would then target Alert Base on Ellesmere Island in Northern Canada. Since there was nothing there but an airstrip and no settlements of any description for hundreds of miles around, the detonation of the warhead would serve only to eliminate the capacity for fixed-wing aircraft to land in the middle of a frozen wasteland. After this prelude Hunt once more launched into the main thrust of his proposal.

"In order to dissuade me from instigating all-out war, you must achieve the following two objectives, and in fairly short order. Firstly, I want a Doppler radar survey conducted on the entire Antarctic continent from an appropriately equipped orbiter, in a manner similar to the Doppler radar surveys that have been conducted on Mars and Venus in recent years. I am fully aware that NASA is in possession of the necessary technology to achieve this first objective within a matter of a few weeks. The results to the survey will be transmitted to me so that I may study in detail the layout of the land masses underlying the Antarctic ice. Secondly, you must construct an orbiting graviton field generator similar to the type utilized in the classified experiment that was carried out two years ago by the United States Navy, and which involved the British destroyer HMS *Wildcat,* under the command of the then Commander Dawn DeFaller. Now I expect you are wondering how it is that I have come into possession of knowledge of this highly classified experiment, but that matters not for now. Simply believe me when I say that I am fully aware of what transpired during that unfortunate and misguided foray into warp field technology, and indeed the unexpected and unintended outcome. That *Wildcat* and her crew were inadvertently projected into the past, rather than trans-located across the globe as had been the intention. Be advised also that I understand the theoretical issues that led to this problem and can instruct your scientists and engineers on how to avoid a recurrence of the same problem again. I can also provide full details on the subjects of the construction and operation of the graviton generating orbiter. I am fully aware that senior officers of the militaries of both the United States and the United Kingdom will state categorically that all records and blueprints regarding the construction of a warp field generator have been destroyed. But this is in fact not the case, as I am certain that both the President and the Prime Minister can verify. I want an orbiter constructed and launched by NASA that can direct a beam of graviton energy at a specific series of co-ordinates in Antarctica, probably in an area of Queen Maud Land, pending the results to the Doppler radar survey. The intention will be to rapidly vaporize the ice covering that area, an area approximately one mile in diameter, so as to reveal the structures that I have deduced almost certainly exist underneath."

Hunt spread his arms apart, somewhat theatrically.

"I promise you this. If you acquiesce to my plans, you will see an era of global peace, health, prosperity, and almost limitless energy. However if you do not, the extinction of humankind from the face of the Earth will be considerably accelerated. Please indicate your acceptance of my terms by arranging for a generalized blackout in the city of London, England, for a period of one hour between 10.00pm and 11.00pm GMT, on July 21. Which as I may remind you, will be thirty-six hours following the destruction of Alert Base in Northern Canada, as I promised earlier by way of a demonstration of my abilities. Thank you, gentlemen, for your attention."

With that, Hunt's message came to a conclusion.

CHAPTER 20

A hastily formed Summit Committee of senior naval and air force officers, as well as the President of the United States and the Prime Minister of the United Kingdom accompanied by several other representatives from the two respective governments was convened in the decidedly neutral territory of Reykjavik, Iceland. Dawn had been ordered to attend also, although she found herself the most junior officer present and as such had felt that her influence over the outcome of events had been precisely zero. What she perhaps had not realized was that everyone else, including respective heads of state, had felt exactly the same way. Following much discussion and speculation regarding the possibility of locating and destroying Hunt's ship, it was reluctantly concluded by all except USAF General Robert Webster that this was not going to be realistically possible. Webster, spouting off in his purposely exaggerated drawl, had clung to the notion that 'no imperialist limey upstart in one pissant little British destroyer was going to hold the world to ransom, and especially not the armed forces of the United States of America'. But when pressed for details as to how exactly he proposed to deal with the problem, Webster was unable to come up with anything resembling a workable strategy. It seemed as if Commander Hunt of the Royal Navy was in a position to call the shots, at least for the present. The Prime Minister had finally decided, after close consultation with the President, to arrange for a blackout to strike London at the time specified by Hunt in his presentation. The President also informed the Canadian Prime Minister that all personnel and equipment should be evacuated from Alert Base. The President felt he had no choice but to inform him of the reason; that an ICBM from a US or UK land-based nuclear arsenal may be launched by terrorist action and be directed there for detonation. He had apologized for the situation having been allowed to develop, and had pleaded with him not to allow this information to leak to the press, but privately, did not feel entirely confident that this could be avoided. The Canadian Prime Minister for his part had reacted, predictably, with an outburst of righteous anger. How could his country, which had harmed no-one, be left open to such a strike? Why didn't the Americans have a proper plan in place to prevent this sort of thing from occurring? Where was the USAF? Why was there not an effective American anti-missile defense battery that could be utilized to stop this incoming ICBM? And what the hell were the respective governments of the United States and the United Kingdom thinking anyway? Were they really going to be so weak as to simply give in to terrorism in this way? He was going to call the British Prime Minister and give him a piece of his mind, too. The American President had done his best to be patient, but finally was moved to suggest that had the Canadians actually bothered to put some serious resources into building up their armed services beyond the frankly token force that it was at present, then they wouldn't need to keep on asking the United States for protection but could instead presumably take care of the threat themselves. And in any event, what were they talking about here but a practically disused airfield from the Cold War era that was home these days to nothing but a few polar bears? A base, the President reminded the Canadian Prime Minister that was funded and for the most part administered by the US government during the time it had been operational. With that, the Canadian Premier, exasperated, had simply hung up the phone.

Inevitably during the Summit the issues of how the US government was to liaise with NASA also came up, along with a reluctant admission by the President that at least one copy of the secret van der Meer dossier which was supposed to have been destroyed, was still in existence, much to Dawn's chagrin. He followed up with an immediate warning that this information was strictly classified and not a word was to be repeated to anyone outside of the room, regardless of military rank or position within government.

CHAPTER 21

Nuclear Missile Silo Tartan Three Alpha, Beauly Firth, Scotland, July 20, 2008, 0955Hrs GMT

Nuclear weapons specialist Lieutenant Bob McConnal was on the verge of panic as he practically screamed into his telephone. His computer console was indicating that one of the Trident 3 ICBM's stationed within the silo was counting down to launch and, if nothing was done to prevent it, within minutes its engines would fire and it would leave the base.

"What? Yes sir! I don't know what the hell's going on! It's counting down for launch! No, this was not authorized! The system is ignoring all of our inputs! Sir! There is nothing we can do! Can you over-ride? Oh God! Oh my God, no! It's locking on to a target in . . . northern Canada! Northern Canada, for Christ's sake! We have to stop it!"

But try as he might, there was nothing he could do. At precisely 10.00am GMT the Trident 3 fired up, its rockets roaring as its massive gray bulk lifted off from the silo. Moving slowly at first, seeming almost to hang in the air, it rapidly gained velocity and within seconds was coming close to breaking the sound barrier as it climbed almost vertically upwards on its way to the ionosphere. A small number of civilian observers happening by on their way to work that morning observed its sleek shape, spewing fire as it reached for the sky. As it cleared the cloud cover the missile entered a climbing turn to the north north-west, all the while continuing to accelerate. Within approximately three minutes from launch it had achieved an altitude of one hundred five thousand feet and was hurtling towards its target at around 5,000mph, or more than six times the speed of sound. It covered the 1,800 miles to northern Ellesmere Island in approximately twenty minutes, after which time its main engine cut and the missile nosed vertically downwards, commencing its final death plunge. A minute later it was positioned about one half mile above the deserted form of Alert Base, although because of prevailing meteorological conditions would not have been visible to anyone on the ground. Still moving at Mach 6.3, its 3 megaton warhead detonated. In a blinding white flash, followed by a tremendous roar and a rapidly growing mushroom cloud, the whole of the northern end of Ellesmere Island was wiped from the map. Considerable blast damage to the uninhabited frozen wastes of northern Greenland also occurred within seconds of detonation. After all was said and done, Alert Base, that component of the Cold War early-warning system so vital for the defense of North America during the Soviet era, was gone forever. The subsequent report to the British Government confirmed that a very sophisticated but unknown hacker had managed to break into the UK Ministry of Defence Nuclear Missile Master Control System and orchestrate the launch, confirming the claims made earlier by Commander Hunt that he had the power to launch any ICBM at will from any site he chose.

The city of London, England the following night experienced a severe blackout between 10.00pm and 11.00pm. Official news reports transmitted by the BBC cited a 'sudden, unexpected, and power overload' as having been responsible.

CHAPTER 22

Cape Canaveral, Florida, 0600Hrs, EST August 7, 2008

The space shuttle *Atlantis* stood ready on the launch pad, coupled to her booster rockets and giant external fuel tank. Her crew of five astronauts were already aboard in readiness for launch which was to proceed on schedule that morning forty-five minutes later. The *Atlantis* was also carrying a very special top-secret satellite, the like of which NASA had never before constructed. Following release into parking orbit, which was to be around seven hundred miles above the continent of Antarctica, the satellite itself was to join with an earlier satellite that had already been positioned in that area, one which carried on-board a Doppler radar topographical scanning system with which NASA had been intensively building up a detailed picture of the land masses underlying the ice sheets covering the continent. Everyone at the agency had been aware of the nature of this previous endeavor, which had been undertaken in an open manner using standard equipment, but this new satellite had been constructed and handled in an atmosphere of abject secrecy. Only a very few select individuals were aware of the details of the workings of its on-board apparatus. Indeed, most engineers at NASA understood only that it was some kind of field generator. A considerable proportion of the generator apparatus itself had been manufactured by a highly secret branch of the United States Navy, and only a very select few senior NASA officials were allowed to be present when naval officers appeared at the Cape to discuss specifics of how to modulate construction of the device so that it would function optimally in space. Two of the five crew aboard the shuttle would be responsible for the correct positioning of the satellite in orbit, and assisting in conducting initial tests to insure that it was operational before *Atlantis* returned to Earth. But from that point on it was to be operated from a control room at the Houston Space Center under the direction of the same small cadre of senior NASA officials and naval officers. No-one else was to be allowed to be privy to its operational details. Or its mission.

CHAPTER 23

An encoded communiqué from Hunt to the President of the United States received in the White House on the morning of August 27 had urged him to compare the results of the Doppler radar survey of Antarctica with the map drawn by Admiral Piri Reis back in 1513. All of the cartographers who examined and compared the two were forced to conclude that Admiral Reis apparently had been in possession of detailed knowledge of the underlying geographical features of the continent, as the areas indicated on his map corresponded perfectly with those same areas rediscovered during the recent survey of the continent from space. The air forces and navies of both the United States and Britain had of course continued in their attempts to track HMS *Diamond,* but all efforts continued to meet with absolute and complete failure. For all anyone could say he may have long-since departed the Indian Ocean and may presently be on any ocean or sea in the world. The plain fact was that Hunt continued to possess the upper hand and his determination that the government of the United States should see this project through to the end had shown no signs of ebbing or waning.

The communiqué had gone on to outline details of an area of Queen Maud land, inland about 60 miles from the edge of the ice shelf, lying along the Greenwich meridian, that was to be exposed to a full burst of energy from the orbiting graviton generator. The intention was to vaporize a circular area of ice, one mile in diameter, all the way down to the underlying land mass. The mechanism that Hunt had explained to the scientists and engineers who had constructed the generator was that the matter/anti-matter reactor aboard the device would yield sufficient energy such that the coupled graviton generator would then be able to produce a gravity beam, which could be focused, and would be so powerful but precisely modulated such that the water molecules making up the ice crystals in the target area would simply be vaporized while simultaneously trans-located through a wormhole to another point on the planet. A point in fact within the deep ocean of the middle of the South Atlantic. Hunt had finally explained that the principle was precisely as that which was supposed to have trans-located HMS *Wildcat* from the North Atlantic Ocean to the Indian Ocean during that ill-fated experiment two years before, but which had failed to work properly because of incorrect frequency modulation. The frequency modulation of the energy beam would be such that nothing else besides ice would be forced down the wormhole. Nothing else would be damaged or even disturbed in the slightest way.

Hunt had ended his communiqué with the instruction that bombardment of the target area begin at 0700Hrs GMT the following morning.

CHAPTER 24

The President of the United States himself had insisted on giving the final order to commence bombardment of the Antarctic ice. At precisely 0700Hrs GMT the orbiting device was energized. As instructed all spotter aircraft had been pulled clear of the area, as well as all Antarctic Station Personnel so that the target would be clear. Hunt's instruction had been that the graviton beam would need to be operational for a period of only twenty seconds, after which time it should be deactivated. Aircraft suitably equipped with cameras would then be sent in to fly over the area so as to confirm the successful trans-location of the ice sheet.

The instructions were followed to the letter. All US government cabinet members were present in the Oval Office, glued to the TV monitors that had been set up so they would be able to obtain a first-hand glimpse of the results of their handiwork. At the appointed time the orbiting device had been duly activated. At 0726Hrs GMT, when the vapor and dust had settled sufficiently to enable the spotter aircraft to enter the area and return pictures, those gathered around the monitors gasped in what could only be described as muted awe. Clearly visible was a neat and perfectly circular hole in the ice, precisely one mile in diameter that penetrated down to a depth of approximately three thousand feet. And at the bottom, which became clearer as the cameras' zoom lenses started to operate, was what appeared to be the center of a giant city. On first inspection it appeared to resemble a large collection of ancient Egyptian edifices, replete with large pyramids, several hundred feet tall, as well as columns, temples, and statues. And yet everything appeared in good order, as if it were all contemporary and new. There was no evidence of decomposition or ruination to be seen anywhere.

The President himself seemed overtaken with shock.

"Oh my God. Oh my God. He was right. Hunt was right."

CHAPTER 25

Over the course of the following weeks investigative teams of scientists from the US and Britain, and a number of other countries, traveled to Queen Maud Land to witness first-hand the city that had been revealed there after enduring millennia buried beneath thousands of feet of ice. Or at least the four-fifths of a square mile of what appeared to be the center of what had once been a bustling metropolis, for it seemed that the city extended in all directions into the ice that had not been cleared. Within the revealed section there were roads and what appeared to be some kind of tracks that may have been intended for cars or vehicles of some sort. And the buildings, of which there were many, were all packed in closely but apparently designed in such an intricate manner that the largest possible number of them could be comfortably situated in the available space. The design of the buildings themselves seemed to owe a lot to the designs of the Mayans of Mexico and the Incas of Peru, as well as the ancient Egyptians. The central pyramid stood at least three hundred feet high and about the same along each edge of its base. Another strange thing was that all portals which acted as entry ways into the interiors of the structures were around twelve feet tall and three feet wide, as if they had been purposely created for beings considerably taller than ordinary humans. And as it turned out the internal ceilings were all between fourteen and seventeen feet from the floor level, on each and every story of every construction. And within the pyramid, itself a beautiful, gilded structure, made up of thousands of perfectly fitted marble-smooth blocks of stone that must have weighed many tons apiece, was an immense central chamber that could be easily accessed from a portal on one side of the base. And in the precise center of the chamber stood a series of what appeared to be marble cuboid-shaped objects, each of which stood around twenty feet in height. There were thirty six of them in total. Their purpose, if indeed they had a purpose, was not clear. Further investigations had simply shown that all attempts to scan them with X-ray or ultrasound equipment revealed precisely nothing of their internal structure. And no tools of any kind, not even an industrial-strength drill, laser, or blow torch could make so much as the slightest scratch or scorch mark on any one of their surfaces. It was concluded therefore that, despite their appearance, they were obviously not made of marble, but in fact of an unknown substance seemingly impervious to all forms of human investigation.

The strange large blocks remained a mystery.

CHAPTER 26

Dawn was home on leave in Boston after having been placed on standby to return to duty at short notice in the event that renewed attempts were to be made to locate Commander Hunt and his ship. But for the moment the discovery of the ancient city beneath the Antarctic ice, as well as Hunt's communication with both the President of the United States and the Prime Minister of the United Kingdom, had temporarily quelled the sense of immediate need to locate him. That coupled with the fact that he was still proving to be completely elusive. The truth was that there seemed to be absolutely no way to locate him or his vessel.

Since returning home Dawn had had time to fully study and absorb the news reports of the attacks on London and Riyadh. The sinking of the *Rohollah Samimi* had been chilling in of itself, but these murderous attacks on civilian populations had struck her as simply evil. In particular the destruction of the city blocks in the British capital around the American Embassy with a thermonuclear device had left a sense of shock within her that ran deep. It was not that she especially loved London. As a native of Plymouth she was West Country through and through. But this attack had cut to her very soul. She reflected too on the fact that this was the first time that nuclear weapons had been used to kill since the end of the Second World War. It was as if the world had entered a new phase of destructive madness. News reports also made periodic mention of the destruction of Alert Base in northern Canada, but since prior to the detonation there had been nothing remaining in that area except a runway, Dawn, as most others, saw this incident mostly within the context of a cold-war style nuclear test, rather than an outright attack. The only exception seemed to be the Canadian Prime Minister who still had not tired of making public appearances around his nation, the main purpose of which seemed to be to continue to direct complaints against the President of the United States for his 'failure to prevent this outrageous attack on Canadian territory'. But by this point he was finding himself, unsurprisingly, largely ignored, even by his fellow countrymen.

Dawn looked around the den, contemplating the ornate interior plasterwork, and the fact that she had first set foot inside this house in 1776, well over two hundred years ago. She was so absorbed in her thoughts that she didn't notice the taxi cab pulling up outside on the street. A few moments later her husband, whose house this had been when they had first met, was approaching the front door. When she heard him coming in she rushed to meet him. She smiled warmly when she saw him turned out in his dress uniform, as he always was when returning from a trip at sea.

"Matthew! It's good to see you."

She rushed up to him and embraced him before stepping back and continuing.

"You heard the news, about what happened in London?"

"Yes, I did indeed. A horrific business. Quite terrible and appalling. Why should anyone want to do such a thing? Commit such a random act of mass killing? Of civilians? Of women and children?"

Dawn simply shrugged.

"Welcome to the 21st century, Matthew. We are technologically more advanced at this time than at any point in our history. But, I am sorry to say, no wiser."

"From what I can gather relations between the Eastern and Western worlds seem rather strained. The attack on London was seemingly a retaliatory strike for the sinking of the Iranian cruise

ship, the *Rohollah Samimi*. I sincerely hope that this does not lead
to more conflict."

"I sincerely hope not either, Matthew. Although there was also
the attack on the Kingdom Centre in Riyadh, Saudi Arabia."

"Ah, yes. That too." He shook his head in disbelief. "Dreadful.
I still cannot conceive of an aircraft pilot intentionally crashing his
machine into a building. It surely must have been an accident."

"That is not what they are saying on Al-Jazeera, Matthew.
And a pistol was discovered in the wreckage which had been
recently fired. A matching bullet was found embedded in the
head of the co-pilot." Dawn hung her head. "Remember too what
happened seven years ago on September 11, in New York City
and Washington DC."

Matthew seemed momentarily troubled.

Dawn made as if to say something more, but then instead,
sensing his need for reassurance, decided to kiss him and guide him
towards the den. Once there they made themselves comfortable
in the large soft leather couch. Dawn sighed.

"So, have you heard about the discovery of the ancient city in
Antarctica? It was found underneath the ice."

"Underneath Queen Maud Land, if I am not mistaken."

"Correct. What are they saying about it on the news?"

Revere cocked his eyes sideways and upwards for a moment,
as if he were straining to remember what he might have heard.

"They say it is the greatest archeological discovery of the age.
That certain professors at Yale University were able to calculate the
probability of the existence of significant archeological remains in
that location, and working in co-operation with NASA . . ."

But Dawn was shaking her head, and smiling.

"No, Matthew. The discovery had nothing to do with any
professors from Yale. I'm not supposed to tell you this."

She hesitated. She considered her privileged position regarding
the specialist knowledge to which she and only a small number
of others, including the President of the United States and the
British Prime Minister were privy. She decided to share some of
the information.

"The existence of the ruins was postulated by an officer of the Royal Navy who had been involved in an experiment, whereby he took an intelligence enhancing drug."

Under no other circumstances would Dawn reveal details of secret military operations to unauthorized personnel, but she had come to know that Matthew was possessed of an exceptional discretionary capacity, such that he could be trusted absolutely to repeat what he had heard to no-one. In this case she felt safe breaking this rule. And in any event she could not bear to keep the information from him entirely.

"But there's a problem. He has since disappeared and, until recently at least was threatening to start what could amount to a third world war, unless the United States built an orbiting satellite system that was capable of trans-locating away great swaths of Antarctic ice in an instant. In much the same manner as *Wildcat* was transported through time back when we were engaged in our little experiment in the North Atlantic. The satellite was built and the ancient city was revealed. It seems he was right, but what it all means I am not at all certain. Senior American and British naval officers are still debating about whether or not further attempts should be made to track his ship using sophisticated infra-red spy satellites. But it would be enormously expensive to mount such an operation, and no-one really knows if it would work anyway. Given his current level of intelligence he may well have the capacity to frustrate any such attempt. Also, finding him may not be so important, now that he has been able to demonstrate the presence of the Antarctic city, as he went to considerable pains to prove. Perhaps for the time-being he is satisfied with things the way they are."

Revere furrowed his brow in thought.

"An intelligence enhancing drug?"

"Yes. Although it is highly experimental and the long term effects have yet to be worked out. But it seemed to work very well indeed. He became impossible to beat in ship-to-ship combat during an exercise in convoy protection, and later, when he disappeared, he was able to jury rig a whole series of additional devices, apparently using only his own shipboard stores, that enabled him to slip away unseen. All the way into the Arabian Sea, in fact. And despite the best efforts of both the United States and the British navies we have not been able to locate him."

Revere looked at her blankly.

"I am beginning to see what you mean about being no wiser."

She smiled wanly at him, barely concealing her sarcasm.

"Thank you for that, Matthew. Thank you very much."

CHAPTER 27

A week following its discovery, a group of Swedish scientists who
had made the journey south to witness the great city lying
beneath the Antarctic ice had been the first to witness the strange
phenomenon that had commenced suddenly, and without warning.
Five men and two women, all archeologists from the University
of Uppsala, had been making measurements on the marble-like
blocks when, without warning, and in absolute unison, a soft even
yellow glow had commenced emanating from their very interior, as
if they were lit from within by some unknown light source. A quiet
deep humming sound also commenced a few seconds later as the
Swedes had looked on in astonishment, without understanding
the event they were witnessing. Over the course of the ensuing
two weeks these glowing humming blocks had a profound effect
upon their surroundings, and, as soon became apparent, upon the
planet entire. For incredibly, global power grids were no longer
deriving their electrical energy from the power stations that fed
them, but instead were receiving power from these blocks, or
'Star Machines' as they were soon being dubbed by the world's
news media. The machines themselves seemed to be channeling
energy from some extra-terrestrial source, although how they were
doing so nobody could explain. Perhaps this energy was coming
from the sun, perhaps outer space, and was being converted to
electrical energy and then somehow dumped wirelessly into the

grids, despite the fact that the involved power was rated at many terawatts. Further study did suggest that the strange blocks were channeling energy from space in the form of radiation, converting it to microwaves, and then beaming those microwaves directly to the global electrical grids. The grids however were receiving them, in an entirely unknown manner, as alternating current electrical energy, of an appropriate frequency and voltage. Because of the activity of these 'Star Machines', the world's power stations found themselves with no demand. And yet there was at all times an abundant source of gratuitous power available. With all of the free electricity apparently now available there was no longer any need to burn oil or other fossil fuels in power stations. In consequence much of the world's oil was directed towards the world's ailing airlines, causing them to quickly become profitable once more. Saab, the Swedish car manufacturer, came out with a production model of a steam and electric powered hybrid car which could run on a battery, and water. The car looked just like an ordinary saloon car, but instead of an internal combustion engine was equipped with an electric motor, and a boiler the size of a regular car battery. The latter could produce, from electrical current passed through its heating elements, from a now gratuitously rechargeable battery, enough superheated steam to run the car at up to 135mph within thirty seconds. Cheap transport that did not damage the environment had finally arrived, and the idea had caught on, for Saab and soon the other major car manufacturers including Ford, Chevrolet, Vauxhall, Mercedes, General Motors, BMW, Rolls-Royce, Volvo, and Toyota were selling the new steam/electric hybrids like hotcakes across North America and Western Europe. There was increased interest too in construction of high speed electric rail links, operated from the global grids, to connect major cities in the United States and Canada, for the movement of both passengers and freight. And marine engineers had started discussing in earnest the possibility of replacing ships' engines with giant electric motors that could derive their power directly and wirelessly from the Antarctic machines.

CHAPTER 28

O ver the course of the ensuing months Hunt, who by now
had revealed himself to the world, had quit HMS *Diamond*
and installed himself in his new home, the great city under the
Antarctic ice which he had quickly dubbed Atlantis, after the
mythical lost city, and also the space shuttle which had assisted in
its rediscovery. He had brought *Diamond* in close to the Antarctic
coast, still under the cloak of both visual and radar invisibility and
arranged for one of his helicopter pilots to fly him over to Queen
Maud Land. On his arrival he had quickly disembarked, releasing
the pilot to return, and then the ship was to make for her home
port in Greenock, Scotland, under the command of her Executive
Officer, to be handed over once again to the authorities for return
to regular service with the Royal Navy. Even as *Diamond* was
making her way home Hunt had contacted the President of the
United States and the Prime Minister of the United Kingdom
to inform them of developments and to extract assurances from
them both that *Diamond* would be allowed free passage home
and her complement of officers and crew would not be held
accountable in any way whatsoever for what had transpired over
these last few months.

Taking up residence in his new surroundings, Hunt had
also arranged for the orbiting satellite carrying the warp field
generator to trans-locate progressively more and more of the ice

covering the city, until it was completely ice free and revealed to the world in all of its glory once again. All of this had taken but a matter of hours under the control of the machines that Hunt was able to somehow influence, from the central chamber where he spent most of his time. Indeed it seemed that once ensconced in Atlantis, the city now fully alive with heat and light, Hunt was effectively surrounded by an impregnable fortress. He was at once able to communicate with any agency on Earth, and at any time influence any machinery he chose, having it do whatever he wished. Within a matter of hours it also became apparent that, in conjunction with his machines, he was in absolute control of all of the planet's weapons systems. So even although his location was now no longer a secret, he was for all practical purposes, untouchable.

And yet it was becoming clear that, despite the earlier atrocities committed against the Kingdom Centre in Riyadh, the United States Embassy in London, and the liner *Rohollah Samimi,* he intended, somewhat paradoxically perhaps to use his enormous power for the greater good of humanity. He saw to it that the machines continued in their task of energizing the global electrical grids, providing an almost limitless source of energy for the entire planetary population. This in turn created a tremendous reduction in demand for over-strained petroleum reserves. This of course effectively impoverished overnight the formerly mighty petroleum economies of the Middle Eastern States, principally those of Saudi Arabia, The United Arab Emirates, Yemen, as well as Qatar and Bahrain, and even Iran and Iraq. Global demand for oil had slumped and the crude that was being sold now could command a price of perhaps seven dollars per barrel on the international markets as opposed to the recent level of one hundred and forty-two. The Iranian President had spoken in blusterous terms of yet another example of Western imperialism, but was rapidly subdued when he and his people came to the realization that, despite the oil from the region having been economically devalued, the Middle Eastern countries for the first time in history were able to meet all of their energy needs through the global energized grids.

As Hunt's power to heal the broken planet apparently grew, he became progressively less shy about announcing his presence to the world on television by way of special transmissions, as well as numerous websites. As time went on he started to become revered as an object worthy of special attention, even to the point of worship, by progressively growing numbers of Christian churches in the United States and elsewhere, a reverence that Hunt himself did everything within his power to encourage. Typical Sunday services in some of the more charismatic Baptist churches across America would commence with the congregation intoning, *All praise be to Him that brought us out of the darkness, All praise be to Him that brought us peace, All praise be to the Messiah, come back to His people at the appointed hour!* The Messiah. For his services to humanity, and perhaps also his charisma, Hunt had finally been recognized as a deity by many of the more Christian faithful of the Earth. Hunt turned his attentions to the performance of miracles, which he could achieve in person or from distances of thousands of miles. He was of course manipulating the energy fields being produced by the machines and directing them to a highly specific focus at particular points in space and time, with the effect of rendering instant and precise repairs to the damaged or diseased bodies or minds of those afflicted. But despite some speculation to this effect from various academic quarters, the Catholic Church too had been convinced of his Messianic status. For the Pope had decided that he must seek an audience with this man as a matter of supreme spiritual importance. The Holy Father had decreed that this was the man who had united in brotherhood the Judeo-Christian world with the Islamic world, as well as Hindu, Sikh, Jain, Buddhist, and the other myriad of the Earth's religious and spiritual denominations. Indeed because Hunt had publically confessed, within a few days the Holy Father had issued an official Papal pardon for his earlier atrocities, which were anyway rapidly receding in importance in the minds of the majority of the world's population.

When the Pope and his entourage had arrived in Atlantis, they had first of all marveled at the sheer size and wondrous beauty of the city, which stretched for four miles in every direction from its center, in a circular pattern occupying a total area of fifty square miles. They marveled too at its light, warmth and agreeable climate, despite the harsh Antarctic conditions outside. And the city itself was truly beautiful. Long and wide palm tree-lined boulevards connected every part of the city with every other. There were temples, meeting rooms, pyramids, obelisks, statues of mythical beasts, and what could have been dwelling places everywhere, laid out in a mathematically efficient yet elegant manner, that could only be described as an architectural masterpiece. A wonder to behold, made of gold and silver and shimmering giant carved granite blocks that all fit together perfectly, as a colossal jigsaw puzzle. And there were energy conduits running every which way, but of a technology that was not understandable to the visitors, which conveyed heat, light, and electricity wherever it was needed and at whatever level of power required.

After witnessing all of this, and considering what a transformation the world had enjoyed, the Pope had decreed that God had answered the prayers of the world's faithful.

At long last all of humanity was truly saved.

CHAPTER 29

The letter that came through the door seemed like a regular naval postal communication that would ordinarily be classified as suitable for carriage by civilian postal services. Or so Dawn thought when Matthew handed it to her at the breakfast table. It was sealed in a large manila envelope, printed with the usual British Ministry of Defence Royal Naval markings and was addressed to Dawn in her official capacity as Capt. D. DeFaller, RN, DSO. But when she opened it all semblance of normality evaporated as she cast her eye over the missive within. For the message was from Commander Hunt. There were also three other smaller envelopes contained inside, all held together with a rubber band.

August 27, 2008

Dear Captain DeFaller.

I hope that this communication finds you well. I have no doubt that you cannot have failed to take notice of recent developments regarding the new source of global energy provision and the obvious benefits derived therefrom (all of which has been made possible as a consequence of my cognition enhancement). I nevertheless would like to express my sincere condolences in regards to the loss of human life and the destruction of property that was unfortunately necessary in order to bring this to fruition. I especially regret the necessity for the nuclear attack on the British capital, which although limited in its scope, did result in the irreplaceable loss of fine examples of classical Georgian architecture. However I would hazard to guess that as a Devonshire girl, in your heart of hearts the welfare of the great city of London is perhaps not of paramount concern. But please trust me when I tell you that this was the only practicable methodology for forcing the governments of the United Kingdom and the United States of America to work with me, rather than against me, as in my judgment they most certainly would otherwise have done.

I also write to you now with a special request that you make the journey to Queen Maud Land and join me in my new home in the city known to contemporary popular culture as Atlantis. I have already made arrangements with your superior, Vice-Admiral Sir Phillip Bailey, that you make the trip to Antarctica. In addition, the Prime Minister of the United Kingdom and the President of the United States are both fully aware and supportive of my desire that you join me here.

Your old command, HMS *Wildcat*, will be docking in the port of Boston within a few more hours from your receipt of this notification. You will please make ready to join her on the morning of August 29th at 0800hrs, for sailing at 0845hrs. You will make for the Southern Ocean as a passenger; Commander Malcolm Callaghan will be in command. On reaching a point one hundred miles off the coast of Queen Maud Land (the precise co-ordinates of which are known only to Commander Callaghan at this time) you will be flown alone, by helicopter, to Atlantis where I will be awaiting your arrival. Please allow me to reiterate that my invitation is open to you only. In aside to its crew, the helicopter shall be carrying only you as a passenger, and will depart immediately following your safe delivery with me. The purpose of your visit shall become clear upon your arrival.

I remain ma'am, your obedient servant,

Garry Hunt

Garry Hunt, Commander, RN
City of Atlantis
Queen Maud Land
Antarctica

Also included in the smaller envelopes were standard orders issued by Vice-Admiral Bailey that she was to present herself at 0800hrs on the morning of August 29th at Pier Number 4 at Boston Harbor for embarkation on *Wildcat,* for a voyage to the Southern Ocean, just as Hunt had said. Bailey had also, somewhat unusually, added the request that she call him at his desk when she received this latest order. The remaining two envelopes, which both looked very official, bore letters, one from the White House in Pennsylvania Avenue, Washington DC, and the other from No. 10 Downing Street, London, England. The content of each was much the same; they took the form of appeals from the President of the United States and the British Prime Minister that she give of herself wholly and completely to this mission that represented without a shadow of a doubt the most important of her entire career. Both ended with sincere expressions of gratitude for her devotion to her country and her duty. On finishing Dawn felt not so much privileged to have received personal letters from the British and American premiers, but rather a sense of indignant outrage at Hunt. For despite his new-found fame as the harbinger of global peace, harmony, and limitless gratuitous energy, he was, as far as she was aware, still a serving officer in the Royal Navy, and technically her junior. How dare he issue orders to her, his senior officer, no matter how politely expressed? And the way he had gone directly over her head to Vice-Admiral Bailey and the President and Prime Minister, without her knowledge. This only served to leave her with a sense of annoyance. Nor did she particularly appreciate his reference to her as a girl, Devonshire or not. By the time she spoke to Matthew about it she was visibly fuming.

"I fully appreciate that Commander Hunt has exhibited a modicum of impertinence," he had said, "but as I see it there is nothing to do but execute the order."

Matthew was anticipating being off-duty for the next fifteen days and so had asked if he might accompany his wife on the voyage south aboard *Wildcat*, and then return to Boston thereafter. Dawn was honestly not certain if his presence would be welcomed but she was sufficiently angered at this point that she could not care less.

"Yes Matthew," she responded. "I will inform their lordships that you are most definitely sailing with us. And you will be returned home at the expense of the Royal Navy. Or else I myself will not be going to visit with that murderer. I don't give a damn what anybody says."

CHAPTER 30

It had been a full five days on the long voyage south before *Wildcat* had reached her station off Antarctica. The voyage itself was uneventful, the weather having been for the most part reasonably calm and pleasant, although as they had pushed south between the Falkland Islands and South Georgia temperatures had become noticeably colder, unsurprising for this time of the year at such southerly latitudes. At this point too Matthew and Dawn had stood out on deck together, bundled up against the cold, and had enjoyed on two consecutive evenings the beautiful early September light show of brilliant red, green, and blue created in the night sky of the Southern Hemisphere by the Aurora Australis. In all of her travels Dawn had never before beheld the Aurora, said to be one of nature's most beautiful, wondrous, and romantic spectacles. Matthew as it turned out had seen the Aurora Borealis once during a brief stay on Iceland during a fishing expedition back in 1759, although he repeatedly stated that this time around the experience was better than the last which had involved only a shimmering green curtain effect, and which he had witnessed, of course, without his wife by his side.

As it had turned out Matthew's presence aboard *Wildcat* had been welcomed by Vice-Admiral Bailey, and of course by all other officers and crew aboard. Callaghan had been especially happy to see him again, spending long hours with him in his cabin, reminiscing about old times. For Dawn it was a little strange being aboard *Wildcat* purely as a passenger. But Callaghan had done everything in his power to ensure that things ran as smoothly and pleasantly as possible for both her and Revere.

On reaching their station in the Southern Ocean, Callaghan had informed Dawn that they had arrived, and ordered a helicopter crew to make ready for the short flight to Atlantis. Dawn had spent the last thirty minutes with her husband in an unusually emotional state, reassuring him that all would be well and that she would see him again soon, despite her growing sense of foreboding about what the immediate future would hold for her. But they both knew that Hunt had not yet made his intentions clear, nor had he given any indication as to how long he wished Dawn to remain with him.

They had then both walked to the helicopter deck on *Wildcat's* stern and Dawn had climbed aboard the waiting Lynx, its screaming engines already fully warmed up and ready. She kissed him once more, before he stood back and waved her off, as the pilot applied power and collective pitch to the main rotor assembly, and the machine slowly rose into the air, as if in defiance of the laws of gravity.

CHAPTER 31

Approximately forty-five minutes later the helicopter was already hovering over the enormous deep depression in the Antarctic ice at the bottom of which lay Atlantis. The pilots overflew the city, swooping down until the ice towered above them on all sides like a colossal mountain range. They zig-zagged up and down until they located the landing pad marked with a large illuminated white letter 'H' that had been set aside for them, whereupon they slowed their machine to a hover before setting it gently down. Dawn then jumped out into the cold minus fifteen degree Fahrenheit air, withdrew, and immediately made the 'OK' sign with her right index finger and thumb, and waved the pilots off. She watched the Lynx rise once more and moments later it was disappearing over the ice peaks high overhead on its journey back to *Wildcat*.

She now found herself quite alone, and facing a large pyramidal edifice, perhaps three hundred feet tall at its apex, and constructed from a very smooth dark stone of a type and texture that she felt certain she had never before beheld. At its end, directly opposite her and clearly visible, was a set of double doors. As per another of Hunt's directives, explained to her by the co-pilot during the flight, she approached. On passing through she found herself entering into a long chamber. Stepping inside, she noticed immediately that the interior air was warm and dry, a very comfortable contrast to the freezing conditions of the Antarctic outside. She unzipped her now unnecessary coat, and once her eyes had adjusted to the relative gloom, the sight that met her resembled nothing so much as a throne room belonging to a medieval castle from Europe, or the British Isles of the Middle Ages. As she walked further she noted that the walls on either side were made of very smooth stone, behind which a soft bluish-yellow light seemed to be emanating in a gently flickering manner, as if lit by medieval flaming torches, except try as she might she could not see any torches visible anywhere. The floor was also made of the same smooth stone, and yet strangely there seemed to be no visible joints in its construction, as if it was entirely carved from the solid bedrock.

Dawn suddenly stopped and took a sharp intake of breath in response to what she now could see. For at the other end of the long chamber, the somewhat grandiose figure of Commander Garry Hunt reposed. On studying him further, Dawn noted that he seemed to be completely at ease. He appeared to her in fact rather much as a king seated upon his throne, casually surveying all that was his. He eyed her regally as she approached. When she finally drew close to him he rose to meet her. The awareness suddenly struck her that he was no longer dressed in his military uniform, but instead resplendent in long, flowing, gray and brown robes. He indeed resembled a ruler from some ancient but nondescript time. And his posture, his countenance, the texture of his face, all seemed to suggest a profound change had come over him, as if the enhancement of his mental capacities had also manifested as a concurrent enhancement of his physical presence. His piercing, brilliant brown eyes seemed charged with an energy of sorts. They almost seemed to glow, and yet . . .

Her musings were cut short when he finally spoke.

"Antarctica in early September. Quite hostile, and yet, possessed of an immense beauty that cannot be matched. I do apologize, but I deactivated the external heating since the Holy Father departed back for Rome. It is therefore quite cold in the outside areas of the city. You witnessed the Aurora Australis earlier?"

He framed this last sentence as a question, and yet somehow he simultaneously managed to make it seem more like a statement of fact. As if he knew that she had indeed enjoyed the most spectacular light show on Earth. For some reason her normal confident disposition seemed to be failing her; she felt quite unable to speak. It was as if Hunt's mere presence was surprisingly intimidating to her, causing her to regress to an almost child-like state. When finally she recovered her powers of speech she could manage but one word.

"Yes."

Her voice felt diminished, small, inadequate. Hunt's visage visibly softened.

"Various early civilizations believed that the Aurora were a visible manifestation of the souls of unborn children, dancing in the night sky."

His features then adopted a more logical, rational, calculating attitude, which to Dawn was a little disagreeable.

"Of course they were mistaken. The Aurora are in fact nothing more than the result of protons and electrons streaming in from the sun, typically during periods of enhanced solar flare activity, interacting with the magnetosphere and the ionosphere, as we modern humans with our euphemistically-termed advanced civilization have been able to divine."

His features grew naïve, innocent, boyish.

"But you know, that information was known to the ancients who built all this that you see around you here."

He fixed her in a quizzical, if penetrating gaze.

"More than ten thousand years ago."

He paused to allow the import of that last statement to strike her. As she mulled the words over in her mind, she could not help but stare involuntarily at a door portal located somewhat to Hunt's right, a portal standing around twelve feet in height. He seemed immediately aware of what she was thinking.

"In ancient epochs giants roamed the Earth. There are many confirmatory references to be found in all of the major religious texts."

He made this statement very casually, as if he were commenting on the weather.

"Genesis, chapter six, verse four, for example. *There were giants in the earth in those days; and also after that, when the sons of God came in unto the daughters of men, and they bare children to them, the same became mighty men which were of old, men of renown.*"

Dawn could only stare at him, completely unsure as to how she should interpret this statement.

When he spoke again he changed tack completely.

"What do you suppose would be the most fitting and appropriate punishment for Sheikh Osama Bin Laden, for his crimes against humanity, for planning the September 11th attacks against the United States, for his wild embrace of Wahhabism with its attendant strict interpretation of Sharia law?"

During idle moments Dawn had given this issue some thought, more especially since her personal experiences those two years before with the French Prime Minister Alain DuLac to whom she had been introduced aboard the carrier *Samuel de Champlain.* But she dared not speak her thoughts now. But no matter, for in a flash she saw that Hunt was apparently reading her mind, and recreating what he saw there before her very eyes, in the form of some kind of three-dimensional vision, rather much as if a hologram was being projected before her. She witnessed what appeared to be Bin Laden himself caught and held in a secure location, being questioned by CIA officers, being told coldly what fate awaited him. Then she flashed rapidly to the next part of the vision. Bin Laden was undergoing enforced surgery, quite against his will. She could see him clearly, strapped to a gurney, being wheeled into an operating room. The surgical team were ready. He was prepped, anesthetized, and soon the procedure commenced. An operation to switch him from male to female. A gender reassignment procedure. Afterwards she witnessed his weeping and agonizing as he, or she, was again locked up in a cell, alone, except during the brief but frequent periods when he was visited by medical staff and their orderlies who periodically forced powerful hormone injections upon him, as well as food down his throat. Her throat. Next she saw how he, or she, was transported to a poor tribal area of eastern Afghanistan, by now appearing, externally at least, just as a woman, where he/she was dropped off from a helicopter, there to be brutally assaulted and raped by a band of rough men, before being dragged, bloodied and bruised before a makeshift Sharia court, overseen by a small group of Shi'ite clerics, who pronounced their inevitable sentence of death upon him, upon her, as a defiled woman. A woman who had brought shame upon the community in the sight of Allah, his cries, her cries of protest that he, that she was in fact Sheikh Osmama Bin Laden, falling on deaf ears. Dawn saw how Bin Laden was buried waist-deep in the dirt and then pounded with rocks and stones as he, as she, screamed and shrieked, until his skull, her skull, was broken open by the sheer vicious savagery of his, of her, beloved religion.

Dawn felt sickened by what she saw. Hunt instantly recognized her revulsion.

"You recoil, Captain DeFaller. But yet this is what you yourself imagined. I am revealing to you nothing more than a window into you own mind."

"But . . ."

She could not muster any kind of a meaningful argument.

"Tell me, what think you of Adolf Hitler?"

"What?"

"Specifically, during his period as Chancellor of Germany, from 1933 to 1945?"

Dawn considered the question for a moment.

"He was a madman, an insane fascist."

"A madman? A fascist, you say? He was neither, you know. Fascism is merely democracy run out of control."

Dawn was not at all sure what he meant by that last statement but felt disinclined to press him for an explanation.

"Hitler was not mad. At least not at first, to be sure. And he was no democrat. In fact he came to hate democracy, especially after witnessing sessions of the Austrian parliament in progress. He believed in social reform, universal health care, and the dismantling of the hated class system. Of course he also believed in the self-evident supremacy of the Aryan race. And the self-evident criminality of the Jewish international financial conspiracy, which he believed existed for the sole purposes of first enslaving and then later ruling the world. In his view the primal and absolute responsibility of the state was to protect and preserve the Aryan master race. None of these latter points he believed required any expounding, justification, or explanatory argument. To Hitler they were but unquestionable and self-evident truths. Anyone who failed to see that was in his estimation a contemptible fool. His famous, unnecessarily long, repetitive, and pregnant tome, *Mein Kampf*, is peppered not infrequently with shrewd, astute observations of humanity, even occasional flashes of genius. It was Hitler who recognized that to reach the masses one must present, orally and not in writing, a simple, packaged argument, all sides of which can be easily seen simultaneously, even by the most unsophisticated of minds. Anything more complex is doomed to be considered only in the minds of the bourgeoisie and intelligentsia, and therefore be forever relegated to cultural irrelevance."

Hunt all of a sudden seemed bored, as if he had had enough of all this small talk.

"But Captain DeFaller, I digress. I am simply making idle chit-chat. Please allow me the privilege of explaining my reasons for asking you here."

He peered skyward while outstretching his arms.

"In a nutshell, Captain DeFaller, what I want of you, is this."

He stared at her in an extremely focused and highly intelligent, yet almost lupine manner. Dawn imagined that this was the stare to which Lieutenant Devlin had been alluding earlier in her description of the man when she had met with him aboard *Diamond*.

"I want you to oversee my project to terraform the planet Mars."

CHAPTER 32

Dawn thought this to be some kind of joke.

"I'm sorry?"

"Captain DeFaller, I have already demonstrated an ability to design and have built, under my direction, an orbiter that can utilize warp field technology to create a deep hole, initially one mile, and now eight miles in diameter through the Antarctic ice. It is really a very simple matter indeed to design a warp drive for a space vessel such that a trip to Mars would be well within the grasp of humanity."

"But . . . Mars is so very far away. Much further than the moon. It would take months, years, to get there."

"Around thirty-five million miles, or about one hundred and forty times as far away as the moon. However with a suitable warp drive the transit time would average out at eighteen plus or minus two seconds."

Dawn was aghast. "Really, Commander Hunt, I don't see how . . ."

"And once in orbit there, Captain, you will activate a terrestrial warp field from your ship, which will create a small but entirely livable bubble on the surface, around one quarter of a mile in diameter. Oxygen and nitrogen will be introduced from your ship and thus there will be a breathable atmosphere inside the bubble, which will also be maintained at a suitable temperature. And because of the nature of the bubble, it will grow, slowly at first but in a mathematically exponential manner so that after a period of three months the entire planet will possess an enriched oxygen and nitrogen atmosphere, and become significantly warmed. At that point Mars will be ready to receive photosynthetic plant material and the process of turning the surface of the planet green will begin. Again, using warp field technology, local terrain will be prepared and then large fields of plant matter will be transported there from Earth, once suitable receiver ports are established on the Martian surface. The atmosphere will be seeded with water vapor in a similar manner, leading to rains which will fill up the lower lying areas to form lakes and oceans, which of course will be very important for the establishment and maintenance of global weather patterns. The whole process from start to finish will take about six months, after which time the building of towns and cities can begin in earnest. Humans can then start relocating there, especially from the poorer areas of Earth, and the current pressures of overpopulation and limitations of global resources will be relieved."

But Dawn just stared at him as if he were mad.

"But why me? Why am I to be the one to have to conduct all of this?"

"You have previous experience of dealing with situations outside of the normal human realm of existence, specifically, when you traveled back in time to North America of 1776. Also, your body does well traveling through warp fields. I will not bore you with the reasons, but I can say categorically that this is not true of everyone. And, by the standards of a non-enhanced human you possess a remarkable ability for handling completely new situations. As for myself, I cannot leave Atlantis for the time-being as I must remain here to co-ordinate everything from Earth. I am after all the brains behind the operation. But for this project to work someone will need to travel to Mars in order to implement the practical aspects of the scheme. But have no fear, Captain, this will be for a matter of months only. At the conclusion of the initial part of the project, many other people will be sent to Mars to build the first cities and towns, and you will be free to return to

Earth, or remain there, or travel between the two as many times as you please."

"So how long will it take to build the ship?"

"I have already submitted detailed design specifications to Northrop Grumman Corporation. They are working on the design even as we speak, and have been for about a month. The ship is in fact almost ready, and should be completed in approximately twenty four hours. Following that it will be flown here by its on-board computer."

"Twenty-four hours?" Dawn was having a hard time believing what she was hearing. "And how long will it take for the ship to fly here?"

"About twenty minutes."

"Twenty minutes. From North America to Antarctica?"

"Yes, Captain. That is correct."

"And what about my husband? Will he be coming to Mars too?"

"Not initially. After the terraformation is complete, you may invite him to join you there. If you so choose."

Dawn stood and stared at Hunt in silence. His ideas seemed utterly incredible, and yet, he had achieved so much already. Indeed many, if not most, up until a matter of a few weeks ago would have dismissed his notions as fanciful nonsense. Perhaps this was even a good idea in the end. More living space, more resources for humanity. Where was the potential harm in that?

"I would like you to remain here until it is time to commence your journey to the Martian surface. A room has been prepared for you. I believe you will find everything in order."

Dawn considered reminding Hunt that she was in fact his superior officer and that she could technically require that he surrender himself to her and accompany her back to London to face a Court Martial for his crimes. But something told her that this would be a futile gesture. Hunt did not seem inclined to be willing to surrender to anyone. And in any event he seemed to be operating with the full support of the respective governments of the United Kingdom and the United States.

CHAPTER 33

Dawn awoke to the gentle but insistent sound of Hunt's voice informing her that it was time to rise, make ready, dress in the jumpsuit laid out in her room, eat breakfast, and then report to the area where he had first spoken with her the day before. The room where she had spent the night was indeed very comfortable. She had felt as if she had been sleeping in a five-star hotel. As she rose and dressed, and especially later as she sat down to the meal that Hunt had brought to her room, she began to contemplate seriously what she was about to get herself into. A flight into space. A visit to another world. Was such a thing even possible? Hunt certainly seemed convinced that it would be so.

A little later, when she was ready, following her meal of grapefruit and cereal, toast with butter, jam, and two cups of coffee, she made her way back to the area where Hunt was patiently awaiting her. Despite the huge size of the complex, and its apparent deserted state, she found that she experienced little difficulty navigating her way around. It seemed to be laid out in a remarkably logical manner, with landmarks included everywhere that jogged the mind to just exactly the right degree, as if its designers had considered every possible directional contingency.

When she arrived she found Hunt waiting for her. On seeing her approach he positively beamed.

"Ah! Captain DeFaller! Come with me please!"

He waited for her to reach him and then commenced walking briskly down a corridor. Dawn immediately fell into step behind and followed him, as if that were the entirely natural thing to do. After a few moments the corridor opened out into a very large open-area chamber, but closed over with what appeared to be a roof that looked as if it could be opened, about one hundred and fifty feet above their heads. In the center of the vast expanse of floor area sat what Dawn guessed would very shortly be introduced to her as Hunt's spacecraft. It somewhat resembled the Space Shuttle orbiter as operated by NASA, but was perhaps twenty percent smaller, as well as substantially better looking, sleeker, with stubbier wings, and seemed to be entirely given over to crew accommodations, as opposed to possessing a large cargo bay as in the NASA version. But attached to its base, and upon which it seemed to rest, were two long pods, approximately four feet in diameter, that ran its entire length and which to Dawn resembled some kind of flotation devices. The entire ship appeared to be finished in a highly polished surface of silver and gold.

"Captain. This is your ship. She was actually completed a few hours earlier than expected by Grumman Northrop and flown here under my direction last night. Every system I have personally tested and assessed. I can say with confidence the vessel is fully functional and operational. You will find all the necessary amenities aboard for a comfortable stay. You will be the only crew member, however there will be step-by-step instructions clearly provided for you by way of the on-board communications equipment, which will place you in touch with me, so you need not ever feel alone. A full space suit and two complete spares, and a life support system with two redundant back-up systems are provided aboard. You should not at any time need the space suits. They are there only in case of mishap or emergency; for example, in the event that you may need to move outside the ship while in space to effect repairs. But that should not be necessary. If it does become necessary however, the ship's computer or I myself will provide you with full and clear instructions."

He turned and smiled at her. Dawn realized that this had been the first time she had seen him do so. In fact he seemed altogether friendlier and more like a normal social human being, if rather a lot more animated, than he had the day before.

"And now, Captain, all that remains is for me to ask you to go aboard, and bid you good luck. Once you are settled in the computer will show you a video presentation and issue some simple instructions."

She was surprised.

"There is no training that I first of all need to complete?"

"No," he replied emphatically. "The ship's computer will handle all of that."

"Very well, then, Commander Hunt. I shall board now, as you wish."

A panel on the side of the ship opened smoothly, causing a short set of folding steps to descend down to ground level. Dawn stared at the steps for a moment, then at Hunt. He simply gestured for her to climb aboard. She stared at him a moment longer. And then, taking hold of the hand rail, commenced climbing the steps.

"Good luck, Captain. And *bon voyage.*"

On hearing this latter platitude she shot Hunt a parting glance. She wondered if this was in recognition that her paternal grandfather had been French. A language that he had been at pains to impart to Dawn when she had been young, quite successfully as it had turned out, as she was indeed a fairly fluent French speaker. As the steps folded and the panel closed again she imagined that this was exactly the kind of thing of which he would be aware.

CHAPTER 34

Within its interior the ship was surprisingly spacious and luxurious; it felt to Dawn rather much like being inside a sizeable modern and thoroughly efficient trailer or recreational vehicle. All excepting of course that once the outer and inner airlock doors closed behind her, she found herself in a mostly windowless environment, with the exception of the four small windows in the cockpit area, to which she noted she did enjoy free access. Immediately behind the cockpit there was an area much like a small sitting room, replete with a couch and a reclining armchair, although she noticed that the latter was equipped with a harness. A soft, female voice suddenly addressed Dawn.

"Welcome aboard, Captain DeFaller."

Dawn looked up and around in surprise for a moment, but of course, there was no surprise really. She was being addressed by an artificial voice, which she surmised was most likely the ship's on-board computer. The voice sounded mostly human but had a quality of gentle smoothness that rendered it a little artificial.

"Please do not be alarmed. I am the ship's computer. I answer to the name Danielle. You may speak with me at any time, simply by addressing me by name. I am programmed to answer any question you may have regarding the mission. However first of all I must ask that you approach the chair immediately in front of you and fasten yourself into the harness for take-off."

My gosh, Dawn thought. A talking computer, replete with a personality. Hunt must have designed her too. And had her built along with the vessel, by Northrop Grumman. The man truly was a genius. Dawn surmised that Danielle must be watching her, most likely through a series of cameras.

"I will shortly take the ship into orbit around Earth and, once there, will explain to you further the nature of our mission and the systems aboard this ship. At that time I will also be ready to answer any questions that you may have."

Dawn suddenly remembered that she had forgotten to ask Hunt the name of the vessel she was now aboard. Perhaps it didn't have one, but she was curious.

"Danielle?"

"Yes Captain?"

"Does this ship have a name?"

"Affirmative, Captain."

There was a pregnant pause. Did Danielle need to be asked everything directly?

"Then what is it?"

"This ship is named *Vega,* after a loose transliteration of the Arabic word *wāqi,* meaning 'falling' or 'landing', which comes from the phrase *an-nasr al-wāqi,* meaning 'the alighting vulture'. And, of course, *Vega* is also the name of the brightest star in the constellation Lyra. Please Captain, approach the chair and affix yourself in the harness."

Dawn did as she had been requested. She settled into the chair, which was surprisingly comfortable, and adjusted the straps on the harness and pulled them over her body, and fastened them in place. Not much different from the seatbelts one finds on the seats in an airliner, except there were additional elements running over both shoulders. Much as one would expect pilots to wear.

"You will now feel the thrusters fire. Do not be concerned that no-one is at the controls in the cockpit. I am in full control of the ship, and will be at all times during the mission."

At that point Dawn felt a growing vibration arising from the very frame of the ship, accompanied by a low pitched roar.

Within seconds her forward-facing chair inclined backwards as the ship angled upward and she saw through the cockpit windows the roof panel she had seen earlier ranged across the top of the chamber start to slide slowly back. Behind it lay the clear blue cool morning Antarctic sky. Approximately twenty seconds later the ship accelerated upwards and in a matter of seconds had cleared the open roof and was climbing steeply, not quite on the vertical, all the while continuing to accelerate hard. The sensation was not unlike that one experiences during take-off while aboard a regular jet airliner, but with the very high angle of attack the ship was gaining altitude at several times the typical rate of climb of fifteen hundred feet per minute of a large passenger jet. The roaring sound she could hear was also quieter and smoother than that of even the most modern and advanced civil aviation jet engines. Within the space of five minutes the blue sky she could still make out straight ahead had now started to adopt a significantly deeper hue, despite it still being morning down below on the ground. About a minute following that she thought she could make out a few stars shining like pinpoints of light through the field which by now had adopted a very deep and dark blue coloration indeed. The appearance of the sky reminded her of the experience she had once had while diving off the coast of Cozumel Island in Mexico, when at about a hundred feet below the surface she had moved off the edge of an undersea cliff and peered down into a cavernous abyss almost two thousand feet deep. The dark blue of the water below appeared to gradually merge with utter blackness, creating the impression that the abyss was bottomless. The same merging of the dark blue with blackness outside the ship finally occurred about forty-five seconds later. The sky now appeared as it does from the ground on Earth, but at night, its appearance studded with the usual array of stars. At that point the ship began to reduce its rate of climb as it continued its ascent more gently. The roar of the engines diminished somewhat as they were throttled back a little, and Dawn heard Danielle's gentle voice addressing her once again.

"We have now achieved an altitude of one hundred thousand feet, Captain. We will continue our climb more slowly and gently until we reach an altitude of five hundred and twenty-eight thousand feet, or one hundred miles. We are also currently moving at a speed of Mach seven point two, but will continue to accelerate until we reach a speed of Mach twenty-four, or around twenty thousand miles per hour, a speed sufficient for us to enter orbit."

It was another twenty-three minutes before *Vega* achieved her target altitude and speed. Just as the ship's acceleration ceased and her speed stabilized, Danielle announced that there would be a brief period of weightlessness as they entered orbit, but that would last for only nineteen seconds until the artificial gravity was engaged. In the meantime Danielle requested that Dawn remain harnessed into her chair, until the operation was complete. Dawn did indeed feel herself floating as free from her chair as her harness would allow, as if she were underwater, but then, as the artificial gravity came on-line, she once more felt herself settling back into her chair as her body again had weight. Danielle had further instructions.

"Captain, we have now entered orbit and you may remove your harness and move freely about the cabin."

Dawn gingerly undid her harness and stood up. The roar of the engines had now ceased and the ship no longer felt as if it were moving. She moved over to the cockpit area and climbed into the co-pilot's seat on the right side. The view of the Earth far below, brightly illuminated like a brilliant shining marble set against the black infinity of the cosmos was remarkably beautiful. She could clearly make out oceans of cloud and weather patterns covering the South Atlantic that they were now passing over. Parts of eastern South America and western Africa were clearly visible.

"From up here everything looks so pure, so clean and fresh." She wondered if Danielle would understand or care for such a comment. She sat staring at her home planet for another five full minutes, by which time they were now passing over Saudi Arabia and the Red Sea before Danielle interrupted her again.

"Captain, if you are ready, I would like now to explain the nature of our forthcoming mission. Please make yourself comfortable on the couch and I will lower the video screen."

Reluctantly Dawn pulled herself away from the cockpit and moved to the couch.

"Before we start, would you like some coffee?"

"Yes, please."

A panel slid open on the wall, and there was a steaming mug of black coffee sitting inside on a small tray, along with some creamer and sugar. Dawn took it before sitting down on the couch.

"Danielle, you may proceed with your presentation."

"Thank you, Captain."

A video screen dropped down from the ceiling and positioned itself approximately five feet directly in front of Dawn.

"Commander Hunt has I believe appraised you of the essential nature of this mission?"

"Yes. Apparently we are to terraform Mars, that is, render the Martian environment habitable by humans. And in a matter of just a few months."

"Approximately three months, Captain. As you correctly and succinctly put it, terraformation of Mars is the process by which the surface of the planet will be purposely altered such that it will become habitable by human beings, as well as other animal and plant life currently residing on Earth. When the process is complete, most of the planet will be suitable for colonization. The process of instigating this terraformation has been within the technological grasp of humanity now for a little over a decade, however to execute such a program would have required the economic and strategic co-operation of all of the major governments in the world, not to mention a number of the more minor ones. For this reason, and also the fact that the process would have taken at least a century to reach completion, the project never got under way, at least thus far. But Commander Hunt devised a very much faster and more efficient methodology, consisting of essentially similar steps but relying on warp field technology to make it work. Warp field technology with which you are in essence familiar, which made it possible for you to journey backwards in time. A technology based on matter/anti-matter reaction combined with graviton generation."

"Yes. That proved to be quite an unexpected adventure."

"In the future it is projected that continued human population growth on Earth will increase pressure to colonize new areas, such as the surface of the oceans, the ocean floor, Earth's orbit, perhaps also Earth's moon. In addition, other planets or moons in the solar system may be mined for raw materials. And eventually, of course, although not for a very long time, the sun itself is expected to both cool, and expand, eventually to approximately one hundred times its present diameter. If humanity has not found an alternative home by then, extinction of the entire species will inevitably occur. If on the other hand there are settlements on Mars, then there will be some extra time, to the tune of several centuries, before Mars itself becomes too hot and the species has to move further out into the solar system in order to avoid annihilation. Eventually of course the sun will become a red giant and at that point humanity will have to have spread out to other star systems if it is to survive, but that is a very long way in the future indeed. As it stands currently, Mars possesses many of the materials required for the terraformation process, in the form of minerals within its soil. In addition, there are substantial quantities of water trapped just beneath the surface as permafrost, as far as latitude sixty degrees from each of the poles. The poles themselves incorporate variously water ice and carbon dioxide ice. There may even be more water ice deeper in the crust, although this is speculative and relatively unimportant for our purposes. And during the summer months, as polar carbon dioxide ice sublimes into the atmosphere, that is, going directly from the solid phase to the gaseous phase without passing through the liquid phase, it leaves behind some water. Fast atmospheric winds moving at around two hundred and fifty miles per hour then pick up this water and throw it up into the atmosphere where it forms cirrus clouds, mixed with surface dust. Gaseous oxygen is present only in very small trace quantities, but is present in much larger quantities chemically combined with metals within the rocks and soil. The soil itself also incorporates a quantity of perinitrates, a chemical complex of oxygen, nitrogen, and other elements."

Dawn was beginning to wish she had paid more attention during her chemistry classes she had experienced as a youngster.

"The soil also incorporates perchlorates, which may be used to liberate oxygen in chemical oxygen generators. And also electrolysis of Martian surface water when released from the permafrost would liberate both free oxygen and hydrogen. All that would be required to instigate this process would be a plentiful source of electrical energy."

Dawn had a question.

"If we succeed in terraforming Mars, would the planet remain stable after the process was complete such that human life could exist there indefinitely?"

Danielle digested the question for a moment, almost as if she were thinking about the most appropriate response. But then Dawn thought to herself, machines cannot really think. They possess no true sentience. Unless of course Danielle, as another of Hunt's creations, was different from other computers in some fundamental way, such that at her heart lay a true artificial intelligence.

"Mars has no plate tectonics, and never has as far as is currently understood, based again on geological surveys that have been undertaken to date. This being the case, then the recycling of gases locked up in sediments back into the atmosphere occurs at a reduced rate as compared with Earth. Mars also has no magnetic field. Both of these features of the planet may exist as a consequence of its being approximately half the diameter of Earth. Therefore its interior is cooling more rapidly than the corresponding rate for Earth. But despite these observations the planet offers a ninety-eight percent probability of maintaining a habitable environment for humans for considerably longer than human civilization is projected to last, within the solar system at least, according to some mathematical models. Enriching the atmosphere to acceptable parameters for maintenance of human and animal life will, on a planet the size of Mars, lead to a slow rate of bleeding off of atmospheric gases into space, according to calculations. But artificial generation of oxygen and nitrogen at the appropriate concentration will be sufficient to counter this. Does that address your question adequately, Captain?"

"Yes, it does."

"Good. Then I shall continue. It is believed that conditions on Mars were at one time, probably millions of years ago, similar to those on Earth of today. Similarities extend to the thickness of the Martian atmosphere and the presumptive presence in the past, based on geological surveys of the planet, of liquid water. A considerable proportion of the Martian atmosphere has been lost to space since that time, and also, because of plummeting surface temperatures, another fraction has been frozen at the poles as carbon dioxide ice, also known as dry ice. To terraform Mars successfully will entail essentially two major changes. The atmosphere will have to be built up with oxygen and nitrogen, to a total pressure of just a fraction under thirty inches of mercury at datum."

"Datum?"

"A value corresponding to sea-level on Earth, Captain."

"Ah. I see."

"Also, the planet will need to be heated because as it stands it is too cold. The Martian atmosphere is thin compared to that of Earth and has a low pressure at datum of slightly less than one-fifth of an inch of mercury, or about one hundred and sixty-eighth of that required. In addition, the Martian atmosphere currently consists of ninety-five percent carbon dioxide, three percent nitrogen, one point six percent argon, and traces of water, oxygen, and methane. Thus the atmosphere consists mostly of carbon dioxide, which is a greenhouse gas. Once the planet starts to warm, more carbon dioxide will enter the atmosphere from the reserves frozen as dry ice at the poles, which will increase the greenhouse effect. Thus the two processes of building the atmosphere and warming the planet will complement each other, which will assist greatly in our terraforming protocol. In order to build the atmosphere, water will have to be deposited on the planet. There could be several sources for this water, but we will be beaming it to the planet's surface through a focused wormhole, using as a source some of the many ice asteroids that orbit the sun between Mars and Jupiter. Now, at this stage it will become expedient to import hydrogen which will be assembled from protons and electrons present in the solar wind. Again, our warp field generator will assist greatly in amplifying and accelerating this process. We will commence this so that, when sufficient hydrogen has been introduced into the Martian atmosphere, the hydrogen can be induced to react with the by-now increased levels of atmospheric carbon dioxide via the Sabatier reaction, to yield methane and water. Methane will also be invaluable for the purpose of inducing a rapid increase in atmospheric pressure. Additionally, methane can be utilized in the production of more carbon dioxide and water, necessary for initiation of photosynthesis, by reaction with ferric oxide. Are you still following me, Captain?"

Dawn nodded her head.

"Yes, I believe so."

"Good. Now, as planetary temperatures continue to climb, more polar dry ice will sublime into the atmosphere and further add to global warming. At this point there will be large dust storms caused by moving atmospheric gases. This will seem violent but in point of fact will be harmless to you as you will be protected, and will further assist in the effort of warming the planet, via direct absorption of solar radiation by the atmosphere itself. Soon after this, dry ice will cease to form at the poles because the temperature will be too high at all times during the Martian year. However there will still be no liquid water because the pressure will be as yet insufficiently high. Following subsidence of the dust storms, the planet will now be warm enough to receive certain species of photosynthetic bacteria and algae, such as those that currently live on Earth, in Antarctica. These will be introduced to the Martian polar regions via warp field technology where there will exist sufficient quantities of water ice for them to thrive.

The algae will be introduced further around the planet and will propagate themselves rapidly, causing the surface to darken and thus promoting more planetary sunlight absorption, thus further warming the atmosphere. The algae will by now be contributing oxygen to the atmosphere, however there will not yet be enough for maintenance of human or animal life. But the atmosphere will grow steadily denser, until the pressure climbs to around thirty inches of mercury. At this point, Captain, you will, while wearing ordinary clothing, be able to don a breathing mask and an oxygen tank and take walks outside the protected zone. However, a buffer gas such as nitrogen will be required in large quantity also. This will be achieved by beaming in ammonia-rich asteroids into the atmosphere and exploding them with high energy laser bursts, which will liberate nitrogen and hydrogen from the ammonia present. The oxygen content of the atmosphere will continue to increase, until after a period of a few more weeks only it will have reached sufficient levels."

Danielle stopped her monologue for a moment, before starting up again.

"The final stage will be to position large mirrors in geosynchronous orbit above the poles. This will increase the absorption of sunlight in these regions and thereby contribute to melting of water ice to yield steam, another greenhouse gas, as well as warming the planet still further. More sustained planetary heating will occur later as the first human settlers commence mining fluorine-rich minerals from which chlorofluorocarbons and perfluorocarbons can be manufactured, and then released into the atmosphere as very efficient greenhouse gases. But this will not be part of your remit, Captain. Ozone will also be produced in electrical apparatus and released into the atmosphere at high altitudes as a shield against cosmic radiation, but again, this will not be your concern. And that, in summation, Captain, is how we shall terraform Mars to render it suitable for sustenance of human and animal life."

Dawn shook her head from side to side.

"Well, Danielle. All that will be very impressive, assuming we can indeed manage it. But I do have one question. What about gravity? Isn't the gravitational field on Mars significantly less than on Earth?"

"It is indeed, Captain. But you will be experiencing normal gravitational force, as inside the protected zone gravity will be artificially generated. Should you leave the protected zone, however, then you will experience Martian gravity until you return. But for the long term it is not expected that human settlers living on Mars will suffer any ill effects as a result of exposure to the lower gravitational field. And they will find certain tasks, such as walking or running long distances less tiring, as well as lifting what would on Earth be quite heavy loads. Experiments will have to confirm that, of course, and if it turns out that Earth-like gravitational conditions are required, for example, to prevent excessive muscle wasting, or conformational changes in blood cells that are typically seen after weeks in weightless conditions, then graviton generators will have to be built and human activity restricted to areas where the higher gravity exists, although as more generators are built these areas would expand. But again, Captain, this will not be your concern."

Danielle changed the subject.

"And now Captain, for the voyage to Mars itself. This ship is equipped with warp drive, and as you have seen already, artificial gravity is also provided inside the crew compartment. The gravity will not only hold you against the floor, but can also be brought to bear longitudinally, by focused devices called the longitudinal gravitational dampers, or LGD's. The LGD's will, at the appropriate time, perfectly cancel the effects of extreme acceleration or deceleration, so that during our jump to warp drive you are not crushed to a viscous gelatinous mass."

Dawn could not help but smile a little at this last remark.

"I am glad to hear that."

But Danielle apparently had failed to appreciate the humor inherent in her last statement. She simply continued, as before.

"In order to make the ride feel a little more realistic, the LGD's will function a tiny fraction of a percent less well than optimally, to create a comfortable illusion of acceleration and later, deceleration, but, I hasten to add, this is strictly an illusion. And during the acceleration phase, you will also experience a brief episode of time dilation, that is, time will run more slowly for you than for anyone outside of the ship's warp field."

"How much more slowly?"

"By a factor of around one hundred. So, for example your acceleration for transit to Mars will appear from your perspective to take around five seconds, but to an outside observer, it would appear to take five hundred seconds, or eight minutes and twenty seconds."

"And how long will the transit time take?"

"Approximately thirty-eight seconds, however there will be another additional five second period required for the deceleration as the warp field disengages. However because of time dilation issues, your total transit time including acceleration and deceleration will be in the region of eighty minutes from an outside observer's point of view. But from your point of view, aboard the ship, transit from Earth's orbit to the region of Martian space will take around forty-eight seconds. There will however be an additional thirty-six hours required to align with the planet at conventional speeds and enter orbit."

Dawn was a little taken aback by this explanation.

"Thirty six hours? That is an additional day and a half. Why so long if the transit time is so brief?"

"We cannot enter Martian orbit at the equivalent of super-light speed, Captain. We would be instantly destroyed. So instead we must drop out of warp at a distance of approximately one quarter of a million miles from the planet. From there, using conventional ion rocket thrusters, we will be able to generate a speed of some seven thousand miles per hour, and will be able to reach planetary orbit within approximately thirty-six hours."

"You say the equivalent of super-light speed? What did you mean by equivalent?"

"During warp the ship will not actually be moving, Captain. Instead our warp drive engines will be compressing space ahead of us such that we simply drag the compressed destination towards ourselves, using the enormous gravitational field that our graviton generator can yield by harnessing the energy derived from our on-board matter/anti-matter reactor. To actually move at five times light speed would be a physical impossibility, since as one approaches light speed, one's mass increases towards infinity. The German mathematician Dr. Albert Einstein was the first to postulate and then prove this theoretically during the early twentieth century. He was indeed absolutely correct, as practical experience has since confirmed."

"And the ship's on-board graviton generator and matter/anti-matter reactor, this is the same design as the apparatus used in the experiment whereby my previous command was pushed backwards through time?"

"Yes, Captain, except approximately five hundred times more powerful."

"Are you absolutely certain we will not be projected through time by accident?"

"Yes Captain. Absolutely certain. With our given energy bands and settings, that would be a mathematical impossibility, except of course for the ordinary time dilation that you will experience, effectively a trip into the future, but amounting to minutes only."

Dawn stared through the cockpit windows into the dark void beyond.

"So, Danielle. Are you ready to take us to Mars?"

"Yes Captain. Navigation is plotted and the course is laid in."

"Then let's do it."

"Please once more harness yourself into your seat. After you are secured, we will depart."

CHAPTER 35

Danielle had been absolutely accurate in her description of the acceleration to warp speed. Dawn had noticed a moderate sense of artificially rendered acceleration, promoted only by the action of the LGD's, for a period of five seconds, a feeling rather much like the acceleration one experiences while aboard a passenger jet on take-off. She did notice however out of the cockpit windows that as soon as the warp field had been engaged, the ship had become surrounded by a giant sparkling cloud, glowing beautifully with every color of the rainbow, and exhibiting what appeared to be intense coronal discharge rather much as one might witness during a severe thunderstorm on Earth. Except that the stars, which ordinarily appeared as pinpoints of light, seemed to become suddenly greatly elongated, and almost immediately the ship was surrounded by what appeared to be a tunnel through this disturbance, through which they appeared to be traveling at immense speed. Following the sense of acceleration there was a thirty-eight second period where the ship felt as if it were moving at constant speed, quite smoothly and uneventfully through this tunnel, and then another five second period of an artificial sense of deceleration. Following that the tunnel vanished, the brilliant colors and coronal discharge, which had reminded her of that fateful experiment in which she had engaged in the North Atlantic Ocean, were no more. All that lay outside the ship now was the blackness of empty space, apparently stretching to infinity, in all directions. But as Danielle brought the ship about, a small reddish-brown orb appeared in Dawn's field of view. It looked to be perhaps twice the diameter of the moon as viewed from the surface of Earth.

"Danielle. Is that Mars directly ahead of us?"

"Yes Captain. We will enter Martian orbit in approximately thirty six hours."

Dawn felt the ion rockets fire.

"We will now accelerate to seven thousand miles per hour, conventional speed. That will take around ten minutes. When the acceleration is complete, you will be free to move around the cabin once more, Captain. I suggest at that time you partake of some food and drink, and perhaps take some rest. I will take care of the remainder of the journey."

A short time later Dawn was reclining on the sofa with a cup of black coffee in her right hand and some food in her left. She had briefly sat in the cockpit and stared out into space. But apart from the stars she could see nothing, except for Mars herself, and the gray forms of her two tiny and aspherical, asteroid-like moons, Phobos and Deimos, ranged appositionally around their parent planet, very slowly growing larger in her field of view.

CHAPTER 36

Entry into orbit proved to be smooth and uneventful. There had been a degree of acceleration to approximately eight thousand five hundred miles per hour as Danielle had positioned the ship in orbit, but it had not felt particularly noticeable. By now Dawn was seated back in the cockpit again, after having spent the last thirty-six hours variously eating, sitting looking out into space at Mars as the planet slowly grew in her field of view, or, when she had grown weary of that, relaxing again on the couch in the main cabin area. She had even had time to watch a movie and sleep for a few hours, but now Danielle had placed the ship in a parking orbit around the planetary equator, at an altitude of three hundred miles above the plain of Lucus Planum, and was ready to begin the descent to the surface.

Looking out at the planet below, which at this point now entirely filled her field of view, Dawn could make out the reddish-brown appearance of the surface, along with various upland and lowland areas, as well as the edge of the thin and wispy looking enveloping atmosphere.

"Look below at the surface of the planet, Captain. We are above the plain of Lucus Planum. To the north, framed by the tops of the cockpit windows, you can make out the Martian equator and the impact crater of Apollinaris Patera. To the south, Gusev crater and the canyon system of Ma'adim Vallis. To the east and west you will see mainly a large cratered field. Our landing site will be near the equator, due north of Gusev crater but due south of Apollinaris Patera, about half-way between the two, or approximately eighty miles from each geographical feature."

Danielle waited for a few minutes while Dawn spent some more time peering down at the surface of the planet below.

"It looks so big, Danielle."

But Danielle ignored Dawn's last comment.

"We are now going to begin our descent to the surface, Captain. Please sit once again in the chair and insure that your safety harness is properly fastened."

Dawn complied, and shortly afterward she felt some thrusters fire and the ship started to decelerate, before the nose pitched downwards by a few degrees and the descent commenced. A few minutes later Danielle made a further announcement.

"We are about to enter the Martian atmosphere, Captain. When we do you will notice that the ride will become a little choppy."

Just as Danielle had said, when the ship entered the planetary atmosphere, about thirty-five miles above the surface, the smooth silent descent morphed into a noisy, jostling, altogether rougher experience. Dawn also noticed that, through the cockpit windows, natural daylight was now flooding in, replacing the darkness of space, albeit with somewhat lower light levels than those to which she was accustomed on Earth. She also noticed the slightly reddish, otherworldly ethereal hue.

"We are now slowing our rate of descent in preparation for touchdown, Captain."

As the ship started to decelerate Dawn could make out for the first time a mountain range off in the distance. At this point she felt as if she were aboard an aircraft, looking down on a slightly alien version of the dry deserts of California or Nevada, from perhaps thirty-five thousand feet. But as they continued their descent to the surface Dawn found herself all of a sudden experiencing a sense of real fear, as if she was launching herself into the unknown, and who knew what awaited her imminent arrival on the surface of the great plain below. Strangely she had not felt any sense of trepidation throughout the flight from Earth, but now, as the reality of the alien world, which had slowly grown all around her until it filled her whole experience, the feeling had reared its head. Inwardly she wished that Matthew were here.

"We are about to land, Captain. Touch down in thirty seconds."

The ship started to decelerate at a noticeably greater rate.

"Touchdown in twenty seconds."

The deceleration continued.

"Five. Four. Three. Two. One."

There was a brief soft thud and the ship shuddered to a halt. Their journey was over. She had actually arrived on the surface of Mars. As the ship powered down, all machinery whined to a halt. But then, without any warning from Danielle, the lights and all the computer panels winked out, as if the power had been cut. Dawn found herself sitting in darkness and utter silence, inside a hardened metal box, alone on a deserted plain on a lifeless alien world.

"Danielle?"

There was no response.

"Danielle? Danielle?"

Nothing. Attempting to stem a rising surge of panic, Dawn picked up the communications handset which connected her with Hunt, back on Earth.

"Hello?"

But the set was completely dead. Was this a trick? Had she been sent to Mars simply to be marooned there to face a slow and lonely death?

"Hello? Hello!"

Outside the darkened silent ship Dawn could hear some wind start to howl quietly.

"Danielle! Hello?"

CHAPTER 37

About four minutes and thirty seconds later the lights and panels suddenly came to life once again. And when Danielle spoke, Dawn experienced an enormous sense of relief.

"You may disengage your harness and move about the cabin now, Captain. But please be advised that for the next few minutes I will keep the airlock hatch closed until I have established a life-support envelope around the ship which will sustain you at a comfortable temperature and pressure, with an appropriate atmosphere."

"Danielle! What did you just do? Why did all the power go off?" Dawn was close to shouting.

Danielle seemed to pause before responding. Almost as if she had something to hide. But Dawn dismissed the thought as soon as it entered her head. For despite her apparent personality, Danielle was only a machine, after all. She possessed no emotions.

"I experienced a momentary, sudden and unexpected power surge on landing. To avoid the potential for damage, I powered down all systems so that I could run a general diagnostic check before rebooting and continuing with the mission, Captain."

"What caused the power surge?"

Again, the strange pause.

"I do not know, Captain."

Dawn found that answer strange, perhaps even a little frightening.

"You have absolutely no idea? Can you make a guess?"

Another strange, uncharacteristic pause.

"No, Captain."

Dawn sensed that there would be no point in pushing Danielle further for details.

"Well please inform me beforehand if you are going to do that again. You scared me. Very badly."

"I apologize, Captain. It should not be necessary to repeat that procedure. But I will certainly inform you if I am going to do so, unless I am obliged to do so with such a degree of rapidity that there is insufficient time to issue a warning."

Danielle continued.

"I am now in the process of forming the life support envelope outside the ship. The process will be complete in about ten minutes. In the meantime please don the boots in the locker."

A locker door by the floor flipped open smoothly and Dawn could see what appeared to be a regular pair of hiking boots. She pulled them from the locker and took them to the couch and sat down. She started to put them on. They turned out to be high quality and fitted her perfectly. In fact she found them to be extremely comfortable.

Ten minutes later Danielle spoke again.

"The life support envelope is now fully formed, Captain. Are you ready to become the first human being ever to step onto the surface of Mars?"

Dawn inhaled deeply, and then did so again. Fortunately by now her sense of fear had given way to a growing feeling of rising excitement.

"Yes Danielle. Please proceed."

"A word of caution. When I open the airlock, you will be able to step outside the ship and walk on the surface. Gravity will feel normal to you, as will the temperature, which will be the same as the temperature presently maintained inside the ship. The air will consist of eighty percent nitrogen and twenty percent oxygen, at a pressure of exactly one bar, or twenty-nine point nine-two inches of mercury, in other words average atmospheric pressure on Earth at sea level. But you will see the edge of the envelope about twenty feet from the ship in every direction, which will appear much as a wall of water, held back by an invisible energy field. Notice that it is not actually water, but simply an optical refractive effect as a result of the envelope containment force field. You will be able to step through the edge of the envelope at any point. To do so would be harmless in of itself, but you would of course find yourself outside the protective envelope and then exposed to a temperature of around minus sixty degrees Fahrenheit, in an atmosphere of mostly carbon dioxide, set at a pressure of around ten millibar. Gravity will also be less than half of that to which you are accustomed. If you spend more than a few seconds outside the envelope you will lose consciousness. If you are ten feet or less from the edge of the envelope, I will be able to adjust the extent of the envelope in your vicinity, by shifting its footprint from elsewhere to recapture and revive you. However if you range further, I will be unable to assist you. You will be on your own. I repeat my warning. If you are exposed to the conditions on this planet as they currently stand, you will lose consciousness within a few seconds, and you will not survive for more than a few minutes. Do not be fooled into a false sense of security by the planet's apparent similarity to Earth. If you must, step just outside the envelope by no more than six feet, for the experience, but for a maximum of ten seconds only. However I assure you, you will find it neither comfortable nor enjoyable. Do you understand?"

"Yes, Danielle. I understand fully. Thank you. Please proceed."

The airlock doors slid open, the steps unfolded, and Dawn stepped slowly through. She looked around at the terrain facing her. It looked so familiar. She felt as if she were about to step outside into a desert environment on Earth. It really did not appear at all dangerous, but of course, that was an illusion, for outside Danielle's envelope, there was only a freezing, gasping, hypobaric death.

After a further moment's hesitation, Dawn stepped outside the ship, descended the steps, and became the very first human being to stand on Martian soil. As she did so she thought of Neil Armstrong's famous quotation as he became the first human to step onto the surface of the moon, back in 1969, a little over thirty-nine years ago.

That's one small step for man, one giant leap for mankind.

CHAPTER 38

As Dawn's feet touched solid ground once more since leaving Earth, she instinctively looked around. The great plain of Lucus Planum formed a vast panorama all around the spot where Danielle had chosen to put the ship down. Here and there the vast flat expanse was broken by the appearance of gentle mountain ranges on the far horizon, appearing as if they were perhaps fifteen or twenty miles away, but in the main this whole region of the planet was a quite flat desert. The ground underfoot was gravelly, a little rocky in places. Small dark reddish-brown boulders were strewn liberally all around, but there were also areas of very fine red oxide colored gravel that took the appearance in places almost of sand. She looked up. The sky was tinted with a reddish-blue hue, rendering it quite Earth-like and yet strangely alien in a subtle kind of a way, but from this vantage point it did in fact appear fairly normal to her. Here and there she could make out thin cirrus clouds, apparently quite high up in the atmosphere, moving slowly towards the east. She looked down once more at the small boulders beneath her feet, and on closer inspection noticed that they were coated in a thin layer of frost, although that seemed to be rapidly melting within the confines of Danielle's gravity/air envelope. Looking out from beyond the envelope, the edge of which she could see gently shimmering, with an almost water-like quality to it, as Danielle had said it would, she became aware that the frost seemed to be covering much of the rocks and some of the fine gravel, extending out in all directions. The planet must indeed be quite cold, if the little bit of atmospheric water that had vaporized from the polar regions had formed a frozen layer on the surface. She approached the edge of the envelope, and, remembering Danielle's warning about the need to remain inside, she gingerly extended her hand to touch the edge. It felt velvety smooth, with the quality of liquid in a way, but yet not. She extended her naked hand all the way through to the other side. Immediately she felt a bitter cold clamp against it like the jaws of a vice, as she experienced the temperature external to the envelope itself of around minus sixty degrees Fahrenheit. The cold was so extreme that it almost burned. Danielle had been right. After a few seconds she had had enough and pulled her hand back inside the protective warmth of the envelope once more.

CHAPTER 39

Revere sat alone in his cabin aboard *Eagle*. He had just commenced another cruise with a fresh load of cadets, each of which had joined his ship as eager youngsters, hopeful for a career with the United States Navy or the United States Coast Guard as junior officers. *Eagle* herself had sailed days earlier from Boston under the interim command of Lieutenant Commander Hackett, but Revere had been transferred aboard after *Wildcat* had made a pre-arranged rendezvous with her in the South Atlantic Ocean. The rendezvous itself had taken place just twenty three hours following Dawn's departure for Atlantis.

He had been writing the ship's log entries for the day, all the while amused at how even this simple act had changed so much over the centuries since he had begun performing such a task on a daily basis. For at one time, such as those years he had been master of the fishing schooner *Jawn Henry*, or later captain of the frigate USS *Connecticut*, the log had been an actual large notebook, a diary of sorts, which had to be filled out by hand with a quill pen and a bottle of ink. Now the log took the form of a computer terminal, sitting on top of his desk, into which he spoke via a microphone, the speech-to-text software doing the rest. Indeed he had noticed that over the period he had spent in the 21st century, the quality of his penmanship had somewhat declined. He glanced over at the chronometer mounted on the wall of the cabin. It was half-past eleven at night, and yet he wasn't in the least tired. He sighed. Everything aboard *Eagle* was so efficient, so clean, so easy to get perfectly correct, and yet there was a certain something he could not quite place but which he missed about life aboard his earlier commands. The soft glow and aromatic odor of the oil lamps to which he had been accustomed before his jump forward two hundred and thirty years to the world of instant light, instant heat, instant power, instant gratification, all at the touch of a button. The light in his cabin now was not at all unpleasant, he even had had dimmer switches installed along with soft yellow bulbs, that created something of the soft glow which he preferred at night, but yet the whole scene, that of the lights, the ship's log taking the form it did nowadays, the running water, the fully equipped bathroom, the telephone, the intercom, the television, the DVD player; it was all so, for want of a better word, sterile. There were times when he no longer felt quite as fully alive as he once had, existing in this artificial world, where few if any natural materials or problems for that matter presented themselves.

He felt at once at a loose end and also a sudden nostalgia for the past. He had thought that in order to indulge these feelings he had been entertaining of late he might devote some serious effort to writing something significant, perhaps even a novel. But about what should he write, exactly? However as he mulled the idea over, his mind wandered once more. He thought back to his conversation he had had with a senior naval officer, an Admiral Grierson, who had called him earlier that morning to inform him that Dawn had been sent away on a top secret mission and that he would not see her again for several months. Although, the admiral had added, in about a week he would be able to receive e-mail messages from her, transmitted directly to his ship, and would therefore be able to converse with her. At this point she would doubtless answer all of his questions, with the exception of course of those few that might still remain classified. In the meantime all that could be stated to him was that she was safe and well. For the next seven days her duties would continue to be secret, but following that, it was expected that much would be revealed. He allowed himself to think about her for a moment, about the nature of their initial meeting on the North Atlantic Ocean, how he had mistaken her for an enemy and had fired upon her ship. How he had lost his ship and his entire crew for his trouble. He envisioned her beauty, her intelligence, her intensity when working, the way she gave of herself, and yet at the same time she was possessed of an intensely feminine side, how she enjoyed from time to time the sweeter things in life. He truly loved her even more now than when they had first fallen for each other, in the scullery of his house on Boston's Beacon Hill, back in 1776. He smiled as he reminded himself that in reality he had fallen for her much earlier than that.

But once again his mind returned to the question as to what to write about. Thoughts of the American Civil War had briefly entered his mind, but this of course had all played out more than eighty years following 1776, the year he had left Massachusetts for the 21st century. What he knew of this event he had gleaned from historical accounts written by a variety of authors. He had not been entirely surprised to learn that the war had taken place, although accounts of the loss of life and destruction of property that had ensued as a result had been somewhat shocking to him. As he understood it, the conflict had evolved out of a relatively minor issue but had risen to encompass the slavery question, cotton exports from the southern states, chiefly to Britain, and cessation from the Union of a number of states to form a separate Confederated States of America, apart from the United States and overseen by its own government under President Jefferson Davis, located in the Confederate White House in Richmond, Virginia. Relations between the United States and the United Kingdom had also been strained during this period, the possibility of war between the two nations once more having reared its head, on several occasions. The politics of the war had proved to be immensely complex. Revere had even been quite surprised to learn that Confederate ships had been built in Scottish yards, and a not-insignificant number of Irish, Scottish, Welsh, and English seamen and soldiers had either been pressed into service, or even voluntarily made the journey across the Atlantic so that they could join with fighting for either the Union or the Confederate armies, although the British government had for its part remained officially neutral. Some had stayed on following cessation of hostilities, others had returned home. Slavery itself had also been something of an enigma to him. He had seen examples of it during his early life of course, but Massachusetts had abolished this vile trafficking in human beings very many years before the war itself. He had never really understood the reasons why the southern states had been so reluctant to relinquish this disgusting, backward, and blatantly racist institution, even despite the arguments that without it local economies would collapse. As it turned out they did in the years immediately following the end of the conflict, plunging the south into terrible poverty. But in time they were able to rebuild.

No, he decided. He would not focus on the Civil War. He entertained a certain degree of interest in the period but had no desire to dwell upon it. He had always cherished the ambition to write a perhaps semi-historically accurate story of sea-farers of old, based upon the demise of the Vikings of Scandinavia during the latter part of the 13th century following their occupation of parts of Scotland. This would be the subject matter for his writing project. He had always held a fascination for Scotland. Such a small and yet such an influential country as she had been over the ages. Absolute historical accuracy for Revere over the production of such a piece of work was not so much important to him as the simple act of producing a finished work on his own, from start to finish. He had often felt that each person who had lived a worthwhile life had at least one novel in him, or her. If he could discipline himself to write in a concerted manner over a significant span of time, this might be his.

But how to start? With personal computers and word processing being so available today in the early 21st century, not to mention their truly marvelous levels of advancement, as well as the oceans of information at the fingertips of almost anyone who cared enough to spend a few seconds looking, it should be positively easy. He tried to imagine explaining the situation in which he now found himself to one of his contemporaries should he ever be transported back to his own time, but had long since given up on the idea as utterly hopeless. There simply would be no common frame of reference. He stared at the blank screen of his computer, trying to think of a way to introduce a story. But he could not. Instead he decided to kick back for a little and switch on the television. Perhaps the diversion would help him clear his mind. When he hit the power button on his remote control device he found himself watching *Real Talk with Robert Valentine.* Valentine himself Revere enjoyed; the man was possessed of a keen sense of humor and a quick, intelligent wit. But why he would waste his time pursuing some of the activities he did, for the entire nation to witness, was beyond Revere. Here for example he was engaged in a skit known as *Robert's Q&A,* where Valentine would walk the streets of downtown Burbank or Los Angeles and stop passers-by at random in order to ask them some simple general knowledge question or other, based upon variously, the Constitution of the United States, a simple issue relating to global geography, or some aspect of contemporary American pop culture. Revere watched as Valentine walked along a sidewalk and stopped a woman who appeared to be in her late twenties.

"Excuse me, ma'am," Valentine asked her, as he approached with a hand-held microphone. Ma'am. Revere would never grow accustomed to addressing ladies one did not know well in this casual, almost flippant manner. But such was the way of the times.

"Excuse me, ma'am. Would you mind telling me who was the first President of the United States?"

Revere watched in abject disbelief at her vacant expression, which told him and all others watching that she was unfamiliar with the simple response required to correctly answer the question.

"Woodrow Wilson?" Her eyes conveyed a brief flash of hope, that perhaps against all odds she might actually have guessed the correct answer.

"No ma'am, I'm afraid not." Valentine smiled in his big and disarming manner. "Would you care to try again?"

"Uh . . . Richard Nixon?" She seemed genuinely confused.

"No ma'am. It was George Washington. Can you perhaps tell me this. How many stars are incorporated in the American flag?"

At that moment the camera panned onto a US flag flying from the roof of a nearby building.

"Uh, . . . I can't count the stars on that flag, it's flapping about too much in the wind."

Valentine stopped another passer-by, a man perhaps in his thirties, although he could have been older, Revere could not tell for sure as people now often looked young even into their fifties, an age that not so many managed to attain in the 18th century.

"Sir? May I ask you a couple of questions? Which countries border the United States?"

"Uh, Australia, oh, no, actually it's New Zealand, and . . . I'm sorry, I can't remember the other one."

Valentine spoke slowly and deliberately as he repeated the response to the camera. "New Zealand. A country that borders the United States."

"Yeah. I got it. You were hoping I'd say Puerto Rico, but it's a trick question. The other one is actually Guam. Right?"

Another woman was stopped. Perhaps also in her thirties.

"Could you tell me ma'am, through which country runs the Panama canal?"

"Hawaii?" The same vacant look in her eyes said it all.

"What is our nation's capital?"

"Chicago? No! New York! It's definitely New York. That I do know."

"In what country would the inhabitants speak Gaelic?"

"San Francisco?"

"What do the letters 'BYOB' stand for?"

"Uh . . . bring your . . . own . . . uh, uh, . . . bitch? Bring your own bitch!" With that she started laughing.

Revere switched off the set in disgust. How could people with such easy access to information, such as had never been seen before in all of human history entire, be so damnably ignorant? But then again, he mused, perhaps this ease of access, to virtually anything, was precisely the problem. Knowledge and goods of the most marvelous quality and craftsmanship came so easily now that people lacked motivation. Or anything even remotely resembling appreciation for all that they had. He sometimes felt like weeping for the future. What was to become of America if its young people kept on down such a road?

Perhaps the original purpose of his having switched on the television set had been realized after all. For suddenly he felt sufficiently inspired that he turned to his computer terminal and started typing.

CHAPTER 40

Lucus Planum, Mars, September 11, 2008.

Dawn was standing atop a small rock approximately one mile from the ship, staring out at the distant hills surrounding this part of the plain. The bubble had been expanded by now, over the course of no more than one hundred and sixty-eight hours, or one Earth week, to a radius of around a mile and a half further out from where she stood. And beyond its protective envelope she could see the atmosphere literally thickening as it underwent the compositional changes and increase in density as part of the terraforming process. It was also glowing and sparkling as if a giant planet-wide fireworks show were in progress, all the colors of the visible spectrum were continually flashing before her eyes in a light show so beautiful as to make the Aurora back on Earth seem like only a supporting act to this main event. Danielle had explained to her before all this had started that the visual disturbances were a consequence of the localized warping of space-time and the resultant effect on matter-energy inter-conversion. Dawn had been immensely impressed with the progress that Danielle had managed to orchestrate since their landing. However at first she had wondered why her presence here had been necessary at all. But as things progressed she had found that there had been several points now during the process which had required her to liaise with Hunt back on Earth, periodically appraising him as his 'person on the ground', so to speak, as to precisely what was happening, and then him having her, at his instruction making some modifications to Danielle's programming. She smiled at herself. Danielle. Danielle was of course simply a machine. Albeit a very sophisticated one. But already Dawn had psychologically anthropomorphized her—it—this computer which had ultimately been designed and programmed for taking *Vega* to Mars and commencing the task of terraformation, by a singular man back on Earth. Commander Garry Hunt, of Her Majesty's Royal Navy. A man who had been cognitively enhanced via the use of a selective pharmacological agent. But a man nonetheless.

But now Danielle was calling Dawn back to the ship via the wrist communicator with which she and Dawn were also able to talk with Hunt back on Earth, instantly using a warp field to transmit the carrier radio wave, so that there would not be the slightly more than three minute delay between her speaking from Mars and his receiving the message on Earth.

"Captain, I would like you to return to the ship. There is something I would like you to do. Thank you."

"Very well, Danielle. I am returning to the ship now."

Dawn took her eyes off the sparkling light show in the upper atmosphere and started walking back to the ship, over the hard and gravelly rocky brown terrain.

Twenty minutes later Dawn stepped inside *Vega*.

"Captain. I have just received news from Commander Hunt that you may now contact your husband. Please use the computer terminal and compose a message for him. You may share with him any information you wish, including details of your present location and a summary of how you arrived here."

"I may say anything at all? Nothing is classified?"

"That is correct, Captain. When you are finished, I will of course scan your message for any possible edits that may be required, but I do not anticipate that any will be necessary. Following that I will arrange for your message to be sent as e-mail via the warp-field modem."

Dawn sat down at the terminal, just as a blank screen appeared, ready for her to type her message to Matthew. She sat for a few moments, feeling a little like she had done in college when a term paper had been due, not quite sure how to start. But then a flash of inspiration came over her and she commenced typing.

Matthew,

I am sorry I have been out of contact for these last seven days however I am now at liberty to tell you all about what has been going on during this time. I hope you have been well and have not been too concerned about me. You won't believe where I am contacting you from. Matthew, at this moment I am on the surface of the planet Mars! Commander Hunt sent me here in a spaceship of his own design named *Vega* that he had engineers at Northrop Grumman construct and deliver to him to Atlantis in Antarctica. I set off one week ago and landed on the northern area of the plain of Lucus Planum, near the equatorial region of the planet. Commander Hunt and the ship's computer, Danielle, who can talk, and with whom I have been enjoying many fascinating conversations, have a scheme for terraforming the planet. That is, to render it suitable and stable for human habitation. The whole experience has been so utterly exciting and frankly incredible! I have actually been able to fly in space and see planet Earth from orbit. I have also orbited Mars and become the first human to set foot on the Red Planet! And Matthew, it's so beautiful here. Utterly desolate and uninhabited, of course. But very, very beautiful. Danielle tells me that the terraforming process will be complete within another month. And after having seen it go now for a week (an Earth week, that is, to avoid confusion Danielle maintains Earth-time here) I can confirm that it is indeed happening so very fast! It has to be seen to be believed. I have even been outside the ship and walked around on the surface, within a zone that Danielle has set up in a protective bubble (her term) containing breathable air and set at a suitable temperature and pressure, and with a gravitational field equal to that on Earth. But soon the whole planet will be like that. Once the process is complete you will be invited to come here too for a visit if you would like, and we can spend some down time here together. I know how interested and excited you are in astronomy, you will just love it. I will have to remain here for another month but we can communicate now by e-mail whenever you would like. Send your messages to my address at: <u>dawn.defaller@</u> <u>marsterraformproject.com</u>

I hope you are well and enjoying your trip.

Love you and miss you much,
D.

"When you are finished, Captain, just click on the 'Send' icon in the usual way. Or just tell me you are ready and I will send it for you."

Dawn looked over her message for another moment, and then hit the 'Send' icon. The words flashed from the screen.

It took only twenty-five minutes for Matthew's response to appear in her InBox.

Dawn,

I am very glad and relieved to hear from you and to learn that you are safe. However I must confess to finding myself astonished, not to mention nonplussed and utterly amazed on learning of your current whereabouts. I am of course aware of the moon landings that took place during 1969 through 1976 and so am fully cognizant that our species has by now mastered the art of traveling in space. But nevertheless I was unprepared for the news that you are now a resident of the planet Mars, if even only on a temporary basis. The idea of rendering another planet habitable to humans has before occurred to me. I had also wondered while still living in the 18th century as to whether Mars or Venus for that matter may in fact already be suitable for human habitation and indeed often pondered on this while observing the night sky through my telescope. But now I have a wife located on Mars and with whom I am engaged in correspondence. Please forgive my rambling on the subject but you must understand that this news has captured my imagination in a manner that little else could. I am aware of course that Commander Hunt has become very highly intelligent but despite this I still find myself dumbstruck at what is now possible using modern technology. I do hope however that he is taking proper care of you and that he has given due consideration to your safety during the course of the mission. I would consider it the utmost privilege to be able to make the journey to Mars to meet with you there, this would in fact be the culmination of my wildest dreams. But above all else I wish for you to return safely to me here on Earth when this mission has reached its conclusion.

To change the subject of my missive for one of a much more pedestrian nature; I have commenced the process of writing my first novel. At the moment I have only the first chapter completed. The intended story, semi-historically accurate, is based upon the Viking raids on Scotland during the 13th century, about five hundred years before my time. The ability of the Vikings to navigate at sea over long distances without the use of sextants, modern compasses, or chronometers, in primitive sailing ships has always been a subject with which I have found myself quite fascinated.

I am wondering if it might be possible for you to send me some photographs of your current location? I should very much like to see what the region of Lucus Planum in which you now find yourself looks like. I must confess to being a little worried for you, Dawn. Please above all else come back to me.

Your loving husband,
Matthew.

CHAPTER 41

Dawn was quite taken aback upon reading the latter part of her husband's email. Matthew? Writing a novel? She had never considered the idea that he would be interested in such a thing. She hoped that he would soon offer her the opportunity to read what he had written.

"Captain DeFaller."

"Yes Danielle? What is it?"

"I need you to be ready to accept some algorithms which I will momentarily send to the computer terminal. The task should be simple enough, and according to my estimate should take you approximately seven minutes to complete. But I will be unable to accomplish it without your help. After that, I would like you to harness yourself into your seat once more as we will be taking a brief flight into orbit so that you may see for yourself the state of the terraformation process. You may think of this as a sight-seeing tour, if you will."

Precisely seven minutes and thirty-five seconds later, much as Danielle had predicted, Dawn was strapping herself into her chair as Danielle was closing the ship's airlock and preparing to lift off from the surface. The computing task had indeed proven elementary. Danielle had simply sought Dawn's opinion on which specific colors of water resulting from different mineral mixtures being brought to the fore in various lake beds would appear most natural to the human eye. She apparently possessed no means of making such an assessment.

As the ship climbed gently but rapidly through the Martian atmosphere, which was already brighter and more given to subjecting the ship to occasional turbulent bumps, Dawn could tell already that it was thicker and denser than it had been just a week earlier when she had landed here. A few minutes later Danielle adjusted the ship to what felt like a more level pitch and announced that they had now achieved orbit at an altitude of one thousand miles and invited Dawn to unbuckle herself and take a look at the thus-far terraformed planet from this vantage point.

When Dawn stepped forward into the cockpit and looked out at what she saw her breath was taken away. From this point in high orbit, Mars appeared now not red, as it had seven days earlier, but blue. An Earth-like blue, with a dense oxygen/nitrogen atmosphere and earth-like weather patterns obviously visible. Danielle cut in, like a documentary narrator.

"Directly below us are the recognizably visible landmasses of Aonia Terra, Arabia Terra, Terra Meridiani, Tempa Terra, Sinai Planum, Solus Planum, and Tharsis. The lower-lying parts of the great plains of Chryse Planitia, Xanthe Terra, Acidalia Planitia and Vastitas Borealis are now large oceans. And the plain of Aram Chaos is now a large lake."

It was strange for Dawn to think of such a thing within the context of the planet having been virtually dry as it had been so recently, and yet it was now in possession of enormous bodies of water. And all of which had come into existence very rapidly indeed. Dawn could see that into these oceans flowed mighty rivers, coursing through Ares Vallis and Valles Marineres, the latter of course being the great Martian canyon system that at a length of approximately two thousand five hundred miles utterly dwarfed the Grand Canyon in Arizona back on Earth. Valles Marineres was as long as Continental Europe in fact, extending nearly one fifth of the way around the planet, and in places reached down below the surface a distance of over four miles.

"So what is your opinion so far of our work, Captain? How does Mars appear to you? Does the planet present a pleasing and natural visage?"

Dawn had to struggle to find the right words.

"It's beautiful, Danielle. Absolutely beautiful. You have all but achieved terraformation of Mars, and in a matter of days only. From what little I have read about this before, I had come to understand that at a minimum the project would have taken contemporary science at least one hundred years to achieve, perhaps even as much as one thousand. And it was not apparent, from mathematical, engineering, or even economic considerations that such a scheme would be practical. Or even possible. But if it had been possible, it would have represented by far the grandest project ever attempted in the whole of human history. But you have achieved it. And in days only."

If Danielle enjoyed the compliment being paid to her she certainly did not show it.

"The planet is now almost ready to receive photosynthetic bacteria."

Dawn indeed felt that the planet had become very beautiful. But as she looked out onto its marble-like appearance, she felt a sudden wave of depression falling over her. Human beings would soon come to these pristine new lands. They would quickly swell their numbers, and inevitably despoil the environment with their power struggles and politics, national boundaries, religious incompatibilities and intolerance, crime, pollution, toxic waste, greed, and war.

She peered down at the great bulging plain of Tharsis below, which would surely become a tourist attraction, as upon Tharsis sat a number of huge shield volcanoes, not unlike those in Hawaii, but a great deal larger, and very much older. Included in their number was the massive bulk of Olympus Mons, the largest known in the entire solar system, which rose to a height of over sixteen miles above datum, over three times the height of Mount Everest on Earth. She imagined how tourists might travel out to see this geological feature, perhaps even spend time hiking or camping there. She realized now that Mars would never again be peaceful and undisturbed. Her natural resources would in the very near future be exploited by giant corporate mining and drilling conglomerates, operating purely for profit, until eventually they too would approach the point of exhaustion. Perhaps by then humans would be looking for other planets to terraform, creating yet more environments upon which to reproduce and exploit for their own selfish ends.

Danielle interrupted Dawn's thoughts in her silky smooth, feminine voice.

"Captain, I would like to return the ship to the surface of Lucus Planum. Please once more harness yourself into your chair."

Dawn took one last look at the stunningly beautiful view of the now blue planet below.

"Yes Danielle. I-"

But her next statement was cut off by a sudden violent lurching of the ship, followed by a sense of spinning out of control. Dawn, not yet in her harness, was sent flying across the cabin. She came to rest head-first against a bulkhead. Fortunately she was able to pick herself up. Her head was bruised, but otherwise she seemed unhurt. She rushed across to her chair and was able to get her harness fastened around herself just before the second lurch that gripped the ship, even more violently than the first, as if a giant hand had grabbed a hold of the vessel and was shaking it from side to side.

"What the hell was that, Danielle?"

But Danielle did not answer. Dawn became more nervous.

"Danielle!"

The lights dimmed and from her chair she could see some of the instruments on the cockpit dash panel flashing off and on, indicating various altered states within the systems they were designed to monitor. There was a third lurch, but then this time the ship stopped spinning and seemed to start moving with an apparent sense of purpose, as if Danielle had regained control.

"Danielle?"

Finally Danielle responded.

"It appears we have been subjected to the same energy field that affected us momentarily upon initial landing on the planet. We are now apparently returning to the surface of Lucus Planum. As far as I can tell, Captain."

"As far as you can tell?"

"I am not currently in control of the ship, Captain."

Dawn was aghast. And a little frightened.

"Danielle? You are not in control? Then who is?"

"Insufficient data to make such a calculation, Captain. But the agency that is now controlling this ship is emanating from the surface of the planet and seems to be associated with the high energy field that has engaged with us. Its source is the southern polar region of the planet, however based on the ship's current speed and trajectory I compute that we are being returned to the same co-ordinates on Lucus Planum at which we landed earlier, Captain."

With that, Danielle went suddenly silent.

"Danielle? Danielle!"

But the ship's computer did not respond. All Dawn could do was sit in her chair and wait for *Vega* to land.

Approximately ten minutes later the ship made its final approach to the precise spot from which it had taken off earlier. But just as she was touching down, all the lights went out, leaving Dawn in gloomy darkness, in which she could see only with difficulty. As the vessel settled on the ground, she heard the engines power down and the life support systems shut off. The airlock opened, but this did little to alleviate the darkness as by now night was falling on this part of the planet, the sun having already set at these co-ordinates nearly an hour previously. Then everything went silent.

"Danielle? Danielle?"

But it was hopeless. Danielle would not answer. The ship lay lifeless. And apparently helpless.

Dawn felt an urge to get up out of her chair and move outside. As she stepped through the airlock, she felt a very noticeable difference in the quality of the air. There was also a quite strong breeze blowing from the north-west, and she estimated that the temperature was now at around sixty-five degrees Fahrenheit. The sky was quite cloudy too. In fact it looked as if rain might even be possible. She descended the steps and moved away from the ship. Strangely, despite Danielle's apparent non-operational status, gravity felt normal, as if she were on Earth. Perhaps Danielle was not entirely out of commission.

But Dawn was wholly unprepared for what happened next. For standing directly ahead of her, at a distance of some twenty-five feet, were three shimmering figures, each of which stood around twelve feet tall. One of the figures took a small step forward and a she felt a voice addressing her.

"Dawn DeFaller."

The voice seemed to be present more in her mind than her ears. And looking directly down at her was a human-like, but not quite human, face. For a moment she imagined herself caught up in some kind of nightmare, as if her brain was beginning to shut down and she was hallucinating. The voice addressed her again.

"Dawn DeFaller."

To her horror, her mind finally accepted the reality that she was not alone on this planet. This was no hallucination. Standing outside the ship were other, obviously alien beings. One of whom at least that could speak her language.

She felt herself losing control as she gave way to her rising and by-now intense fear. She heard herself scream.

Then everything went black.

CHAPTER 42

All at once a powerful calming feeling came over Dawn, as if the shock and the fear were suddenly lifted away, just as her consciousness returned. Perhaps it was some kind of telepathy, some kind of trick, but as she felt herself returning to her senses, she stopped screaming. The three beings kept their eyes silently fixed on her. She felt her ordinary persona rapidly reassert itself, and for a moment she started casting her mind around for anything that might be useful as a weapon. But the one who had spoken with her seemed to already anticipate this response.

"Dawn DeFaller. I acknowledge that our presence here is both unexpected and frightening to you, and our physical appearance may be unsettling. But please understand. We are here to converse with you only. We mean you no harm."

"Who are you?! Why are you here?"

"My name is Vari. These others here with me are Loki and Wotan. Together we represent the remaining old ones of the peoples of this planet. Please, come, and we can talk."

Vari stood before her, extended to his full size he was indeed around twelve feet tall, perhaps a little more, as were his companions. His body appeared strange to her, composed of neither corporeal matter nor pure light energy, but rather, something in between those two extremes. She noticed that all three figures gave off a soft greenish-yellowish glow. When Vari talked it was not at all clear to her whether he was actually speaking, or simply directly influencing her mind.

"We have taken the liberty of disabling your ship's computer, Dawn DeFaller. Although in the meantime we have taken over its function of ensuring optimal atmospheric composition, pressure, temperature, as well as a gravitational field strength equal to that on Earth. And please accept my apologies for hijacking your vessel's normal navigational mode while it was in orbit and forcing it to land here. But no matter. That will be put right later. But for now, it is our desire to converse with you."

Dawn felt finally safe enough and sufficiently at ease with the situation to approach Vari.

"Who are you?" she asked as she came within a few feet of him.

"As I said, I am Vari. Loki, Wotan, and I are the three surviving ancient ones."

Dawn straightened her back, craned her neck, and faced Vari directly. As if she were his equal.

"What do you want with me?"

Vari smiled. "Ah, that is much better. Your spirit is returning. But you know, it is not so much what we want with you, Dawn DeFaller. But rather, what do you want with this planet?"

"I came here in this ship at the behest of its designer in order to render this planet hospitable to human life."

"At the behest of Garry Hunt, yes?"

"You know Garry Hunt?"

Vari smiled once more.

"Dawn DeFaller, there is much I must share with you. You will understand better when I am finished. But before I do that, please first of all tell me, what think you of religious philosophy and doctrine as it currently exists on planet Earth?"

Under the present circumstances Dawn considered this an odd, peculiar sort of a question. Nor was she at all sure how to respond. But a moment later she surprised herself with the answer she was able to offer.

"Well, I am no expert on the matter, but it seems to me that there is a surprising degree of faith among the peoples of Earth at this point in our history. More especially now since we have made all kinds of scientific discovery that has cast considerable doubt on the validity of the major religious texts that exist on our planet."

"Those major religious texts to which you refer being, the Christian Bible, the Jewish Tanakh, and the Islamic Qur'an. Yes?"

He said this as if he could see directly into her mind.

"Well, yes, I daresay, but what we now know is that none of these texts agree, at least entirely, with current scientific dogma."

"And you accept this as an axiom?"

Dawn considered the question for a moment.

"Well of course. I mean for example, in the Bible the Earth is stated to be no more than ten thousand years old. But we know that it is much, much older than that."

Vari silently surveyed her features much as she remembered her father doing when she had been a young child.

"But you are assuming, are you not, that time has always flowed at the same rate, at least locally, on your planet?"

"Well of course it has. What does a statement like that even mean?"

"The famous scientist of the early 20th century, Albert Einstein, demonstrated that time itself is relative. And this in turn was based on the notion that the speed of light was a demonstrable constant, regardless of the spatial attitude or velocity of the observer. But what if I were to tell you that the speed of light has not been a constant, but instead, has been diminishing since the beginnings of the universe? If those circumstances were to hold true, then your science that has extrapolated linear time backwards into the past could well have over-estimated the age of your planet, perhaps even by as much as the discrepancy that exists between your people's scientific estimation of the age of your planet, and the age quoted in your major religious texts."

Dawn simply stared at Vari. She really wasn't at all certain she followed his line of reasoning.

"But in any event," Vari continued. "None of your major religious texts were intended to be taken as literal truth. They were written as allegorical interpretations of a phenomenon that lies quite beyond the human experience and therefore cannot be adequately described to your primitive intellects in any truly meaningful way. And you know, on Earth during ancient times, this was all quite acceptable and normal thinking. In fact, were your modern literal interpretations of religious texts, interpretations that are currently giving rise to so many problems for your human society at this time, to be espoused to peoples from Earth of two thousand years ago, these interpretations would be regarded at best with dumbfounded bemusement. You see, there is rather much a tendency among contemporary humans to assume that the peoples of Earth have always thought about religion, and God, for that matter, in largely the same manner as is currently imagined, despite the fact that human science has irrevocably altered the planet, and its peoples' view of it. Allow me to elaborate. Despite their technological advancement, the peoples of Earth now are more concerned with God than at any other time in their entire history. As such, there is much discussion and discourse, a great deal more in fact than there has ever been in the past. And yet, never has such discussion been more devoid of depth and perspective. It is as if the entire human race has failed to advance spiritually but instead has devolved in a retrograde manner to a much more child-like state. In the so-called Western world especially, with its rather unique and recent ideas of democracy and human rights, there exists now an unshakeable view that the Creator God must necessarily be included within the scope of these rights and is therefore by design, readily available to all, simply by virtue of their wishing it. Leaders of nations justify their decisions by stating that God has given His approval for their actions they are about to unleash, most especially when other groups are in consequence certain to be injured or even killed. But very few members of contemporary humanity have any awareness that in ancient times the concept of God was very unlike that held up as unassailable truth at present. And those few who do realize it either choose to remain silent on the issue, or else risk public ridicule. But those of ancient cultures understood that the very concept of the Divine was virtually unknowable within the context of ordinary human experience. I guarantee that such peoples would be astonished, regardless of their religious background or culture, if they were to be suddenly exposed to this modern human practice of religious fundamentalism, self-righteous piety, the certainty of being in possession of literal truth. It is of course the case that humans of all ages and epochs have sought a meaning and purpose beyond the drudgery and often pain and suffering of their daily lives. It has always been the case too that some have rejected religion. Contemporary humans are generally beset with the notion that this is a recent phenomenon, correlated with scientific and technological discovery and advancement, but in fact nothing could be further from the truth. But even such individuals, at all times in history, have sought meaning by substituting other pursuits, for example, music, public performance, or art. Indeed the musicians, artists, and actors of today are no different inwardly than at any other time in Earth's history. They are all seeking to fill a deep spiritual void that they feel within themselves."

Vari stopped talking, as if he were done for the time-being. Wotan picked up the narrative. But just as with Vari, it seemed as if he were communicating with Dawn telepathically rather than with actual speech, although as before, she could not be entirely certain.

"You are doubtlessly unaware Captain DeFaller, but approximately six thousand five hundred years ago, there existed within the ancient Aryan peoples certain populations who rejected the concept of a singular sentient God. Rather, they saw within all matter, both living flesh and inanimate material, an intangible non-descript but very real life force. As time proceeded, certain descendants of these Aryans had spread out to that part of Earth known to you as India. Many in contemporary India still believe in this life force, which they have dubbed *Brahman*. But nowhere in this cultural background will you find any evidence of attempts to speak directly with *Brahman,* as *Brahman* is not recognized as a conscious entity. Thus the idea of praying to *Brahman* and asking for help with or approval for one's endeavors is simply not done. Indeed even to propose such a course of action would be seen as madness. To such peoples *Brahman* is simply the force that binds and animates the cosmos."

"I see," said Dawn.

"I am not entirely convinced that you yet do, Dawn DeFaller, but I shall continue nevertheless."

Wotan peered down at her in a somewhat reproving manner.

"There were other ancient cultures that entertained similar concepts. For example, ancient China held to the view of the binding and animating but impersonal cosmic force to which they referred as the *Dao.* As with *Brahman,* one could not and would not even expect to converse personally with the *Dao*, any more than a contemporary human would expect to be able to converse with the force of gravity, or the forces that bind an atom and cause it to hold together. Such forces have no recognition of or interest in the daily minutiae of human existence or experience. Other peoples evolved their own words to describe this cosmic force. Some tribes in the Middle East spoke of *ilam.* From *ilam* was derived the word *ellu.* Indeed in ancient Israel, the Hebrew word for *ellu* was, and is to this day, *Elohim.* But even the ancient Israelites felt no personal connection with any creator God. There was only *Elohim,* or the recognition of that cosmic force which was holy, of being of God, so to speak."

Wotan momentarily stopped addressing her, as if to allow her a moment to digest all he had said, before resuming his monologue.

"Tell me, Dawn DeFaller, are you familiar with the story of Adam and Eve to be found in the Book of Genesis in the Christian Bible?"

Dawn responded to the question verbally, but it seemed as if Wotan had seen the answer in her mind before her lips had had the opportunity to utter it.

"Yes, of course."

"Indeed. Well, you know, almost every culture that either has existed on Earth or currently exists now, and certainly all of those of which modern peoples are aware, and several of which they are completely ignorant, have or had their own legends. Legends of a lost land regarded as a paradise in which all peoples at one point had the opportunity to reside for eternity. And once there they would have enjoyed a harmonious and peaceful existence. Things such as senescence, disease, and death would have been unknown. But in each and every such legend, a singular representative human or sometimes several or even whole groups of humans disobeyed a clear direction and the result was permanent ejection of the entire human race, for all time, from the paradise state. The story of Adam and Eve with which you are familiar is but one of very many such stories that have existed at one time or another over the whole span of human existence on Earth. But each and every one of these stories, without exception, has been intended only as allegory. They are not and were never intended to represent an accurate account of a series of actual events. They are only myths. The account of the Creation with which you are doubtless familiar too is also such. It was never intended to be taken as a factual account. But this is where modern human science misses the essential point, as it concludes that such accounts cannot be true. You see, Dawn DeFaller. Such stories were only ever intended to possess allegorical significance as to the nature of humanity and the relationship between humanity and the Divine. For the specifics of the literal Creation of the cosmos and the Earth and of human beings themselves is simply beyond the ability of people to understand. It lies beyond human ken, and simply cannot be adequately related. Indeed no less so now than at any time in history. The main message underlying religion, a message that was recognized several millennia ago, in fact, was the idea that only those who shed such things as self-absorbance, selfishness, and greed will ever find peace and spiritual tranquility. It is ironic in an age when human beings have never been in possession of more knowledge than at the present time, but yet they increasingly experience terrible problems born of these negative personality traits that all religions of the world have counseled all peoples to eliminate. All religious traditions present on Earth at this time agree with this axiom. For example; Buddhism, Confucianism, Jainism, and Daoism. As well as the more latter monotheistic faiths; Judaism, Christianity, and Islam. Each has its own version of truth as well as its own version of myth, and yet none possesses all the answers. But they all agree on the one principle that religion is not and has never been a matter of empirical legalism, which, no matter how earnestly pursued, will contribute precisely nothing to the elimination of suffering, pain, and death. Do you see my point, Dawn DeFaller?"

Wotan fixed Dawn in a hard constant gaze, the way one might when attempting to train a dog. She craned her neck and looked into his face.

"Yes. I do believe so."

He said nothing, but continued staring at her, as if he were probing her mind for a confirmation of her verbal response. But presently he seemed satisfied, for then he stepped back, and Loki moved forward and took his place. A moment later he commenced speaking.

"But let us focus on the monotheistic religions, those being, of course, Judaism, Christianity, and Islam? You possess a basic understanding of each?"

"Yes."

"Good, for that will assist in my discourse. Monotheism, or belief in a singular sentient creator God, as a concept first arose approximately two thousand eight hundred years ago as you would understand it. In the first instance this belief system was not viewed seriously by many, but in time, monotheism established itself as the principal religious philosophy of the peoples of Earth. The Israelites were the first to attempt to present their deity, Yahweh, as the sole representation of the ultimate. In order to assist with the promulgation of this belief system, a creation story, the story of Adam and Eve, was devised."

Loki stopped for a moment as if to assess Dawn's state of readiness for his story. He seemed satisfied, and continued.

"The story of course is one with which you are familiar. At the beginning of time, the first created human being, or *adam* in Hebrew, arose to discover that he was in the Garden of Eden, also a creation of Yahweh. Now Eden was a beautiful place, including a beautiful proto-river, which was the source of the Tigris, the Euphrates, the Pishon and the Gihon. The rest of the Earth was animated by these rivers coursing out of Eden. Adam, a man, had been created by Yahweh from simple and abundant substances taken from the Earth itself, and was the only human being present in Eden at that time, although there were also a variety of created animals. As the only human being in Eden, Adam was thus the de facto steward of the land. He was in a position where he could have chosen an easy and plentiful life in this land of paradise, where there was no pain or death, nor suffering of any kind. But planted in the middle of Eden, were two trees, those being the Tree of Life, and the Tree of the Knowledge of Good and Evil. And unfortunately, also residing in Eden was a talking serpent, a snake that within the context of the story represents the concept of antagonism of Yahweh's will, or evil as you may more comfortably call it. Because the serpent had the power of speech, he would talk with Adam from time to time. But despite the companionship of the animal, Adam found himself growing lonely. Yahweh of course recognized this, and so one day, as Adam was in the garden, Yahweh gently breathed upon Adam, thus causing him to fall into a state of unconsciousness, a deep sleep if you will. Yahweh then cut open Adam's chest and removed one of his ribs, which he used to create a female human companion for Adam. Adam was delighted with his new companion when he met her for the first time. He named her after the Hebrew *Havva*, or *Giver of Life*, thus calling her Eve. You are familiar with this story, Dawn DeFaller?"

"Yes I am. I expect that you would find most contemporary adult human beings to be so."

Loki almost smiled as he peered at her. She still could not shake the strong feeling that he was reading her mind.

"But please allow me to continue. The myth of Adam and Eve is borrowed from another Upanishadic legend of a singular and lonely man who decides to remedy his unfortunate state by cutting himself into two separate halves. One of the halves grows to become a complete female companion, he himself as the remaining half grows to form a whole man once more. So you see that the creation story is nothing more than legend. Each version that has ever existed shares many common traditional elements with the others. The creator fashions Adam from abundant base elements to be found on the Earth. Adam is placed in an environment replete with two sacred trees, four rivers that together flow out to the whole earth, and a serpent with human-like understanding and the power of speech. Adam grows lonely and so a female companion, Eve, is fashioned for him. And as you know, Adam and his companion were forbidden to eat any fruit produced by the Tree of the Knowledge of Good and Evil. But the serpent skillfully deceives Eve in debate over this issue, thus persuading her to eat some of the fruit of the tree. Eve then persuades Adam to do likewise. In anger and as punishment, Yahweh banishes Adam and Eve from Eden for ever. And thus humanity, at least for the duration of its time on Earth, loses its chance for experiencing a perfect existence. Indeed, from that point forward men are to toil and scratch a meager living from the soil, women are to bring forth children into the world in pain and suffering. But the purpose of the creation myth is only to assist human beings to fully appreciate what they are in the spiritual sense, and in what direction their lives should be headed. To help them make sense of such issues as: for what ultimate reason is life punctuated with back-breaking labor, emotional and physical pain, agonizing childbirth, disease, and death? Why do human beings feel so very alone and separated from one another?"

Loki stopped for a moment once more.

"Do you understand, Dawn DeFaller?"

"Yes. You are saying that the creation stories that human beings have related to one another down the generations are only allegorical and should be treated as such, rather than interpreted literally."

She looked up at him, hoping that he would be satisfied with this response.

"Yes indeed."

At this, Dawn felt a sense of relief.

"However a very large number of contemporary Christians, especially in the Western world, take the story to be an entirely accurate and literal account of the original sin that plunged humanity into its present state. But this entirely interpretive ideology was first proposed by Saint Augustine of Hippo during the early part of the 5th century. This was never recognized by traditional Jewish nor Orthodox Christian traditions in the ancient world. But modern humans do have a tendency to view these stories and myths from the point of view of knowledge of subsequent historical events. They also fail to appreciate that their beliefs as they currently stand are emphatically and qualitatively not the same as those of the ancients, and because of this they misinterpret the meaning of ancient texts. Indeed, contemporary Western society embraces the principle of reason and judgment, and because of this, many read the Christian Bible as if it were a literal account of human origins and history. But you know, until quite recently, in historical terms, both Christians and Jews maintained that it was neither desirable nor even possible to interpret the holy texts in this manner. The story of the Garden of Eden as related in the Book of Genesis is merely a metaphorical account of the early stages of development of the human race. In Eden, Adam and Eve represent the gestational state of humanity. They have yet to grow up, and the chief function of the serpent is to act as a guide, showing them, that is, the human species entire the difficult and painful road to maturity. Indeed; to become familiar with suffering and desire, to recognize that both are inextricably linked, to become acutely aware of one's own mortality, these are all ultimately inevitable consequences of existence within the human condition. In the principal players of our story we see representations of various faces of the human being. Eve represents the burning desire within humans for freedom from a regulated, inhibited existence, coupled with the constant and insatiable need for more knowledge. The serpent represents the tendency to question authority, to mistrust, and to rebel, especially against that which is in humankinds' own best interests. And in Adam is embodied the spirit of apathy and the inherent reluctance of human beings to accept responsibility for their actions. And thus within the paradigm of the human condition, knowledge is bound up with both good and evil, which are thus linked and inseparable. Hence the story reflects the manner in which great knowledge can promote tremendous benefits but at the same time can promulgate terrible harm. But the fall of Adam and Eve is not a disaster that has literally befallen humanity as many today believe. The darker side to human nature is an essential component of being, which facilitates such essential features for survival as ambition, aggression, competitiveness, even jealousy. Virtually all of humanity's greatest works are based upon these elements, and could not have been otherwise achieved."

Loki peered at Dawn once more, as if to see how she had absorbed all that he had said. It seemed for a moment he might ask her a question, but then he simply continued. His narrative became a little more negative in its flavor.

"However, be that as it may, modern humans have nevertheless reached a crisis point. They have become more sectarian and argumentative over minor points of theology than at any time in their history. They argue vehemently about trivial matters that are impossible to prove one way or another. Many, especially the most highly educated of your time, have become incapable of giving serious consideration to any new idea or concept because they believe that they already know everything. In their self-importance and pride, their sneering chauvinism, their desire to display the imagined superiority of their own intellects, they cannot accept any kind of reasoned or constructive critique. They display inappropriate concern for their own reputations, and often use their power and influence over others in a manner that may only be described as weak and contemptible. Now I will not deny that human achievement has reached dizzying heights. But unfortunately, many of these heights represent only the height of evil. For example, the Second World War demonstrated human abilities and propensities for violence and mayhem as never before, which of course ended with the detonation of two atomic bombs over the Japanese port cities of Hiroshima and Nagasaki. This ended the war, but also underlined the nature of human beings to destroy themselves. The atom bomb was a brilliant and crowning technological achievement, but in its use, humanity has demonstrated itself to be incapable of governing its aggressive tendencies. What say you, Dawn DeFaller?"

Dawn could only respond with the stock answer to which she was familiar.

"The atomic bombs dropped on Hiroshima and Nagasaki did end the war, and had they not been used, many more lives may ultimately have been lost."

"Then consider this. Approximately six million Jews were murdered in concentration camps and at other locations on the order of the Nazi government of Germany during the war years. How does this support the notion of human progress?"

Dawn remained silent.

"Indeed to prosecute their genocidal aims, agents of the Nazi government took full advantage of modern industrial age technology. Examples would include the well-developed roads and railways, management and bureaucratic processes, the pharmaceutical and chemical industries. Concentration camps were set up and run as if they were factories, but factories in this case producing only death. Nationalist fervor, mistaken for patriotism, energized the German populace to such an extent that all Jews had to be expelled, or exterminated, within the framework of a kind of perverted and deviant social planning project in which each and every member of society had to be reduced to the lowest common denominator of a singular ethos."

"But the Nazi era was an exception," Dawn protested. "Nothing quite like it has ever happened before, and the hope is that nothing like it will ever happen again."

"Nothing like it will ever happen again? Are you so sure and certain of your future, Dawn DeFaller? Humanity's future? Look to your own time. Your planet is experiencing an ever-burgeoning growth of religious fundamentalism. And the fundamentalists that this creates are proving themselves quick to condemn anyone who holds even just moderately different theological views as being at hazard with God. Many Christian fundamentalists consider that those of the Jewish and Moslem faiths are headed for eternal perdition. Jewish and Moslem fundamentalists often espouse a similar but opposing stance. And many fundamentalists from all three groups regard Hinduism, Daoism, Jainism, and Buddhism as false religions. The fundamentalist sees his or her own religious doctrine as the only true faith, while all others are erroneous or worse."

"But is all of that necessarily a bad thing? I mean, does it really matter to which religious doctrine a particular individual holds?"

Loki pondered on the question a moment.

"Fundamentalism is invariably fiercely reductive. In many parts of the world, Moslem fundamentalists have succeeded in bringing down lawful governments. And often, within their number, may be found extremists, bent upon wreaking terrorist acts on society. But their attempts to defend the traditions which they hold so dear invariably leads to grotesque distortions of their central tenets, tenets which are based not really upon scripture, but upon such values as love for ones fellow creatures, tolerance, consideration, humility, charity, and such like. Instead the fundamentalist focuses only on pure reading of scripture, a purpose for which scripture itself was never intended, as I have attempted to explain to you. The fundamentalist also invariably adopts an extremely selective stance when conducting such readings, while encouraging others to do likewise. For example, Christian fundamentalists are often to be found reading and quoting from the New Testament Book of Revelation, and are often deeply excited by its depiction of the tribulation of the so-called End-Time period. They also consider that they and they alone are privy to the details of precisely when and how these events will unfold. But there are many other verses to be found in Christian scripture that speak very differently. The New Testament Sermon on the Mount is an excellent example, in which the Christian Savior encourages His followers to live in peace, to refrain from sitting upon others in judgment, to love their enemies, and to turn the other cheek when wronged. The fundamentalists of the Jewish tradition have a tendency to focus on the Deuteronomist sections of the Old Testament, but what of the direction that exegesis should bring one to charity? Islamic fundamentalists focus almost exclusively on the violent and aggressive suras of the Qur'an. But they ignore the calls for peace and tolerance, often citing the principle of abrogation by way of justification. Far from fighting in the interests of the Divine, fundamentalists are in fact drawing away from the Divine. They preach of such absolutes as *Family Values, Islam, The Holy Land,* as if they were earthly representations of the sacred. But these things are purely human and historical phenomena, and thus the fundamentalist is guilty of idolatry. And, as so often happens, the idol which they worship demands that its worshippers do away with everything and anything that is not in perfect agreement with its perceived position."

Loki then faced Dawn once more, but as he did so his demeanor grew visibly stern. Gone was his relaxed, almost friendly air of seeming nonchalance. When next he spoke the voice she heard in her head had become clearly more accusatory in its tone, bordering almost on the hostile.

"Dawn DeFaller. It is our desire that as humanity's representative, you will now answer to us, as His representatives, for the failings of your species. He has laid specific charges against all of humanity, as follows: Failure to follow His laws as laid down by Him, Rammsihaar, the Architect and Creator of the universe and all things within. Failure to worship Him in a rational and practically meaningful manner. Failure to oversee the planet provided for your species with due care and attention. Failure in your species' role as stewards over all other living things existing upon that planet. Religious division. Religious extremism. War. Wanton genocide. Wanton xenocide. Empire Building. Excessive pride."

His words came across as harsh. Severe.

"What? What do you mean?"

"You have been brought here to answer for the crimes and offenses of your species against the Creator, known to us by His one true name of Rammsihaar. We as His Guardsmen will hear your pleas and explanations. We will consider the merits or otherwise of your statements. But be advised. If you fail to convince us of the merits of allowing your species to continue inhabiting your planet, Earth, as your species has named it, you and all other members of your species will be exterminated in His name, like the infestation that you have become. And so it shall be done."

Dawn was shocked and dumbfounded. But she had only a few seconds before the formal proceedings commenced. This time Wotan spoke. But as he did so, it appeared to Dawn that a newsreel movie was playing before her eyes, but one which followed his statements, as if he were narrating while the crimes of humanity were laid out before her. She saw images of Hitler's *Schutzstafel,* or Waffen SS, marching across Europe, subjugating entire cities, and of course hunting down all Jews, wherever they were to be found, rounding them up, and herding them off into trains to be taken to concentration camps where many of them would be murdered, often in the most awful manner imaginable. Some were forced to watch as SS men hacked off their fellows' arms with machetes, doused them in gasoline, and then set them on fire, finally releasing them to run screaming and shrieking in agony down the street, before death took them. Next came images of those thousands of souls murdered by Josef Stalin in one of his many purges, followed by massacres of the Hutus in Rwanda, the Chinese in Indonesia, and the Chinese citizens of Nanking suffering death at the hands of the Japanese Imperial

Army. She witnessed the handiwork of *Madame Guillotine* during the French Revolution, the cries of children burned to death at Chechnya, the death-throes of the victims of the World Trade Center attacks in New York City.

Vari spoke.

"Your species, despite all commands to the contrary, engages in endless, meaningless, and mindless genocide. You are cruel and murderous. You repeatedly visit holocaust upon your fellow humans, and always in His name, as if even in your wildest dreams He would condone or wish or command this. What say you, Dawn DeFaller? How do you answer this charge?"

Dawn remained silent for a moment, not quite sure how best to proceed. She had to deal with the fact that she was rather shocked. But then some ideas started to flow.

"Our species is capable of great violence, that much is true. But we have also achieved much that is good. Consider advances in modern medicine. Public health. Our efforts to feed, clothe, and house our ever-burgeoning population. Our efforts to bring recognition of individual human rights to those in our world who are oppressed by their respective governments. Western ideas of democracy. Freedom of expression. Freedom of speech. Civil rights. Presumption of innocence until proof of guilt is ascertained by a jury of one's peers, within the context of an adversarial system. And in the Western world at least, violence is perpetrated against those who first engage in violent acts themselves. I must argue that despite our being imbued with a potentially violent nature by our Creator, those of us in mainstream society in the West have been able to overcome this tendency in a constructive and mutually beneficial manner."

Dawn stared at her three inquisitors as she responded, but they seemed not to be swayed by her answers. Wotan took up the line of questioning.

"The manner in which humans now worship the Creator has risen to levels of fanaticism not ever seen before, not even within the continent of Europe during the dark ages of mankind, with its many burnings of alleged witches and heretics. Many at this present time are ready to destroy, maim and kill in His name. Even to immolate themselves, by various acts of selfish lunacy, such as witnessed in New York City on September 11th, 2001, or at the Kingdom Center in Riyadh but a short time ago. The famous words of Joel Moody have never been as true as at the present time:

Men of generous culture or of great learning; women of eminent piety and virtue from the humble cottage to the throne have all been led out for matters of conscience and butchered before a mindless rabble lusting after God. Their limbs have been torn from their bodies, their eyes gouged out, their flesh mangled and slowly roasted, even their children have been barbarously tortured before their eyes. And all in the name of religious opinion.

Tell me, Dawn DeFaller, do you seriously imagine that He is in any way impressed with this outrageous behavior? Are you not aware that destruction of human life in His name is viewed, without exception, as the most heinous of crimes?"

Dawn responded with a ready robustness.

"I for one have never believed that any Deity would be impressed with murder and mayhem carried out in His name. Although it has to be said that the major religious texts in the contemporary world do include passages which urge the faithful towards acts of violence, especially against those which the texts themselves deem unworthy of life. For example, according to the Old Testament of the Christian Bible, in the Book of Exodus if I am not mistaken, one will find the clear command that the faithful shall not suffer a witch to live. This command has given rise over the ages to the execution of many women, and even a number of men, by being burned to death. One can scarcely imagine a fate more awful. And do not certain verses of the Qur'an, the Islamic holy book intone that there will be no peace in the world until the Jewish people have been utterly annihilated?"

Once again, Vari, Wotan, and Loki seemed unimpressed with this answer. They betrayed no emotional response whatsoever upon hearing it. Dawn could only guess as to what they might be thinking. Wotan simply continued with the prosecution.

"The planet Earth is presently suffering in a state of pollution unknown at any time in its previous history. Your science of organic chemistry has created tens of thousands of compounds that are now present in the environment in varying degrees of concentration, many of which act as toxins and poisons to all living things. Regulation and understanding of many of these compounds are hopelessly inadequate. Even your food is polluted to ever-greater extents. Crude petroleum is being extracted by drilling and utilized at ever greater and greater rates. Damaging oil spills are repeated occurrences, causing great distress to sea and coastal creatures. Radioactivity is omnipresent and ever-increasing, in many forms, such as the ether net, cellular telephones, radio and television waves. Proportionally speaking, more and more of you suffer from cancers than at any time in the past. Your protective ozone layer is being depleted, subjecting your species to exposure to ultraviolet and cosmic radiation. Your species is slowly poisoning its own environment. If this process is allowed to continue you will become extinct within the ensuing three hundred years."

"But once again, our species has been imbued with the intelligence and ability to question and investigate what we are, and to attempt to improve our lives through applied study, science, and engineering. We are not perfect and it is inevitable that we have made, and will continue to make mistakes. But this is what we are. What you have described lies at the very core of our nature. It is the way we were created."

"So you cannot help yourselves acting and behaving in the ways that you do, despite commands to the contrary emanating from the Creator Rammsihaar Himself?"

Dawn hesitated before answering.

"I suppose so, yes. What else can I say really?"

Wotan's next question seemed a little odd to Dawn.

"Dawn DeFaller. Given the unimaginable vastness of the cosmos, do you imagine that there might be life forms on other planets with a level of intelligence and abilities similar to your own species? In this or any other galaxy, and/or time-frame? Present company being excepted, of course."

"Perhaps. I would not rule out the possibility."

"And yet, to your knowledge, you have never been visited or contacted by any other species?"

"As far as I am aware, but I really cannot say."

"And why do you imagine that might be so?"

"Well, I would guess that distances are too great to traverse. Other civilizations may exist but may be unaware of our existence. Or they may exist, relative to humanity, only in the distant past, or the distant future. But I really do not know."

"What do you suppose happens upon death? Do you believe that there exists a human soul or spirit? And that this spirit or soul persists beyond the end of the existence of the corporeal body? Do you believe in conventional notions of heaven? Or hell? Or purgatory?"

"I have not devoted much thought to the issue."

"You should. Although might I suggest that you forget about the conventional religious texts and instead utilize your own wits and mind. All of the salient information is to be found preprogrammed there, as in all humans, indeed, as in other sentient animals. Humans are peculiar in that some members of your species have usurped this programming and developed some exceedingly absurd ideas, whereas others have not. A phenomenon incidentally which is not to be found in other earthbound species. It is indeed a consequence of your higher intelligence levels, but may also prove to be your eventual undoing."

Dawn was beginning to become a little impatient. She addressed Wotan impetuously.

"Why do you choose this time to bring up all of these issues? Why do you address all of your questions to me in particular?"

"Because, Dawn DeFaller, your species has discovered the secret of travelling through time and space. This you know. And you are the specific member of your species to come here to this planet. If you are allowed to continue to exist, you will inevitably spread your culture first of all throughout the solar system, and eventually the galaxy entire. Indeed you are already in the early stages of transforming this planet into a habitable environment for humans, a process that we have thus far chosen not to interrupt, and which continues as I speak. It is precisely because of this that we question you, and, in the process, attempt to divine the deeper meaning behind the fundamental animating forces that drive you."

Vari then spoke once again.

"Dawn DeFaller, we have heard your testimony. We will now retire to consider our verdict. Please await our return."

Vari, Loki, and Wotan's bodies appeared to coalesce into a singular ball of pure glowing energy, and then faded away into nothingness. A moment later it was as if they had never been. Dawn found herself waiting, quite alone, as if this whole episode had been a dream. But approximately eight minutes later, they returned, in a manner much as the reverse of the process by which they had departed. When their bodies had reformed, Vari addressed Dawn once more.

"Dawn DeFaller, we have considered the responses you have given to our questions. Our response to you is this. You must rescue your species before it is too late. The man who sent you here to us, Garry Hunt, was quite correct in surmising that there existed a civilization on your planet preceding ancient Sumer, on the continent that you know as Antarctica. It was within this civilization that the one original and true philosophy was recorded and distributed. Although a written copy of it was many centuries later discovered by the Ancient Greeks and hidden from all humanity as the Hellenized texts. A sign which will direct you to the still-extant remains of this record now exists in the form of a tablet to be found in a very specific location within the Borobudur temple, underlying a panel of stone decorated with a very specific design. Before it is too late, you must locate this tablet and follow the directions that you will find inscribed upon it. We will provide you with details of the appearance of the stone panel that you must locate. To this end I have programmed your ship's computer with a likeness of the design borne by this panel, under which the tablet lies. You must locate the panel at the temple which bears this specific design and recover the tablet lying underneath."

Vari's next statement somewhat took her off guard.

"I must also warn you of Garry Hunt's desires to rule the planet."

"Rule the planet. What do you mean?"

"Garry Hunt entertains quite serious designs upon global domination. Soon his moves to that effect will become apparent to you. Be advised that if he succeeds in carrying out his plans, utter catastrophe will befall the world and your species will face total destruction."

Dawn didn't answer.

"And consider this. Make use of your husband. Listen carefully to what he has to say, and consider his advice from different angles. His origins from within another time bestow upon him several advantages that modern humans almost without exception are lacking, although he himself is unaware of this special talent. Travel to the Borobudur in the company of your husband. But refrain from discussing with him the deeper reasons for your journeying there. This will keep his mind more pure and receptive, and ready for the tasks that you will face."

Each of the beings regarded Dawn carefully for a moment longer, and then once more they slowly coalesced and faded out.

Dawn felt in no doubt that her audience with Vari, Loki, and Wotan, the apparently self-styled Guardsmen of Rammsihaar, had come to a conclusion.

CHAPTER 43

D awn awoke to find herself lying on the couch inside the main cabin of the ship. Danielle was addressing her in gentle soothing tones.

"Captain. I am sorry to waken you. But we have arrived back on Earth. I am engaged in the final phase of landing at the base in Atlantis."

"What? How long have I been sleeping? What happened? Where is Vari? Where are the Guardsmen?"

Danielle remained silent for a moment, as if she did not understand Dawn's question.

"I am unaware of that to which you are referring, Captain. I can report that you returned to the ship after an absence of thirty seven minutes and fourteen seconds, during which time you were scouting the surface of the planet. On your arrival back with the ship you contacted Commander Hunt and he informed you of a change of plan in that it was now no longer necessary for either yourself or this ship to remain on the surface of Mars as the terraformation process had now achieved chain reaction status, a phenomenon that he had failed to anticipate, but which was most pleasing to him. So he ordered you home. Through me you commenced the return flight to Earth and then you decided to sleep, which you have been doing until I woke you but a few moments ago."

Dawn was nonplussed. Had she been away from the ship for only thirty seven minutes? It had seemed like much longer.

"But, Danielle, what about the beings I encountered. Vari. Loki. Wotan. They introduced themselves as the Creator's Guardsmen. I was talking with them, for a substantial period of time."

Danielle was silent for a moment.

"Captain," she finally replied. "I reiterate that you were away from this ship for thirty seven minutes and fourteen seconds. And during that entire time I monitored your every action. You were alone. At no time did you interact with anyone, except me. I can replay the recording of your actions during your time away from the ship if you would like."

"Please do so."

Danielle played a recording that showed Dawn leaving the ship as she remembered, but instead of her strange meeting, she simply seemed to have spent the time wandering around and looking about. Just as Danielle had said, a little over half an hour later she had returned to the ship, answered a call from Hunt, and then instructed Danielle that they would be leaving and returning to Earth. Then she lay down and slept, until Danielle had wakened her upon re-entry into the Earth's atmosphere. There was absolutely no sign of Vari or the other Guardsmen, or of her inquisition. She sighed. Her interaction with the Guardsmen had been real, of that she was certain. It had not been a dream or a hallucination. All she could surmise was that perhaps at some point Vari had lifted her out of time, so to speak. Placed her in some kind of bubble where time did not flow but instead stood still. And then later, returned her to the normal flow of time upon the conclusion of their interaction with her, in such a manner as to render the whole episode invisible to Danielle. Her experiences with warp field technology had taught her that such things were indeed entirely possible. She thought about this for a while, but then concluded, especially after thinking of Vari's final warning, that she would not relate anything of the latter to Hunt when she would be meeting him once again in just a few minutes. She did however retrieve from the on-board printer a hard copy of the design described to her by Vari, of which, tellingly, Danielle apparently had no knowledge. She glanced at it briefly. It resembled some sort of intricate stone carving from the ancient world. She folded it carefully and secreted it in her clothing.

Moments later the ship slowly descended into the large chamber in Atlantis from where it had taken off just over a week previously and effected a soft landing on its pad. When the engines powered down, Danielle opened the airlock, and Hunt stepped aboard.

"Captain DeFaller! Welcome home! And I am very glad that you could return sooner than expected!"

"Commander Hunt. I did not expect to see you again so soon. I have to report that your project to terraform Mars has proceeded already to a point that I can only describe as marvelous and incredible. It truly has to be seen to be believed."

"Our project, Captain," he corrected her. "You have been quite deeply involved in the whole affair at least up until this point. But please, you must be exhausted after your journey. Walk with me to your room which has been prepared for you where you can rest and freshen up."

The thought of a proper rest did sound appealing to her. She started to follow him down a corridor, away from the ship which was by now in the process of being stowed inside its bay, the roof already having completely closed over it.

"But tell me. As the first human being to have set foot on the Red Planet, what were your initial impressions?"

She hesitated for a little, thinking of the Guardsmen, and how they had obliged her to face an inquisition. She also remembered how they had left her with a dire warning of the consequences should she fail in her present mission back here on Earth. Foremost in her mind too was Danielle's failure to have made any record of her ever having met these beings. She clung tightly to her resolution to avoid any discussion of her involvement with them.

"Captain?"

Dawn was jolted back into the present.

"I am sorry, Commander. I think I am actually quite tired. Mars was quite simply stunningly beautiful. More especially after the terraformation process got under way. The planet was also most fascinating from the point of view of its geography. I think in time Mars will make a very fine home for future settlers who journey there. I could not help but notice that when I first arrived the soil was clearly a reddish brown color, with a pinkish-brown sky. But when Danielle—the ship's on-board computer—took me up into orbit for a sightseeing tour, the planet appeared blue, much like Earth. And when we landed again I was able to step outside wearing nothing more than the clothes I have on now, and breathe normally, in a comfortable temperate environment."

They arrived at Dawn's room. Hunt opened the door for her and bade her enter. He then told her she may remain there as long as she pleased. When she was ready, he would arrange for her to travel home once more to Boston.

CHAPTER 44

To Dawn, sitting at home in the den at the house on Boston's Beacon Hill, so soon after her recent experiences felt a little peculiar. To be surrounded by that which was thoroughly normal and familiar, immediately following her brush with that which was truly fantastic and out of this world, left her with a sense that she was not on an entirely even keel. And in aside to all that, try as she might, she could never quite get used to the idea that this house had been Matthew's, centuries before she had been born. She had of course experienced the house briefly as it had been in 1776, the first time she had entered it, in fact. And it was also quite true that it had not changed so very much in the intervening period, other than having been modernized.

But she was struck with the feeling that she had witnessed already more than any singular human being should. Perhaps her recent conversations with Vari, Loki, and Wotan had left her unsettled. She also felt an inexplicable but strong compulsion not to discuss her experiences with these beings with anyone. Not even with Matthew, at least not for now. She could not say precisely why she felt this way. The feeling was not born out of a sense of secretiveness, for such was not a natural state for Dawn. Perhaps Danielle's insistence that the meeting had never taken place had left her feeling that others may judge her to be mentally unsound. She would of course discuss her impressions of Mars itself with

Matthew, and show him all of the photographs that she had taken using the camera aboard *Vega,* as well as discuss the workings of *Vega* herself, and the flight in space, and the terraformation of the planet. But a little voice in the back of her head told her not to touch on the subject of Vari, Loki, and Wotan with another living human being.

The news that was emanating from the television set in the corner of the room should have been truly amazing to her, but she found herself unfazed by continual reports of initiation of a process that would lead ultimately to Mars becoming suitable for human habitation. For her, of course, having seen the whole process first hand, the protracted explanations of the news reader and other commentators were not so impressive as they might otherwise have been. And she noticed immediately several flaws and inaccuracies in the statements that were being made, often very authoritatively, by various experts from such bodies as NASA and the European Space Agency.

She glanced at the clock on the opposite wall. It was nearly nine in the evening. She was really just sitting up waiting for her husband to get home from the naval base where he had arrived earlier that day. At this moment he would be involved in the final stages of organizing his leave and that of his training vessel's crew, but he would doubtlessly be home very soon. And there he would stay, until it was time to take out a fresh crew of cadets. At that time the training process would have to begin anew, all over again.

After the discussion of the Martian terraformation process, she had gradually lost interest in the news, but the next item caused her to sit up and take notice.

"We interrupt this report to bring you a special bulletin. NBC is receiving information that just a few minutes ago, an event of enormous significance to the Moslem world is alleged to have taken place. Previous stories reported on NBC and other major news outlet channels dealing with the issue of the possible re-emergence of the prophet of Islam, which have come to light over the past few weeks, have now apparently been confirmed as almost certainly genuine."

The mention of previous reports in connection with this news item caught Dawn's attention. She had not seen or heard any such reports, and was not clear on what was being presented. This latest story must have developed and unfolded while she was away on the surface of Mars.

"According to numerous eye-witness accounts from underneath the world-famous mosque in the Iranian city of Jamkaran, from the historic so-called Well of Occultation, the principal living prophet of Islam, the 12th Imam Mahdi, has arisen and is about to reveal himself to the people of the world."

Dawn's initial reaction was to consider this to be yet another religious stunt, some kind of scam, the purpose of which was simply to influence the masses within the Middle East. But she continued to listen. The celebrated reporter, Kristiana Amanziz, was apparently on location at the mosque in question in northern Iran. It appeared to be early in the morning, the sun having just come up. She was talking in a quite animated and excited manner in regard to this latest occurrence.

"In Islam, the coming of the 12th Imam Mahdi has been predicted for centuries. It is prophesied that he will come to Earth, emerging from the Well of Occultation, located under the present-day mosque here in the city of Jamkaran in northern Iran, where he is said to have resided for centuries, awaiting the right moment to re-appear to humanity. His coming will coincide with a period of great peace and prosperity on Earth, which many are maintaining has already begun with the discovery of the ancient lost city of Atlantis under the ice of Antarctica, the apparent solving of the global energy crisis, and the commencement of the terraformation of the planet Mars. This latter process has been under way for just over a week now and according to NASA spokespersons will proceed to the point where the planet will become suitable for human habitation, incredibly within a matter of only a few more months. It is said that the Mahdi will further work to institute a single global government and will put right all of the mistakes of mankind, both spiritual and technological."

At this point Ms. Amanziz changed tack.

"Reports that the Mahdi was to reveal himself to humankind started coming through just five days ago, following a statement to that effect made by the President of Iran. At first these reports were dismissed as just another empty promise like so many that have gone before in regard to the Mahdi's reappearance, but this time there were a number of accompanying signs, described by many as miracles, signs that were taken by the faithful as proof of the Mahdi's existence and his intent to save all of humanity. These signs are said to be as follows: Imam Mahdi will reappear on a Friday on or around the autumn equinox, and it is indeed Friday here in Iran as I speak. And of course, we are within a few days of the autumn equinox. Imam Mahdi will appear suddenly. And finally, he will be joined by three hundred and thirteen of his most devoted followers who will reaffirm their loyalty to him. Of course, there have been dissenting voices, particularly amongst Jewish and Christian groups. Many are suggesting that the Mahdi's reappearance heralds the end of Israel, and a number of Christians have expressed deep concerns that the Mahdi is an impostor, or antichrist, who means to hide the face and light of Jesus, the only true ruler of the Earth according to Christian theology, from the people of the world."

Dawn watched all of this unfold with utter bemusement. How could the world of the 21st century, with all of its education and technological advancement, believe in such utter nonsense? How could people seriously credit the notion that a man had existed in a state of immortality, down inside a well, of all places, for centuries, waiting for the most opportune moment to reveal his presence to the world? And how could a journalist of Kristiana Amanziz' proven and obvious professional stature consent to represent these events, euphemistically termed, in this manner that could only be described as childish and puerile?

"Of course the Mahdi has not yet revealed his face to us."

Well of course. How convenient.

"But he will be making his appearance on this balcony at any moment now. And here today in the city of Jamkaran are assembled a crowd estimated at one hundred thousand faithful Moslems, waiting to catch a glimpse of the 12th Imam when he makes his reappearance."

The camera panned over to a balcony leading off an upper level of the mosque, situated between its two minarets, above the expectant crowd which was indeed truly enormous, an ocean of people, filling the streets as far as the eye could see. Without warning, Ms. Amanziz started literally shouting, rather uncharacteristically, in excitement.

"And here he is! The 12th Imam Mahdi, making his return appearance after centuries in occultation. Praise be to God! Praise be to Allah!"

Praise be to God? Praise be to Allah? Dawn could not quite believe what she was hearing.

Dawn watched as a figure clad in white robes appeared from behind a curtain and slowly made his way to the edge of the balcony, as the wild cheering rose to an almost insane crescendo, one hundred thousand voices raised in unbridled ecstasy. As he proceeded, he slowly pulled the veil from his head, revealing his face, while batteries of cameras panned in for close-up shots.

What Dawn saw next caused her blood to run cold in her veins, for she instantly recognized the face of the 12th Imam Mahdi, as he leered at the cameras thereby revealing himself in all of his glory to the peoples of the world. This despite his fairly heavy disguise, in the form of a full beard and slightly darkened skin, no doubt in place so that he would not be recognizable to any who might know him. But to her, his piercing brilliant brown eyes that suggested highly focused energy and intelligence, and his intense lupine stare, was absolutely unmistakable. This was a face that she knew.

It was Hunt.

CHAPTER 45

In his first official act in his capacity as 12th Imam Mahdi, Hunt effectively united the Moslem world into a singular political entity. He did so, quite literally, overnight. And this had proven to be very easy indeed, for as the Mahdi persona he found that, precisely as he had surmised, the leaders of all of the Middle Eastern nations behaved towards him in the most obsequious and servile manner, and were ready to carry out his every whim, no matter how inappropriate or even downright absurd it might be. He commanded, de facto as well as de jure, the sovereign governments of Saudi Arabia, The United Arab Emirates, Iraq, Iran, Yemen, Qatar, and Turkey, to form a single council, subordinate and answerable to him alone, which was to meet in a new building to be constructed in Istanbul, the center of the ancient Ottoman Empire and in which the last Caliph had ceased to rule back in 1924. The building was to house the World Islamic Senate, or WIS, and construction work was to be commenced immediately. The former seven nations were to form a single power bloc, which was to be henceforth known as New Arabia. Also to be included were the former independent entities of Oman, Abu Dhabi, Kuwait, and Bahrain. All other Islamic nations on Earth were to become satellites of New Arabia, governed from the WIS to which they would each send a number of representatives, the exact number varying from one nation to another, for a total of three hundred and thirteen, all told. The practical aspects of all of these sweeping changes were commenced literally as soon as Hunt had finished issuing the relevant proclamations, for the Mahdi had spoken and no Moslem anywhere on the planet would question his word. For the Mahdi was next only to the Prophet himself in importance, as his living representative on Earth.

In his second act as 12th Imam, Hunt ordered the leaders of Israel to promptly assemble before him. He forced them to listen to a diatribe, televised and broadcast to all corners of the globe, in which he explained, amongst other things, how the Jewish peoples of the world were to henceforth behave and deport themselves. As Jews they were to be afforded the luxury of continued existence merely as a consequence of Allah's good graces. They would be offered the opportunity to convert to Islam, the final corrective and therefore most pure of all the world's monotheistic religions. But any who failed to heed the call must live in subservience to the Ummah, according Moslems special respect wherever and whenever they encountered them. And, of course, there was the matter of payment of the special *jizya* tax, in return for which, their security would continue to be guaranteed, for a time, at least, if not for an indefinite period. Any willful violation of these terms would result in swift and terrible retribution. And to prove the point, an impressive flotilla of nuclear powered submarines of the SSBN type, ready to launch inter-continental ballistic missiles, appeared in the Persian Gulf, apparently belonging to New Arabia and under the control of the WIS. This latter revelation stunned leaders of Western nations, as they were all utterly nonplussed as to how any of the former Middle Eastern nations had been able to construct and/ or purchase such formidable weapons in a completely clandestine fashion, and so quickly. However to their relief, not to mention surprise, the Western nations were left relatively untouched by the new Mahdic proclamations. Indeed the Mahdi simply intoned that there would be no specific demands leveled at any Western government. All Western Christian nations were informed that they may continue as before, but on the understanding that New

Arabia was starting an advanced weapons development program and any attempt to interfere would be regarded as an act of war and would result in armed conflict. At the very next meeting of the United Nations Security Council, notable because of the absence of representatives from Israel as the Mahdi had immediately forbidden Israel continued UN membership, there was significant discord as the representatives of the United States adopted an, 'I told you so,' stance in regard to recent developments, while the leaders of the European Union were much more circumspect and non-committal, issuing statements such as, 'let the record show that the leading EU nations wish to maintain constructive dialogue with the World Islamic Senate and to reach appropriate and lasting agreements with regard to global trade.' The French and the Germans seemed particularly interested in presenting such a face, although not the British, much to the chagrin of the UN leadership. The Russians for their part seemed to be watching events unfold with a detached bemusement. Representatives from the African nations simply complained about how their nations would, as always, be downtrodden and forgotten while the rest of the world moved on to ever greater and more glorious heights. Indonesia intoned that even although they were the world's most populous Moslem country, they had enjoyed secular self-government for a long time, and were most unhappy about having to kowtow to this New Arabia, which would undoubtedly attempt to impose considerably stricter Islamic values on their country, most especially in the form of Sharia law. It was this latter issue that was of special concern to the Indonesians. Sharia was, they argued, nothing more than a form of political totalitarianism masquerading as a religious edict that, if instigated, would be a disaster for their country which was in its present state peaceful, productive, and reasonably successful. The only support for Indonesia came from the United States, Australia, and Egypt. The Egyptian representatives identified with the Indonesian position of an Islamic population governed by a secular government. But all other nations, including Canada, urged restraint and less of this 'offensive and inflammatory' type of talk. Mexico, Costa

Rica and Peru complained that the Indonesians had nothing to complain about when their respective nations were in dire need of economic aid. They were in effect suggesting that the Indonesians and Egyptians should simply be quiet, recognize the new world order, and fall into line. As in several other aspects of recent global developments, the United States and Australia were alone amongst the advanced Western democracies in their refusal to acknowledge this new world order; all other leading nations, especially those within the EU, it seemed, simply could not acknowledge it quickly enough. And indeed they declared their intention to issue a formal statement to that effect to the representatives of New Arabia when they were to formally take up their seats at the UN Security Council before the week was out. The United States warned that it would not be long before this new World Islamic Senate would commence a descent into a whole catalogue of human rights abuses. The EU representatives retorted in their high-minded manner that the government of New Arabia was without doubt cultured, educated, cultivated, and sensitive to the human condition and physical, psychological, and spiritual needs of the individual. In all probability they would quickly build a society more equitable, superior, and just than existed in even the wildest dreams of George Washington, Thomas Jefferson, or Abraham Lincoln. Indeed all the more so now that they were being guided by the 12th Imam, seen by many, if not most, as God's living representative on Earth.

The New Order in the Middle East received a mixed blessing from the ordinary peoples of the world. As to be expected, Moslem populations within Canada, Western Europe, and Australia welcomed the new developments with open arms, stating repeatedly that it was a miracle. A miracle that the Western powers were about to be brought to their knees once and for all, for the good of planet Earth and all of her peoples. And the Jews were finally being put in their proper place. *Allah hu akbar!* Ordinary indigenous Western Europeans were much more reticent, even hostile, deeply concerned that this could spell the end of their free societies as they had come to understand them. Nor did the reduction of Israel in status to a subservient *Dhimmi* state sit well with non-Moslem Western European populations. And despite all assurances by New Arabia that they would not seek armed conflict with anyone, many felt that a major war, even a holocaust, may be imminent. A sizeable and growing proportion of the US population felt that now was the time to launch an all-out nuclear offensive against the Middle East, the inevitable casualties and collateral damage be damned. If weapons development inside New Arabia continued at the pace recently revealed to the world, quite soon there would be nothing left to do except negotiate, as the sun set on the Constitution and the Bill of Rights. Indeed there was even a lobby group set up in Congress with the express purpose of pushing the agenda, and fast, of all-out war. Increasingly high profile militia groups sprang up all over the nation, from Oregon to Florida, New Hampshire to Nevada. Arms sales rocketed; within a week and a half they had mushroomed by around eight hundred percent.

And as to the very recent belief of many of the peoples of the Christian world that Garry Hunt was the Messiah; there were many who still held privately to this belief, but had rapidly learned to keep their mouths shut about the issue now that the world was subjugated to the 12th Imam Mahdi. However there seemed to be almost no-one who realized that Garry Hunt and the 12th Imam were one and the same person, although perhaps not entirely surprising given his quite heavy disguise combined with his very limited appearances in public or on television. This point was not lost on Hunt himself. He took care to place watch on those few individuals who had met him personally, including the Pope. Indeed he had a sophisticated plan in place for the rapid elimination of the Holy Father and any other person who might threaten to reveal his true identity. Should this course of action prove necessary.

CHAPTER 46

The 12th Imam proved to be true to his word, for over the ensuing days New Arabia's military machine went into production overdrive. By the time two weeks had elapsed since the Mahdi's reappearance on Earth, and with his assistance, the conventional and nuclear capacities of New Arabia had exceeded that of even the United States in virtually every arena. By official accounts the US still had about twenty percent more helicopters within its army, and twenty-eight more minesweepers in its navy, but in all other respects New Arabia was the biggest military juggernaut on Earth and it was widely believed by virtually all observers that there was no force left which could seriously challenge its superiority. New Arabia it seemed had become the new global hegemon.

As far as day-to-day life in the Middle East was concerned, there were a number of instituted changes that, while not so different from daily life in Riyadh under the previous Saudi Wahabbist regime, in more northern and previously secular cities such as Istanbul these changes were harder for incumbent populations to accept. For example, a generalized ruling went out from the WIS that all homosexuals were to be relentlessly hunted down and executed. The newly formed police forces of New Arabia were ordered to expend considerable effort on obtaining records of all individuals who might have been known for having previously engaged in such activities, irrespective of whether they were doing so at the present time or not. They were to be arrested, and, after a show trial, delivered up for execution by beheading. The heads were then to be placed in suitably sized reinforced jars filled with preservative solution, and incorporated into the walls, lobbies, and stairwells of public buildings throughout the length and breadth of the kingdom, as a constant reminder to all of Allah's prescribed punishment for those who might feel tempted to commit 'unnatural' acts. Prayer five times per day, every day, became mandatory, on pain of imprisonment and heavy fines. Men were required to wear full beards, while women were required to be veiled in the burqa such that no part of their bodies, not even their eyes, would be on display while they were outside the family home. And of course while they were outside on the streets, they were to be continually escorted by their husbands, or failing that, a male relative, whom they must walk at least three paces behind at all times. No girl was to be allowed to continue her formal education beyond the level of the ninth grade. At mosque on every Friday, attendance at which was mandatory for all, women were to be segregated and reminded that hell was populated mostly with unbelievers and women, especially those of the latter group found at the Day of Judgment to be in possession of a university education. Under Sharia law, the testimony of a woman was given half as much weight as that of a man. And very rarely would anything other than verbal evidence be considered by a court operating under Sharia principles, since presumptively no Moslem man would damn himself by deliberately lying. This would render it very difficult, in fact almost impossible, for a woman who had suffered a sexual attack to bring her attacker or attackers to justice, especially so since in such a case, were she to fail to prove the charge against the defendant, she herself would be accused of adultery and, after a show trial, put to death by stoning.

But this was the new order, and the people of New Arabia and other Moslem nations would simply have to make the adjustment.

For the Mahdi had spoken. As Allah's living representative on Earth, and King of New Arabia, he was infallible and just. His words defined the beginning and the end of law and wisdom in all of humanity's earthly concerns.

CHAPTER 47

Despite their fatigue as a result of the fourteen hour flight from Los Angeles' LAX airport, from where they had flown from Boston, Dawn and especially Matthew found the experience of taking an early morning walk along Orchard Road, Singapore's main shopping thoroughfare, an immensely enjoyable experience. They both felt that the city exuded marvelous qualities of cleanliness and freshness, so rarely found in big urban areas in modern times, but readily apparent from the moment they stepped off the plane at the very contemporary Changi airport. They would be spending one night in the city before returning to Changi the following day just after lunch to catch the on-going connecting flight to Surabaya, Indonesia. Dawn had visited Singapore several times in the past, but for Matthew this was his first time setting foot on the island lying just off the southern tip of the Malay Peninsula. Dawn herself always marveled at how British in character the island seemed, with its road signs, traffic lights, street layouts, and road vehicles, which drove on the left, just as in the UK. Even electrical outlets were of the British design, supplying 230 volts at 50Hz AC. For her, Singapore resembled a union between British and Chinese culture, and the result was visually at least most pleasing. She could sit happily in a hotel restaurant in the city, soaking up the ambience while watching the BBC World Service. She also enjoyed immensely the friendliness and innate courtesy of the local people, who were invariably bilingual, speaking a form of grammatically perfect English with a polished, old-world British accent, and also Mandarin, as a matter of expediency. Some were also fluent in Malay. Of course things had not always been this way. During the Second World War Singapore had been desperately poor and had become the field of the most humiliating defeat for the battered British army under the command of Lieutenant-General Arthur Percival at the hands of the Japanese, advancing north from Kota Bharu, Malaya. Indeed Churchill himself had called it the worst disaster and greatest capitulation in British military history. On that fateful day on February 15, 1942, some 130,000 British, Indian, Australian, and Dutch troops became prisoners of war, and Britain's respect as a great power in the Far East was permanently diminished. Many were subsequently transported and set to work as slave labor on the Burma-Siam railway. The railway was to claim an appalling 250,000 lives, mostly from the effects of tropical disease, malnutrition, or extreme brutality at the hands of the Japanese army. And as if that were not enough, General Percival had also presided over the greatest loss suffered by the Royal Navy in a single action; the sinking of both the battleship HMS *Prince of Wales,* and the cruiser HMS *Repulse,* fifty miles off the coast of Kuantan in Pahang by a force of Japanese bombers.

But those days were long gone, although the infamous Changi prison was still in existence, with an accompanying museum, where at one time many British prisoners of war had met a brutal and painful end. Matthew had expressed a desire to visit sometime before catching their on-going flight. So Dawn would have to organize that, along with the city tour she wanted to take with him, which would include a brief but reasonably thorough visit to the city's Chinatown, as well as its harbor, replete with old statuesque lions standing lonely sentinel, and the old British colonial law court buildings, contrasting with many modern skyscrapers. She also planned to take him out to dinner in one of the city's many fine Chinese restaurants.

Although Singapore had begun during the 3rd century AD, and had risen during the 14th through the early 17th centuries under various Srivijayan rulers until its destruction at the hands of the Portuguese, Matthew of course knew nothing of the later history of Singapore as a dependency of Britain. That had not come about until 1819 when Englishman Sir Thomas Stamford Raffles established a British seaport on the island itself. Under British Colonial rule Singapore had grown in importance as a centre for both trade from India and China, and entrepôt trade in South East Asia. Thus it had rapidly expanded to become a major port city. The surrender of the Japanese following detonation of the atomic bombs at Hiroshima and Nagasaki in 1945 resulted in Singapore reverting to British rule once again. Between 1945 and 1963 increasing self-government was granted to Singapore however and thus in 1963 the island merged politically with the Federation of Malaya to form Malaysia. But political disputes between the Singaporean People's Action Party and Malaysia's Alliance Party led to Singapore being expelled from Malaysia, thus rendering it an independent Republic in August 1965. At that time, there was a severe shortage of housing, and high unemployment, but a very aggressive modernization program was embarked upon which led to strong manufacturing industry, good public education, and increased public housing. The economy started to grow at the rate of around nine percent per year, and thus by the 1990's the country had become one of the world's most prosperous nations, with strong international trading links, a highly developed free market economy, and, behind Japan, the highest per capita gross domestic product in Asia.

The following morning, after a good breakfast at their hotel, Dawn and Revere had climbed into a taxi which had then sped along the Pan Island Expressway, reaching the airport in good time to catch their on-going flight to Surabaya.

Later, while in the departure lounge awaiting boarding, Matthew and Dawn relaxed for a little in one of the airport's several coffee shops.

"Tell me, Matthew. What did you think of the tour we took through the city yesterday afternoon?"

"I found it to be quite fascinating. I am still quite amazed at how modern Singapore has become. I had never envisioned this part of the world thusly."

"Tell me about Changi prison museum. What did you think of that?"

Dawn had not accompanied her husband to the prison. She had been too busy making arrangements.

"It seems that the servicemen incarcerated there by the Japanese during the early 1940's experienced a terrible regime, replete with starvation, various tortures of the most brutal sort, as well as dysentery, yellow fever, dengue fever, and malaria. Many of them did not survive."

"These were terrible times Matthew. Terrible."

She changed the subject to that of their intended destination for which they would be departing in approximately two and a half hours.

"Have you ever been to Indonesia before?"

"No, I have never before made the long voyage to any port within that country. However an associate and contemporary of mine did make the voyage, I believe on two separate occasions, if memory serves. The country was not then known as Indonesia however but as the *Nederlandsche Indie,* or Dutch East Indies."

"Yes, the country was known that way until 1949, after which it gained its independence from Holland."

"My associate I believe sailed to the Javanese port cities of Batavia and Surabaya. Sailing there at that time involved a voyage of many weeks."

As instructed by Vari while on the surface of Mars, Dawn had not explained to Matthew the reasons why they were now making the long flight to Indonesia. Only that it was imperative that they do so, and that the reasons would become clear to him in the fullness of time. She had added that they would be travelling to the Borobudur temple in Yogyakarta and to that end would be meeting with an archeologist specializing in ancient Buddhist structures and artefacts from the University of Surabaya, Dr. Ari Bambang, with whom she had recently been put in contact. Dr. Bambang was to meet them in Surabaya and travel with them both to the temple. Beyond this she could not reveal her motives for the trip, but she had asked that he trust her. She need not have, of course, for as in all things, he trusted her without question.

Eastern Java, Indonesia was but a two and a half hour journey from Changi aboard the large Airbus airliner that made the flight. The plane was surprisingly full, Dawn thought. Sitting in a window seat, she was able to peer out below from thirty thousand feet through the clear, cloudless air as they crossed over the Sunda Strait, lying between the islands of Sumatra and Java. In her mind's eye she imagined the volcanic island of Krakatoa which had existed in the Strait until that fateful day in August 1883, when it had erupted, resulting in the biggest explosion in all of global history. The attendant explosive force, equivalent to the simultaneous detonation of many atomic bombs, had caused six cubic miles of solid rock forming Krakatoa itself to be instantly vaporized. This had also triggered a tsunami that had killed nearly forty thousand people, and a shock wave which had encircled the entire globe more than seven times, for a total distance of around one hundred and seventy-five thousand miles. The sound of the explosion had been heard as far away as Zanzibar in Eastern Africa. Indeed following the tsunami, bodies had been washed up there. Even in Southern England there had been slight but measurable disturbances in the surface of the sea.

On their final approach to Surabaya, from the aircraft Dawn first of all noticed the abundance of small dwellings with red-tiled or thatched rooftops which seemed to be everywhere all around the area of the airfield itself. About one minute before touchdown on the runway, she became acutely aware of the seemingly haphazard manner in which the buildings below appeared to be laid out, as if many had been constructed without much consideration for town planning or congruity of appearance or function. She found herself somewhat startled when the aircraft finally crossed the runway threshold and she could clearly see that the adjacent grass was waist-high, and was apparently supporting a substantial complement of grazing livestock, principally goats and cows, all held in check by nothing more than the presence of a single farmer wearing a simple cloth suit and an old world coolie style hat. He did not even glance up at the jet as it thundered past at one hundred and twenty miles per hour on the runway just feet from him and his animals, its spoilers raised and engines powering up into full reverse thrust. A few minutes later the Airbus finally pulled up at the terminal building. A sign bearing the legend, *Welcome to Surabaya* was clearly visible, but in aside to that there seemed to be nothing to indicate that this was a modern international airport. The terminal building resembled nothing so much as a long terraced house, with a simple red-tiled roof. There were no jetways, no modern-looking gate number indicator signs, none of the typical modified and specialized road vehicles that one ordinarily sees here and there on big airport aprons. The large jet in fact had pulled up some distance from the terminal itself, and a mobile ladder had been run alongside its main entry door on the port side, immediately behind the cockpit. When she and Matthew finally exited the plane, the first thing that struck her was the stifling heat and high levels of humidity, the like of which she had rarely experienced except in a very few of her tropical voyages she had made a number of years before. As she started to descend the steps, she experienced a momentary desire to turn around and retreat back into the aircraft's cabin, with its modern equipment and furnishings, as well as highly effective air-conditioning, rather than continue on into this unknown world that was rapidly beginning to seem quite primitive to her Western sensibilities. Steeling herself, she glanced over at her husband. But it was apparent that, if he was experiencing any of the same immediate emotions as she, he was not betraying them outwardly.

On arrival at the terminal itself, the contrast with the very modern and highly efficient Changi Airport in Singapore could not have been any more stark. The deplaning passengers were first of all shepherded into a small room, the entrance to which opened directly off the apron area, which appeared by all accounts, judging by its very badly peeling paint and general period appearance, to have been last decorated perhaps around the year 1940. Its interior furnishings seemed to date to around the same era. Along its left side were several glass-faced wooden counters, each replete with an official-looking individual sitting dutifully and patiently behind. It seemed that this was the Immigration Control Checkpoint. Signs posted on the glass windows exhorted arriving passengers from foreign destinations to purchase a visa appropriate for the duration of their intended stay in Indonesia. The lines were rapidly building, but Dawn and Matthew were close to the front so they had not long to wait before being able to deal directly with an official, who took their passports, affixed a sticker, and collected the fee which could be paid (cash only) in Indonesian rupiah or a variety of foreign currencies, including British sterling, Singapore dollars, or US dollars. But to Dawn's immense surprise, payment in US dollars was only acceptable if the bills were new and in virtually mint condition. She was fortunate that she had sufficient Singaporean dollars to cover the fee for both Matthew and herself, as her credit card would have been quite useless in this situation.

Next, they had to line up at a series of high wooden counters, again looking as if they had been built during colonial times, and wait for their turn to present their passports bearing the new visas to yet more officials, who wanted to know the reasons for the holder's trip, how long they would be staying, from where they had come, and so on. On finally clearing this area, they then passed through another doorway into a larger but even dingier, poorly lit International Arrivals Area, in which a large and rapidly-growing crowd of people seemed to be thronging and congregating around the single dirty and ancient-looking baggage carousel that opened through a hole in the wall to the Aircraft Parking Apron outside. Dawn noticed for the first time that, although the men were dressed normally by Western standards, all of the local women were clad in the burqa, as per the directive to all Islamic nations recently issued by the WIS. How they could stand it in this heat and humidity she could not even begin to imagine. Bags were already being delivered to the carousel, but it was immediately apparent that there would not be sufficient space on the device's conveyor belt for all of the checked baggage aboard their plane, not to mention the several other aircraft that were also simultaneously off-loading baggage. Indeed the scene seemed rather chaotic, but somehow, things actually worked. Deplaning passengers were very rapidly identifying their bags, taking them, and moving away to the exit port, where customs officials were waiting to open random bags, presumably checking for drugs. Also, Dawn noticed, these officials were insisting on passing each arriving bag through a filthy and very old X-ray machine that had surely seen better days, before allowing it to proceed with its owner to the open part of the airport. The reasons for subjecting baggage to another X-ray examination, when it had just been pulled from an incoming aircraft and was destined for the parking lot she could only guess at.

After finally clearing customs and passing out of the International Arrivals Area, the scene that greeted Dawn and Matthew was one of utter pandemonium. Hundreds upon hundreds of people were rushing around everywhere, many holding up placards upon which were written the names of those they were there to meet.

Dawn turned to Matthew.

"There should be a driver from the hotel in Surabaya here waiting for us. Keep a look out for a sign with our names written on it. His name is Mr. Anton, I believe."

Before he could even respond, a man approached them.

"*Taksi, Pak?*"

Revere was able to respond immediately.

"*Tidak, terima kasih.*"

Dawn stared at him, genuinely surprised.

"Matthew, you speak Indonesian?"

He laughed.

"No, but I took the opportunity to read up on as much of the language as I was able before we made the journey here."

"Bapak, perlu taksi?"

Again he was able to deal with the enterprising cab-driver's attempt to purloin him and his wife as passengers.

"Tidak, terima kasih."

But then another man, holding up a sign bearing the legend, **MATTHEW REVERE AND DAWN DEFALLER,** made his way over to them.

"Excuse me sir," he started in slightly halting, heavily accented English. "You are Mr. Matthew Revere?"

Revere immediately bowed slightly towards him.

"Ya. Apa anda Bapak Anton?"

"Betul. Senang bertemu dengan anda."

"Saya juga."

"Selamat datang di Surabaya. Saya dari Hotel Mandarin."

Matthew immediately introduced Dawn.

"My lady, this is Mr. Anton, from the hotel where we will be staying in Surabaya. Mr. Anton, this is my wife, Dawn."

"Anton's features spread into a beaming smile. He immediately extended his hand to both Matthew and Dawn.

"I am very pleased to meet you both." And to Matthew he added, "You speak excellent Indonesian."

"Thank you, Mr. Anton, that is most kind of you to say so, but really it is not the case. I know only a very little of your language. It is you who speaks excellent English."

"Thank you sir, thank you very much." He looked down at their luggage. "Are all of these yours?"

The moment they responded in the affirmative Anton clapped his hands loudly and called out for assistance. Instantly two young men appeared and picked up all of their bags, and started carrying them outside to the parking lot. Anton led the way.

Immediately on exiting the terminal building, Dawn and Matthew became aware of the multitudes of people lining the side-walk, many of whom were trying to sell items of food or small souvenirs to passers-by, and the continuous, ultra-slow moving jam of traffic that made it seem as if exiting from the airport in a vehicle of any kind would be nigh-on impossible. Anton led them to a smart new metallic red Mercedes saloon sitting outside in a parking spot. The porters loaded their bags into the trunk. Anton then tipped them both and they disappeared back inside the terminal. He opened the doors of the car and invited them to climb inside.

The Mercedes was able to exit the airport parking lot much more rapidly and easily than either Dawn or Revere would have expected, given the continuing mass of very slow moving traffic jamming the entrance and exit roads. Anton simply turned out in front of other vehicles and joined the traffic flow, forcing other drivers to stop at the last possible moment in the process. It was but minutes before they had picked up some speed and were driving along the airport approach road. First they came to a large roundabout upon which sat a vintage propeller-driven aircraft, painted light blue, probably a trainer of some sort that looked as if it dated to the Second World War era. Traffic on the roundabout was chaotic, but cars seemed to move aside to allow the Mercedes to enter and proceed on its way. As they exited the roundabout, Dawn noticed that although they were on a road marked quite clearly with two lanes, other drivers seemed to be taking advantage of the fact that their vehicles, many of which were Japanese, were small and narrow enough to allow for driving as if there were three lanes. At various points she felt a pang of alarm as the cars adjacent to theirs, all moving at thirty to forty miles per hour, might be as little as three or four inches away. For the most part traffic did not seem to move any faster than this, but it did seem rather dangerous. She felt that she herself would have difficulty driving here, if only because she would not know what would be expected of her in a given situation. She leaned forward and addressed the driver.

"Mr. Anton?"

"Yes Miss?"

"Who constructed these roads? Were they built by the Indonesians?"

"No Miss. These roads, in common with most in the country, were constructed by the Dutch, during the second half of the 19ᵗʰ century and the first half of the 20th. Indonesia was colonized by Netherlanders at that time. But after 1949 of course, when the Indonesian people won independence from Holland, the Dutch people departed, along with all of their engineers and city planners. So in consequence, all of the roads, bridges, and town planning, not to mention railways that were once so ordered in our country, have entered a phase of continuing decline. It is as you say in English, Miss, a great pity."

"Thank you."

"Thank you, Miss."

Dawn resumed looking out at the passing scene. They were a little further from the airport now and everywhere it seemed, ranged along both sides of the road in great numbers, were makeshift sackcloth or polythene tarpaulin shacks, supported on rickety frameworks of sticks and squalid and filthy, with entry-ways often just inches from the traffic speeding along the road. They would be acting as small roadside restaurants or shops, selling everything from meat, often an entire animal carcass, as well as fruit and vegetables, or, as she noticed, gasoline in glass bottles that looked like they had recently held soft drinks. More shacks were set up as news stands, and some seemed even to function as tiny drive-in service stations, with supplies of tires, windshield wipers, spark plugs, air filters, and a variety of other car parts stashed outside. And the mopeds, mostly of Japanese manufacture, seemed to Dawn to be everywhere. She noticed too that often one moped would be carrying an entire family of two adults and two small children. She noticed that often the adults would be wearing crash helmets, the women wearing them over the head dress part of their burqa, but not their offspring. In addition to the mopeds there were also very many bicycles, some ancient-looking specimens, which were often being used to transport enormous loads, such as a wardrobe, a piano, or even part of a car body. There were also many small Suzuki vans that had been converted into minibuses and appeared to be in service as regular city buses. They were so tiny, and yet ten to twelve passengers could squeeze into the back, sometimes sitting on each others' laps, Dawn noticed. There was even room for concertina-style automatic doors in the side of the vehicle from which passengers could board and alight.

A small Honda saloon car driven by a teenage male passed them in a lane it had made for itself. Dawn noticed to her amusement across the back window in high-contrast white letters was emblazoned the legend *TOTAL ASSY.* Anton, looking in his rear-view mirror, noticed her reaction and seemed to guess the reason for her amusement.

"It means total assembly, Miss. At the factory, the car is completely assembled prior to delivery to the customer."

"Oh, I see." She smiled awkwardly.

The roads were also home to a variety of full-sized buses and heavy trucks, the only large vehicles on the roads. The trucks, or lorries as they were apparently called here, were nearly all very old, and in general grossly overloaded, with sacks of produce stacked so high that the rear bed of the truck stood twice as tall as its intended ten feet. Not infrequently there might be one or two young men sleeping on the top of this precarious heap. The full-sized buses, also very old in appearance, seemed to be driven by crazed maniacs, but this made them stand out as the only truly belligerent drivers on the roads here. They would speed down hills in their five to ten ton vehicles, without slowing even when the road ahead was blocked by slow-moving cars. Instead they seemed to expect that everyone would get out of their way before they arrived.

And yet despite all the apparent bedlam, Dawn nevertheless felt that everyone, with the exception of the drivers of the large buses, was very friendly and accommodating on the roads. Even although drivers used their horns almost constantly it was as a genuinely friendly and respectful reminder of one's presence in a lane, real or invented. There was very little of the selfishness, hostility, emotional immaturity, and downright infantile belligerence that frequently bedevils North American or Western European highways. Nor did there seem to be any sign of people driving unnecessarily large vehicles simply for the hell of it. Almost all the cars and vans were compact or even sub-compact, with everyone making do quite nicely. After a while Dawn began to feel that driving here was really not so bad after all. There was a distinct order to the chaos, and the friendliness and laid-back approach was better for one's blood pressure. By this point it was becoming amusing to her that the very few traffic lights that existed, probably a throw-back from the Dutch colonial era, were largely ignored. A green light would change to red, but dozens of mopeds, cars, and minibuses would just keep on coming by as if it were not there. But then, for some reason that she was unable to fathom, drivers would suddenly all decide in unison to stop, and then wait until the light changed once more to green.

Revere was even perplexed.

"Mr. Anton, how do people know when it is time to stop for a red light?"

Anton just laughed.

"It is considered correct practice to pass a red light for a while, but then stop. It is hard to explain how one knows when to stop and when to keep going, but anyone who grew up here just intuitively knows. The system works, we have very few accidents."

"It must make things difficult for foreigners who attempt to drive here."

"We recommend that foreigners do not drive here, Miss. Our rules for driving are a little different from elsewhere, I think."

He laughed again.

"Mr. Anton, why are those houses built in that river bed? That is a river bed, isn't it?"

"Yes Miss. That is a river bed. People who have enough money to construct a proper house but who do not have enough money to afford the best land often build in a river bed. They are dry most of the time and land is cheaper there."

"But what happens when it rains?"

"They sometimes get washed away. But there is a smaller channel that still cuts through between the houses that can carry river water as long as the flow is not too great. So most of the time, the people who live there will be all right. And if they are not, they will simply rebuild."

Dawn looked again at the many haphazardly built and arranged small dwellings jammed right next to each other in the river bed. The houses all looked distinct from each other in appearance and seemed as if they had been built by the people who lived in them. There seemed not to be any planning or adherence to building regulations whatsoever, nor use of the services of architects or builders. In fact much of Surabaya seemed that way. It was as if an enormous population had been gathered up into a small area, given access to building materials, and then told to get on with the job of constructing residences for themselves.

"The smaller houses in the river bed form a district known as a campon, Miss. Campon houses are small, perhaps five hundred to seven hundred and fifty square feet, but comfortable, they may house a family of up to ten in one or two rooms, sometimes one above the other, sometimes side by side."

Dawn balked at this statement, but Matthew seemed unfazed.

Finally, after about forty five minutes, they had arrived in the city's busy central business and premier shopping district. Gone was the seeming poverty and squalor that they had witnessed in great quantity just moments before, for they had now entered a world of great opulence and luxury that would compare very favorably indeed with downtown Manhattan, San Francisco, Paris, London, Rome, or Madrid. Suddenly all the men visible on the streets were wearing expensive tailor-made suits, the women without burqas but instead smart ladies' business suits with skirts. The Mercedes turned into Jalan Tunjungan and pulled up at a large and beautiful colonial structure.

The sign affixed on its side read, MANDARIN ORIENTAL HOTEL MAJAPAHIT SURABAYA★★★★★

CHAPTER 48

The following morning Dawn and Matthew rose early, so as to be ready in the hotel lobby in time to meet with Dr. Bambang, who had arranged to pick them both up personally. She had telephoned him shortly after they had settled into their room, and she had found him ready and willing to immediately meet with them. Indeed, it was Bambang who had, upon hearing of their impending visit to Surabaya, made all the necessary arrangements for Dawn and her husband to stay at the Mandarin Oriental. And what a hotel it had turned out to be. Dawn in truth had entertained a modicum of trepidation as to the standard of accommodations she could expect to find in a country such as Indonesia, but the accommodations were quite simply magnificent. The building was not new, having first opened its doors for business almost exactly ninety-eight years before in 1910, but the graceful colonial style structure had been recently renovated and was in beautiful condition in every respect imaginable. Over the years the leaders of many of the world's nations had stayed there, enjoying no doubt its luxurious and elegant old-world charm. The hotel too Dawn noticed was located very close to the premier shopping districts of downtown Surabaya, and despite its thoroughly-deserved five-star rating, in general the rooms cost only nine hundred and forty-three thousand rupiah, less than the equivalent of one hundred US dollars, per night.

At eight o'clock she and Matthew were ready. They went downstairs to the dining room to enjoy a breakfast of Indonesian coffee, eggs, ham, pineapple, and fried bananas. At half past eight they moved to the lobby with the intention of waiting for Dr. Bambang to arrive, only to find that he was in fact already there, waiting for them. On seeing them he immediately rose to his feet from the chair in which he had been sitting, and extended his hand in greeting.

"Captain DeFaller! Captain Revere! I am Dr. Ari Bambang, of the University of Surabaya. I am so very glad that you have made the journey to Indonesia! Welcome!"

Dawn took the initiative, and introduced them both.

"Dawn DeFaller, pleased to meet you, and this is my husband, Matthew."

"Dr. Bambang." Revere gave a polite bow.

In common with so many of his compatriots, Bambang was of shorter stature, perhaps five feet six inches in height, but slim, of a dark complexion, and in excellent health.

"Please, this way," he said, motioning for them to move outside. "My driver is waiting."

Sure enough, as they exited the main door from the hotel lobby, there was a very polished and quite exquisite blue BMW saloon car waiting right outside. Dawn and Matthew got in the back, while Bambang got in next to his driver.

"If it meets with your approval, I was thinking that we could go directly to Yogyakarta, where I can give you a personal guided tour of the Borobudur temple."

"That would be perfect, Dr. Bambang. Thank you."

"I must advise you however, that, as a woman, you will fare much better when travelling outside of the well-to-do urban areas of our country now if you wear this covering." He motioned to the plain black burqa that was folded neatly, lying to one side on the rear shelf of the car. Inwardly Dawn groaned as she realized that there would be no getting away from the issue. She would indeed have to cover herself up completely when out in public. She shuddered as she thought of the sweeping changes that Hunt had been able to bring about in the world, from his political base at the WIS in Istanbul, and in so short of a time. She remembered Vari's warning regarding his designs to rule the entire planet. Dawn had been hoping that as a Western woman she might not be required to don the burqa, but this was apparently not to be. She was going to have to wear it while travelling through the more rural parts of Indonesia, and remain at her husband's side at all times, as well as behave in a manner that indicated, outwardly at least, total submission to his will in all matters. She felt an immediate sense of anger welling up inside of her, an emotion that was betrayed in her tone of voice and general demeanor when she asked her next question to Bambang.

"Must I put this on now?"

"No, we have darkened glass on the side windows of the car, so there is no need to wear the covering until such time as you alight from the vehicle."

Bambang's features fell as he peered sorrowfully at Dawn.

"I apologize, from the very bottom of my heart. Indonesia, although mostly Islamic, has traditionally always embraced the values of individualism and never the values of hard-line religious edicts. But now as we are ruled by the new regime from New Arabia, as it is being called, this has simply become law. You must protect yourself, or else face arrest and imprisonment, possibly worse. But please believe me when I tell you that we Indonesians hate this as well as many other rulings that we have been forced to accept of late. Until just a matter of a few weeks ago, the burqa has never been forced upon Indonesian women. But at the present time we find ourselves quite simply with no choice in the matter."

Somewhat angrily, Dawn pulled the still-folded burqa from the rear window shelf and placed it beside her.

CHAPTER 49

The city of Yogyakarta turned out to be a large metropolis, easily equivalent in size and scale to many large North American and Western European cities. Neither Dawn nor Matthew had expected that there would be such a large population living within a relatively small area. The city consisted of a curious mixture of modern steel and concrete skyscrapers, office blocks, condominium apartments, and Western-style hotels, but intermixed with many campon areas, often backing right up against a modern office building or hotel wall. For Dawn it was strange to see such a mixture of wealth and poverty, often within a singular city block. The journey there had been relatively slow, taking most of the day to travel the one hundred and fifty miles from Surabaya, as Java possessed only very few freeway-type roads. Most of the thoroughfares on which they drove were instead simply country type roads with only a single lane in each direction, divided by nothing more than a painted white line. During their journey they had passed through many small towns and villages, the appearance and ambience of which seemed always to be about the same. But Yogyakarta, as in common with other Indonesian cities, was a distinctive mixture of old and new, rich and poor, with still a hint here and there of the old Dutch colonial influence.

On their arrival in the city, Bambang had driven them to the Novotel Yogyakarta located on Jalan Jenderal Sudirman in the city's central business district. There they were to spend the night before journeying on to the Borobudur temple the following morning. Their room had turned out to be very comfortable and the hotel sported an upscale walled-in courtyard which included a beautiful and imaginatively designed swimming pool, but looking out from the rear of the building Dawn could see only an ocean of campons. The campons were populated by the ordinary inhabitants of the city, as well as by chickens, goats, and sheep. To Dawn, the latter were very strange sights indeed to see within a densely populated downtown metropolitan area.

The following morning they had breakfast in the main dining room. Dawn then went back to her room and once there, covered herself with the hated burqa in readiness for the trip to the Borobudur. In Yogyakarta she had noticed that within the hotel, Western standards of dress seemed to predominate for women, but outside on the streets women were completely covered in the strange and vaguely hostile black garments. She detested the claustrophobic feeling, the uncomfortable heat, the closeness of her sweat, as well as the inability to move or even see freely. To her it felt as if she were dressed in a tent. And what grated on her the most was the idea that women must dress this way when outside, regardless of their own personal wishes, merely to satisfy some religious edict written in an ancient holy book.

When she was ready, she joined Matthew and Bambang downstairs once again in the lobby. On seeing her approach Bambang immediately had some more advice for her.

"Captain DeFaller. We will soon be entering an area where the police will be present in considerable force, ready to ensure that all Islamic laws and customs are being upheld. Unfortunately, this will especially apply to women. When we are out, and especially when we are at the temple today, please remember at all times, unless you are absolutely certain that there is no-one else observing our party, to remain silent unless spoken to by one of us, remain close to your husband, and to walk three paces behind him. Once again, I apologize profusely for this, but to act otherwise will invite unwanted attention from the authorities, and possibly arrest, which could lead to heavy fines and even imprisonment."

This comment had angered her, but there was absolutely nothing to be done about it except comply.

The Borobudur Temple turned out to be located some miles distant from central Yogyakarta, located within a park near Magelang which incorporated some other buildings and historical national monuments built in more recent times. The park area was pleasant but seemed to be populated with an army of local hawkers, trying earnestly to peddle their various goods. There were probably as many of them in fact as there were actual tourists. And the tourists themselves, mostly Australians, New Zealanders, British, Dutch, French, Belgian, German, and North American, were literally swarmed by as many as five of these people at a time as they moved around, who were apparently all but desperate to sell their various wares which they would literally push into a person's hand, and then insist on payment. The situation was not really dangerous, although pick-pocketing may have been rife, but was clearly intimidating for anyone unaccustomed to such a hard sell. One thing Dawn noticed however was that the burqa-clad women without exception were entirely free from this form of harassment.

As they walked through the park area towards its rear-most aspect, Dawn, walking dutifully behind Matthew, saw the Borobudur temple rising before her. It was a sobering sight, appearing larger and more massive than in the photographs of it that she had seen. Upon approaching the structure she was suddenly very aware of the ancient nature of the temple and felt a strong sense of connectedness to the distant past. Bambang commenced a commentary as they came close, for he possessed expert knowledge of the Borobudur.

"There is a proper manner in which one should ascend the Borobudur temple. The orientation of the structure is based on the cardinal points of the compass, and one should begin from its eastern aspect. The location of each of the five hundred and four statues of the Buddha are also oriented on the cardinal points of the compass. There is also a series of one thousand four hundred and sixty relief panels, which should also be approached from the east."

Dawn groaned.

"One thousand, four hundred and sixty? Do we really have to inspect all that many?"

"Yes, I am rather afraid that we will, for many will appear very similar. I am sorry, Captain, but with the three of us working systematically, it will not take so long as it might seem. Now it is true that the Borobudur has four entrances and exits, but the main and true entrance lies to the east. After entering, one should turn either to the right or *Prasavya,* or to the left or *Pradaksina,* complete one circuit of the temple, then climb to the next terrace, and repeat the same pattern. During each circuit one should systematically inspect each of the relief panels that surround the entire lower part of the temple, symbolizing its spiritual guards. In this way we should be able to find the panel that matches the description that you have. I expect you will find that there will be several that superficially appear to match, but we can examine each one in detail until we locate the one that is a true match. Please notice also that reliefs showing sitting and squatting *Boddhisattvas* are alternated by reliefs of a man and a giant flanked by a woman and a goddess, which can be seen on the balustrades. Such reliefs surround the entire lower part of the temple."

As they entered the temple by its east gate and Dawn saw just how many intricately carved stone panels there actually were built into its walls, she started to realize that this search would probably turn out to be anything but simple.

CHAPTER 50

Almost four hours later the trio had climbed only to the second gallery of the stepped pyramid that constituted the main part of the temple. Dawn and Matthew had carefully examined and compared each panel that even remotely matched the description given to Dawn by Vari that Danielle, albeit unconsciously, had been able to download and print for her, in surprisingly high resolution such that it appeared more like a fine line drawing. She had made copies of the image on heavy duty plastic-impregnated waterproof and tear-proof paper, and each of them was carrying one. But despite having examined over three hundred panels they still had failed to locate the correct one. Just as Bambang had said, many seemed at first to be a match, but then on close inspection it became clear that they were not. It was hot work, the temperature being nearly one hundred degrees, and under her burqa, Dawn was becoming very tired and irritable. She had to force herself to continue with the task at hand. Although she understood that it was neither the fault of her husband nor Bambang that she had to wear the damned thing, she could not help but feel resentful towards them both. Here she was, fully dressed beneath this personal tent on a very hot day, made of heavy black material, the worst of colors for insulating against the heat, while even with her eyes covered, trying to search for an obscure ancient artifact of the utmost importance. And all the while the men were free to wear anything they wished. It seemed so horribly unreasonable and unfair.

"Come," said Bambang, finally, as he finished inspecting the last panel of interest on the second terrace. "Let us climb up to the third. Perhaps we will have more luck there."

"Dr. Bambang."

Dawn was polite but her tone belied her ragged patience. She also knew that she was addressing a man without first having been addressed, but she had had it, and anyway, there was no-one within earshot other than her two companions. To hell with protocol.

"How about if we split up? Matthew and I could proceed to the top of the structure, and work our way down, while you could keep on working your way up. Hopefully one of us will locate what we are looking for rather quicker that way. What do you think?"

Bambang considered the question for a moment.

"I daresay that could work, as long as you do not think that you might accidentally miss something. There are some panels that are harder to locate for the uninitiated, especially around the small stupas on the top gallery."

"Well, even we do miss something, where would be the harm? We would get to it eventually after meeting you as you work your way upward."

Something in Dawn's tone told Bambang that it would be best simply to agree to her request.

"Yes, Captain DeFaller. Excellent idea. I suggest that you pursue that very course of action."

Dawn's idea had turned out to be a very good one, for approximately forty five minutes later, on the top gallery she and Matthew were just about finished when they hit upon a panel that looked different from the others. On initial inspection, it seemed to fit the description. Revere had seen it first.

"Dawn! This one here! Look! I believe this may be the one for which we are searching!"

Dawn peered closely at the design, comparing it carefully with the design reproduced on the copy she was holding in front of her. After a moment she became quite excited.

"Matthew! You're right! This is it! Let's fetch Dr. Bambang!"

With Bambang's assistance, along with the selection of tools he had brought with him, they were able to carefully work the panel loose. The process of so doing consisted of one person standing guard while the other two worked on attempting to prise the stone panel from its mountings to which it had been attached with a primitive but highly effective form of cement. Fortunately the panel itself was located behind a small stupa nearer the top of the whole structure, in an area in which few other visitors, or the monument caretaker staff or police, for that matter, seemed interested in looking. There were occasional individuals who walked over that way but Bambang, who was assisting Dawn to move the panel, was playing the part of a university professor with a special interest in the inner structure of the Borobudur. This seemed to assuage the curiosity of even the most determined of those who were intent on trying to see what was going on.

When at last they had succeeded in removing the panel, Dawn examined the reverse side, but found it to be simply flat and smooth. There was no evidence at all of any design other than the one carved on the front side. But just as Dawn was beginning to think that they had perhaps removed the wrong one after all, she noticed what appeared to be a small latch underlying the area over which the panel had been lying. She reached out and pulled on it. At first nothing seemed to happen. It appeared as if it was merely incidental, perhaps a simple support for the stone. But when she turned it first of all to the left and then to the right, a trap door opened unexpectedly and apparently under the influence of some kind of unknown power source. The opening that was revealed was perhaps around twelve inches by sixteen, and behind it was a simple red button, made of what looked like polished marble.

"What do you think?" Dawn asked both the men. "Should we push this?"

Neither of them seemed entirely sure. After a few seconds of indecision she decided to ignore them and proceed on her own. She reached down and punched the button. Immediately there was a quiet humming sound, followed rapidly by the opening of a slot rather much like a letterbox, through which a slab was dispensed, smoothly and quietly. Dawn retrieved it as it appeared. After that, the trapdoor closed again.

She examined the slab. It was made from some sort of shiny hard alloy, and incorporated an intricate design etched into its surface. The design showed a map of, rather incredibly, modern Egypt, as well as a pyramid, and a series of numbers. It seemed to Dawn that the numbers might denote many things, but Bambang was of the opinion that they were spatial co-ordinates describing the location of the pyramid shown on the design. There was also a design showing what appeared to be a map of part of the internal structure of the pyramid, indicating a series of corridors and passageways, as if it were directions of some sort.

"What is it?" asked Matthew.

"I cannot be certain of course," Bambang said in reply, "but in my opinion this is a set of instructions."

"Instructions?"

"Yes. I will need to return to my university department to be sure, but in my opinion this is an instruction to the bearer to journey to another ancient monument, most likely one of the Egyptian pyramids. But before I say anything further I need to seek the expert opinion of one of our archeologists specializing in Egyptology, back at my college. We should have a definitive answer within the next two to three days."

Bambang was as good as his word. Back in the Mandarin hotel he sent word two days after they had returned that the slab did indeed bear a set of instructions, directing the bearer to a specific corridor within the Great Pyramid of Giza, in Egypt. When he met once more with Dawn and Matthew, for the final time before their departure from Indonesia, he put it succinctly.

"You are intended, Captain DeFaller, to journey to the Great Pyramid and locate the passages indicated here, leading to the chamber shown. Within that chamber I believe you will find the answers that you seek. I suggest you take this slab and journey to Cairo."

CHAPTER 51

The latest CNN interview with the 12th Imam Mahdi, broadcast live to every corner of the globe afforded him the opportunity once again to clarify a number of points of theology. During the course of the interview he was at particular pains to explain in some detail theological prophesy regarding the reappearance of Jesus (peace be upon him) as the Mahdi's lieutenant. But of course Jesus had thus far apparently not made his reappearance on Earth. However the Mahdi assured the peoples of Earth that, just as prophesied in the Hadiths, Jesus (peace be upon him) would indeed be coming, and soon. But he did comment that here we saw yet another piece of evidence that the Christian religion is at fault, based as it is upon an inaccurate holy text, when it cannot correctly predict the sequence of events relating to the return of its supposed Savior of humankind to Earth. And as the Mahdi was keen to point out, this inaccuracy of Christian theology was of course understood by every faithful Moslem.

The Mahdi then went on to announce plans to commence the initial wave of human colonization of Mars, but only by faithful Moslems. He revealed for the first time plans to build many large space ships. The purpose of these vessels would be to convey settlers from Earth to the newly terraformed Mars. Upon arrival they would commence the construction of the first Martian city on the great plain of Tharsis, in the shadow of Olympus Mons, the giant but extinct volcano. They would build homes and basic infrastructure, and, most importantly, a huge mosque. Islamic engineers, Islamic architects, Islamic scientists, Islamic doctors, Islamic dentists, and Islamic clerics were to be dispatched in the first wave, as well as sufficient skilled laborers to turn the dream into a reality. The Mahdi explained how in this way, the newly terraformed Mars would be won for Allah and Islam. There would be regular supply flights to keep essential items coming in, but the settlers would be sent there to stay.

And thus the first baby steps of humanity to expand into the cosmos would be taken. As history rolled on, human beings would learn to colonize other planets also, and eventually colonize other star systems in the galaxy. And thus the problems associated with the limitations of planet Earth would be solved. And the 12th Imam Mahdi would go down in history as the one who started this whole process in motion. A process made possible only through the good graces of Allah Himself.

CHAPTER 52

The Great Pyramid of Giza, the largest and oldest of the three pyramids at the Giza Necropolis loomed larger than life to Dawn and Revere as they stood before it. It was a giant structure, some four hundred and fifty-five feet tall and seven hundred and fifty-six feet along each edge at its base. Dawn marveled at the sheer effort that must have gone into its construction, more than forty-five centuries before. Even to build it today would represent a gargantuan effort, and, somewhat disconcertingly in her mind, may well prove to be beyond the limitations of even modern technology.

"Shall we begin?"

Samir, their Egyptian guide who had driven them both out here from Cairo, was anxious to get on. Dawn and Revere were staying in a local hotel in the city, posing as Drs. Richard Heigel and Helen Marchand of the Department of Archeology from Yale University. Within the context of their alias personae they were friendly but not married, so, to complete the ruse, they had booked separate rooms, although at the same hotel. All of the appropriate paperwork, including fake passports and other identification documents, had been arranged in advance and sent on to the authorities in Cairo, as well as the Faculty of Archeology at Cairo University, allowing them to make a special supervised investigation into the Pyramid of Giza. Upon their arrival there two days earlier they had met with a Dr. Hosni Sharaf, an archeologist at the university who had provided them with Samir as their guide. He had apologized about his being personally unable to join them on their investigation, but had given them a thick sheaf of papers outlining all of the regulations they were to abide by, as well as limitations of activities which they were permitted to undertake while within the structure of the pyramid itself. Dismantling of constructs within the chamber they proposed to visit were to be permitted, but care had to be taken that all deconstruction was carefully reconstructed at the end of their investigation. Nothing was to be damaged. Nor was anything to be removed from the site.

Their initial meeting with Dr. Sharaf had been a little awkward for them, despite their intensive home-based study of ancient Egyptian Archeology, as they had been quite concerned that he might ask them to explain or elaborate on some aspect of their work which would be beyond them both. But as luck would have it, Sharaf was cordial and courteous, but not particularly searching. He seemed to assume that they knew their business well enough, which was just as well. For although on the surface Dawn and Matthew could pose as professional archeologists, there was very little substance behind their front, a reality of which they were both painfully aware.

Dawn responded to Samir.

"Yes. Let us get to work as soon as possible. We have only today and tomorrow, before the pyramid is once again open to the public. We are not yet certain as to how long our investigation will take."

Matthew smiled inwardly as he remembered that the Great Pyramid, a national treasure and monument, had been temporarily closed to the public on the order of local government, purely to accommodate them both.

Samir smiled.

"Then please, follow me."

Samir led them both up some stairs which brought them after some minutes to a rough stone portal, incorporating a door.

Producing a large bunch of keys from his pocket, he proceeded to unlock the iron door, a contemporary looking structure.

"This door, this is not an original structure?"

Dawn glared at her husband. But Samir, surprisingly, did not seem to find the question odd.

"No, Dr. Heigel, this was added about forty years ago in order to maintain a semblance of security. This is not the original entrance to the Great Pyramid but is the entrance used nowadays. This entrance is known as the Robber's Tunnel. It was dug by workmen in the employ of Caliph al-Ma'mun, around AD820. When we enter you will see that the tunnel is cut straight through the masonry of the pyramid itself, but will meet with the ascending passage."

"Ah yes, of course. The Robber's Tunnel." Revere made a sincere attempt to sound sage and knowledgeable.

Samir swung open the door.

"Please. Follow me."

They entered the interior of the base of the pyramid and commenced walking along a narrow level passage that after a hundred feet or so commenced sloping downwards at an incline of about ten degrees. The passage itself would have been dark but for the presence of many electric light fittings which had been added to the walls. However as a precaution each one of them also carried a flashlight, just in case there was a power failure. As they penetrated deeper and deeper into the bowels of the monument itself, Dawn started to feel a strange sense of foreboding, as if she was leaving the world of light outside and entering another realm. According to the map on the slab that they had found hidden at the Borobudur, the chamber that they ultimately sought lay deep underground, directly beneath the pyramid's center. The walk there was definitely not one to be attempted by anyone suffering from claustrophobia.

"Do members of the public come down here very often, Samir?"

Dawn's question was really in response to the stifling heat and stuffiness that she was now beginning to feel. She was trying to take her mind off the discomfort she was feeling. But at least, in here, away from the prying eyes of the public, she was not required to wear the burqa.

"Actually no, not very often. As this chamber is somewhat more difficult to reach, only the most dedicated members of the public make the effort to visit this part of the pyramid, although all are welcome."

After walking on a downgrade for what seemed like at least another three or four hundred feet, and negotiating several right-angled turns, at which point the narrow passage narrowed even more, they finally reached what seemed like the end of the passage, and another iron door. This one was securely padlocked.

"A moment please."

Samir produced his keys again. He removed the padlock and swung open the door, to reveal a ladder that extended vertically downwards for about sixty feet into the gloom. He motioned to them both to start climbing. After a moment of trepidation, Matthew went first, followed by his wife. Samir came down after them, closing the door from the inside as he went. Dawn noticed to her great relief that he had brought the padlock along with him.

On reaching the bottom of the ladder, they found themselves standing in a small poorly lit vestibular area, of perhaps around six square feet. Another portal faced them. But this time there was no door.

"Walk through straight ahead and you will have entered the antechamber to the Chamber of Kings. Turn to your right and walk again through the second portal and you will be in the Chamber of Kings itself.

"You are not coming?"

"Local law states that I must remain outside as long as there is anyone inside either the antechamber or the Chamber of Kings, Dr. Marchand. And also, as I am sure you are aware there is the curse of the Chamber of the Kings. I am not a superstitious man, Dr. Marchand, but I feel that there is no reason to tempt fate."

Dawn smiled. Samir was of course referring to the ill-fated expedition that had come to this part of the pyramid in 1924 but had left rapidly and prematurely after having been apparently very badly frightened by something. Or so the story would have one believe. In fact the members of that expedition had departed in so much of a hurry that they had left most of their equipment behind, much of it quite valuable. She had come upon this during her research for her role. But in any event this had proved to be an unexpected piece of luck. She was not afraid of ghosts or demons or other preternatural phenomena, but up until this point she had been concerned about how they would deal with anything they might find with Samir standing sentinel over them. But apparently he trusted them to know what they were about. And he was quite content to let them get on with it. Alone.

They looked at each other, and then stepped through into the antechamber. It turned out to be a plain room about ten feet by seven feet, with a fifteen foot ceiling, dimly lit with more of the same type of light fixtures. As Samir had said, to their right stood another portal, beckoning them to come on through. Dawn stood aside.

"Well, I think you should go on through first, don't you?"

Matthew smiled at her.

"Then let us see what lies inside."

With that he stepped through the portal.

Matthew found himself standing inside another, slightly smaller chamber. He pointed his flashlight at the walls and the ceiling. At first he noticed nothing out of the ordinary, they seemed plain and unremarkable, but then he noticed the small alcove on the far side of the chamber. On approaching it, he noticed that inlaid in the wall about three feet from the floor, was a carved smooth stone panel, approximately three feet tall and six feet wide.

"Dawn! Come on through! I think I have found something!"

Moments later she was standing by his side, peering at the design on the panel. It appeared to depict the sun and the inner planets of the solar system at some point during history.

"Look, Matthew! That's the Earth, and there, that's Venus, and Mercury. And behind them. The planet Mars. What do you think? And look, the Earth's moon and the moons of the other planets are depicted as well."

Revere seemed to be deep in thought.

"I agree. This does appear to be a depiction of the inner planets. But I am trying to think of a specific time in history when they were all aligned thusly."

"Isn't this simply an alignment that they were in relative to each other at some point in the distant past? Around the time when the pyramid was constructed perhaps?"

"I do not know. It does not seem to fit any pattern I can envision."

"Well how do we know for sure that the planetary alignment depicted here actually ever occurred anyway? Shouldn't we confirm the information against established records, if possible?"

"Of course. But remember too that I am trained and experienced in the art of navigation by the stars. Planetary alignment comes into play as well, but this alignment depicted here does not appear familiar to me."

"Yes, well let's take a few photographs for our records. Do you think there might be any way we can get inside or behind this panel?"

"Yes, I am thinking about that, but I do not see anything yet." He studied the edges of the panel with considerable care.

The flash of the first photograph Dawn took with her digital camera went off. Without warning there was the combined sound of what seemed like a dozen or so hidden bolt mechanisms sliding back. The panel itself then slid slowly downwards, revealing another small portal, just large enough for them to climb through. They both looked at each other in surprise.

"Perhaps one of us should remain outside in case this door shuts again?"

"Good idea, Matthew. You stay here. I will go inside."

Before he had time to protest, Dawn had stepped over the three foot wall and had entered the further chamber inside. The moment she did so a soft glowing green light appeared to emanate from the walls, becoming sufficiently bright within a few seconds so that she could turn off her flashlight. She quickly noticed in fact that the system of lighting appeared to be similar to the one she had encountered inside the temple in Atlantis. The walls of this chamber were smooth and clean, in fact the whole chamber belied a powerful sense of newness, as if it had only recently been constructed, and had not endured since ancient times as the rest of the pyramid. But of course this was more than likely purely an illusion. This chamber had probably never been opened since the date it was originally sealed, over four thousand years before.

Running the length of the chamber was a stone plinth. At first it appeared plain, with a smooth, unremarkable surface, but then Dawn noticed some indentations running along the underside of its edge, into which she found her fingers would fit. On placing her fingers in position into every indentation simultaneously, she was able to activate a locking mechanism, which disengaged and caused the whole plinth to be released from its surface, rather as the lid of a case opens when the latches are undone. Gingerly she pulled up the plinth and looked inside, and noticed that there were a number of small cylinders within that looked as if they were made of some kind of metal, perhaps copper, or bronze. On lifting one of them out, she was able to open one end of the cylinder and peer into its interior. With the aid of her flashlight she could make out rolled parchment, bearing a large quantity of writing that had been scribed by hand in ink. From what she could see it looked like ancient Greek, although she could not be certain. She reached in to lift another of the cylinders, but as she did so a series of laser-like beams started shining and converging to a point within the chamber just a few feet from where she stood. Seconds later something resembling a holographic three-dimensional image formed to show the face of one of the Guardsmen that Dawn had encountered while on

Mars. A moment later the image started to address her, but in some kind of automated manner, as if it were a recording that had been purposely left here, waiting to be discovered. It did not seem to have any awareness of her existence. As with her experiences with the Guardsmen, when it spoke, she was uncertain if it was actually audibly verbalizing, or simply communicating directly with her mind.

"If you have successfully opened this chamber, I congratulate you on being the first human being to have done so since the time of the Pharaohs. Inside each of these cylinders you will find fragments of copies of the original Holy book, as penned by the Hellenistic sages and mystics of Ancient Greece. This book has been suppressed for millenia, but must be once again exposed to the world for all of humanity to appreciate. For within its passages lie the solutions to the greatest dilemmas of the present age. Take this book and place it in the hands of your greatest living scholars. And inside the shorter copper cylinder you will find a cut jewel, resembling a large diamond, but which is in fact harder and heavier, and made of a material unknown to human science. Take this jewel, known as the Eye of the Pharaohs, and insert it into the receptacle to be found atop the plinth inside the edifice known as the Great Hall, within the rediscovered complex built on that continent lying at the bottom of the planet. Upon so doing a resonance frequency will be set within the global internet systems that will greatly facilitate the dissemination of the message of the book to all of the peoples of the Earth."

At that, the message abruptly ended.

Dawn was immediately struck with the impression that this recording must have been made millenia ago. But she had received the message loud and clear. Moments later she stepped back through to where Matthew was waiting patiently for her, carrying the entire collection of fourteen metal cylinders that she had found.

"Matthew. I have no time to explain but we must hide these cylinders in our packs and get them out of here."

A few minutes later Dawn and Revere had all of the fourteen small copper cylinders in their possession, carefully hidden in their packs, and had resealed the plinth, the subject of which they had agreed to remain silent about to Samir. They exited the chamber and made their way back to where he was waiting for them.

CHAPTER 53

Political stability in the world started to be seriously challenged as a new round of directives from the 12th Imam started to be heard. For example, at midnight on September 14th, 2008 the state of Israel ceased to exist as a political entity. At that time it instead became known by its new Arabic name, Al Quds, actually a reversion to its name that it had borne in ancient times. Shortly thereafter in the new state of Al Quds, all those Jews who would not convert to Islam were closely monitored by the authorities for evidence of lack of righteousness, in particular their frequent failure to pay the Jizya tax that had now been levied against all of Al-Quds' non-Islamic citizens. At first the punishment for such transgression of Allah's law was simply a reprimand issued in the form of a letter to the concerned parties, but suddenly and without warning the authorities swooped down and commenced mass arrests of members of Jewish families. Mass beheadings soon followed at the guillotines set up in every town and city within the state. Within a matter of a few weeks around twenty percent of the Jewish population of Al Quds had been thusly eliminated and it seemed only a matter of time before the remaining eighty percent would be wiped out. On a further directive, all musical performances within the Islamic world were to be banned, as was the playing or learning to play of any musical instrument. Prayer was now to be enforced five times per day, every day, without exception, for all Islamic people, on pain of death.

In Britain, Sharia law started to make its presence felt ever more strongly. The British Parliament received notification that they were to henceforth treat all Jews resident in the UK in the same manner as they were being treated in Al Quds. They were to be offered the chance to convert to Islam, or face the requirement to pay the Jizya tax and submit to surveillance, which would inevitably in some cases lead to execution for unrighteousness. The WIS however left the preferred method of execution to the discretion of the British judiciary. London's Buckingham Palace also received a directive from the WIS that henceforth the palace buildings were to fly flags from its highest flagpoles depicting the Star and Crescent of Islam. And Queen Elizabeth was to declare a national holiday every Ramadan during which she was to deliver a televised announcement to the British people. In this announcement she was to officially recognize her inferiority and absolute subservience to Islam and the global Umma. Similar political maneuvers in Scotland had led to a modicum of rioting and civil disobedience, and in consequence the WIS had issued an edict directly to Edinburgh City Council regarding the 'offensive' nature of the edifice of Edinburgh Castle itself, since it was an extant symbol of British colonial power and expansionism belonging to an age that was now long past. The WIS added that it was high time that Moslem people could walk the streets of the Scottish capital without being reminded of their subjugation by Western imperialist forces of the 18th and 19th centuries. And as if on cue, the leaders of the by-now majority Islamic Edinburgh City Council, in particular one Seoras Galway, MP, could not bend over backwards far enough nor quickly enough to accommodate these complaints. Before the week was out, Galway had deemed as a matter of law that Edinburgh Castle should be immediately demolished to make way for a new super mosque. And of course all work, including demolition and construction of the new Islamic house of worship, would be paid for by the non-Islamic

Scottish taxpayer, by way of the Jizya. Stirling City Council soon followed suit with plans to convert Stirling Castle beyond all recognition into yet another mosque. Stirling went one better than Edinburgh and also announced plans to issue an official apology to all of the Islamic controlled English City Councils for the 'offensive and wholly unnecessary' violence that took place on the field of nearby Bannockburn in 1314, when Scottish forces defeated those of England in a bloody pitched battle. A battle in which one English Knight, Sir Henry De Bohun, had had his skull cleaved in two at the hands of the Scottish king, Robert the Bruce, while wielding his battle axe. Bruce, the Stirling councilors had said, had been a rank infidel whose very name represented extreme offense to Islam.

Perhaps unsurprisingly, these moves proved less than popular with the indigenous Scottish populace, and gave rise to several terrorist organizations, the most prolific of which became known as the Scottish Army for Freedom, or SAF. The SAF had come about some months earlier as an underground organization, existing mostly within the cultural background and political fringes, but with these latest announcements the senior leader, an erstwhile novelist turned guerilla announced plans to kidnap the Islamic apologist Seoras Galway and murder him in a highly publicized campaign. His head was to be set on a spike at Edinburgh Castle, while his torso and limbs would be placed at Stirling. The SAF simultaneously issued a dire warning that the same would happen to anyone who so much as moved a single stone of the structures of the castles of either Edinburgh or Stirling, these proud icons of Scottish culture and history.

Over a very brief period the SAF made tremendous strides in their popularity. Soon the popular cry on the streets the length and breadth of the country was *Just Say No to Sharia!* Unsurprisingly the WIS was quick to declare the SAF a terrorist organization, and placed a price of the heads of its leaders, as well as outlawing membership of the organization. But despite their best efforts, the stage was set for a confrontation between the ordinary people of Scotland and those who would rob them of their hard-won freedoms. It seemed that within Europe, the Scots at least had had their fill of theocratic totalitarianism and rank cowardice from their political leaders.

CHAPTER 54

South Atlantic Ocean. September 25, 2008

To Dawn, the sound of the sea rushing aside as USCG Cutter *Eagle* pushed through the waves had a satisfying, very natural feel. This was one of the few times she had been aboard a ship under sail, its hull being moved through the ocean by nothing but the power of the wind. Her only other similar experiences had been as a visitor to the latter part of the 18th century, as an invited guest aboard her husband's ship USS *Susquehanna.* Matthew presently joined her on the deck after he had taken care of some immediate business on the bridge with the officer of the watch.

"How are you feeling now? Does your head still trouble you?"

"No, Matthew, I'm feeling a lot better now. I think those painkillers did the trick."

She was referring to the pounding headache that she had experienced soon after they had set sail from Boston harbor. It must have been the stress, she thought. For although *Eagle* had departed on a regular training mission, she and Matthew had between them planned an unscheduled diversion to the Antarctic coast, whereupon they both were to disembark and make their way to Atlantis. Dawn had been extremely careful to stow the strange jewel that she had taken from the secret chamber deep within the Great Pyramid of Giza. The Eye of the Pharaohs the holographic recording had called it. No-one aboard *Eagle* yet knew of their plan, however at some point during the voyage Revere planned to discuss his temporary leave of absence with his executive officer, Lieutenant Commander Hackett. The plan was that, after being dropped on the Antarctic coast as near to Atlantis as possible, Hackett would continue the training voyage as acting commanding officer, while Revere and Dawn would travel to their intended destination on the two snow mobiles that they had arranged to have loaded aboard *Eagle* while she was still berthed in Boston. The machines were carefully concealed in crates, the latter without any identifying labels or marks, such as to render them effectively invisible to any members of *Eagle's* crew. Once in Atlantis, the plan was to find the plinth within the temple specified by the hologram that Dawn had witnessed in Egypt, and simply place the jewel in position. After that, Dawn had no idea what would actually happen, if indeed there would be some great event that would affect the peoples of the Earth or not. But she was clear that this was what the holographic message had specified that she should do. In any event, she and Revere would then travel back to the coastal area where *Eagle* would rendezvous with them once more. They would come back aboard, Revere would resume command, and the mission would proceed as planned. They anticipated that they would be away from *Eagle* for not more than twelve hours. All records of this diversionary activity would be judiciously kept out of *Eagle's* log. Revere was confident he could secure Hackett's agreement to maintain secrecy by telling him that he was under orders to carry out a highly classified mission that was to be discussed with no-one. Indeed Revere and Dawn's departure from *Eagle,* and later re-boarding, would be witnessed only by Hackett himself. Dawn thought once more of the jewel itself, hidden in Matthew's cabin. She had carefully removed it from its container and studied it in her hands. It did indeed resemble a cut diamond of sorts, about the size and shape of an egg. It sparkled brilliantly with every color of the visible spectrum. Dawn had rarely if ever seen quite this effect produced by any other diamond that she had encountered. It was also very much heavier than one would expect, for it weighed about as much as it would have done had it been made of solid lead. Or even gold. She remembered that the hologram had informed her that although the jewel resembled a diamond it was in fact made of some other harder, unknown substance. All this she found easy to believe upon her cursory examination. Whatever the jewel was made of, it was as beautiful as it was mysterious.

"Matthew? How much longer before we reach the coast of Antarctica?"

"If the wind holds, around forty-six hours. And of course, if it does not, we can use the engines. However in this part of the world the wind rarely if ever subsides."

"So Matthew, how-"

But her question was cut short by an announcement over the ship's tannoy system.

"Captain to the bridge immediately! Captain to the bridge immediately!"

He glanced over at the loudspeaker from which the announcement had just emanated.

"Sorry, I must attend to Mr. Cunningham's request. I shall return presently."

When Revere stepped onto the bridge, Lieutenant Cunningham immediately informed him of the situation that had developed.

"Sir! We have received a signal from a vessel identifying itself as a frigate of the Royal New Arabian Navy. She is on a converging course with us and orders that we stop immediately and await the arrival of a boarding party."

"What do they want?"

"Sir, they wouldn't say. But I can place you in contact with her captain."

"Then please do so immediately."

Moments later Revere was talking with an unfamiliar voice at the other end of a radio link.

"This is Captain Matthew Revere of the United States Coast Guard Cutter *Eagle*. We are on a routine cadet training voyage.

Please identify yourself and state the nature of your request. Over."

There was a brief pause, before the response came.

"Captain Revere." The voice sounded Arabic, but the speaker obviously had a good command of English. "This is Captain Ali Sharifi of the frigate *Al-Tariq* of the Royal New Arabian Navy. I am currently seventy-five nautical miles north-west of your position, but am headed in your direction. I order you to stop immediately and hold your position."

"For what purpose?"

"We have orders to board and search your vessel. We have reason to believe that you are illegally conveying an ancient artifact which you intend to transport to the continent of Antarctica. We are required to search your vessel and seize this artifact. You will hold your position and await the arrival of our boarding party. We will be joining you within three hours. The search will take no more than thirty minutes, after which time you will be free to proceed. I must warn you, however, Captain Revere, that if you fail to comply, I am under orders to sink your vessel."

Revere put down the microphone and thought for a moment. How could the RNAN possibly be aware of the presence of the jewel aboard *Eagle,* or the fact that he and Dawn intended to transport it to Antarctica? Was this just a lucky guess? A bluff? Would he have any chance of outrunning a frigate? Was there any coastline in which he could hide before *Al-Tariq* caught up with them? But it was hopeless. They were presently much too far from land. Even with their engines running and all sails set, he could not possibly hope to outrun a fast warship. He decided that his only option was to stop as ordered, and wait.

"Captain Sharifi. This is Captain Revere. I am stopping and holding position as ordered, and am awaiting your arrival."

The response, when it came, sounded cold and uncaring.

"Good, Captain Revere. We will join you presently."

After ordering Cunningham to stop and hold position, Revere informed Dawn of the situation. She was immediately annoyed.

"How the hell did they know about our plans? Did someone leak the information?"

"I do not know. But the fact remains, we have been detected. We have no hope of outrunning a modern frigate." He thought hard for a moment. "I suggest instead that someone take the jewel and submerge in a diving suit just before *Al-Tariq* converges on our position. And wait there until their search is over. Then the diver can surface and we may be on our way."

"Do you have any certified divers aboard?"

"Yes. Lieutenant Smallwood. We can have him make ready, and at the critical moment hand him the jewel wrapped appropriately so that he does not see what he is carrying, and have him stow it securely in his suit. He can go down, and wait. In the meantime I will entertain our guests. Hopefully they will be gone within half an hour as Captain Sharifi stated. But Smallwood will be able to stay down for up to thirty minutes, as long as he avoids exertion and does not exceed a depth of two hundred feet."

"Thirty minutes at two hundred feet? That's a long time to linger at such a depth. What will he be breathing? Trimix?"

"Trimix, yes."

Dawn was not happy with this plan, not least because even if Smallwood remained submerged for half an hour, it would still quite possibly be cutting things close. But she could not think of anything better. To her it seemed possible, perhaps even probable, that if the RNAN knew of their mission and current location, then they may have some sure way of detecting the jewel once they were aboard *Eagle*.

"Well whatever happens Matthew, Smallwood had better not lose the jewel. The water here is deep."

"Approximately ten thousand feet."

"If he loses it, it is gone forever."

"Indeed."

Neither of them said anything more but they were both fearful of the consequences of the loss of the jewel.

Within twenty minutes of the expected arrival of *Al-Tariq*, Smallwood was on deck, dressed in his full diving gear and receiving final instructions from Revere.

"Take this package," Revere said to him. "Stow it very securely about your person. Do not open it under any circumstances. Do not surface until you receive the signal to do so from me personally. The boarding party from the RNAN will be with us shortly. It is my belief that they are looking for the contents of this package. It is absolutely imperative that they do not find it."

Revere stated the next part of his instruction with great care and emphasis, fixing Smallwood in the eye as he did so.

"It is also imperative that you bring it back to the surface following your dive."

"Yes sir!" Smallwood was young, perhaps some twenty three years of age, and very keen. "I will await your personal signal before surfacing. And sir?"

"Yes, Lieutenant?"

"Assuming I merely have to descend and hold position at two hundred feet without moving about, I can conserve my air and so may be able to extend my bottom time to approximately thirty-eight minutes. About eight minutes over the nominal half hour time limit. My dive computer will confirm the precise time but I believe I can do it."

Matthew was most impressed by that response.

"Thirty-eight minutes. Excellent, Lieutenant! That should be more than enough."

They waited until *Al-Tariq* had closed to within a mile of their position, her gray wolf-like form visible off their port side, and then Smallwood entered the water, facing away from the oncoming vessel. He waited until the latter was within minutes of reaching them before commencing his descent.

"*Eagle!* This is the frigate *Al-Tariq* of the Royal New Arabian Navy! Stand fast and prepare to be boarded."

Revere was expecting the voice over the loudspeaker but nevertheless it engendered a feeling of depression in him. His mind was cast back to the incident during 1776 while aboard his earlier command, USS *Susquehanna,* when he had been stopped following a bloody sea battle with the British frigate HMS *Bulldog,* only to be faced with apparent certain arrest at the hands of one Vice-Admiral Sir Charles Eastleigh-Grant, and probable execution. Only the timely intervention of the Lynx helicopter with her Exocet missile from HMS *Wildcat* had saved the day. Revere watched as *Al-Tariq* came a short distance alongside, before powering down her gas turbine engines to idle. Within moments an inflatable was launched from her side, and almost immediately it was speeding over to meet them. He could see that the boat was carrying three men, two of them dressed as officers. Approximately thirty seconds later the boat had arrived at *Eagle's* side. Some American crewmen helped her tie up, and presently the two officers climbed up the steps on *Eagle's* side and stepped on to her main deck. Revere stepped forward to meet them, extending his right hand in greeting.

"Good afternoon, gentlemen. I am Captain Matthew Revere, officer in command of this vessel."

The older of the two men surveyed him with detached coolness for a moment, before taking Revere's outstretched hand in his.

"And I am Lieutenant-Commander Ali of the frigate *Al-Tariq.*"

"How can I help you, Commander?"

Ali came straight to the point. "Captain Revere. We have reason to believe that you are transporting an artifact which does not belong to you, but rather, is the property of the peoples of New Arabia. Return it to us now, and we shall depart."

Revere maintained a façade of nonchalance.

"I am rather afraid that I do not know to what you are referring, Commander. This is an American training vessel, on routine patrol with a complement of naval cadets. We are transporting no cargo."

Ali became impatient. He pulled a device from his pocket, about the size and shape of an iPod. Staring at it as he manipulated a dial on its front face, he looked up at Revere with an expression of pure malice in his features.

"Where have you hidden the artifact? According to my readout it is in fact aboard. You are an infidel and a liar, Captain! Where is it?"

Revere felt the hairs bristling on the back of his neck. This man was beginning to annoy him. But he gave nothing away. Instead he simply reiterated his story.

"We are transporting no cargo."

"Infidel dog! Where did you hide it? Tell us! Tell us now!"

But Revere would not.

"Tell me! Or I will tear this ship apart!"

But Revere had nothing further to say. Ali clapped his hands and barked out a brief order in Arabic and instantly his two companions commenced running around *Eagle's* deck, submachine guns readied at their hips, looking for doors and companionways. It was not long before they were conducting a fairly thorough search of the living quarters of the vessel. But a search of nearly twenty minutes' duration, and including the use of their small devices, which apparently sped the process greatly, yielded nothing.

Commander Ali finally ran out of patience. He gathered his men and they quickly returned to their launch. As they sped away Ali yelled over to Revere.

"You had your chance, Captain! Now you die!"

Revere noticed Ali was speaking with a radio microphone, more than likely to one of his crew aboard his ship. As if on cue, *Al-Tariq* loosed three torpedoes just moments later, one after the other, which came speeding over to *Eagle's* side. The resultant explosions, moments later, were terrific. Mercifully Dawn and Revere both were blasted into unconsciousness, just as the first of the three tin fish reached their target.

Revere awoke to the feeling of cool, lapping water striking him gently but repeatedly in the face. It took him a few seconds to regain his bearings, but presently he realized that he was in the water. He looked around for *Eagle,* but could not see her anywhere. *Al-Tariq* was gone also. What had happened? Had they been torpedoed? It seemed he was quite alone, in an off-shore region of the South Atlantic ocean. *Dawn!* Suddenly he remembered his wife. Where was she? He could not bear to imagine what might have become of her. Somehow he managed to find the energy to call out her name.

"Dawn! Dawn!"

There was nothing. No response. It seemed that indeed, he was quite alone. He called out again.

"Dawn!"

Mercifully this time she returned his call.

"Over here!"

At first he fancied that he was imagining things, hearing what he wanted to hear. But as he spun around in the direction from where the sound had emanated, he spotted a deployed life raft. And leaning from the side was Dawn. He started swimming weakly towards her as she used the paddle to bring the raft over to his position.

As she hauled him aboard, he stared at her weakly.

"What happened? *Eagle?* Where is she?"

"Matthew. *Al-Tariq* torpedoed us before going on their way. I saw torpedoes coming our way just before I passed out."

"What about Lieutenant Smallwood?"

She jerked her thumb over to one corner of the raft. There, lying behind the toolbox, was Smallwood. Still dressed in his diving suit.

"Is he all right?"

"He was injured by sinking debris from *Eagle.* I think his leg may be broken. But he managed to surface and he was able to return the jewel."

She slid the jewel over to him, still tightly wrapped in its covering.

"For now I have given him morphine. He's asleep."

"So how did you manage to procure the life raft?"

"I came to in the water and found the raft floating in an undeployed condition. At first I thought there might be something wrong with it, that perhaps it had been damaged by the explosions. But when I pulled on the painter line, it inflated."

"How are you feeling, Dawn?"

She sighed.

"I have felt better, but I am OK."

With that, Revere passed out once more. Dawn decided to leave him.

He slept for four hours.

CHAPTER 55

Revere was awakened from his slumber by the sharp retort of a Very pistol being fired. He slowly opened his eyes, only to realize that night had already fallen and they were surrounded by darkness. But as he came fully to his senses, he realized that the darkness was broken in one direction by the presence of a large ship, possibly a cargo vessel, running perhaps six or seven miles south of their position. Dawn had attempted to attract the attention of the passing ship by sending up a flare. She had waited until their paths had intersected as closely as their relative positions would allow before firing. There were five more flares packed in the raft supplies, but she wanted nevertheless to maximize their chances of being seen. She need not have been concerned, for no sooner had the flare burst overhead, lighting up the entire area and glowing like a star shell, than she saw immediate signs that the officer of the watch aboard the ship had seen their light. She watched as it very gradually altered course, turning towards their position, and started to slow. She reloaded the pistol so as to be ready for when the ship approached their position, although she knew that if the bridge crew were alert they would already be scanning the surface of the sea with their short range radar. They should also already be picking up the signal from the raft's transponder that was currently energized by the salt water, and they had almost certainly seen the raft's flashing white beacons. She waited out the twenty or so minutes as the ship grew larger and larger. Presently she saw a small fast launch being put down over the vessel's starboard side. Moments later the latter was making straight for their position at well over twenty knots, displaying as many lights as a Christmas tree and training two powerful searchlights straight ahead. Dawn by now could see that the ship was an oil tanker, and was truly enormous. Even although she had traversed approximately six miles since the initial sighting of Dawn's flare the ship was still making headway, despite the fact that her engines were doubtless idled, or even running in full reverse.

"Ahoy there! Stand by! We will be with you presently!"

The launch idled her engines as she pulled up alongside. Despite her obvious relief at having been rescued, Dawn maintained her professionalism.

"I am Captain Dawn DeFaller, British Royal Navy, and this is Captain Matthew Revere, United States Navy. And we also have a casualty, Lieutenant Justin Smallwood, United States Navy, lying over there in the corner. I gave him some morphine earlier and he is still sleeping."

But Revere himself had drifted back into unconsciousness. He was obviously exhausted and Dawn was becoming a little concerned about him.

"The three of us are the sole survivors of an attack on our vessel, the United States Coast Guard Cutter *Eagle,* a cadet training ship. Our vessel was boarded illegally and then torpedoed by *Al-Tariq,* a frigate of the Royal New Arabian Navy. We need immediate assistance. Lieutenant Smallwood needs the attention of a doctor. I believe he has a broken leg. Can you help us?"

The response was immediate and in the affirmative.

"Of course we can. Please take a line from us and secure your raft. We will ferry you to our vessel."

"Certainly. But may I know your name?"

"Oh I am sorry, Captain DeFaller. I am James Pearson, senior bridge officer."

"What is the name of your ship?"

"We are an Exxon VLCC. The *Saskatchewan Star.*"

Dawn could not believe her luck.

"The *Saskatchewan Star?* Captain Bryan King?"

Pearson stared at her, somewhat taken aback.

"Captain King, yes. You are acquainted with him?"

Dawn smiled disarmingly.

"Yes. Captain King and the *Saskatchewan Star* were involved in an Anglo-American joint civilian-naval operation a number of months ago. Codenamed Operation *Ankara.*"

"*Ankara,* yes. I was not on duty during *Ankara* and so I missed it. But I understand things went off very well."

"Indeed they did, Mr. Pearson. I was the naval commander in charge of *Anakara.*"

Pearson's eyes widened in surprise.

"Then it is very fortunate that we found you, Captain."

CHAPTER 56

O nce safely aboard *Saskatchewan Star* and installed in a comfortable cabin it was not long before King took the time to visit. He found Dawn there alone.

"Captain DeFaller! What an unexpected surprise! When I heard that the survivors aboard the raft included you and your husband I came just as soon as I was able. How are you? Has the doctor had a look at you both yet? What happened?"

"It's very pleasant to meet with you once again, Captain King. And yes, the doctor has seen us both, as well as the young lieutenant who was with us. Me he discharged immediately, but my husband, Matthew, is still with him. He called about fifteen minutes ago to say that everything is fine. Matthew just needed some intravenous fluids and some rest. And Lieutenant Smallwood was treated for a broken leg. He is also suffering from a mild case of decompression sickness."

King listened with courteous civility.

"I'm very glad that everything has worked out for the best. But please, once again, I would ask that you call me Bryan. I know that you and your husband are naval officers and are accustomed to formal rank and titles, but aboard the *Star* we do not stand on ceremony. It's strictly first name terms, on the bridge, even when we are amongst the crew. Nothing has changed since you were last here."

Dawn smiled.

"Bryan. We were most fortunate that you came along when you did."

"Indeed. Quite a coincidence. Listen. Later on, when Matthew has been certified as fit by the doctor and released, I would like to invite you both for a tour of the ship."

"I know that Matthew would be absolutely fascinated."

"Excellent. So it's settled, then. I will go directly to the sick bay and find out what is taking so long. Our medical officer is good but a little young. He tends to err on the side of caution, to the point of keeping someone with a cough confined to bed for a week."

Dawn laughed.

"Well, you can laugh, but I expect he'll insist on keeping your young lieutenant in bed with his broken leg until we dock."

CHAPTER 57

To Revere, the view from the bridge of *Saskatchewan Star* was mind-boggling. He could not believe that such an enormous ship could be built and operated safely. Just standing looking out on the ocean they were well over one hundred feet above the surface of the waves, higher than even a lookout in the crow's nest would have been aboard his first naval command, the USS *Connecticut.* Since the commencement of their tour following breakfast the next day, in which he had partaken voraciously, he had done nothing but ask a myriad of endless questions and quiz King on all aspects of the day-to-day operation of his ship. On a couple of occasions Dawn had gently reminded him that his manner of questioning was leaning towards the interrogative. But King would have none of it. As ever, he was the perfect host.

"Not at all," he would say. "I would be happy to talk about the *Star* and nothing else for a week."

But after discussing the workings of the navigation computer and the ways in which King was able to communicate with the Engine Room, as well as giving Revere the opportunity to sit in the Captain's Chair for a spell, he had them both join him in the chart room just off the main bridge itself, and take seats at the table, which he cleared.

"So," he began. "If I may inquire, how can I help you?"

Revere responded initially.

"Well, sir. We were en-route to a particular destination when we were intercepted by the RNAN and sunk."

King seemed to immediately see what he was driving at.

"Well, if you would like me to, say, divert course in order to drop you at a specific destination, I could arrange that, as long as it did not involve more than say, three days additional sailing time. You see, we are presently running empty, in ballast only, from Buenos Aires to Bahrain. Once in Bahrain the *Star* is to be handed over to the government of New Arabia. We do not know for certain what will happen following that, but it seems likely she will be decommissioned as a tanker and converted for another purpose."

"And what about you and your crew?"

"Oh, we expect we'll be kept on by the new owners. They'll need an experienced crew to operate the ship. But our days of transporting large quantities of crude oil over the world's oceans seem to be over, more especially now since the global economy is no longer dependent on continued supplies of enormous quantities of petroleum, because of the unearthing of these strange machines in Antarctica. That's why Exxon has decided to sell this ship, along with many others like her. I believe the other major oil companies, mainly Shell, British Petroleum, and the Indonesian company Pertamina are looking to do the same thing. Although I've heard that in some cases ships are simply being put up for scrap. But because the *Star* is relatively new and high-tech, and can be converted for another purpose for a fraction of the cost of a brand new vessel, we are lucky. Nothing much will change for us in practice, just the company name on our paychecks, and the cargo which we end up transporting. For any merchant seaman, that is a more than fair proposition."

Revere had another question.

"So you would not be averse to diverting course for a few days?"

"Absolutely not a problem."

"But how would you explain your tardiness to the authorities in Bahrain?"

"Oh, that would be easy. We could feign engine trouble, or a navigational computer malfunction, or something of that nature."

Revere decided to elaborate on the nature of their mission prior to their sinking. As he started to speak, he glanced at Dawn to see that she was in agreement with his doing so, but she made no visible signs of objection.

"We put to sea around five days ago aboard *Eagle,* a sailing training vessel of the United States Coast Guard. We had a crew of thirty-five Naval Academy cadets from Annapolis, Maryland, and four commissioned officers, including myself as captain, as well as seven non-commissioned officers. A total of forty six officers and crew. Plus my wife, technically travelling with us as a passenger. We were on a sailing training voyage out of Boston, Massachusetts, to head down into the South Atlantic Ocean, past the western coast of the Falkland Islands, and thence to cruise off the coast of Antarctica for three days. Following that we were to return to Boston, where we were due back some two weeks after our initial departure. That much is straightforward. However, I had planned an unscheduled stop along the coast of Antarctica's Queen Maud Land, where Dawn and I were to alight for approximately twenty-four hours. The ship was to proceed to within twenty miles of the coast. We were then planning to take a small boat to the nearest beach head, and in secret. In the meantime I was to leave *Eagle* in the hands of my Executive Officer as acting commander. Only he would be aware of my temporary absence from the ship. Once ashore, using two snowmobiles that we were to bring with us aboard the small boat, we were to make a rapid transit to the excavated site that has become known as Atlantis. There we were to make a brief visit to a specific temple within the complex of unearthed buildings. The purpose was simply to place an artifact that we have in our possession in position at an altar contained within. The placement of this artifact, we have reason to believe, will result in enormous benefit to the state of international relations all across the globe. I am not at liberty to discuss or divulge the reasons for this belief, but we both feel it to be a mission of vital importance for the sake of world security. But as you are aware, five days out of Boston, our ship was intercepted and sunk by a frigate of the Royal New Arabian Navy, the *Al-Tariq*. At first we were boarded; it seems that the RNAN was aware of our secret mission to Antarctica and of the artifact that we were transporting, although I have no explanation as to how they came to know of this. We successfully hid the artifact by sending it down two hundred feet below the surface of the ocean with a diver, Lieutenant Smallwood, who is presently in your sick bay. When they were unable to find the artifact, the boarding party returned to *Al-Tariq* which thereafter torpedoed our vessel, which was consequently destroyed. All remaining hands were lost, save for Lieutenant Smallwood, who was underwater at the time, and Dawn, and myself. In fact, both my wife and I are quite surprised that out of everyone aboard, we were the only two to survive the blast. I believe it may be because out of all aboard, Captain DeFaller and I were the only people standing on deck near the vessel's stern when the torpedoes struck."

King listened to Revere's story with intent.

"I'm very sorry to hear what happened to you. What a dreadful situation. I'm very sorry about your crew."

"Yes indeed, as am I. They were a fine collection of officers and seamen, and of course most of the crew were cadets, who did not deserve to be placed in harm's way. But such is the way of things sometimes. Thankfully Lieutenant Smallwood survived, but his right leg was broken by debris from our sinking ship, and while he was still under water. It must have been very difficult for him to maintain sufficient presence of mind under such circumstances to avoid drowning before reaching the surface once more. Although he did not spend sufficient time on his safety stops and so that would be how he contracted his decompression sickness."

"Well it is impressive that he was able to save himself at all. I don't know how I would have fared under such circumstances. You still have the artifact to which you were referring?"

"Yes. By lucky chance it is still in our possession. But of course, we no longer have the snowmobiles or the small boat with its stock of provisions which we had planned to use."

King appeared pensive for a moment.

"I could easily divert to a point twenty miles off the coast of Queen Maud Land. We could give you one of our motor launches, provisioned with food and water sufficient for twenty people for a period of up to three weeks, replete with a heater and air conditioner, as well as a radio, echo sounder, transponder, and computer navigation system. As well as suitable warm clothing, goggles, and medical supplies. And, as luck would have it, we are transporting a cargo of six snowmobiles, complete with fuel, as well as a set of tools and spare parts for emergency field repairs. They were intended for the government of New Arabia, but you are welcome to any two of those. We could drop you more or less as you had planned, and then feign engine trouble for a period of twenty four or even forty eight hours while you carry out your mission. Following your return to the coast, you could make your return trip back out to the *Star*. With the navigation computer and radio aboard your launch that would be an elementary task. We would then recover you from the ocean, along with the snow mobiles, and be on our way. When we arrive in Bahrain, we could arrange for your return to Boston."

King looked at both of them, back and forth.

"How does that sound?"

Dawn broke out into a broad grin.

"That sounds wonderful, Bryan. You are sure that you are prepared to take the risk?"

"Absolutely. I am in no special hurry to hand over my ship to the Arabians. As far as I am concerned they can wait for a few more days."

Revere had another question.

"There is one more thing."

"Yes?"

"Would you have any objection to allowing me the use of your radio so that I can report the loss of *Eagle* and her crew to the proper Coast Guard authorities in Boston?"

"Not a problem! In fact, I will take you to our communications console right now."

CHAPTER 58

The journey from the coast of Queen Maud Land to Atlantis was proving to be harder going than either of them had imagined. The ice over which they rode aboard their snowmobiles was packed solid, but was not especially even. In places great cavernous holes gaped out at them, like large mouths waiting to swallow them whole. The ride was decidedly bumpy and uncomfortable and they both had to be constantly on the lookout for anything that would bring their ride to an untimely end, more especially slight depressions in the snow that as often as not indicated an area where the underlying ice was weak, betraying the potential presence of a deep fissure into which either of them, or even both of them, could unexpectedly fall. Such a fall could bring their mission to a sudden end, and could even prove fatal. Atlantis lay some sixty miles inland. At an average speed of around fourteen miles per hour it would take over four hours to reach their intended destination. But there was nothing to be done about it. They would just have to keep pushing their way carefully in the direction indicated on their GPS units built into the snowmobile control consoles. As they went, Dawn thought about the *Saskatchewan Star,* anchored off the coast in the freezing Arctic waters, patiently awaiting their return. Assuming they did successfully negotiate the ice to their target, would they in fact be able to carry out their mission without let or hindrance from opposing forces that may have anticipated their moves and gathered against them? And would they be able to get back to the shoreline unmolested and without incident? She certainly hoped so.

As the hours rolled on, one thing did start to become more apparent. They were operating their snowmobiles with ever-greater skill and speed, and the remaining distance to Atlantis had shrunk greatly. Finally Revere was the first to spot their destination on the horizon.

"There it is."

He indicated by pointing with his right arm extended, as he drew his machine to a temporary stop. Dawn looked but still could see nothing except ice and snow, although her GPS unit was indicating that Atlantis was indeed very close at hand. But she trusted her husband's judgment, for she had come to realize that he had a very keen appreciation of the subtle nuances of various geographical features viewed from all kinds of positions from the sea and the land. He also possessed very sharp eyesight.

Approximately thirty minutes later they were making their way on foot down the long narrow staircase, constructed soon after the uncovering of Atlantis, by a group of Norwegian contractors that ran down the face of the excavated ice all the way towards the uncovered ancient settlement below. They had hidden their machines near the edge of the excavation, by the top of the staircase, in a trench that they had dug. All the way down Dawn was thinking about the layout of the altar that she would be seeking inside the central temple which she could make out below. She placed her right hand inside her pack and grasped the wrapped package containing the jewel, to reassure herself that it was still there.

Some forty-five minutes later they reached the base of the staircase. Dawn groaned inwardly when she contemplated the long climb back up that they would have to make later. Her current level of physical fitness was not as high as she would like it to be, but her days at sea and her time engaged earlier in off-world travel had rendered that somewhat inevitable.

She stood for a moment and looked around, but it seemed as if the entire complex was deserted. Perhaps this really was going to turn out to be straightforward after all. Satisfying themselves that they were alone, they commenced walking towards and then around the various buildings between them and the temple. On finally reaching it some seventy-five minutes later, they walked around to the entry way. They looked at each other for a moment, hesitating, before stepping inside. Dawn went in first, Revere following directly behind her.

At first the interior of the temple seemed poorly lit and completely quiet, as if they were utterly alone. But after they had walked about forty feet, without warning the interior of the temple lit up like a Christmas tree. Almost immediately a familiar voice called out in the gloom.

"Captain DeFaller!"

CHAPTER 59

" Captain DeFaller. And Captain Revere. I have been expecting you. Please. Do come in."

"Commander Hunt. I was not . . ."

"Not what, Captain? Expecting to find me here? You were laboring under the impression that I would be in Constantinople, were you not?"

Dawn just stared at Hunt, incredulous.

"You see, Captain, you reckoned without my intelligence quotient being presently at around three times that of Doctor Albert Einstein, even when he was at the peak of his illustrious career. And of course combined with my capacity for telepathy at this point there is nothing that the ordinary human mind can conceptualize or imagine that is not already known to me. In short, Captain, with my intelligence being what it now is, I anticipate your every move. And with my telepathic powers, or powers of clairvoyance, one might say, I actually *see* your every move. And I have seen the reason as to why you have journeyed here in the first place. You are here to place the jewel you have brought with you, known if I am not mistaken as the Eye of the Pharaohs into the receptacle at the base of the altar at which I am presently standing. In so doing, you will cause an interference pattern in local space-time that will generate an instant readjustment of attitude in the minds of the faithful all across the surface of the

Earth, specifically that the principles of all faiths, including Islam, are founded upon Hellenistic ideologies and philosophies of love, mutual respect, forgiveness, and tolerance. Indeed the cylinders you found in the Great Pyramid of Giza actually bear an early written copy of the Hellenistic holy texts. And you have diligently placed these cylinders and their contents for safe keeping at secret locations with leading academicians in London, New York City, and Melbourne. These Hellenistic scriptures will suddenly find themselves much in demand by all Moslems everywhere as they reject the traditional Qur'anic notions of salvation by works and adherence to Hadithic tradition. People of other faiths will be very interested in reading them too. Am I correct so far, Captain?"

"Commander Hunt, I-"

"Please Captain. Address me as Imam Mahdi."

This last request annoyed Dawn.

"But you are no more the Imam Mahdi than I! You are an impostor! You are and always have been Garry Hunt, presently a Commander in the British Royal Navy! Your mind has been very greatly enhanced by prolonged treatment with Chotone-"

Hunt interrupted her again.

"In point of fact, Captain, I have no further need for Chotone, and have not for some considerable time now. Through the enhancement of my intellect I was able to devise a simple chemical modification to the drug such that, following a brief dose regimen, the effects become permanent, as well as even more pronounced. I had already achieved that before I disappeared during the final phase of *Ankara*."

On hearing this Dawn simply exhaled in exasperation.

"But Commander Hunt, intellectual enhancement or not, you are for all practical purposes the man you always were! In fact I really do not understand why you feel the need to insist on continuing with this ridiculous masquerade!"

Hunt cocked an eyebrow at her.

"Ridiculous masquerade, Captain? But don't you see what this ridiculous masquerade, as you put it, has done for me? I am now the ruler of planet Earth, and soon shall be also the ruler of Mars. A fair achievement for a naval commander, wouldn't you say?"

"So you are the ruler of Earth. And perhaps you may rule Mars as well. But at what price? You have managed to hoodwink a sizeable portion of humanity into believing that you are who you purport to be. But of course, you are not. You have committed mass murder in order to prosecute your agenda. Despite your intelligence, Commander, you really are no different from any of the other despots in the history of the world."

"And with which of history's despots do I especially compare, in your considered opinion?"

Dawn hesitated as she conjured up the images of some suitably despicable individuals in her mind, over the years the details of which she had devoted considerable study.

"The sometime premier of Uganda, Idi Amin. Or to refer to him by his full, self-awarded titles, President for Life, His Excellency Field Marshal Doctor Idi Amin Dada, LLD, VC, DSO, MC, Conqueror of the British Empire and King of Scotland. An illiterate junior officer in the King's African Rifles who saw the chance to grab power and unearned military and academic titles, but in the process caused the suffering and death of hundreds of thousands of his countrymen. Or what about Adolf Hitler, Chancellor of Germany during the Second World War and for the twelve years of the Third Reich? An inadequate megalomaniac obsessed with his own philosophy, even to the point of his writing it all out in his book, *Mein Kampf,* that he had published and then all but forced upon the German people. A man responsible for the murder and cruel oppression of literally millions of people. Saddam Hussein, another power monger and killer of his own people. Another despot who deprived his people of freedom and liberty. Nicolae Ceausescu, First Secretary of the communist Romanian Workers' Party Central Committee, as well as a tyrant and mass murderer? Nero Caesar, Emperor of Ancient Rome. A particularly vile example of humanity at its most base. Josef Stalin. Sometime Premier of Russia and responsible for purges leading to even more deaths than those caused by Hitler.

Ghengis Khan of Mongolia. Kim Il Sung of North Korea. The Cambodian Communist Party leader Pol Pot. Augusto Pinochet, Commander-in Chief of the Chilean armed forces and police, and military junta. You see, Commander? The common themes with all despots are selfish power, greed, cruelty, oppressive control, and murder. In your case, you have simply utilized religion as the engine for the advancement of your political agenda."

"But religion is such a useful tool for exerting control over the hyper-religious, is it not? Consider how easily I was able to persuade that fool of an airline captain to purposely crash his Federal Express freighter into the Kingdom Centre in Riyadh. I employed a simple mind trick to which the especially pious are extremely susceptible. He was utterly convinced that he was doing the Lord's work. Right up until a few seconds before the end, but by which time of course it was too late."

Dawn found this last remark especially shocking. But she continued, unwavering in her resolve.

"But you are no different in principle from any other of history's violent, powerful men. And if you continue in this way you will meet your end, just as all those others met their untimely ends in one way or another. Your obvious intelligence and abilities notwithstanding."

Hunt stared at her as if ruminating on what she was saying, while yet remaining wholly unperturbed.

"You know, that imbecile of a captain aboard the *Al-Tariq* had the rank stupidity to come and inform me personally that he had torpedoed the sailing training vessel on which you were travelling. And that you were dead. I had him killed on the spot for his idiocy."

He faced Revere.

"I am indeed quite sorry that your ship was sent to the depths, and specifically I feel that I owe an apology to you, Captain Revere, more especially for the loss of your crew."

Revere just stared at him impassively, betraying no emotion. If he did have some thoughts or feelings on the matter he was not revealing them. Hunt either ignored this, or more likely simply did not consider it worthy of note.

"You know, Captain DeFaller. I have always admired you. For an ordinary human you really do stand out amongst your peers. Indeed, I have a proposal for you."

"And what would that be?"

"I propose that you leave this blithering half-wit that you call your husband and come with me. I will make you as I am intelligence-wise, and in no time we can be happy ruling both Earth and Mars together, as Emperor and Empress."

Dawn stared at him in utter contempt. More especially since he had just apologized to Revere, apparently in a sincere manner, and yet now he was insulting him.

"You are serious? You really expect me to leave my husband just so that I can be your companion in this moral degeneracy?"

"I promise you, you wouldn't miss him, any more than one might miss a less favored pet rodent. Most certainly you would come to see that, and quickly. I promise you, if you were to see things as I see them, you would be permanently changed."

"Well I am afraid I must decline your offer, Commander."

Hunt stared at her.

"Yes, I expected you would respond that way. Not one of your more impressive decisions, Captain, but I was ever hopeful that you could be persuaded to see the light. However as far as the Eye of the Pharaohs is concerned, I must warn you that I have no intention of allowing you to position it beneath this altar. For you see, even although you say you wish to refuse the opportunity to become the most powerful woman in the entire history of Creation, I myself am very happy and content to be, and remain, the most powerful man."

He fixed Dawn in a stare.

"You know, you have done very well indeed to have found the one and only extant copy of the Hellenistic texts and the Eye of the Pharaohs, and quite without assistance, with the exception of your loyal lapdog that you inadvertently and quite by chance pulled from where he belongs in the 18th century."

That last comment intrigued Dawn, for it suggested to her that Hunt knew nothing of the Guardsmen whom she had encountered while on Mars, as she had hoped but not dared believe. She determined to try not to dwell on the issue, lest Hunt see the thoughts forming in her mind. He had already claimed to possess at least some powers of telepathy and she had no reason to disbelieve him.

"You know I could return your husband to his own time, his memory erased of all that he has witnessed since meeting you. It would be a kindness, returning him to a limited and primitive paradigm but one in which he possesses a modicum of social standing, comprehension, the illusion of control over his destiny, and respect from his peers. I could similarly erase all knowledge of ever having met him in your mind too, if that would ease the parting?"

"Commander Hunt, you really have failed to understand my psychology if you imagine for even one moment that such an offer could possibly be appealing to me."

"Well, Captain. I rather fear that it is, as they say in tactical circles, your move."

Dawn felt powerless to finish the job she had come to do. She felt that any move towards the altar would prove hopeless. Hunt would doubtless have a hundred different effortless methods at his disposal with which he could stop her. Instead she decided to try to appeal to his better nature.

"What about the people of the Earth? Why do you care to exert power and authority over them? Are your technical achievements not enough? Consider your insights into science and technology. Your ability to rapidly terraform an entire planet. Why do you need to control the lives of every individual with threats of death for anyone who does not wish to follow your rules and regulations?"

"You ask me what about the people of the Earth? So what about them? They are to me as overly aggressive chimpanzees, with delusions of grandeur. You ask of my desire for control. The answer is to be found not only in the personal satisfaction it brings me, but also the order that I can now bestow on a world that was previously disordered and chaotic. You know that the Second Law of Thermodynamics states that left to its own devices, all matter tends towards a state of maximal entropy, or disorder, and so it tends to be with ordinary human societies. Indeed it has been this way all throughout time. Because of advances in science and engineering, amongst other things, the problem has grown particularly acute of late and prior to my intervention had threatened to extinguish all human and much animal and plant life on the planet. But I have restored order. I have also discovered an almost limitless supply of alternative energy that more than makes up for the petroleum that was humanity's greatest source of power but the affordable aspects of which were simultaneously dwindling away in the face of an ever-burgeoning population. And more and more of that population were demanding their share of American President Woodrow Wilson's much touted self-determination, coupled with a higher standard of living. Such people could not thus live in peace but instead were driving ever more towards division and disharmony from one another. Indeed was it not another American, the Secretary of State in the Wilson Administration, Robert Lansing, an unusually perceptive individual, for an ordinary man, who put it thusly: 'The phrase, self-determination, is simply loaded with dynamite. It will raise hopes which can never be realized. What a calamity that the phrase was ever uttered! What misery it will cause!' And you know, a number of years later, Walter Lippman, another of the more prolific individuals produced by the United States of America during its zenith, denounced President Wilson's doctrine of self-determination as barbarous and reactionary. He said: 'Self-determination, which has nothing to do with self-government but has become confused with it, is barbarous and reactionary. By sanctioning secession, it invites majorities and minorities to become intransigent and irreconcilable'."

Hunt talked as if he were patched in to some external source of information that was being directly streamed to his brain.

"'It is stipulated in the principle of self-determination that individuals need not be compatriots because they will soon be aliens. There is no end to this atomization of human society. Within the minorities who have seceded there will tend to appear other minorities who in their turn will wish to secede.' One might very well make the case, as Lippman did, that President Wilson's doctrine of self-determination destroyed the Western empires during the latter half of the twentieth century. But I have done away with all of that, through the power of my mind in association with an opportunity that I and I alone have been able to see."

He uttered the word 'I' as if he considered himself to be God's finest and noblest gift to all of humanity.

"If the price of all of this has been a lessening of personal liberties and civil rights, and a small reduction in the human population in percentage terms, then so be it. If I am not in fact truly the Imam Mahdi, if he even really exists at all, or did ever exist, does it even matter? So long as the people of the world believe that I am?"

Dawn shook her head slowly from side to side.

"You talk of a lessening of personal liberties and civil rights, a small reduction in the human population in percentage terms. You sound just like any of history's mass murderers. You are perpetuating a religious doctrine that perceives women as second class citizens at best, little more than cattle at worst."

"Come Captain DeFaller. I am beginning to weary of this little discussion. I think it best if I simply show you how it feels to be as I presently am."

With that, Hunt pulled some kind of device from his clothing, a silver object made of metal, perhaps polished stainless steel. Before Dawn had any time to react, he had aimed it at her, and activated it. Immediately she began to feel herself becoming sleepy. Within seconds the blackness was threatening to take her, but then she felt something, she knew not what, working to mitigate Hunt's attempt to rob her of her consciousness. Stumbling, but somehow managing to remain on her feet, she saw an image of Matthew advancing towards Hunt, and engaging him in combat. What was this? What was she witnessing? Didn't he realize that he could not defeat Hunt in this way? The man had become far, far too powerful. But yet Matthew seemed to be prevailing against him. He had succeeded in moving him from his position behind the altar, had thrown him against one wall of the temple in a violent maneuver. As Hunt was struggling for breath, Matthew advanced upon him once more and kicked him squarely in the solar plexus. Hunt groaned and choked in extreme discomfort as the wind was knocked clean out of him. He seemed to be immobilized for the time being.

Dawn.

Was someone calling her name? In her semi dream-like state, she couldn't tell. What was happening? Was this a hallucination brought about by the device that Hunt had activated only moments before? What was going on?

She felt a sharp stinging smack across her face.

"Dawn!"

What? Was this Matthew? Had he slapped her? She felt a second stinging slap in the same place as the first across her right cheek.

"Dawn! Waken up! The jewel! Get the jewel and place it over here! Do it now, while Commander is Hunt is still unconscious!"

But Dawn did not waken. Or at least she did not return to a state of normal consciousness. She felt herself lost, dreaming, as if in a trance. In her mind's eye she saw a giant wall standing before her, damming back a huge body of fluid that in its entirety represented the sum total of all knowledge and understanding in the universe, and perhaps other universes also. The tiny hole in the wall that allowed just a trickle to come through represented to her how limited was human perception and ability to comprehend. But the wall she noticed was beginning to fail. Cracks were starting to form around the tiny finger-sized opening, but soon spread to encompass the structure entire. Then, as inevitably it must, the wall collapsed. Not in a violent manner, instead it simply vanished.

And Dawn was instantly awash in knowledge. Comprehension. Understanding. In a trice she saw the mathematical computations delineating relativity. She looked up at the ceiling of the chamber and could instantly envision the precise fractal equations describing its complex patterns. The strange hieroglyphics inscribed there made sense to her. An unleashed torrent of ideas flooded through her mind. She noticed that the tiles on the floor of the chamber had been laid in a pattern that could be approximately described by a Fourier transformation. Ideas occurred to her relating to how best to attain and maintain global peace and harmony. Cultural and religious issues. Language and its myriad of limitations. Western musical modal scales suddenly made perfect sense to her. The processes underlying the genesis of the very stars she could see with perfect clarity. Even an understanding of the origins and ultimate fate of the universe formed clearly in her mind. And all of this occurred without the slightest mental effort on her part. Hunt, who was once more standing before her, interrupted her in her musings. His features betrayed a gloating self-satisfied smile. Revere attempted to tackle him again, but Hunt easily parried off his attacks as if her were dealing with a child. Had Hunt's apparent earlier discomfort at having been kicked simply been feigned? Had it been nothing but a ruse to distract Revere? Dawn calculated that it was. Hunt cried out triumphantly.

"Dawn! My Dawn!"

It was true. She regarded him differently now. With the device he had brought to bear just moments ago he had successfully transferred at least some of his enhanced intelligence to her.

"Dawn," he said again. "Now you see what it means to think as I think. To perceive as I perceive. To comprehend as I comprehend. Before you were blind but now your eyes have been opened. The mysteries of the universe have been laid open before you. You can engage in any intellectual process or thought experiment. You can solve any problem. Ordinary human beings understand nothing more of your mind than a Boston-based cockroach would understand of the intricacies and details of municipal government in Shanghai."

He extended his hand to her.

"Join me. Leave this man you call your husband. Join with me and together we can rule the Earth and the Red Planet. Dawn! You will be Queen of all you survey!"

Dawn regarded him with a considered eye, carefully taking account of every possible consequence, and consequences of the consequences, of her decision. She took his hand. When she spoke her voice sounded strange. As if she was no longer ordinarily human.

"I accept your offer. I do see now. You were right and I simply had not the mental capacity to appreciate that. Ordinary humans are as animals. They know not what is in their own best interest."

Hunt watched her, a smile breaking out on his lips. He was elated.

"Ordinary human beings need to be led."

"Dawn! I knew that once you saw the truth you would join with me."

When she spoke again, Dawn sounded as cold as ice, as if all feeling had departed from her soul.

"You have a holding cell for Captain Revere?"

"Yes indeed."

In a trice Hunt had flicked his wrist and the device with which he had transformed Dawn now rendered Matthew paralyzed but still fully conscious and able to breathe normally. He was not in danger but was unable to move any part of his body. Not even his eyes.

Dawn approached him, her expression utterly without feeling.

"Then let us move him. We can wipe his memory and return him to his own time in due course."

Matthew heard every one of Dawn's words, and saw plainly the expression on her face and heard the iciness in her voice. He was devastated. He wanted to cry out in protest, to try to get her to come back to her senses, but he could not utter a single sound from his throat. His tongue felt as if it were a lifeless block of solid lead. What was wrong with Dawn? What had this monster done to her, to render her thus? Why was she all of a sudden intent on ending their marriage and erasing all of his memories of her?

"When will Mars be ready for colonization?"

"In a matter of two weeks only. I have ships being built even now that will transport the first wave of colonists there."

"They are all to be selected on the basis of their strong adherence to fundamentalist Islam?"

"Of course. That is how we shall control them, as you so correctly noted even before I changed you. People with strong faith are easily led, as you will soon discover. The first wave of colonists will arrive on the fully terraformed Mars and commence creating infrastructure there, initially in the form of cities, replete with roads, railways, power grids, hospitals, schools, manufacturing bases for all of their basic needs. And of course, mosques."

"I look forward to being the supreme military, political, and spiritual leader of the Martian colonists."

Hunt just shook his head with joy. He had created so much during the last few months, but of all of his creations, Dawn was by far his greatest.

"I look forward to that with eager anticipation."

As he was talking Dawn walked casually around Matthew's still-paralyzed body.

"I cannot imagine what I ever did see in him," she commented carelessly. She ran her eye up and down his body as if she were looking at an animal caged in a zoo. "He is so, primitive, in every sense of the word."

She stepped around him a couple more times, and then casually approached the altar that had very recently been her intended target.

"And to think, I would have actually dropped the Eye of the Pharaohs into the receptacle down there."

"You have the Eye?"

"Indeed I do. I have it here. Let me uncover it and we can destroy it."

"My thoughts exactly."

Dawn slowly reached into her pack attached to her belt in which she carried the jewel. She wrapped her hand around the jewel's massive bulk, and pulled it out, still in its wrappings. She started to unwrap it, and in a moment it shone out in its surroundings like a beacon, as if it were energized from some external power source. Hunt noticed this latter phenomenon.

"The Eye senses the proximity of the altar with which it wants to join, with which to become one."

"It is indeed beautiful."

And indeed it was. It shone in beautiful colors, much more so even than the finest of cut diamonds.

"How will you destroy it? Fast neutrons? A Quiller beam?"

"Indeed yes. Just as you say. I will expose it to a beam of high energy fast neutrons. A modulated Quiller beam."

"I see."

All of a sudden Dawn made a move wholly unanticipated by Hunt. She dropped down and stepped rapidly towards the altar. Before Hunt had even registered her intentions, she had dropped the jewel into position into the complex groove into which it fitted, in just exactly the correct orientation. Immediately when it engaged, a powerful humming sensation filled the entire chamber.

Hunt's expression turned to one of utter horror. For a moment he was speechless. Utterly without understanding at what she had just done. Then he screamed.

"No, no, no!"

She ignored his cries and screams of protest, which were rapidly morphing into shrieks.

"No, no, no, no!!!"

But the deed was done. The jewel, and then the surrounding plinth, and then the altar entire illuminated with a warm orange glow, as the humming grew louder and filled the entire space, penetrating their very sense of being.

In that moment, as Hunt realized that he had forever lost control of Earth and all manner of human activity and artifice, he looked at Dawn with utter contempt.

"You have betrayed me! You fool! You simple minded fool!"

"Did you really imagine that I would join with you in your cold hearted cruelty? Yes, your intelligence levels have reached fantastic heights, but your morals unfortunately have descended to the point where they are now plumbing the depths of degeneracy! I gladly choose to forfeit my own enhanced intellect rather than destroy my marriage and the lives of other human beings all for the sake of personal power, wealth, and gain!"

Matthew started to sense normal feeling and then capacity for movement returning to his body. Moments later he stepped beside his wife, Dawn and he presenting a united moral front to Hunt. Hunt stared at them both one more time in utter disbelief, and then bolted like a frightened horse from the temple. Within a moment he was gone. Dawn knew not where, but she felt no inclination to follow after him or make any attempt to determine where he might be. She just knew, as if by some sixth sense, that for all of his intelligence and power, he had suddenly melted into utter insignificance.

She did however feel a sense of deep humbling wonder as before the intensely glowing altar there appeared the unmistakable form of a humanoid being. About twelve feet tall, not proportioned as a human, precisely, nor made up of solid matter exactly, nor pure energy, but something perhaps in between.

"You have done very well, Dawn DeFaller."

"Vari!"

She stared up at him in surprise, not having expected to ever see him again.

"You saw what just happened?"

"I have been watching you all along. You were simply unaware of the fact."

He motioned towards Revere.

"This is your husband?"

He made the statement as if it was a question, but Dawn knew he was simply pronouncing a fact.

"Yes. This is Matthew."

She turned to him intending to prompt him to introduce himself to Vari, but she saw once more that he appeared to be caught in some kind of a trance. Vari seemed to notice her concern.

"Have no fear for your husband, he is temporarily suspended in time, but only for the duration of my manifestation here with you. He will be released unharmed upon my departure. It is however imperative that he does not see me, or have any memory of my visit after I am gone."

Dawn felt relaxed once more, her concern subsiding.

"It was however most fortuitous that your husband was here with you these few minutes past. For you see, Dawn DeFaller, as humans you are made of matter, but your husband belongs in another time. And thus the vibrational energy of the sub-atomic particles from which his body is constructed do not match with the present era in which he now finds himself. As you humans put it, his quantum signature does not match that of the present era. It is precisely for that reason that when your nemesis, Garry Hunt, subdued him with the frequency resonance modulator device that he held in his hand, instead of the destructive interference he had intended to bring to bear to destroy his mind, there was in its place a constructive interference event. This had the effect of transferring some of Garry Hunt's artificially enhanced intelligence to him."

"So what happened to me? It seemed Hunt attempted to render my intelligence enhanced also. Did he in fact achieve this?"

"Yes indeed, Dawn DeFaller. As I am sure you are aware. And I might add that the enhanced levels of intelligence that both you and your husband now possess will remain with you for the remainder of your lives."

Dawn gasped at this news.

"I must add that neither you nor your husband will ever be as intelligence-enhanced as Garry Hunt. But as preternaturally intelligent as Hunt has become, there were some things he still failed to realize. For example, he reckoned without the effects of time, as we saw with the result of the use of his device on your husband."

Dawn could swear Vari was actually smiling at her.

"He also failed to recognize the strength of the human spirit within you. For even although you were tempted by his offer of all things in this world and on Mars, just as Christ was tempted by the Devil during his forty day and night sojourn into the wilderness, your sense of morality nevertheless prevailed, and you declined. Despite the fact you had no clear idea of the consequences of this decision. And, of course, Hunt failed to recognize my existence and influence. In fact in his mind he had utterly rejected the notion."

Dawn regarded Vari with a quizzical expression.

"So what happens now? With the world?"

"A good question. Your pursuit of righteousness has resulted in a flood of realization amongst the peoples of the world. When you leave this place you will find that the philosophy of the Ancient Greeks, the Hellenized view of rationality, individuality, and reason, as well as values of tolerance and mutual respect have overtaken the senseless destructive pious fundamentalisms that have been the bane of humanity for the previous two millennia, and more particularly in the last century. Because of your efforts, you have truly saved the human race from its own machinations. The Hellenized holy scriptures, the written copy of which you have arranged to have deposited with various agencies around the globe have already started to be copied and published into books that will be distributed about the planet. Within a matter of days there will be a new religion on earth, a revival of that of the ancient Hellenized world. There will be a new era of true peace and understanding."

"And what of Atlantis? What of the energy source that the world is presently utilizing? What of Mars? What is to happen with all of these issues?"

Vari spoke a touch more soothingly.

"Dawn DeFaller. Garry Hunt did well. Very well indeed to accomplish that which he did. But he was only able to achieve this in a state of artificial cognitive enhancement. The human race is not yet ready to leave the third planet. The time will come, mark my words, but the time is not now. The work that Garry Hunt has done to terraform the Martian surface will be undone. I know you would like to show your husband your handiworks there beforehand, but unfortunately that I cannot permit. You will be deeply disappointed, but the fourth planet will be returned to the state in which you found it when first you landed there. The energy source that Earth is currently utilizing from the machines within this complex that you know as Atlantis must be severed, and indeed the complex itself must be hidden once again under the Antarctic ice. But fear not. For the new age that you have done so much to usher in will yield remarkable new discoveries, but they shall be made by natural human minds, not those under the influence of ultimately dangerous and destructive cognition enhancing agents. Included within this discovery set shall be new and effective alternatives to petroleum."

Vari cocked his head at her in a slightly jaunty manner.

"As I alluded to already, Dawn DeFaller, your husband will be released when I depart from here. He will not however have any memory of me. And one more thing. Be advised that despite humanity's previous issues with religion, as I outlined to you earlier, and as you have now discovered with the Hellenized texts, there is in fact a Creator God. Known to us by His ancient and true name of Rammsihaar. A force far greater than yourselves, or even me. For Loki, Wotan, and I are His Guardsmen. The elevated remnants of an ancient civilization of corporeal beings that once existed on Mars. Just as there once existed an ancient civilization of giants here in this city. We do His bidding, as we have done His bidding now. We seem strange to you, but all of Earth's religions, without exception, speak of us, but by a variety of different names. You have in fact heard of us before. You may advise your friend, Thomas Powers that which he already knows so well, that he will indeed be reunited with his wife and son when the time is right. From a spiritual perspective, Thomas Powers represents a prime example of how humanity can be at its best and strongest. As do you, Dawn DeFaller. All peoples of Earth would do well to emulate his and your examples."

With that, Vari smiled at Dawn one final time, acknowledged her with a gentle tip of his head, before he vanished in a flash of light and was gone from her forever.

CHAPTER 60

As Hunt boarded *Vega,* he rapidly punched in a series of numbers at a keyboard near the entry hatch.

"Danielle! Take me to these co-ordinates! Immediately!"

Hunt's frantic demands were perfectly juxtaposed against Danielle's soothing dulcet tones.

"Commander Hunt. You are aware that these are the spatial co-ordinates for the elevated dry section of the Martian plain of Chryse Planitia?"

"Yes! I must travel there now! As fast as you can take me. I have lost Earth. But I shall not lose Mars! As soon as I arrive I will take control of the planet and clear the way for the arrival of the first wave of settlers!"

"Yes Commander. Please strap yourself into the chair."

Approximately twenty minutes later, after *Vega* had cleared Earth's orbit, Danielle engaged the warp field generators and the ship was able to rapidly make the journey to a point in space relatively close to Mars. Then at that stage ensued the necessary period of thirty-six hours as Danielle took the ship under conventional ion rocket power to the edge of Mars' orbit. Hunt found the waiting almost intolerable, in all that time he did not sleep, but he knew there was nothing at all to be gained by pushing Danielle on the issue. He had after all designed all aspects of the functioning of the ship. She had advised him that, if he was not going to sleep, he should at least entertain himself during this time, but he was wholly disinterested. For he was consumed with the feeling that his situation would be salvageable once he reached his destination and he could take command of the planet. When finally thirty-six hours later Danielle spoke the words he had been longing to hear, his frustrations were to some extent mitigated.

"Commander Hunt. I am ready to assume a parking orbit above the co-ordinates you specified on south western Chryse Planitia. May I proceed?"

"At once, yes, Danielle."

Fourteen minutes later *Vega* was in orbit and beginning her descent to the surface. Against Danielle's advice, Hunt unbuckled himself from his chair and stood at the window gazing down on the northern hemisphere of Mars, which since the terraformation had become a very earth-like planet, with white swirling clouds replete with weather patterns, brown landmasses, and blue oceans. Far below he could make out a landmass representing part of the plain to which they were headed. There was nothing there now except virgin land but one day there would be a metropolis, filled with mosques and worshippers who would, without exception, direct their attentions to him and him alone, in his capacity as 12th Imam Mahdi. Just as soon as he could organize the first shipments of settlers to make the journey to this place. Yes! He would be lord and master of this beautiful new planet, this paradise remade by him in the image of the Garden of Eden. Just as God had created the Earth in seven days, so Garry Hunt had created the new Earth in mere months! And it would become his new empire! How magnificent it would be! He looked down at the ground below once again, which was by this time coming into view. He could make out detailed geographical features. Any moment now, the ship would touch down and he would step out onto his new domain as master. Forget about Earth and all of its problems. He had Mars, and what a beautiful planet she was.

Moments later Danielle reduced the descent rate to just one foot per second, and *Vega* made contact with the soil. He had arrived! He was elated beyond description.

"Open the hatch, Danielle! Open the hatch! I want to take in the fresh air of my new world!"

Danielle obliged, and Hunt was suddenly able to sample the cool fresh mid-afternoon breeze. He was truly in paradise! His Eden!

But he was so caught up in the emotional intensity of the moment, the tremendous rush stemming from his visiting a planet other than his native Earth for the very first time that he failed to heed Danielle's warning about the planet-wide energy field that was fast approaching. Indeed he was contemplating the hills in the far-off distance and what he might decide to name them, when it struck. Hunt was afforded a brief glimpse of *Vega's* instantaneous vaporization, and the near-simultaneous and very rapid reversion of this localized region of Mars to the same barren red landscape that it had so recently been, the sky turning once again from a rich light blue color back to its thin and feeble bluish-reddish-brown hue as the oxygen vanished in the blink of an eye. And although deeply shocked by the phenomenon that he beheld, as the nearby ocean boiled away into space, he was yet unprepared for the warp field that by sheer chance pounced upon him, grabbing him up, saving him in the nick of time from being vaporized himself, and hurling him back in time to a point corresponding with the year May 14, 1613, on Earth's calendar.

Commander Garry Hunt, RN, sometime 12th Imam Mahdi, choked and gasped out his last breaths as he lay writhing in agony on the red oxide dust, as his skin swelled and blistered painfully, his lungs collapsed, his eyes turned scarlet and popped, and his blood boiled. And after his final, merciful death, there his remains would lie, slowly shriveling and mummifying in the freezing bacteria-free dirt, with only water ice and light Martian breezes for company for a period of three hundred and sixty three years and two months.

It would not be until July 1976 that NASA's Viking I Lander with its cameras and image transmitters would by chance land adjacent to his still well-preserved and obviously-human corpse, and transmit its gruesome image back to Earth.

CHAPTER 61

Safely back aboard *Saskatchewan Star,* Dawn and Revere relaxed in the tanker's officers' lounge. Their trip back to the ship had been a little bit of an adventure in of itself. They had both been dreading the return journey across the ice, and, as luck would have it, Dawn's snowmobile had developed carburetor problems and refused to run, only minutes after they had left the vicinity of Atlantis. She had broken into the toolkit that accompanied the machine and spent the best part of forty-five minutes in an attempt to address the issue. But she was eventually forced to concede that the problem lay beyond her capacity to cope, and so instead she had summoned the officer of the watch aboard the tanker using the two-way radio with which she had been provided. Captain King had been consulted about the issue, who had then been able to promise that a helicopter which had landed on the ship from a nearby US aircraft carrier only two hours previously would be sent out to their position and would pick them both up. She was directed to be ready to fire a flare when requested to do so by the pilot in order that their precise position would be known as he made his approach. The chopper would also pick up their machines, but would later drop Dawn and Revere at the spot on the coast where they had left their boat, before returning to the ship. Dawn and Revere would in the meantime return a little later, bringing their boat back with them.

Shortly after taking off, they had all been witness to the spectacular event whereby Atlantis was refilled with ice in a matter of seconds only, just as Vari had promised would happen. Watching it occur, and witnessing the sheer power that the event had unleashed, had been awe-inspiring. For Dawn it had been almost frightening.

From the news reports that were being broadcast by all of the major global television stations, it was apparent that this was by no means the only sudden change that had taken place of late. The biggest breaking news story that had captivated everyone's attention was the sudden and inexplicable destabilization of the enhanced Martian atmosphere, and the Martian oceans, that had recently been built up during the terraformation process, as explained by the Imam Mahdi. Astronomers and physicists had appeared, one after another, talking of a mysterious destabilizing energy wave that had struck the planet, probably against all reasonable odds, which had returned conditions to what they had been only months earlier, when Mars was barren, cold, and lifeless. Several other scientists as well as a number of clerics called the whole concept of planetary terraformation into question, suggesting that it was variously too difficult to achieve safely, or that it was against God's will.

The other big story was that major global religions had been deeply affected right down to their very philosophical foundations, and shaken to their respective cores by the publication and distribution of the Hellenized texts. Texts which purported to be the original true and final corrective scriptures, kept in a repository by the Ancient Greeks, but apparently lost to the world when Ancient Greece had been destroyed by the ever-onward march of progress. The effect upon the faithful of all denominations had been immediate and nothing short of astonishing, for suddenly in churches, synagogues, and mosques all across the globe clerics were standing up and begging their God for forgiveness for their erroneous attitudes and ways that had led to so much religious division and strife. Dawn had never dared hope that this would have been the final effect of all of her efforts, but she was truly elated, for this would mean that a new beginning might finally dawn upon the world as all peoples everywhere, regardless of cultural background, could truly commence working together as one.

Also, as Vari had indicated would happen, the source of gratuitous energy beamed directly to Earth had come to an end. But the upshot was that giant new oilfields had been discovered in the South Pacific Ocean, directly underneath the Cook Islands, which were of course a dependency of the United States. There had been almost simultaneous announcements of discoveries of a methodology for industrial scale cracking of water using specific radio frequencies, to yield hydrogen and oxygen, and a foolproof method for initiation and maintenance of cold fusion, the holy grail of physics that for decades had eluded the most intelligent of minds. Long believed to be impossible, and once in 1989 announced by Martin Fleischmann and Stanley Pons, only to prove to be a red herring, the process was now practically possible to initiate on the surface of a palladium electrode. On a small scale at first, over the years it would grow and become eventually an alternative source of clean, safe, and almost limitless energy that would power the world. But all of this would take five to ten years to come on-line. In the meantime there would be sufficient petroleum underneath the Cook Islands in the newly dubbed Oceanic field to power the industrial nations, and to that end the oil companies had now cancelled their plans to sell off their tanker fleet. This last piece of news had elated Captain King, as he had received new orders to turn his ship around and head back to the eastern seaboard of the United States, there to await new orders. He was especially pleased by this as he had not wanted to go to work for the government of New Arabia. He had been unhappy at the prospect of taking a ship designed to carry petroleum into a country where there would be no petroleum to carry, all the while subordinating himself to an alien political system which he secretly believed would have had no love for either him or his ingrained Western values. But the whole issue was now moot, for New Arabia itself was no more, having suffered a complete loss of confidence in the face of the re-emergence of the Hellenized texts, as well as the apparent and deeply disturbing disappearance of the 12th Imam Mahdi, which had led to a massive and extremely rapid political instability in that part of the world. This had resulted in its reversion to its previous state as separate sovereign nations, each with their own much more limited military forces, and which, given the new global religious ethos, were willingly subordinated to the West in general, and the United States in particular, in a manner as never before seen at any point in recorded history. And Israel of course was restored to her former incarnation.

For the first time, planet Earth seemed to have truly found peace, equity, and prosperity.

And as for Matthew, Dawn saw that he apparently had no memory of ever having come face to face with Vari in Atlantis, despite the fact that Dawn could have sworn that Matthew had at one point looked directly upon his ethereal form. She decided that she would say nothing of Vari or of his companions, Loki or Wotan to her husband, at least for now. Perhaps in time she might bring up the subject, but for now an inner voice was telling her it would be best to remain silent on the issue. Matthew for his part, as with everyone else on Earth, as far as Dawn knew, was quite happy with the explanation that the Antarctic ice had filled in once more, and Mars had reverted back to its pre-terraformed state, because of a purported energy imbalance.

EPILOGUE

At home in Boston Dawn and Matthew were enjoying the last few days of their leave before once again resuming active duty. At the coffee table in the den, Dawn was going through the pile of mail that had arrived the morning previously. One particularly ornate envelope had caught her eye, and she had opened it first. On pulling the contents out of its cover, she saw that it was a wedding invitation. She studied it for a moment, before realizing that it had been sent by one Doctor George Wright, and his wife Fiona, currently living in Edinburgh, Scotland, concerning the upcoming marriage of their daughter, Toni, one of the engineering officers aboard *Saskatchewan Star,* to Commander Jack Tylon, the skipper of HMS *Skirmisher,* the SSN that had taken part in Operation *Ankara.* Dawn smiled to herself as she shared the news with Matthew. That first night when the various naval captains had been invited aboard by Bryan King, she had definitely come away with the impression that Tylon and Wright had been very friendly with each other and were both interested in a further liaison. But then the thought occurred to her that being married to the commanding officer of a submarine would be quite a lonely life, at least for a few years until he was promoted to flag rank. Wright too had her own career of course, but still, as an officer of the Merchant Marine she would undoubtedly have considerably more free time than he would as a serving skipper aboard one of Her Majesty's Submarines.

Dawn placed the wedding invitation to one side, as the other issue of her husband's new novel entered her mind once more. Several times she had been casually pestering him about it, indicating that she would like to read what he had written. He had indeed told her that he would let her see it, but so far he had shown her nothing. But now she had decided that she really wanted to see what he had penned thus far. She raised the matter with him again, this time a good deal more insistently.

"So, Matthew. This novel of yours. The one that you had said you had started writing in your e-mail you sent to me when I was on Mars?"

"Yes?"

"May I see it?"

"I have only just started writing it. The first chapter is all that is yet complete."

"Well may I see it anyway?"

He paused, not quite sure how best to answer. Finally he responded.

"Very well."

Revere went through to the study and returned a moment later, carrying with him a small sheaf of papers, loosely clipped together. He proffered it to Dawn.

"Please, I am feeling a little embarrassed, for I fear that my writing is not of sufficient quality for general publication. But read it if you wish."

"Nonsense, Matthew. I am sure it will be very well written. What are you calling it?"

"The First Waterloo."

"The First Waterloo. That's an odd name. How does that fit with the story?"

"Well, I thought it poignant. In much the same way as the French under Napoleon lost the Battle of Waterloo against the British, the Vikings before them lost the Battle for Scotland, when both expected victory."

Taking a seat on the couch she looked down at the papers in her lap, and started reading.

THE FIRST WATERLOO

A Novel by

Matthew Revere

Chapter 1

CHAPTER 1

Coastal Norway, Langesunde Settlement, A.D. 1262

*E*rik stood alone on the side of the cliff, lost in thought, staring silently across the fjörd and out to sea. It had been almost three weeks now since he and his fellow raiders had returned from their last voyage, weighed down with all the loot they could carry, taken from the several monasteries they had sacked in the Isles of the Britons, or Engelund, as some of his compatriots were now naming it. They had sailed south along the north eastern coast of the country, going ashore at various locations in Northumbria where there were whole communities of monks. Holy men living in apparent poverty, but who were known to hoard artifacts of solid gold, as well as chests of gold and silver coins, and precious jewels. Over and over again these monks had pleaded for their lives while at the same time crying like frightened sheep. A few of the more steadfast ones had called upon the name of their Christian god to help them.

Help them? Erik pondered. Help them to what? Did their god really value such men as these? These weaklings and cowards, who cheated the common people out of anything of value, only so that they might keep it for themselves. And all these crimes committed in the name of this god. To Erik's way of thinking, no matter how he looked at it, it seemed contrary to the laws of the true gods, those of the Norse people, to let such men live. Surely their god, if indeed theirs was any *kind of a god at all, must also see things in those terms. Putting such men to the sword and burning their monasteries seemed like an act of kindness, more especially to the ordinary Britons, although not any of the latter group ever seemed to look on the situation that way. Erik frowned. Perhaps it was not reasonable to expect anything else. In his experience all peoples disliked being invaded, no matter the benefits they might derive as a result. Misplaced loyalty to false gods as well as representatives and lords just seemed to be human nature. Generally, on hearing of a Norse invasion, the local populace would mount a defense of sorts, mostly with weapons hastily fashioned from farming implements, a defense that invariably was as useless as it was spirited. The plain fact was that farmers and cottars could not fight the Viking warriors come from over the sea in their long ships. Those who tried invariably ended up suffering the same fate as the monks, although often they died more bravely. Their womenfolk would then suffer the various indignities meted out by the more brutish members of the long ship crews. Erik was careful never to be a participant in such activities—in truth he felt it abhorrent that women were forced to watch as their menfolk were slaughtered, and they were then abused and violated in turn by many of his fellow Vikings, who must have seemed as ferocious invaders to them. But Erik held a minority view. Many if not most of his countrymen were of the opinion that the Britons, as all peoples, had to be taught a lesson concerning the superiority of the Norse race, and that killing the men and raping the women into submission was the only way to achieve this, along with any chance of a lasting peace. There was also the possibility that some might be left with child, thus helping to procreate the Norse race while at the same time breeding out these inferior Angles and Saxons that seemed so prevalent on the Isles of the Britons. And surely this must be a good thing, for the plain fact was that despite the Viking reputation for fierceness, they were farmers as much as they were warriors, and were in desperate need of fertile lands to support their ever-growing population, as much of their own lands were altogether too northerly, cold, mountainous, and barren to effectively grow sufficient crops. Erik frowned again. The Vikings were expansionist, yes, but this they had found necessary in order to ensure the survival of their people. In any event, was not survival of the fittest the natural law? Was it not the way of things? That was what everyone said, at least.*

Erik allowed his mind to consider thoughts of the future, when his earthly life would be over and it would be time to make the journey to Valhalla, where he would stand proudly before Thor, god of war, to receive his eternal rewards. Oftentimes he prayed most earnestly that Thor would find him to be good enough. Brave enough. That he would die in battle, rather than live on to the infirmities and dishonour of old age.

Erik turned and started on his walk back to the settlement.

"Erik!" It was Lars. Lars who liked to boast of his exploits. Lars who liked mead.

"Lars. How goes it?"

"It goes well, Erik." Lars proffered a cup full of mead. "Come, drink with me!"

Erik accepted the cup, and followed Lars inside the Great Hall, a large meeting place constructed from solid slabs of thick granite, and roof beams of stout oak. Inside, a large fire roared, keeping the air warm. For though it was spring it was still cold outside. Within the Great Hall several men appeared to be taking advantage of the opportunity to dry off some of their clothing. Lars and Erik found a place to sit, on wooden chairs laid out with goat skins around a small thick oak table.

"What say you of Haakon's plans for the all-out invasion of Engelund, Erik? Exciting, are they not?"

"If not a little ambitious." Erik could never quite share Lars' enthusiasm for these discussions.

"Oh come, come! Erik! It will be glorious! Just think of all that fertile land, the prosperity, the sheer wealth! We will all of us be able to raise our families in peace without a further care in the world. Those Saxons are as bees guarding a honey pot. Their riches and spoil are ripe for the taking! It will be the battle of ultimate triumph, Erik!"

A smile broke out on Erik's fair features. His blue eyes gleamed a little.

"The battle to end all battles? Is that what you think, Lars?"

Lars considered the question for a moment, and then roared with laughter. Several others in the Great Hall shot them brief glances, before resuming their own conversations.

"You always were quite the jester, Erik!"

At the end of the previous year the Norse king, Haakon the Fourth, had proposed a plan for an all-out invasion of the Isles of the Britons and to take over the tracts of lush fertile land for the Viking peoples. Whether this plan would actually be put into action or not depended much on the results of the raids on Northumbria from which Erik had just returned. And the weather, of course. And both of these had been nothing short of excellent. In addition, this year their crops and their goat herds had thrived. There certainly would be no shortage of provisions to feed and clothe the numerous long ship crews that such an invasion would inevitably require.

But for all that, Erik was less happy about this very ambitious invasion plan than his fellows. For one thing, although Haakon had long and glorious battle experiences, he was growing old. And according to some, perhaps those closest to him, he was also growing weak. Years before, the Norsemen, led by the same King Haakon had taken the Isle of Man on the very western-most side of the Isles of the Britons, and henceforth occupied and farmed it with much success for over twenty years. Haakon had subsequently returned to Norway, but had left his grandson, Magnus, to rule Man in his stead. But recent reports spoke of unrest and rebellion amongst the Manx people. They said Haakon laughingly dismissed this as a small problem that would be dealt with in due time, but Erik felt less than convinced. Although he had never encountered the Manx, he had heard many reliable reports of their character. They were not as the Angles and Saxons to the south of the Isles of the Britons, but a different breed altogether, considerably tougher and much more resilient. They also had a reputation as fierce fighters. But the Norsemen were fired with the spirit of their successes from several weeks before, and had little *time for nay-sayers. Besides, the mystical Wise Woman, one of the most elderly and revered of Erik's people, had issued a most important prophecy that the raids would meet with great bounty this year.*

For now at least, all indicators suggested that the invasion was going to be on.

"Erik!" Lars jolted Erik from his musings. Erik had not noticed, but Lars had now been joined by Helle, his sometime drinking mate and 'special' companion. Helle was sitting on his knee at a jaunty angle, smiling at him with her pretty sea-green eyes. He had his arm around her waist. With his free hand he stroked her long strikingly blonde hair.

"Erik, you were leagues away!"

Both Lars and Helle were smiling at him now.

"Come, Erik! We can find Helga and retire to my hut, just the four of us! What say you, Erik?" Helga was Helle's close friend and even more beautiful than she in the estimation of some. Lars had been trying to get Erik together with her for months now, but thus far to no avail.

"Lars . . ."

Not even knowing how to finish his sentence, Erik just shook his head and managed a weak smile. He held his cup to his lips, quickly swallowed the rest of his mead, rose to his feet, bowed politely to Helle as she fixed him in a gaze of mock-longing, and just walked away.

"That's Erik. Always the gentleman!"

Lars grinned wickedly. Helle started to giggle girlishly, more intensely when he began to fondle her breast, as she made a deliberately useless mock attempt to brush his hand away.

The following morning was very bright and sunny. The temperature was already climbing to higher levels it seemed than on any other day so far that year. All appeared fresh and beautiful; the sea out across the fjörd particularly so, more especially as the sun's rays cut distinct paths across the water causing it to shimmer as if it were a looking-glass.

Erik rose from his cot. He sat on the edge for a moment, shaking off the final cobwebs of sleep before standing and walking to the place where he kept his wooden water tub. He poured some of the freezing cold liquid across himself and then took some in his mouth, washing it around before spitting it out again. He then poured some in a cup for his morning drink and donned his clothes. Next he took a piece of jerked salted goat-meat and started to chew on it, enjoying the smoked flavour as he sipped at the water and looked out from his hut at the beautiful spectacle of the new day. He thought of Lars for a moment, wondering if he had spent the night with Helle, wondering if he would now be suffering from a large hangover for that matter, given how much mead he had probably consumed the previous evening. Erik in fact found it astonishing that Lars, despite his obvious penchant for young ladies—for Helle was not the only one to have received his attentions—had so far managed to avoid becoming a father. Or at least as far as anyone knew. It suddenly occurred to Erik that perhaps there were some fair-haired blue-eyed children running around amongst the Angles and Saxons in Engelund. He smiled briefly, but then stopped when images of abuses of the conquered came into his mind again. He didn't like to admit it, but he knew that Lars was one of the worst offenders during the aftermath of the heat of battle. 'Battle always brings out the worst in people, never the best,' he liked to tell himself, but deep-down he knew that just was not an adequate excuse.

Erik had promised Snorre he would help him mend his fishing nets that morning. He quickly drank the rest of the water from his cup, and then placed it back down by the side of the bed, and tied on his foot-leathers.

He found Snorre on the beach, by the side of a grounded fishing boat lying on the beach.

"Good morning, Snorre." Erik waved.

"Erik! Good of you to come."

Snorre had already laid out a large net across the sandy beach.

"Would you like me to start on this one, Snorre?"

"Yes indeed!"

Snorre handed Erik a ball of twine, and a large needle fashioned from bone.

"That would be very good. You do that one, and I will do this other one here in the boat."

He motioned to the deck of the beached vessel.

"If you would just help me lay it out first, I would appreciate that very much."

Snorre was an older man, and a very experienced sailor and navigator. It was no wonder that he was in charge of the long ship on which Erik sailed during the raids. More than once he had been able to get them safely through a storm in the Great Northern Sea, or Nordsjøen as the Norse people named it, when a man of lesser experience might have lost the ship and all aboard. He also had a rightly-earned reputation as a great warrior, as Erik knew only so well. But during times of peace he invariably would relinquish his tight grip on the running of things, content to be a simple fisherman, friendly and relaxed. But in the throes of battle he became a different man, and woe betide anyone, friend or foe, who tried to stand in his way.

"You acquitted yourself well in the battle for Northumbria, my friend."

This was true praise coming from Snorre.

"I was impressed by your fighting skills." Snorre paused for a moment before continuing. "And the way in which you deported yourself."

Although he did not say it, Erik sensed that Snorre too preferred to discourage abuses of the conquered. Although he could not express this too openly for fear of appearing weak before those under him, he really did not care for such things. Erik had long believed that Snorre, for all of his great skills as a warrior, would prefer to bring the superiority of the Norse peoples to their primitive neighbors by peaceful means.

"Thank you."

Erik waited a moment before asking the question foremost on his mind.

"What think you of this planned invasion of the whole of Engelund?"

Snorre put his right hand up to his beard and stroked it gently before responding to the question.

"My opinion is this, my friend. If we put together a large force of ships, well organized and provisioned, and sail in the late spring, it should be possible. We may, however, be away from here for many months. Perhaps even years."

"But do you not consider that Engelund is a large island and will be difficult to retain, if not gain control over?"

"I think it not so large that a force of say, two hundred ships, with another hundred remaining here in reserve, would not be sufficient. And in any event, we need not control the whole country, just the coastal areas. The indigenous population will not put up much of a fight, especially after we soundly beat them into submission. In time they will come to respect us as their natural leaders."

Two hundred ships, thought Erik. That would be a little over twenty thousand men. Surely enough for the Angles and Saxons.

"But what about the Manx?"

"What about them?"

"Could they not be dangerous for us?"

"I would think if we attempted a landing there, then perhaps they could be. That is, if there be any truth to the tales they are telling in the Great Hall. But we shall simply bypass their Isle and leave them. The Manx feel no fraternity nor kinship with the Angles and Saxons. By all accounts, they are not the same people, but rather, they seem to be simply common Celts, barely more than a rabble. Remember too their King is Magnus, grandson of Haakon, and it is said they swear allegiance to him still."

"But they say these Celts have skills as fighters."

"An organized rabble, then. But in any event, we shall bypass the Manx, and leave them alone, and so they will leave us. We just do not become involved. It will be that simple."

Erik found Snorre's optimism reassuring. He resumed working on his net, and said no more.

Matthew Tobias Revere
Boston, Massachusetts
October 2008

ABOUT THE AUTHOR

J. Cameron Millar was born in 1964 in the United Kingdom in Edinburgh, Scotland. He grew up near Glasgow but in 1980 relocated to the north-east of England where he finished high school.

After a period as a reservist in the British Territorial Army, he attended university in Glasgow where he obtained two science degrees. Since then he has worked in industry and academia in the United Kingdom, Canada, and the United States. He currently resides in Fort Worth, Texas. He has one son.

This is his second novel, the sequel to The Van Der Meer Dossier.